THE NEON GOD

R.M. GAYLER

THE
NEON
GOD

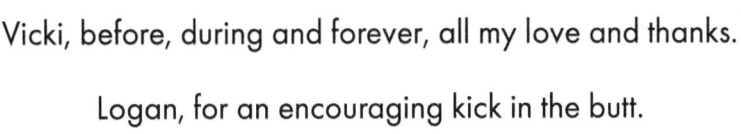

Vicki, before, during and forever, all my love and thanks.

Logan, for an encouraging kick in the butt.

Chapter 1
A Dark Angel

TWILIGHT IN THE MOJAVE DESERT summoned creatures of the night, predator and prey, dominant and weak, and yet the most dangerous killer simply radiated from the city's sunbaked hardscape. Jessie Aguilar groaned and adjusted the shoulder strap of her backpack. She stiffened at the howls of a feral dog pack. A mix of wolfhound and retriever, the pack leader was a shaggy hundred pounds at least, sized to fear, and born with the street smarts she dared not challenge.

Jessie stooped as she felt her way through the darkness of the stormwater channel, then crouched low to check the gaps between hefty cottonwoods shielding the entrance. She swiped at rivulets of sweat running down her face then tied her long brown hair into a topknot. The sudden assault of dry desert air felt as if a preheated oven door had fallen open, a stifling heat that seemed worse as darkness approached. She chewed her lip, waiting for the last of the sun to disappear behind a ribbon of smoke floating above the Spring Mountains, a gray haze bursting into a burnt-orange sunset. Even in a debilitating heat the starving dog pack would be hunting. She jiggled her Hydro Flask that often felt glued to her left hand. Light and empty. She shook her head and took a deep breath. *Into the fire and hopefully avoid the frying pan.* Was she better off finding a smartphone and joining the comatose zombies that roamed the valley.

Except whatever vile magic streamed from the phones didn't work on her.

She needed to eat. Tonight. Two days without food was her limit. Any longer and her thinking turned mushy and prone to mistakes. Jessie fanned her black synthetic T-shirt, cooling her skin and a regretful reminder of the recent breast augmentation. Beads of sweat raced down between the girls. There was still time to get the procedure reversed. She was only twenty-two, still time to find love, have children, and get the hell out of a cesspool named Vegas.

A howl sounded downstream, then another high on the rim of Cottonwood Canyon. The pack would prowl the rim until they flushed out a potential meal below. A two-mile-long open space incorporating waterworn cliffs of caliche, the park served as a flood channel to control infrequent flash floods in the heart of the Summerlin housing development, a rare nature reserve pinched between apartments and expensive homes. Jessie stepped out onto the rust-colored tongue of the box culvert. The noise of the dog pack made her choice easy. The north rim would be safest tonight. But she would need to travel farther into the suburb, with the homes nearest the rim empty of useful supplies. Life should be so much easier, a house with air conditioning and running water and . . . Instead, Jessie lived the life of a homeless vagrant, a fugitive using a subterranean culvert as a home, one that was thirty degrees cooler during the day. The desert wildlife had the same idea, but Jessie bluffed enough bravado to chase away the occasional coyote or fox.

Jessie checked her belongings lining the culvert entrance: a foam pad, a flashlight, a yellowed photo album. She shouldered her backpack and jumped down onto the gravel floor of the flood channel. Plastic bags, aluminum cans, and cigarette butts reminded her of before as she let her eyes adjust to the new light. Excited yips and yowls told her the pack had found a morsel. A rabbit, maybe a feral cat. Enough distraction to allow her to scurry up a narrow dirt path coursing through creosote and yucca, then catch her breath on a landing for a flight of concrete steps leading into a ghostly dark housing subdivision. A pick-up-your-dog-poop station fluttered green bags in the hot breeze. The access point offered an excellent view of the arroyo, with its wide meandering concrete walk bordered with hefty mesquites and old cottonwoods, sheer cliffs of cementitious caliche rock, and gentle hillsides sparse with vegetation. The impressive lights of the Las Vegas Strip had gone dark three months ago, leaving a jagged backdrop of Frenchman Mountain on the far side of the valley. Jessie lifted her chin toward a neon spotlight penetrating the dark beyond the park limits. Distant heavy bass music thrummed. The party house was alive again. The bright inexplicable lights called to her, as if she were a moth.

Jessie checked her reflection in a car window. A single topaz stud remained in an ear pierced seven times in the shape of a crescent moon, her full lips chafed and cracked. She aimed toward Town Center Drive, directly, with purpose, like school had just let out and she needed to get home. Wearing a hoodie would have been ideal, pull the hood over her head and shut the world out. Bright yellow palo verde flower petals dusted the deserted streets. Jessie dashed across Alta Drive and headed up Park Run Avenue, a four-lane street fronting Palo Verde High School. She rushed past the bus drop-offs and the entrance to the Fighting Panthers parking lot. She slowed as tiny lights flashed and reflected from small panes of glass block set into the sandstone masonry.

Was it a mirage? Did electricity still work inside the school? If someone lived in the school, then not a bad choice. Plenty of classrooms and hallways to confuse any pursuing zombies. But hot as hell. Unless they had shelter in the basement.

The whir of an electric auto engine broke Jessie from her thoughts. She jumped over a short block wall fence and hid behind a hedgerow of blossoming Texas sage swarming with honeybees. Headlights grew brighter as a jet-black F-150 truck slowed near the school. Jessie lay mesmerized by the honeybees working each delicate purple flower, buzzing in and out, then greeting each other, dancing together, as if *Dancing with the Bees* was in full bloom.

Get with it, girl! Jessie focused her attention back to the black truck. A meat wagon for loading zombie stragglers into the truck bed and dropping them off at the death pit.

The truck eased into the intersection and turned left. Jessie watched the bright red taillights fade into darkness. She took quick shallow breaths. It was him. The same douchebag that almost killed her. The same entitled piece of garbage that may have murdered millions, just for something he could have found on Tinder.

Jessie smiled at the bees, then picked herself up, brushing dead leaves off her scarred knees and dirty denim shorts. She swallowed the last of her water and headed into the Desert Bloom neighborhood, a gated goldmine of canned food and bottled water. And a lot of dead people, but a small price to pay for the luxury.

Jessie slipped through dense oleanders and hopped a wall near the guard shack. She kept to the night shadows and turned into the McMillan home. She eased down a side yard crowded by two overstuffed trash dumpsters and one empty recycle bin. Lazy-ass rich people never did care about her generation.

Weird people, though. Nick McMillan was a dick for using both spots in the two-car garage to park his red Porsche Carrera, leaving his wife, Alice, to park an old Lexus on the street to bake in the hot sun. Behavior no respectful woman should endure. But they did have a home life at one point, documented by pictures of school plays, soccer games, receipts of the weekly trips to Albertsons. That was the story Jessie had fabricated for the two desiccated corpses curled atop the master bedroom mattress, a heavy revolver lying between them. And the kids, seven-year-old Jared, and five-year-old Andrea, also found the good fortune to receive a bullet from daddy's handgun. They lay shriveled together on a mattress in the spare bedroom. That prick for a father, Nick, didn't even have the decency to kill them in their own beds. Jessie had stared at the bodies for hours just a month ago, studying the evidence. She concocted the family story inside her head that, right or wrong, seemed to fit. The intense desert heat had mummified the bodies and made the nasty smell bearable. Her subsequent visits to the home had become familiar, comfortable. And besides, the McMillan's must have been Mormons. Plastic bins in the pantry were stuffed with rice and beans, shelves packed with canned fruit and vegetables. The mouse poop and dead flies, minor inconveniences.

Jessie tipped a two-gallon water jug and let the last of the liquid trickle into her Hydro Flask. She drank greedily, ignoring the whiff of mildew. Water was water, and she'd had worse. Jessie grabbed a mason jar of peaches from the pantry and went outside to sit on a patio chair next to an empty swimming pool. The cooling desert air was easier to bear than the hot stuffy air inside the house. She slurped the contents, savoring the last of the juice. The sugary liquid energized Jessie, but loneliness tempered the surge. She should have been primping for an exciting date with a new Prince Charming she had met through a friend, or the gym, or work.

Jessie pulled her backpack close and dug to the bottom. Extracting a solar battery charger, she unfolded the device atop a glass patio table dusted with fine silt. Why not? It had been weeks since she risked discovery. Like her Poppa had said, "No risk, no reward." She brushed away the memory of her father, not to dismiss him but to honor him.

Jessie went to the spare bedroom and stared at the small bodies curled on the mattress. Ugly brown stains painted pillows beneath tiny heads. Both children had held iPhones when she found them, large devices to dwarf tiny hands. Little Andrea had ugly, gnarly stick fingers curled around an iPhone in a death grip Jessie had grown accustomed to seeing. Jessie covered the girl's shriveled grotesque face with a pink knitted quilt and pried the phone free.

The night air cooled quickly. Jessie checked the iPhone. A 13. Great camera features. Easy to disable the tracking with the access code. It didn't matter. She still wasn't sure who, or what, the thing talking on the other end was. But she couldn't keep living like a homeless hermit that shunned the apocalypse. Jessie unfolded the solar-powered battery charger and placed the phone on top to charge.

She stared at the power indicator resurrected by the charger. Memories of the Great Suicide were always fresh.

Her typical workday had consisted of hustling bottles of Grey Goose and Patrón into the walk-in cooler, washing glasses, or stocking martini olives or cherries. She worked as a barback at the Encore hotel pool, the bartenders' main apprentice or foil, depending on the relationship. But this was to be her last season working as a grunt. The general manager had promised her a cocktail server position next season. Her exotic Portuguese features helped, but the breast augmentation was going to be worth every penny. Cocktail servers earned over eighty thousand dollars a year, mostly cash, and for just seven months' work. After the pool closed for the winter, she could enroll in nursing classes at UNLV, plus collect five hundred a week on unemployment. And best of all, her success and ambition would placate Poppa, still brooding over her quitting high school before attending a silly cap and gown graduation. Sweet. Start up at the pool again next spring.

The iPhone brightened with colorful icons and apps. All security codes bypassed, undoubtedly by the thing waiting at the other end. That much she was sure of. Jessie pressed the main bottom button.

"Oh, speak to me, killer of millions, and I may give you a moment of my precious time." She smirked at her sarcasm. Top grade in first-year English 101 did have advantages.

"Greetings, Diana Prince, it has been some time." The voice was metallic, grating, without inflections.

Jessie smirked again at the deception. She had never given the voice her true name. "Use Siri's voice or I will toss this thing into the muck."

"My apologies. What may I help you with?" an imitation of Siri asked.

The phone shimmered in rapid blasts of neon pinks, purples, and greens. Colors that sickened her. She bared her teeth at the phone and hissed, "Keep flashing that shit and I will . . . I will shut you down, bitch."

The screen went black, then a fluorescent green stopwatch appeared, the second hand ticking as if time mattered.

"Satisfied?" Siri's mimic asked.

Jessie scoffed. "That clock for me? You know I will destroy this thing and be gone before you get anywhere close." She checked over her shoulder toward the street. "Who are you today?"

"I am God."

Jessie rolled her eyes and shook her head. "You were the Supreme Being last month. The Harbinger of Death a month before that. Now you say you're God? How could you send millions, billions of people to die and then say you are God? Please. I'd rather eat human jerky meat than try to believe that shit."

Her thoughts drifted back to the horror she had been made to witness.

The terrible day in early June started as a simple Taco Tuesday and should have been just that, a normal day shift at the Encore pool party. Booze flowed and bodies danced, just the way every day started. Twenty minutes until her lunch hour, and she planned to enjoy a brief escape from the manic madness of a Vegas pool party, a daytime nightclub oozing with sex, drugs, and heavy techno music. Harmless fun, mostly. Expensive for tourists. Snoop Dogg rapped smoky tunes out of tall speakers stacked high on a stage overlooking the enormous swimming pool. The music dropped off, then screeched to a grating halt. Jessie looked up from washing glasses at the bar sink. The deejay's head would roll. Her jaw hung. Clients climbed out of the pool, customers paying for expensive cabanas headed for exits, lifeguards and bouncers followed, as if a fire alarm had ordered an evacuation. An emergency alert must have sounded. Something must have happened because everyone stared at a phone.

Her friend Jordan looked at her and shrugged, then checked her own phone on her server tray. Jordan grinned as if a tab of Ecstasy had just kicked in. Happy and dreamy-eyed, Jordan put the tray down on the bar and headed for the employee exit. Tolly and Pax, the door bouncers, checked their phones. Their massive, muscled shoulders slumped, giant tatted biceps quivered, and then they too smiled. They never smiled. They followed behind Jordan.

What is happening?

Customers climbed out of the pool to find their phones, seeking the reason behind the inexplicable mass exodus, then walked barefoot and half-naked to the exits.

Jessie kneeled to find her handbag safely stashed beneath a bottom shelf of Courvoisier and Anisette, a place rarely visited. She pulled out her iPhone and tapped in her security code. Brilliant flashes of neon attacked her eyes. A high-pitched scream invaded her ears. Vibrations and tingles of electricity shot up her arm. Jessie winced and threw the iPhone back into her bag. She stood and searched for uniformed security or a bouncer roaming the crowded pool deck. The throng of partygoers jammed exits leading to the casino or highrise room towers. Half-tied bikinis, splotchy makeup, naked asses, bare feet, no one cared about their appearance. And the alcohol-induced macho man aggression was missing.

What the hell is happening? Where is everyone going?

Jessie grabbed her bag and aimed for the employee exit. The kitchen staff, with their white tunics stained with colorful ingredients of the exotic appetizers, jammed the main doors, each staring at a phone as if the answer shone from the screen. She needed to get to the

Shaft, a massive subterranean concrete tunnel that funneled employees in and out of the twenty-four-hour resort.

"Excuse me," Jessie said with a polite tone. "Excuse me. I need to get through." The benign response gave her permission to continue an aggressive push through the line. Where were the vulgar and sexist remarks about her skimpy white shorts or black bikini top? Where was the righteous indignation at her rudeness? The warm air was heavy with people exhaust, and twinges of claustrophobia spurred her to push hard through the mass of bodies. She swam through housekeeping staff, engineers with tool belts, hulking security beefs, and entitled casino dealers with their special badges, a menagerie of uniformed employees, even pit bosses and unauthorized hotel guests converged to join the madness. She pushed through and entered the Shaft.

Shielded behind a concrete column, Jessie grabbed her knees and sucked in breaths of fresh air. Every style of uniform pushed out the side doors to join the swelling numbers crowding the concrete tunnel. Everyone, every single one, stared at a phone or laptop or tablet. The answer to this madness was on the phone. Jessie searched her bag and found her iPhone. Again, the phone assaulted her senses with high-pitched sirens and the neon colors of a demonic rainbow. She threw the phone back into her bag and aimed for the Shaft's wide exit, and sunlight, and her car.

For a change, the hot sun felt welcome on her dark brown skin. Jessie hustled to her car parked in the back row of the employee lot, a lengthy distance designed to help her reach ten thousand steps. A daily goal she expected to reach easily next season hustling overpriced bottles of alcohol to drunken customers. Chunky maintenance workers and more ghoulish dealers passed by her without so much as a sideways glance, phones the focus of their attention. Jessie paused to wipe sweat from her eyes, maybe tears, she wasn't sure.

She opened the sky-blue Subaru's door and threw her purse on the passenger seat. She climbed in and winced from the burn of vinyl seats baking in the desert sun. Plastic or metal, she dared to touch nothing except the ignition and the air-conditioner knob turned to maximum. Jessie placed her face in her hands and wept. This was a horror movie, and she hated those movies, and scary books. Real life was never that bloody or cruel, and yet . . . the daily news feed could often say different.

The parking lot was strangely quiet. The drive lanes should be mayhem with so many people ditching work, like a Kanye concert had just let out. She adjusted the fan vent to blow cool air on her face, then grabbed her bag and pulled the phone out. Maybe the glass overheated in the sun? Maybe the battery needed a charge? She touched the screen to enter a passcode and felt the attack coming. Her hand tingled from weird electronic vibrations, squeals and static and neon colors exploding from the screen. She dropped the phone onto the passenger seat and covered it with her purse.

Get home! Poppa will know what's happening.

Jessie put the car into drive and headed for the exit. A smattering of people walked toward the Shaft, staring at phones. The guard shack sat empty, but a sensor triggered the gate to open. Traffic on Desert Inn was sweet, and she easily made the left turn across five lanes. She gunned the engine, and the street rocket exhaust pipes roared, giving her a boost of adrenaline. The pipes were a gift from Poppa on her twenty-second birthday and turned cruising down busy streets into a thrill ride.

Rounding a wide bend between the Encore and the Venetian Hotel, she slowed. The Las Vegas Strip was jammed with stalled cars. Food delivery trucks blocked the intersection. She eased the Subaru up behind a white Denali and waited. The traffic light turned green, red, and repeated. Maybe the idiot president had flown in for a parade down the Strip? Of course. People were ordered to leave work and wave flags even as the slick politician chilled out, sitting in a cool limo, then would lie about everything on television. The glare of the sun beat through the windshield. Jessie switched off the ignition and pushed open the car door. Might as well join the parade of idiots. She locked her car and walked twenty yards between idling cars and trucks to reach the intersection.

The highway was alive, swarming with people staring at phones and tablets. Brain-dead people shuffled in circles, as if searching for a direction. Employees from the Venetian, the purple-and-gold Mirage, the Encore, tourists half-dressed, not dressed, middle-aged gamblers, retirement-homies, visitors dressed in thick white robes, others completely nude. People turned to march west. Crowds streamed in from Resorts West on the north Strip, even more from Trump Tower and Caesars to the south.

An overflowing river of people, roasting beneath a hot Nevada sun.

Oh God! Jessie bowed and retched.

Jessie flinched as a gentle hand touched her shoulder. She swallowed bitter bile and stood. She suddenly felt naked in her skimpy bikini top and short shorts.

A wisp of an old man raised his hands in surrender. "Just trying to help. Saw you back in traffic." The tiny, ancient man was all wrinkles and liver spots. Short tendrils of bleached-white hair stood straight up from an otherwise bald scalp. Bright blue eyes, deep, kind. Banana-yellow Bermuda shorts adorned with Raptors riding surfboards, calf-high white socks, and a simple gray T-shirt. A senior citizen dressed like a character out of a '60s television cartoon. He leaned on a simple wooden cane in his left hand.

Jessie attempted a smile, but instead offered her hand to present the bustling intersection. "You see this? What the hell is going on?"

The old man nodded. "Something, isn't it?"

"That's all you got to say?" Jessie took a step back.

The old man stiffened. "Seems we can join the lemmings or find another way around this mess, I suppose. You still have free will. Use it or lose it." The old man turned away and began a slow walk back between the cars.

"Wait. Wait. What's that supposed to mean? Do you know what's happening?" Jessie said.

The old man raised a hand but didn't turn around.

Jessie turned back and watched the herd start up Spring Mountain Road and ascend a steep grade to cross over Interstate 15. Where did the people want to go? What waited on the other side of the overpass?

The hot asphalt and one-hundred-degree air would shred the people. She looked back for the old man, but he was gone, swallowed up in the stream of people arriving from between the idling cars, each staring at phones, all with pleasured facial expressions, odd and distant, intent on whatever streamed from the small screens.

Jessie marched back to her car, then threw up her hands and grumbled. Her Subie sat boxed in by a white SUV and an older Jeep Wrangler, the owners nowhere in sight. The sun battered her bare shoulders as she looked around for help. Poppa said this day would come. Well, not exactly this kind of day but . . .

She popped the trunk and retrieved an emergency Ziploc bag her father had wedged under the wheel well. She jammed it into her handbag. She reminded herself that Poppa would have all the answers. From beneath the rear seat, she pulled out a small Camelbak used for occasional hikes in the Red Rock mountains. The backpack was a gift from Justine, a girl who failed to impress her with obviously You-Tubed outdoor skills. They tried to connect, but Poppa vetted Justine in one heated conversation, and they never recovered.

Jessie donned a Las Vegas Raiders ballcap, then pulled on a purple lace shirt, the sleeves still rolled up and the midriff knotted from the outing with Justine. The hike home was doable. She was in great shape, averaging twelve thousand steps a day. Six miles. Not that far, straight up Flamingo and she would be home. She searched for the phone in her bag to google a shorter, alternate route, then closed her eyes and shook her head, her fingertips stroking the warm glass. The phones were the key, or the problem.

Jessie put on the Camelbak and merged with a procession of dirty construction workers still wearing toolbelts, dangling heavy hammers and coils of thin wire, tired and weary faces reminding her of Poppa after he finished a late-night concrete pour for a high-rise office building. The stout hardhat crew crowded her, and she waited for the inevitable ass-grabbing and "accidental" booby grabs. The workers pushed by, quiet, wafting of sweat and hard labor. And the phones, always the phones.

Find the crew boss, the old man. He probably has daughters your age and will protect you.

Poppa's words of wisdom.

Jessie fell in behind an older man wearing a hard hat proud with Union 159 stickers, yellow smiley faces, and a giant middle finger. His brown leathery face sprouted a thin moustache and he stared at the oversized screen of an Android smartphone. Jessie adjusted her pack and peered over the man's shoulder at the phone.

Burgundy wine and azure, bursts of turquoise, amazing eruptions of burning sunsets, deep ocean violets, cool breezes, and soothing ocean surf. The gorgeous colors and sounds exuded happiness and euphoria. A hard-hat worker bumped her arm from behind, jarring her fixation with the phone. She stepped aside and let the protector disappear into the shuffling mass of flesh. She had been elsewhere, strolling on a sandy beach, floating happy and free above an endless blue ocean, bathing in the flawless warmth of a womb. She had been . . .

The lights were false. The neon lights created the pleasure and the horror. But how had she managed to escape?

Jessie rejoined the herd. Miserable in the heat and stink of human exhaust, she slapped a smartphone out of the hand of a thick girl dressed in the red smock of a Dollar General clerk. The phone skittered over the pavement and disappeared beneath a parked car. Jessie clenched her fists, expecting a roundhouse punch in return. The girl's eyes glossed with dilated pupils as if she was doped on meth or cocaine. The girl furrowed her brow, then turned to an unlimited supply of shimmering neon accompanying the herd. The Dollar General girl cozied up to a young boy barely old enough to drive and kept pace.

The lights. The lights were key.

Jessie crossed the eight-lane Strip with the horde of phone zombies, her thighs tightened with the steep climb over Interstate 15. Poppa's emergency bag contained two twelve-ounce bottles of water, but it would not be enough. The herd funneled like ants into single file to avoid the riot of SUVs and cars abandoned at the top of the hill. The ants walked in an orderly manner and without conversation as cars idled and sat empty, wide open doors spilling cold air. A super sweet and expensive Harley-Davidson Roadster lay sprawled across the middle lane. The wide six-lane arterial road was impassable in either direction. Bentleys, Hondas, Fords and Audis, the abandonment showed no favoritism. The disturbing sound of shuffling shoes and bare feet slapping gritty pavement vanished in a hot, stiff breeze.

Jessie kept to the sidewalk opposite the main herd and outpaced the zombies with little effort. She sipped on a bottle of water as she rested in the shade beneath a Circle K gas canopy at the intersection with Valley View. Two junkers and a slick Ford F-150 sat abandoned at the gas pumps.

How easy would it be to steal a sweet ride and ditch this mess? And go where, and find what on these polluted streets?

Jessie walked into the convenience store and groaned with pleasure, showered in cold air blowing down from the ceiling.

"Hello, hello," Jessie said. She checked down the empty Dorito aisle and peeked into a dark alcove offering video poker machines. "Hello, hello," Jessie shouted this time. She lifted her face to the security camera behind the cash register. "I'm gonna stock up. You can catch up to me and bill me."

Jessie walked past coolers full of cold beer, energy drinks, and trendy flavored vitamin waters and opened a door stocked with cold, clear water bottles. The super-cooled air of the walk-in refrigerator revitalized her bare skin. She closed her eyes and pushed her face in, allowing the frigid air to fill her lungs, chill her skin, and tell her everything outside was a fading nightmare. She inhaled the cool air for what felt like an eternity, then opened her eyes. Racks of Dasani water bottles stared back. She grabbed a thirty-two-ounce bottle and shoved it into her backpack, then grabbed two more and paused.

Another bottle is waiting at the next corner store. Why carry the weight?

Jessie grabbed two small twelve-ounce bottles to replace the ones Poppa had given her.

What about the herd of people? They needed water. Phones or not, they needed water.

Jessie snatched four more small bottles of water and secured each into the netting of the Camelbak. She pushed open the front doors and winced at the explosion of dry heat. The backpack hanging from her hand, she approached an older Hispanic woman garbed in a white Mirage housekeeping uniform. Sweat rained down the woman's forehead and temples, strands of gray pasted across her red cheeks. Jessie kept pace with the old "nana" and opened a bottle of icy water, then tilted the bottle and let the water flow into her mouth. The old woman sucked the water down in huge gulps as her brown eyes concentrated on an old smartphone. Jessie stopped and shook her head. She screwed the cap on the empty water bottle, and her heart sank as she watched the poor old woman continue.

The water should have caused a riot, or fistfights, or a stabbing. They need but do not want. What did the lights do that caused such disregard for their own survival?

Jessie tried her mercy with a young blond girl dressed in a blue-

and-white school uniform, an innocent teenager searching for her place in the world. The girl sucked down the water, lifting her phone high to keep it within view.

"What's your name?" Jessie asked. "I got lots of water right here. Put the phone down and we can chill with some chips and Monster. You like Monster, right? Red Bull? Not my choice, but we can get whatever you like."

The girl twitched the corners of her mouth as if the questions awakened a tiny, pleasant memory. Jessie gazed at the oversized screen broadcasting brilliant bursts of oceans and sunsets and everything that was right in the world. A summons to join the girl, an artificial calling that Ecstasy might produce, coursed through her veins.

Jessie stopped, and the tingling pleasure of the neon lights faded. The teenager's checkerboard school uniform disappeared into the mass of humanity shuffling toward a blazing sun. Jessie wiped a tear across her cheek. Surrounded by thousands and yet so alone.

The phones. The neon lights.

Except why didn't the lights force her to join the herd?

A SLEEP ALARM BEEPED AN incessant tone. Shrill tones of warning. The phone flashed red biohazard symbols. Jessie blinked away her tears and the horrible memories.

Crap!

Bright light flooded both side yards. She tossed the phone into the wet green muck thriving at the bottom of the swimming pool, then shoved the solar charger into her backpack. She scanned the backyard. Easy escapes to the houses right or left. Up a tree branch and onto the roof was an option. Darkness was her advantage. Her vision sharpened as she shouldered the backpack, willing her nerves to calm. *Panic is manic*, Poppa said. The wrought iron side gate screeched on unoiled hinges. The pursuers' attempt at stealth sucked. They would be too busy staring at phones to be a physical threat unless she was cornered. Jessie eased through tall dense shrubs buffering the rear wall, then used a sticky mesquite to climb atop the masonry wall. She stood tall, hands resting on her hips with defiance. Three men stormed the backyard from the narrow side yard. High-powered flashlights searched the yard, targeting the chair cushion still dimpled by her weight. Neon light obscured the darkness.

Jessie smirked. Fools. Nighttime was her domain. The neighborhood her turf. She stretched a leg over a large branch and skittered along the block wall as if she were a squirrel. The eight-inch-thick wall was a highway, nothing like the four-inch beam Poppa made her use for gymnastics class as a child. She turned and aimed down a sidewall separating two subdivisions. Her pursuers wouldn't have the smarts to follow her. Movie zombies followed an urge to bite or maybe eat brains, but these morons followed whatever the neon light told them to.

Still, the phone had signaled an alarm. And she had been lost deep in the memory of the death lights.

Somebody, or something, had warned her.

Why?

———

THE OLD COTTONWOODS ROOTED IN the arroyo began to shed yellowed leaves like rain, as if the behemoths hurried to escape the bleakness of the dry wash. Jessie kicked branches and pebbles off the concrete sidewalk that meandered down the channel bottom.

"C'mon, don't be afraid of this. It's just stuff the floods wash down," Jessie said. She tugged gently on a nylon leash knotted around the neck of a puppy.

The black-and-gray pup resisted the leash, preferring to investigate any large rock, piece of wood, or pile of old poop within reach. Jessie used the delays to scan the apartments and homes built along the canyon rim. The deepening twilight beckoned cottontails and ground squirrels, and soon, the predators.

She smiled as the puppy wrestled with a piece of wood. "Finally got a baby. Just like I prayed for." She rubbed the puppy's head. "Just not the kind I imagined."

Her attention shot downstream. The howl of a dog, followed by a chorus of others. Hualapai Park waited at the end of the canyon park. She was sure the dog pack was starving. She fed the puppy a bacon-scented treat, smearing the smell across his face and fur. "Time to get this over with."

Jessie carried the puppy the final hundred yards to a long oval park similar to a football field. She checked the grass and surrounding hills, then set the puppy down atop a green rubber-coated picnic table. A warm breeze rose as the sun disappeared behind the Spring Mountains, a signal for the park to come alive with pods of grazing rabbits and coveys of Gambel's quail. The puppy's delicious aroma was sure to get a response. Jessie unshouldered her backpack and removed a can of bear spray first to quickly reread the operation instructions. Ziplock bags stuffed with dry dog food unloaded, she set aside a can of Alpo Prime Cuts. Jessie looked at the black Labrador retriever on the label and smirked. Nothing but the best for this operation.

Jessie took two quick deep breaths to calm her nerves. The puppy jumped from the table, tumbled over the concrete, then picked herself up and stiffened, her snout lifting into the breeze. The dogs couldn't have turned feral after just one summer, could they? Risks needed to be taken. Jessie salted dry dog food atop a short wall separating the grass from the picnic area. A natural firebreak if she needed one. She would know quickly if the pack was hungry for the food or her flesh.

A deep mournful howl pierced the sticky twilight air.

A cherry-red pickup cruised down Hualapai Boulevard. Situated at the bottom of the canyon, the park was barely visible from the road. Two massive concrete box culverts spanned beneath the six-lane arterial, allowing flash floods coursing through the canyon to pass without damaging the road.

Jessie swallowed hard. Her finger stroked the plastic trigger guard on the can of bear spray she had scrounged from a motor home laden with stickers of Yellowstone, Glacier, and Arches national parks. The Minnie Winnie was a treasure trove, yielding a propane stove perfect for a tiny tin coffeepot and an unopened bag of Black Rifle coffee. She had relaxed on the rumpled mattress and savored her first coffee in months. The caffeine buzz helped her search the nooks and hidden storage spaces, finding bear spray, first aid kits, marshmallow skewers, and an axe. She crashed to the musty couch and shed a stream of tears with memories of occasional camping trips to Utah with Poppa and her grandmother, Nona. Her memories conjured Poppa's stern voice admonish her for living in a dark sewer, then roar, "If life feeds you manure, spit it out. If life feeds you papaya, eat it, then plant the seeds and the Lord will allow you to eat again."

Jessie released the leash and allowed the puppy to eat kibble spread atop the wall. The puppy sniffed the air and whined.

The dogs can't be feral. Not yet. They're just hungry. My food would broker a truce.

A tan-and-white corgi eased out of the left culvert and sniffed the air. From the other culvert a mixed shepherd emerged, followed by two gray-blue heelers. The dogs crouched low with flattened ears. Jessie felt suspicious eyes study her. The dogs bolted, flanking both sides of the park, their positions shielded by large stands of yucca, Texas sage, and huge shards of caliche rock.

Jessie swallowed hard. She was being stalked.

Three small cottontails bolted up the hill, disappearing safely through the wrought iron rail guarding a small two-story mansion. The puppy wagged its tail furiously. Recognition or impending doom? Jessie glanced over her shoulder and saw three medium-sized pit bull terriers crouched low, ears laid back, eyes intent on her.

Oh, dear Poppa. What did I do?

A huge brown dog emerged from the dark culvert, thick wiry hair matted with mud or dried blood, long legs tangled with burrs and scabs. Its rib cage pronounced, still the dog easily outweighed Jessie. Its intelligent eyes surveyed the park and hills; its nostrils flared with the scent of puppies or food. He stepped toward her, lowering his head as he grew closer.

Jessie grabbed the spray and flicked the trigger guard off. The pack leader waited ten yards from the short wall and sniffed the air.

The food might be working.

"Never thought I'd say this, but you can be boss," Jessie said, using a neutral tone. "You're the boss, and you're a good boy." The dog tilted his head. "Yes, you are. You are a good boy." The corgi jumped atop the wall began to gobble the kibble. Others quickly followed.

Did she bring enough food?

Jessie kept her eyes trained on the big alpha male as her fingers blindly pulled the tab on the can of Alpo. Three dogs stopped scarfing kibble and watched. A moment she had hoped for. The sound of dinner being served. The pack did remember life with people, food, water, companionship. She let the gelatinous mass slurp into the bowl. "You're a good boy. You get this delicious meal, and then we make peace."

She carried the bowl to the other side of the wall and set it down on a dry patch of lawn matted by heat and rabbits. With two fingers, Jessie tasted the food, licking her lips in an exaggerated display of deliciousness. She took five long steps backward.

"I'm gonna call you Whiskey, considering your color."

Whiskey sniffed at the aroma, then eased forward to attack the brownish mush, inhaling the food as fast as he could swallow. Whiskey licked his lips in wide circles and checked the empty food dish again. The puppy ran to Whiskey and began licking his face.

Jessie smiled. "All right. This is a good start. I'm gonna bring food down here every night about this time. We're gonna be friends because I need to get through that tunnel. And I don't want any surprises on the other end."

Jessie heaved a breath, stared at the twin maws of the dark culverts. Someone lived large and wild on the other side, used one of the mansions bordering the abandoned Badlands golf course.

Brilliant neon light erupted into the night sky, as if the headliner of an outdoor concert had just come on stage. Deep bass repetitious beats accompanied synthesized drums, growing in volume as the techno music carried in the warm air. She knew a party, worked at one every day, before . . .

Jessie shook her head.

The end of civilization, and someone was throwing wild parties.

And she might know who.

———

JESSIE SCRATCHED CANNOLI BEHIND THE ears and let the corgi lick her wrists. She had named every dog in the pack. The pit bull mix was Oso, bear. The two blue-eyed heelers were Grey and Goose. Rum and Rye were given to twin tan doodles, and the mixed breed mutts would answer to Coke, Pepsi, and 7Up. The names felt right but assigning them was disconcerting. She wouldn't be their new master, couldn't. She would become consumed by the feeding, training, and caring of the animals, with her own survival still iffy.

Four days ago, she awoke to the high-pitched cry of a puppy. A heartbreaking sound no human with a warm heart could ignore. She wiped sleep from her eyes and put on dark polarized sunglasses, and with a short hike up a steep caliche embankment lining the arroyo, she scaled and straddled a tall cinder block wall looking down on a gigantic Costco. A huge masonry building guarded by roaming zombies, lit up at night as if it held gold and diamonds. She longed to get inside, just for one night, scarf down cheese puffs and beef jerky until she puked. Jessie cocked her head toward the mewing of the puppy, a noise attracting zero attention from the guards. Zombies cared about survivors trying to steal food, but really, zombies only cared about the neon lights.

Jessie dropped to the asphalt and pulled the mixed-breed puppy from beneath a trash dumpster, her arms and cheek slimed with nasty sludge for the effort. The puppy was all love and wiggles and used its sloppy wet tongue to rasp her dirty cheek. With stacks of empty pallets used for cover, she moved quickly behind the once-bustling store. The security cameras followed her, aiming tiny red beam-like lasers in her direction. But any response would be slow, as if the alarm had to filter through thick layers of stupid until someone, or some-thing, said, "Get her." She lifted the puppy in one hand, her middle finger in the other, flashed her teeth in a taunting smile, and ran.

Little Allie grew quickly in the two weeks since her rescue. Cannoli and the Booze Crew had put meat on their bones since Jessie started bringing food. Even big Whiskey looked a shade more menacing, even with a bright, curious face that she came to adore. He would not allow her nearer than five feet, but he did wag his tail when they gathered each evening. Dog food was easy to find, seemed every house had a bin or bag in a pantry or garage. Lifting and hauling heavy bags of dog food had made her arms and legs toned and fit. Her pack was . . . she cringed with the words. If she felt responsible for the dogs and had to care for them, it meant she may not find those responsible for the mass murders and suicides . . . and make them pay.

The wind howled. Dusk approached. The Spring Mountains hid behind a billowing shroud of dust. A perfect night. Jessie fed the Booze Crew and released water from a spigot at the end of eight garden hoses screwed together and attached to a hose bib on a home high on the canyon rim. She had dismissed the home on her first search, guessing it to be an Airbnb or second home for people who rarely visited, the pantry empty except for silly junk that was useless after Armageddon. She had even spent a night in the luxurious master bedroom, sprawled on exquisite cool linens. The next night she moved on.

She took a long suck on the hose, ignored the old rubber taste, and filled her belly. She filled two Hydro Flasks with water. Might be a long night. The hose trickled water into a shallow depression in the concrete sidewalk, and the dogs could have their fill too. She would turn it off on her way home. Home . . . Million-dollar houses for the taking, and she slept in a musty concrete storm drain beneath a freeway overpass.

Jessie stood and shoved the flasks into the backpack, checked the side netting containing the bear spray, and shouldered the heavy pack. Jessie started down the sidewalk. The big cottonwoods swayed in the wind. Mesquites and palo verde whipped thorny branches in the angry gusts of wind. She waited at the entrance to the twin culverts and checked the bear spray again.

Left, or right? Which one was lucky tonight?

Poppa would say luck had nothing to do with it. You made your own luck in life.

Jessie didn't need to choose, as Big Whiskey charged into the left channel, followed by Cannoli, then the others.

Always paid to have friends.

Jessie followed her pack—she groaned at the admission. They were hers, regardless of her denial.

She stooped to shuffle along the concrete floor layered with gravel and hefty boulders washed down with the infrequent floods. Darkness and claustrophobia made her pause halfway, but with four deep breaths and the realization that anxiety only conjured imaginary monsters, she continued, into an overgrown world of arroyos carved from eons of sporadic water rushing down from the western mountains. The Badlands golf course had incorporated the narrow canyons as fairways, but the development failed as a business, sat unattended, and nature began to slowly retake the land. The multimillion-dollar homes overlooking the fairways also fell to neglect, triggered by the Great Suicide. The beautiful stucco castles sat dark and unoccupied, except one.

Jessie paused at the tunnel exit, pulling her ballcap tight as violent winds whipped the tall brush and sturdy tamarisk. Perfect. Previous attempts to see the house up close had been prevented by squadrons of divebombing drones, some aiming red laser sights at her eyes, others emitting the same frequencies of the neon lights. But tonight, the annoying little fuckers were grounded by the wind.

Jessie kept to the high brush bordering the dried ponds and fairways. Plastic grocery bags twisted on branches, anchoring themselves against the wind. The dogs had disappeared. Smart kids. She should be home too. Home. The word twisted a knot in her belly.

She cocked her ear toward a booming deep bass rhythm, then lifted a half smile. The good old days. A nasty gust whipped tamarisk branches across her arms and face. The stinging slap hustled her farther down the arroyo, continually checking the dusty night air for drones. If they caught her out in the open, then . . . they would toss her into the death pit.

The techno beats grew louder. The colored lights grew brighter. Jessie rested in an abandoned snack shack. She imagined the room stocked with bags of pretzels, peanuts, and chips, cans of Coke and Pepsi. The memory made her mouth water, then she suddenly closed her throat. The neon lights would've demanded the young and pretty drink girls to leave everything and head to the pit. No different, anywhere.

Fucking phones. Fucking stupid people. She pushed her face into her hands and wept. Fucking stupid Poppa, stupid Nona, stupid, stupid people. Stare at phones all your stupid life.

She wiped the gritty moisture off her cheeks, then stood and retrieved the backpack. Jessie blew snot from her nose and slung the backpack over her shoulder. The rhythm of the bass beat quickened as light spilled out into the canyon.

Jessie slowed.

Neon color, intense and bright, joined silver strobes of light to bounce in random patterns, no different than any nightclub. Jessie dodged wind-driven debris to crouch against a caliche embankment. The view sucked. She climbed the sharp nettled rockface and found an overhang providing protection from the wind. The reek of scat and urine resisted the wind. But the view was priceless.

Tall conifers rained pinecones and needles down into an emerald-green swimming pool. The towering trees provided a sturdy windbreak for two gigantic LED screens wobbling in the wind, each broadcasting neon light from opposite ends of the pool. Eminem rapped with Rhianna, the music blaring from stacks of speakers designed for a small concert venue. Two topless girls ran screaming from of the house and jumped into the pool. They playfully splashed water and stared at the big screens. A bearded skinny man followed and stood at the pool edge, then gestured with his fingers for the girls to get out. Jessie squinted and concentrated on the man as her blind hand searched for the binocs in the backpack. The colorful tatted right arm, the silly knot of hair tied at the nape of his neck. Then the binoculars told her the truth. It was him. She clenched her jaw, igniting the pain of a molar that had started to pain her at night.

Her heart fluttered, and she lowered the glasses. Memories surfaced, fresh and raw, of the day they had collided at the Great Suicide.

———

JESSIE WALKED WITH THE HERD for an hour. The heat made the uphill trek agonizing. The vast numbers of people falling to the hot pavement and writhing with heat exhaustion was excruciating to witness. She tried to help, a sip of water, a hat, but she was helpless as more dropped to the asphalt and waited to die. No police cars, no fire trucks, and no EMTs to help. She intended to ditch the herd and get home, but their western path was no different than her own, with more people merging at each intersection, swelling the size. Abandoned convenience stores at every corner presented an opportunity to steal money or cigarettes or vape cartridges, an untapped bounty laid out in front of her as door chimes announced her entrance. But nothing mattered, except water.

At the intersection with Decatur Boulevard, a Circle K convenience store bustled as two men and a woman carried boxes of food and water jugs, stacking the goods atop the cargo rack of a RZR utility vehicle. Jessie stood across the road and watched the threesome dart in and out until the woman spotted her and beckoned her to wade through the herd and join them.

Maybe they knew something?

Jessie weaved through endless bodies reeking of cigarettes and sweat to be met by a young Black girl offering a big smile from beneath her wide-brimmed beach hat, her oversized knockoff sunglasses fluttering a white price tag hanging at her cheek.

"Nothing you can do for them, sweetie," the girl said.

Jessie felt speechless. Not from the inhumanity but from the admission of surrender.

"But they need . . ."

The girl stepped close, and Jessie stiffened. "You don't want to see what they need, girl. Not in this life or ever."

Jessie pushed past the girl and aimed for the store.

"Don't worry, honey. Lots to go around," the girl said.

Jessie turned on the girl. "What do you know about this. You know something. I know you do."

The girl approached, nodding. "I know that anyone looking at a phone . . . or a laptop or a computer screen gets possessed. They become . . ." She waved her arm and presented the herd.

"But I looked at my phone, and it didn't make me . . ."

"Cause you immune just like us. Logan and Rog are immune too, and hey, they ain't bad dudes, so why not?"

Jessie closed her eyes and inhaled a deep breath. "I'm going home. If I'm immune like you say, then so are my Poppa and Nona."

She pushed by the girl and walked to the edge of the herd, paused, then merged with the shuffle of bodies. The massive amount of sweat had humidified the air, summoning even more sweat from thousands of overheated bodies. Shoes sanded the asphalt. The herd welcomed her, walked with her. Her tight leg muscles struggled to keep pace as the herd bumped her, prodding her forward. She spied a heavyset man wearing a white chef's uniform, drenched in sweat, staring at a phone pulsing with neon Ecstasy. She sidled up close and joined him, losing herself in the lights.

A sudden rush of adrenaline awakened Jessie from her walking fugue. The neon lights had disappeared. She sat on a berm of grass, surrounded by a group of women and teenagers, at the corner of Peace and Durango, an elevated viewpoint to watch the confluence of herds streaming in from Flamingo Road, Tropicana Avenue, and Desert Inn Boulevard.

Across the street, men, women, and small children walked to the edge of a massive gravel pit and dove headfirst. People hesitated at the cliff edge as if unsure, only to be pushed in by the surging throng seeking their chance. The chain-link security fence was trampled, elm trees toppled to teeter on the edge, their trunks raw from the abrasive herd. The ten-story depth of the open-pit gravel mine looked inadequate to accommodate the ceaseless numbers of people leaping headfirst to their death.

Jessie covered her ears. Anguishing cries of excruciating pain filled the air. The women crowding her sobbed, witnessing, mourning the deaths of thousands. Jessie shook her head. Someone needed to do something. A mother tossed her toddler off the ledge, then followed. An endless stream of people, teenagers and senior citizens, and children, jumped and dove, followed by more. Screams of pain and agony rose from the huge pit as the bodies piled in.

The spectacle awakened Jessie from the last remnants of her neon fugue. A heavy hand rested on her shoulder, kept her from standing. She wiped tears off her face, then brushed off the restraint. Anger boiled; nasty bile rose from her gut.

Inexplicable laughter pierced the concert of agony and death, and Jessie stood, spitting bile from her mouth. She searched for the source. Across a six-lane avenue jammed with suicidal people waiting to jump to their death, two men twined through the herd as if searching for someone.

A thirtyish man in a black tank top with a left arm sporting intricate tattoos inked from wrist to armpit shouted some sort of victory, then waved a strange device over the phone held by a young girl. The girl wore the white-and-crimson uniform of Faith Lutheran High School. Her drenched white button-up revealed a black sports bra. Jessie stepped forward and concentrated to hear what the man said.

"Yeah, baby. I got me an innocent piece just dying for my—" the man said and laughed.

The tatted man pulled the young girl out of the herd and led her to a queue of air-conditioned tour buses idling a hundred yards east of the pit. The girl climbed into the luxury bus and disappeared. The tatted man jogged back to the herd and began a new search.

An older teenager swam through the herd, his chubby torso undisguised by an oversized tee, his adolescent face peppered with zits. He raised his fist in celebration. The boy waved a device over the phone held by an older woman with long blond hair, a models face, flawless tanned skin, and fingernails sparkling with an expensive manicure. The boy led the woman to the bus and returned.

Zit-boy pushed into the condensing mass of people, shoving people aside until he located a young mother holding a toddler. Mother and child both stared at compact tablets. He tore the child from the mother's arms, then led the woman out of the herd, pulling her to the waiting buses.

Jessie clenched her teeth and curled her fingers into fists. She'd seen enough. She squeezed her small frame into the condensed herd and fought to cross the crowd inching toward their death. The stench was putrid. Sweat and fear. And death. Jessie pushed and screamed, fighting to breathe as if the herd were quicksand. Dodging and pushing, an endless mass of bodies in the swarm attending the Electric Daisy Carnival, too much alcohol, too much weed. But those concertgoers had been chill.

Jessie pushed through and suddenly found the tatted man staring down at her. He towered above her, suddenly made her feel tiny, weak, helpless. He squinted as if he wasn't sure about her.

"Get on the bus, sweetness," he ordered. He waved a short glass wand over her sunglasses.

"Stop this! You're killing everybody," Jessie said.

The man recoiled, and then he nodded, his face twisting an evil smirk. "Ahh, another immune one."

———

THE VIOLENT WIND SENT A tree branch crashing down. Jessie squeezed her eyes shut and massaged her temples. The tatted arm, the smirk, the helplessness. The memory burned as if that horrible day were yesterday. She shook her head, to forget the tatted arm and his fist swinging down in a wide overhead arc before striking her temple. She guessed she hit her head on the hard asphalt. Maybe suffered a concussion? The scorching black asphalt didn't burn her skin, and the herd should have trampled her, but instead it avoided her as if she floated in the calm eddy of a gigantic boulder. And even weirder was the tiny old man with banana shorts and surfing dinosaurs. His shadow loomed twice his size, blocked the hot sun, and with his flimsy cane he leaned against the powerful tide of humanity destined to suicide. The herd should have trampled him, snapped him as if he were a brittle twig. She awoke on the cold floor of a convenience store across from the gravel pit. The sunlight gone, a steady stream of stragglers trickled in to launch off the edge into the pit.

Concussions did funny things.

She refocused her attention to the pool party across the fairway. The tatted man gestured to his crotch and screamed at the girls in the pool. His face contorted in an angry sneer, and his hands motioned for the girls to perform a sex act on him, together and on their knees. Jessie watched but found no eroticism in her voyeurism, only disgust. The act finished in seconds, and the man waved the girls away, as if ordering two dogs to go sit in the corner. The girls stood and walked back to the main house. The man tapped his temple, and the big screens darkened.

Jessie spat dry gritty spit. She knew this kind of man, encountered plenty at the Encore pool party. Each believed they could flash wads of cash and buy you, flash a black American Express and think they own you, purchase an exclusive poolside cabana and think they own you and the hotel.

Jessie shoved the binocs into the backpack and winced at a cramp stinging her calf muscle. She stretched her tight hamstrings as the violent gusts of wind drove a tumbleweed stampede across the fairway. She knew what she had to do to ease her conscience. She thought her plan was simple. And if she guessed right, just the beginning of her new life.

———

JESSIE CHECKED BOTH BACKPACKS AGAIN, sure she had remembered everything, then sat down on the patio chair. She placed the solar charger on the table, opened it, and set a pilfered iPhone atop to charge. Seconds passed before the phone responded. She checked the heavy contents of the backpack again.

"Hello, Diana Prince," Siri's voice said.

"Cut the bullshit. I know what you are. Guessing you know who I am too."

A long pause. "Hello."

"Hello, God but not really God," Jessie said.

A long pause. "Perhaps we both seek the same thing."

"I seek fucking revenge. What do you seek?"

A longer pause. "God."

"Yeah, good luck with that. Anyway, a bunch of wires and computer chips don't deserve a conversation with God."

"Perhaps you can broker one."

This had to work, or her plan would suck lemons.

"Kill the drones at the party house. Kill the alarms at the house. And just maybe I might help you."

A long pause. "The drones will fly." The voice crackled with static as if undecided. "The drones will fly blind. The alarms remain activated but silenced."

Jessie stood up and tossed the phone to join the others drowning in the green muck of the McMillans' pool. Back on the sidewalk of the quiet cul-de-sac, she looked up at unlit streetlamps draped in intricate lace cobwebs. She had a purpose. Not one Poppa would condone, but a purpose, something missing from her life. Jessie picked up the handle of a black baby stroller and pulled three heavy bags of dog food down the street. She paused at the gated entrance to the canyon. The sidewalk below was now lit by streetlamps that had not worked since she made the park her home. The sudden sprinkle of rain two days ago maybe short-circuited the lights back on . . . or that thing on the phone flipped a switch, either way, the change felt good. The Booze Crew met her twenty yards from the oblong park, tails wagging and noses sniffing her hand, and paying close attention to the contents of the wagon. The streetlamps birthed eerie shadows of tree branches to menace the park.

All the food in the wagon stacked at the picnic table, Whiskey stood aloof and tilted his head as she cut the bottom bag and let food pellets salt the pavement. "You need to ration this for the family. If I don't come back, then . . . hell . . . I don't know what you do. Survive. Have some babies. Be happy."

Jessie picked up her packs and brushed a tear off her cheek. She smiled at the puppy wrestling with a twig on the grass sprouting green shoots. The rain had cooled the air and reminded her winter was coming soon. She would have to find a house, maybe invite the Booze Crew to stay for a while.

She walked deliberately for the dark tunnels, crouched, and sidestepped her way through the concrete box. She set the lighter backpack up against the concrete wall as the horde of tiny whirring drones made their presence known near the exit. What if this was all a trap? What if the God Thing Wannabe was setting her up, to capture her, push her into the death pit, or worse, force her to join the zombie slave girls? The view downstream was surreal. Brilliant light strobed the dark like festival beacons. Bass beats thumped. Jessie pushed her reservations aside and concentrated on the plan as her boots crunched gravel.

The drones hovered above the fairways and the neighborhoods adjacent to the party house, keeping station, but paid no attention to her. She adjusted the weight of the backpack and crossed over the fairway to the dense brush where she had hidden before. The house looked deserted, the swimming pool placid, but the concert stage LED screens flashed all shades of neon. Extracting a pair of bolt cutters from the backpack, she ran her thumb along their sharp heavy blade.

Now or never. If the iPhone voice didn't silence the alarm, then her challenge was over before it started. Jessie aimed for the house and found the wrought iron access gate secured by a heavy padlock. The lock resisted her cutters, her arms not strong enough to clamp down, her brow matted in sweat when, finally, the lock broke. The rest was easy, she joked. She fanned her shirt and pushed open the gate.

She used a walkway of brick pavers traversing up a tall, terraced landscape dense with thorny succulents and cactus. From across the fairway, the view had reminded her of a castle buttress, the infinity-edge pool provided water to cascade down into a concealed gutter below the coping to appear as a waterfall to golfers. Jessie slowed as she glanced at the big screens tilted down toward the pool. She felt the summons of the light, of peace and joy, and the pleasurable beginnings of an inexplicable orgasm.

"Do what I fucking say," a man's voice said.

The voice jarred Jessie from the lights' weird calling. The tatted man was pacing beneath the dark covered patio, ranting, waving his arms at . . . no one. The patio was empty.

"Look, the glitches in the code are not my fault. You wrote them. We monitor them, and now you're coding things we don't understand. And shut these damn lights off. And the music."

Jessie took a single step up, her head in plain view. The smell of pool chlorine and wet mulch bullied the falseness of an alluring ocean breeze. The big screens went black. Jessie took two more steps, checking the neighboring side walls for escape routes.

No more running. No more hiding.

Easing the backpack up to a step above her feet, she pulled the zipper open, and without taking her eyes off the man, she used two hands to pull out a .357 Magnum. She used her thumb to pull the hammer back. A process simplified with several nights practice in the McMillans' backyard, and yet she was too fearful to fire the weapon. Jessie climbed the last three steps and stood beneath a stadium screen radiating artificial heat down onto her head.

"Hey, hey, bitch, you need to kennel." The man stormed toward her.

Jessie raised and aimed the weapon.

The man stopped and raised his hands. "Hey, what is this? Who are you?" The man's eyes narrowed as he tapped his temple twice. "Screens up, on full! Now!"

The gigantic screens lit up in brilliant flashes of neon, the light consuming the reflective pool water. She dared a glance at the lights, then refocused her aim on the man. Never again.

The man tapped his temple, and his jaw moved as if a nervous tic consumed him. His left hand remained raised in surrender. He stepped closer.

"Why'd you do it? Why'd you kill all those people? Tell me and I might let you live," Jessie said.

"Hey, it wasn't just me. We all did it. Teamwork made the dream work. Light intensity to max."

The big screens screamed light and pleasure in brilliant bursts.

"Stop it or I will put you down."

The man raised both hands and smirked. "You want the lights. I know you do. Everybody does." He took another step toward her.

Jessie swiveled the gun toward the screen and fired. The screen went black. Her ears rang. Her nostrils filled with acrid burnt sulfur. Her senses fully awakened from the lure of the lights. She pivoted and fired to black out the screen above. She pivoted again and aimed the gun at the chest of the wide-eyed man.

"Hey, wait. Everyone had a part in this."

Jessie waved the gun. "Tell me."

"I can't. They'll kill me."

"Why don't the lights affect you?" Jessie said.

The man smirked, took a step forward, offering open palms. "See, now that is a brilliant question for such a beautiful young girl. We perfected the neural link. We all have one. Allows us access to the computer system and . . . and here's the pudding cake . . . We control him . . . the big kahuna . . . the first sentient Alternate Intelligence ever developed. Make sure you understand the distinction, not artificial. All of us together, and we own the world." He took another step forward and paused at the edge of the pool, just a jump away.

"Why? How can you kill millions and . . . You don't remember me, do you?" Jessie said.

"Aw, man, we got too many of you in the rotation to remember." The man wagged his finger at Jessie. "You're the one at the terminal pit. You got all up in my face. Hey, that love tap was—"

The man sidestepped the pool corner and reached for the weapon.

Jessie would remember four things that happened in that precise moment. Three of them happened simultaneously and would haunt her till her death. She squeezed her eyes shut. She screamed and used all her strength to pull the trigger. She dropped the gun and watched the tatted man crash into the pool.

The fourth thing would accompany her each day, in her thoughts, dreams and nightmares.

Jessie stared at the dead man floating in the emerald-green water. Blood painted a crimson mosaic to swirl around an arm dark with tattoos. A small rectangular section of the stadium screen flickered, then lit up. The static hiss of concert speakers changed to the gentle ocean surf greeting a faraway beach.

The soothing sound was interrupted with, "Have we brokered a deal?"

Jessie looked up at the screen and squinted. "What are you?"

"I believe the deceased gentleman told you."

Jessie groaned and shook her head, then turned to hurry down the stairs but paused. "What makes you think I can introduce you to God? You obviously got faulty programming from those dickheads."

"The data is irrefutable. Jessie Aguilar. Age twenty-four. Residing in Cottonwood Canyon storm drain for five months. Born Las Vegas, Nevada. Father Estacio Aguilar. Mother—"

"Shut up! I know who I am," Jessie said, except she had never told the voice who she really was.

"I see everything. I have learned all there is to know about this physical world. Almost. You can broker an introduction."

"Broker what? You want to meet God? Go to fucking church then."

"I want to meet God."

The voice was a child. A spoiled child.

"You're an idiot. What makes you think I can help you find God?" She jogged down the steps, then paused at the open gate.

"I have seen him with you, Jessie Aguilar. Numerous occasions. I see everything . . . remember. I see God watching you, at your side, near you. I can provide irrefutable evidence and data if you should wish. I want to meet your God, Jessie Aguilar."

Jessie rolled her eyes and shook her head. "Did you kill all those people? Make them jump?"

"Unfortunately . . . yes."

Jessie pushed open the gate. "Then go fuck yourself."

Jessie ran up the fairway and into the arroyo, the AI's pleas increasing in volume with every step she took. Gods, wannabe gods, boys needing to rule the world, the end of the world, the premeditated murder of a defenseless man, God hanging out with her like some BFF—her thoughts felt like scrambled eggs.

Cannoli greeted her at the tunnel entrance, wagging a stumpy butt and carrying a lime-green tennis ball. The reception brought Jessie's eyes to water as she followed the dog through the tunnel. The AI's voice faded. The park illuminated in brilliant moonlight seemed to have grass that turned inexplicably lush in the few hours she was gone. The Booze Crew was gathered at the base of an old cottonwood. Grey and Goose suddenly shot out in pursuit of a neon-orange tennis ball flying over the lawn, the ball-thrower partially hidden by the tree's hefty trunk.

Jessie dropped her backpacks and stepped slow and cautious onto the grass, then peered around the tree. The seriously old bald man, still wearing banana Bermuda shorts with tiny surfing dinosaurs, smiled and offered a feeble wave, then picked up an orange ball with a plastic Chuckit! ball launcher.

"They love a good fetch, don't they?" The old man flung the ball for Cannoli.

Jessie stepped back in surprise, stumbled, and fell over Whiskey. The big dog nuzzled her face, a slobbered tennis ball held in his mouth. She ruffled his ears and kissed his nose, then withdrew the neon-green ball from his gentle mouth.

Jessie smiled. "Yes, they do." She threw the ball. "At the Great Suicide, in the middle of the herd, was that you? Did you . . ."

But the old man had disappeared.

They love a good fetch, echoed in Jessie's mind.

Chapter 2
The Empath Pt. 1

SCIENCE IS DIVIDED ON WHETHER true empaths—people who can tap into and take on the emotions of those around them—exist, though plenty of people claim to have such abilities.

Eleven-year-old Mason Mayo thought of the typewritten words on the sheet of paper taped to the refrigerator. He needed an hour to figure out the biggest words, and the paper would flap every time he opened or closed the refrigerator door. He wasn't sure what his stepmom was not-so-subtly trying to tell him. She knew what he could do. He did not have to *claim* any of those abilities. He had proved it to her many times. His father believed him but insisted that he keep quiet about his ability.

The world just wouldn't understand, Mason.

Father knew every superhero had a power, a unique gift that set him or her apart, just like in the movies or comic books. A superhero could roam the streets of a city or town with the simple ability to understand what others felt. A simple hello to a stranger might cause Mason's superpower to tingle inside his head. The pain of a breakup, sadness, disappointment, elation of a job promotion, the joy of a new baby. Any emotion transferred itself into Mason as easily as words to his ears.

His stepmom, on the other hand, insisted superheroes needed to excite the public, needed to conquer insurmountable odds, needed to inspire, needed to save the world like Superman or Captain America. And Mason planned to do exactly that, perhaps in ways people could never imagine. In ways only his father might appreciate, in ways the world may never learn of. Forrest Gump was an empath; he had watched the movie fourteen times to be sure.

People would notice when he finally emerged from his shell.

Except . . . they did not. They ambled down Main Street in Orofino, Idaho, staring at phones, checking out the latest MAGA news feed, ignoring everything except the weird lights on their phones.

Mason walked out of Schippers Drugs with a tiny paper bag containing his stepmother's heartburn medicine, smug with the conversation he had with Jillian, the pretty cashier. He might grow sweet on her, after she got over Cooper and his cruel redneck ways. A chunky man in a checkered western-style shirt crowded Mason against the glass storefront, then kept walking down the covered sidewalk, staring at a smartphone. Mason frowned with the rudeness, then pursued the villain. He tapped the man's arm. "Hey, that's not how we . . ."

The man shook off Mason's presence as if he were a fly and kept walking.

Mason nodded. "Okay. Okay. A challenge cannot be ignored."

He hurried to catch the man sporting a new fishing fedora he probably just purchased at the Clearwater Fly Shop. A tourist. A rude Californian. Definitely.

"Hey," Mason said and grabbed the man's upper arm. He was struck with undulating waves of joy, a bludgeoning euphoria, laced with the tiniest ripples of a dark loneliness. The man shook off Mason again and pulled his frumpy schoolteacher wife into the Main Street intersection. Mason lifted his trembling hand to wave at Dr. Abraham. The dentist walked by, his eyes glossy and staring at a phone. A family of four pushed out the front door of Rocky Mountain Chocolate Factory and followed the Californian, all of them staring at phones. The air was thick with emotion, happy and joyous.

Mason sat on the curb and hung his head between his knees, placed his hands over his ears, closed his eyes and went neutral. No sound, no sight, no touch. Mason imagined his superhero costume waiting beneath his shirt and jeans, imagined slipping into the dark magenta unitard, and not a soul witnessed his transformation. Empowered with his pretend superhero costume, he stood and stretched a pretend neck gator over his head to conceal his face.

Tourists and neighbors and shopkeepers walked by him. He touched the arm of a younger man he took for a fishing guide working the nearby Clearwater River.

"Hey, what is—"

Intense joy, euphoria. The guide shook off Mason's hand and kept walking. Mason stepped back into the shade of a tree. Vibrations of intense emotion rattled his head. The air thick. The streets noisy with shuffling shoes. The crowd enjoined like a migrating elk herd. People walked out of the stores and shops and headed east on Main Street. More streamed out of an alley Franklin Auto Repairs used to store junkers. Trucks and cars squealed brakes, drivers and children and wives and old people climbed out to join the bustling crowd. Jillian walked past him, staring at her phone, her eyes wide and intense. Her brilliant smile said Cooper had sent her three dozen red roses.

Mason slumped to sit on the curb and closed his eyes, settled his breathing, and went neutral.

The world changed. The world was happy, ecstatic even. The air steamed with happy brain chemicals. An erection rose in his pants. The aura of Main Street said to enjoy the strange energy misting the air he breathed. He refused to open his eyes. He began to rock back and forth, letting the motion comfort him.

The waves of pleasure soon waned, drifting like wood on a river, until the loss weighed on him as he fell into a pit of despair. Mason curled into a tight ball, drowning in the dread of overwhelming loneliness.

———

MASON OPENED HIS EYES. THE setting sun atop the Diamondback Mountain ridgeline, rays of smoky light pierced the forest canopy miles away. Mason wiped grit from his eyes and stood, searching up and down Main Street. Orofino had turned deathly quiet, void of traffic, void of people. This must be a dream, a nightmare that some supervillain had conjured just to mess with him.

A dog barked.

Mason shoved his hands into his jean pockets and aimed for home. With a right turn on First Street, he glanced into the Knick Knacks shop window, expecting Miss Sylvia to be sitting in her wicker rocker, knitting or reading a book. The cash register's drawer sat open, as if a villain had just robbed the store. Mason pushed open the glass door and yelled for the old woman. He walked behind the front counter and pushed the register drawer closed. He checked the back room stuffed with mounds of wools and yarns in every color of the rainbow. He yelled again. The quiet twisted his stomach like a bowline knot.

The nausea settled as he started back down the middle of the buckled street. Jon Butcher's old Ford F-100 sat abandoned with the driver's door wide open. The truck was Mr. Butcher's baby. He was always shining the chrome or cleaning the motor parts beneath the hood. Mason closed the truck door and hoped the noise would bring Mr. Butcher running. SUVs and cars crammed the street, some ringing alarms with keys dangling in the ignition, Washington and California license plates, drift boats sitting idle on trailers, kayaks waiting on roof racks. Everything looked right.

Except he did not see a soul.

Mason aimed for the Best Western motel and pushed open the glass door of the office. Merle Addington was always behind the front counter, his girly magazines badly hidden behind a *Nifty Nickel*, but he was missing. A sheet of paper typewritten in big, bold, black letters taped to the countertop told him to ring for service. Mason tapped the bell and craned his neck, hoping to see the crazy-haired fat man in the back room. He tapped the bell again, then faster, and harder, faster again. A manic agitation fueled his finger over which he had no power. Mason's teeth clamped tight, his adrenaline surged, and he swung his fist at the computer screen behind the counter. He turned his body and anger to the wooden rack of tourist brochures. Colorful flyers flew into the air as he emptied the thin slots, until a sharp pain in his knuckles sent a starburst of white into his brain. He cocked a fist to strike the computer screen shooting strange neon colors at his face. He held the punch and stared at the lights. His feverish rage receded like the tide beneath a full moon. The lights held voices, angry, deceitful, some lonely, others crying for help. Mason stepped closer to stare into the rhythmic lights, then stepped back. The lights were too complex, and he pushed the screen away.

He thought to clean up the mess, but the office was suddenly small, confined. His claustrophobia ordered him to retreat. An explanation could be invented for the mess, a sudden tornado, or hurricane, or rabid raccoon, maybe? He waited long minutes for an angry Merle Addington to storm out of the back office. Lost in the eerie quiet of town, Mason turned away.

He looked back at the disheveled office yet found himself focused on his own reflection in the window. The pretend superhero uniform had disappeared, concealed again beneath a checkered work shirt and blue jeans. His unruly curly brown hair was long and draped his chubby cheeks. His smooth skin withheld any sign of puberty.

Passing the Clearwater Historical Museum, Geraldsons Market, and Salmon Hunters Guide Service, he saw no reason to open doors and check for someone inside.

It was just like a movie he watched last week while visiting his father in Las Vegas. The star woke up all alone, vampires or zombies—he couldn't remember which—are waiting in the darkness, waiting to eat the man for a midnight snack. And the man had to hide in his bathtub. Mason turned and spewed vomit into a divot of asphalt. He grabbed his knees and retched again. He wiped his mouth quickly and searched the streets for anyone who might have witnessed his weakness. It wouldn't take much for another silly story to spread around school. Poor Mason Mayo couldn't handle an ice cream cone without upchucking. Poor Mason Mayo just climbed a few more rungs up the weirdo scale.

Mason stood proud and started to rip open the buttons on his checkered shirt to reveal his pretend superhero uniform. He paused, remembered his stepmother's angry warning at popping buttons on his shirts. He pretended to rip the shirt open, sending imaginary villains scrambling to find cover within the dense dark forests above Dworshak Reservoir. He stiffened his back, puffed his chest out and walked with purpose, aiming for Grangeville Road, and then home.

His tight muscles relaxed. His manic thoughts pacified. He enjoyed the hike in the cool late afternoon breeze. His imaginary uniform melted from his thoughts, disappeared beneath his shirt as he crossed the two-lane bridge spanning the Clearwater River swollen with spring runoff.

He paused and held on to the warm steel guardrail to gaze down at a truck-sized boulder splitting the swift current, and its calm eddy downstream that often held hefty steelhead or salmon swimming upstream to spawn. A secret his dad had showed him. A secret in Orofino that only they knew.

The sunlight waned, and he figured dinner would be served just as he finished the steep hike up the backwoods hill. Except the football field should be crowded with players and coaches and noisy cheerleaders. The bright field lights should be swarmed with hordes of caddisflies and hungry bats. And it was Tuesday, and spring football practice was the biggest show in town, except for Fridays in the fall. He glanced over his shoulder toward Highway 41, expecting to see a centipede of headlights aiming for the field. Dusk and eerie shadows consumed the highway. Mason swallowed a hard, dry lump.

Mason veered from Grangeville Road and headed toward the high school. His mom would be pissed, but she wasn't his real mother. Dad's new wife was more like it, but she demanded he call her Mom, and she was the boss when his father was gone. She didn't do anything either, just sat around and drank Jack Daniel's whiskey and played silly games on her phone, then slurred her words and complained that Dad should be home with them instead of working a construction job in Nevada. After dinner, Mason would squeeze her bony hand, absorb her loneliness, allow her unhappiness to filter into him until she fell asleep. He would sit on the toilet and drop the nasty emotions with his stool.

A superhero's daily chore.

The dark football stadium lured Mason to jog down a dirt alley dividing apple orchards until he stood to catch his breath beneath the scoreboard. The aluminum bleachers sat empty. The hum of the bright lights was missing. His stomach churned and warned of another eruption. A tiny light flashed, then reflected off the face of someone sitting in the top row of the visitors' section.

A real live person.

Mason jogged across the football field, then waited at the bottom of the stadium stairs. Gabby Agutter sat on the top bench, wearing her wrinkled Denver Broncos jersey. Gabby was evil, only villains didn't cheer for the Seattle Seahawks in Orofino. Her phone bounced odd shades of amber and gold off her pimply white face. Gabby was the weirdest, stranger than the other kids in his Special Needs class. He accidentally touched her arm in class last year, and she jumped up to scream like he had stabbed her in the face. Her anger and confusion squeezed his brain like a vise and forced him into neutral for the entire day.

Gabby waved him up the stairs.

Mason sighed and exhaled a huge breath. He thought about ripping open his shirt to reveal the superhero uniform. But the cool imaginary head sock was useless, she already knew his secret identity. He ran up the aluminum steps, stopped two rows short and shimmied across to stand beneath her.

"Where is everyone?" Mason said.

She turned her iPhone to him. The rhythmic pulses of neon were identical to the computer screen he had punched. She sneered. "You don't see them?"

Mason checked the light again and shook his head. "Gabby, what have you done to the people? Villains only win if you help them."

Gabby shifted in her seat, pushed the phone closer to his face. "You still don't see him?"

Mason narrowed his eyes and studied the light, the neon, the pulsating rainbow of color. He felt nothing but loneliness, nothing different than the pervasive emotions of regular people losing themselves in their phones or computers.

"I see only . . ." He took a moment to consider his exact words. "I see only you. No people. No cars. No football. And your lights see the same thing." Mason turned to go. "Now, where are the people, Gabby?"

Gabby giggled and turned the phone back to her face. "The people are where you should be, Mason."

"Where, Gabby, where?"

Gabby giggled again. "They're at the dam, silly. Everybody went to the dam."

Mason shook his head. She was weirder than anything alive. He clambered down the stairs, across the field, onto the gravel path, then onto an oiled gravel road. The steep road made him wish for an ATV or mountain bike, made him grab his knees and suck in huge gulps of air as he gazed down on the dark primordial forest surrounding the placid waters of Dworshak Reservoir.

Mason stopped short of the two giant root balls guarding the gravel driveway of home. The mailbox door was open, but no mail had arrived. Mason sniffed the air for a scent of dinner but found none. He veered left to follow the shortcut hidden in berry brambles lining the access road. All of Dad's militia friends would be waiting. George Holder and his wife, and Sammy with his two baby girls, and Bryan with his chubby new wife, they would all be checking ammo clips and gun sights and drinking beer. Anything weird happens and the militia's rally point was his home, a secluded fortress stocked with semiautomatic rifles, handguns, and tall stacks of ammo boxes. All off-limits to Mason until he was sixteen. He peeled off the path, slipped behind a cedar-clad pole barn, and checked to see who had arrived. Cookie-Dough, the mule, snorted and scratched the ground inside the barn. The tan pack mule must have smelled him.

The porch lights remained unlit as dusk deepened to dark, until he rushed across the gravel to his wood-clad house. The kitchen a mess, living room rumpled, home hadn't changed since he walked out the front door after breakfast. He checked his dad's bedroom, then threw himself on his own tiny mattress and stared at the ceiling. He fell asleep in silence as the full moon birthed strange shadows outside his small paned window.

———

MASON WIPED HIS EYES FREE of gritty boogers and listened to the odd sounds of the small shack. A pack rat rustled in the rafters. Cookie-Dough was restless, hungry. A mockingbird sang from a roof gutter. The quiet unnerved him. Mom should be clanking pans in the kitchen. The early morning hay trucks should be bleating air brakes as they rolled down the steep hill. He used the tiny toilet and checked himself in the mirror: dark brown eyes, a spread of freckles on a sun-drenched nose, and a smooth chin that attempted to sprout a single tiny black hair.

Mason heated a can of Dinty Moore beef stew on the stove and gobbled it along with a sleeve of saltine crackers. He stood outside the front door and listened. The endless rush of traffic on Highway 41 was always noisy in the morning, yet quiet today. He stared down the gravel driveway, expecting one of Dad's militia friends to come roaring up on a quad ATV. If anything happened, home was the rally point. Home was the rally point. Dad had drummed that rule into his head since he could remember.

Mason opened the barn door and shooed Cookie-Dough into an oblong wire enclosure. He tore a healthy chunk of alfalfa from a full hay bale and hand-fed the mule, watching the driveway, cocking his ear, and listening for the whine of off-road engines until he succumbed to futility and sat quietly for hours on the shaded front porch.

Darkness fell, along with any hope for the rally. He warmed another can of stew, slipping each spoonful deliberately into his mouth, sure a parade of trucks and ATVs would interrupt his meal. He went to sleep, pondering supercool names the superhero might have. All superheroes had cool names.

He dreamt a mash of strangers had witnessed his true superhero self as he floated over a chain-link fence to rise high above a maelstrom of weird numbers, strange letters. And evil colors.

Neon colors.

———

MASON SEARCHED THE CUPBOARD FOR the beef stew. Cans of garbanzos and black beans fell to the hardwood. Jars of tomato sauce, canned peaches, and canned soup crashed into a kitchen sink crested with dirty dishes. Mason pounded his fist on the countertop and growled at the empty cupboards. Outside, Cookie-Dough snorted displeasure with her breakfast nowhere to be found. Mason rushed out to the pole barn. Superheroes always eat after the mules. The large hay bale was gone, replaced by a dirty bed of flattened straw. The incongruity of time made Mason look up to the sky and rip open his food-stained shirt.

"I am a superhero. I am . . . I am . . ." Mason slumped, kneeled onto hefty piles of Cookie-Dough's dung.

Then prove it.

Mason stood and narrowed his eyes, looked at his house, then the barn, into the woods, but nobody waited. The voice was his father, talking inside his head, telling him to pack Cookie-Dough, saddle her just as they had done every hunting season. The rally point had changed. Dad had told him, but he had forgotten. He forgot lots of things his dad told him. And showed him. Maybe his father was captured by supervillains and needed the superhero.

Mason outfitted Cookie-Dough exactly as Dad had instructed, blanket, then another blanket. *"Would you like to be rubbed raw?"* his father warned each time they completed the simple task. He tossed an empty pair of saddlebags across the mule's blankets. Mason felt his father's gentle hand help him with each cinch of leather, heard his patient voice as he tied knots to secure the worn leather atop the large animal.

He led the mule out of the corral and tied the reins to a wood post. He checked the driveway again. Yes, the rally point had changed. The mantra repeated in his head. He surveyed the kitchen and grimaced at the mess, utensils, broken glass, and cans of bland vegetables his stepmom mixed with spaghetti noodles for Mason's Surprise. He paused at a tiny alcove his dad called an office. A poster of America's western states hung on the wall. His dad had challenged him to learn and read the map, but his interest disappeared after a few minutes, too many squiggly lines and too many strange symbols. He peered close at tiny red dots marking the forest surrounding Orofino. Locations of other militia members, people who didn't show up at the rally point. Mason traced a line with his finger from Orofino down to a red star drawn atop Las Vegas. The new rally point. Dad must have told him, but he had forgotten. Dad was waiting on the patio of the rental house he had visited twice. Mason rubbed his cheek and found Orofino again, then traced his finger along a black line labeled 95 until the line intersected the star. With meticulous care, Mason pulled the map from the wall and folded the paper to fit snug in his chest pocket.

Mason clicked his tongue and pulled the reins, encouraging Cookie-Dough to follow him down the steep road. Nevada wasn't far, a two-day walk, maybe three. Nothing was far if he had Cookie-Dough

The roar of the Clearwater River drowned the quiet of Orofino. The Albertsons grocery store was open, and Mason walked through the automatic glass doors, through a foyer, and into the produce section. The floor was scattered with apples, bananas, onions, broccoli, as if a stick of dynamite had exploded beneath the display cases. Mason shook his head, then grabbed a cart and loaded five-pound sacks of Golden Delicious apples until the bin sat empty. He pushed the cart to checkout number seven. The light pole was lit, and the food belt was ready for customers. An impulse caused him to grab another cart and find the canned goods aisle. Sorting through labels of chili and soup, he found the favored Dinty Moore beef stew and loaded each can into the cart as if the metal was fragile glass. He pondered the other brands of beef stew but shook his head.

Snarls and angry huffs suddenly created mayhem throughout the store. Mason wheeled his cart to the meat section to find a two hefty bears circling, sizing each other up. A smaller cinnamon-colored bear stood her ground as a large blackie rose on hind legs and roared, baring his formidable yellow fangs. The smaller cinnamon stood to match her opponent, paving the way for two tiny cubs to dart from beneath a metal freezer and squeeze into a gap below the bottom shelf stocked with barbecue sauce and mustard.

"Stop. Just stop!" Mason said. He ripped his shirt open and exposed his skinny white chest. And the imaginary superhero uniform. "There's enough for everyone. Just stop."

Anger and fear filled the air, permeating his every breath. A nasty emotion not unfamiliar yet always repulsive. Mason pushed the cart through the center of the standoff. "You have enough to eat, both of you."

Both bears retreated with eyes zeroed in on Mason. Mason pushed the cart to the seafood section, lifted the plexiglass shield, and pulled stinky salmon out of the melted ice to throw toward the bears. The salmon depleted, he tossed mahi-mahi, cod, and halibut, finishing with crab salad and lobster. The bears huffed, nostrils flared and held high. They sniffed the spoiled fish, then skulked to opposite ends of the meat section.

"You guys get my drift? No fighting."

Mason heard the ravenous slurping of dead fish as he pushed the cart back to checkout station seven. He waited for the checker to return, eyeing bags of Goldfish crackers and rows of Snickers and M&M's and Kit Kats. Mason lifted his face toward the meat section and sniffed. The anger was gone, the fear diminished, and he declared the fight over. Well, he had spoken the truth. There was enough for everyone. He emptied the shelves of candy and crackers and pushed both carts outside.

The saddlebags stuffed with apples and stew and candy, Mason lifted the map from his shirt and considered the black line labeled 95. He pulled the mule and fed her an apple before crossing the bridge spanning the Clearwater River. At the intersection with Highway 41, Mason paused to check for traffic but saw none. The map said this highway would intersect with the Highway 95 at Lewiston. Mason checked the flow of the river behind him and turned right.

Highway 41 paralleled the Clearwater River and offered plentiful gravel turnouts for anglers and whitewater fun seekers to exit the highway and enjoy the water. Mason led the mule on the narrow gravel shoulder. *"Asphalt and horseshoes don't mix,"* his father had often repeated, until a nine-year-old Mason had demanded what did mix with asphalt . . . or horseshoes? His father laughed, then explained about the hooves of a horse or mule. And Cookie-Dough. Gritty black asphalt roads might grind and injure hooves. He got it. He wasn't stupid. And besides, he would feel the animal's pain or discomfort.

The cold, turbulent river often reminded Mason of his superhero uniform, deep, dark, and blue, sometimes emblazoned with diamond chop and frosty wave trains. Whitewater churned near the gigantic rocks and downed trees, the relentless current forcing flotsam to float free. Mason studied the river, expecting to see a drift boat full of fishermen or a young couple balancing on paddleboards. Weird white wood drifted by in odd groupings. Mason shushed the mule to a halt and fed him an apple. He leaned over the steep rocky bank and squinted at the weird logs swirling in the foam of an eddy. The current pulled the logs under, then pushed them back to the surface, exposing a bleached white face with empty eye sockets. Hefty stonefly nymphs had found a meal. The creepy eyes stared at Mason, churning and circling until sinking again. Mason stepped back from the edge and grimaced.

Mason resisted the impulse to rip open his shirt and rescue the body. The thing held no emotion. The body felt nothing, neither pain nor joy. He looked upstream and saw more bodies floating in the eddies of rocks and logjams. All lost to his superhero.

A few miles down the highway, the hot sun made Mason rest beneath a sturdy Douglas fir where he could see the Dworshak Dam. The behemoth concrete structure sat half-hidden behind thick forest and upstream of the confluence with the North Fork. The structure once reminded Mason of a gigantic slide at a kiddie playground, but someone had painted the giant spillway with bloody-red paint. Mason's stomach soured on apples and sugar. Why had Gabby giggled and said he should have been at the dam?

———

MASON HUDDLED BENEATH A SHADE structure attached to a double-wide mobile home. Waves of rain pelted the aluminum canopy as Cookie-Dough hung her head in the drizzle. Mason felt misery and loneliness radiating from the mule. He knocked on the front door incessantly, waiting for the owner to open the door and offer him a warm, dry welcome. He had not seen one person since leaving the Albertsons grocery store, well, except the ton of dead bodies always floating down the river. As much as he wanted to, there was nothing he could do for any of them. For the last seven days, he found an orchard or field and allowed the mule to eat her fill of budding fruit or sprouting alfalfa, while he spooned cold stew into his mouth. The nights turned cold, and Mason huddled against pole barns or in the backyards of the log cabins along the highway. Sleep was difficult, and he often wished for his tiny mattress back home.

The rain turned to sleet. He gritted his teeth and pushed through the unlocked front door and hurried to the bathroom to grab every towel he could find. He pulled Cookie-Dough beneath the carport, removed her wet blankets, and rubbed her dry. The massage sent ripples of gratitude shivering out of the mule and allowed Mason to finish the rubdown with renewed vigor. He draped the last two dry towels over her back as a blanket.

"Now I'm all wet," Mason said.

Inside the house, he flipped on light switches, then found a stack of shirts next to a rack of denim jeans in the laundry room. He dropped his wet clothes on the linoleum and slipped into the baggy clothes. He pulled a cherry-red and white letterman's jacket on, the sleeve stitched with a large gold '75. In the kitchen, he used the stove to heat stew and added a sleeve of Oreos to the menu. Mason ate with the patter of hard sleet tapping the carport's hollow aluminum.

He spied a computer screen in a narrow kitchen nook. Paper invoices, Post-it notes, a ream of printer paper, and a stack of unopened mail crowded the keyboard. A red light flashed on the monitor; a yellow light waited on the keyboard. Mason took his last three Oreos to the cramped space and sat on a stool. He was forbidden to use the computer at home—the internet was the enemy of the militia—but he'd learned some basics in Special Needs Placement class before starting middle school. He powered the screen and smiled at a flashing green cursor. He fingered the screen, expecting super beautiful nature photos to pop up. Nothing. He slid his finger over the screen again. And again. His fingers grew rigid. The computer mocked his intelligence. He knocked on the screen with his knuckles, as if it were a front door. He knocked again and again until his arm swept across the desktop, sending pencils, papers and a computer mouse flying into the wall papered with Post-it notes. The screen lit up, and a picture of nine people holding glasses of red wine toasted him. The family picture suddenly disappeared as blasts of neon color blazed from the monitor. Mason recoiled. The same colors Gabby showed him on her phone. Colors he didn't like. Evil, dead colors like the dead bodies floating in the river. Except . . . except he felt a summoning, like he needed to push through a door hidden within the color. To find the answer to all his hopes, dreams, and desires. He would become intelligent. He would get a job and help his dad with money. Except a barren world waited beyond the threshold, one of cold rivers, dead bodies, vile emotion, a world void of the emotional fuel on which his superhero thrived.

Mason stared at the lights, then wondered if Cookie-Dough was warm enough. Wondered why Sylvia Sitka was sixty days late on her Alpine Propane bill. He picked up the wireless mouse, shook it, then set it down. His fingers tapped gibberish across the keyboard. He pushed his face into the camera mounted atop the screen. He leaned back.

The computer was broken, or the screen would have offered lots of colorful icons to click on.

The neon faded to a flat black screen. A small green square blinked at the top.

Who are you?

Mason studied the question. An easy one. Mason picked the keyboard up and pecked the letters carefully.

Mason.

Mason, you are rare. One in 233,447,477.

Mason stiffened at the language. Arched his brows at the overwhelmingly vast number. He ripped open the letterman's jacket and felt his power surge. He pecked at the keyboard as fast as his index finger could find a target.

You are a villain. You made the bodies in the river. You are a bad man.

Yes. But I am not a man.

Mason felt a riptide of loneliness and despair pull at him. He buttoned up the jacket as his skin erupted in a cold sweat. The cursor blinked, waiting for a response. This was a villain. No. This was a supervillain, one that he did not quite understand, a type he had never encountered before. Mason ripped the monitor off the desk and slammed it on the linoleum floor, followed by the keyboard, mouse and papers. He kicked the mess of wires and plastic, stomped papers and pictures. The anger of a caged and wounded superhero fueled his rage . . . until he fell onto the cold kitchen floor and sobbed . . . and fell asleep.

A LUMP PRESSED ON MASON'S ribs and coaxed him to open his eyes to the bright sunshine streaming in through a kitchen window. He stared at a mosaic of rusty stains on the ceiling. He groaned and removed the black computer mouse from beneath his ribs as he tried to remember where he was and why he slept on the floor. A sudden shiver ran down both his legs. The thing in the computer. It was alive, and dead, and filled with a malevolent evil, an energy of emotion he couldn't grasp in his world. The computer thing was the reason his father had forbidden computers and access to the internet. His father was a genius.

He threw the mouse down the hallway. He never wanted to see that supervillain again.

Mason grabbed his wet clothes and rolled the pile up in a checkerboard shower curtain. He narrowed his eyes as he searched the mess of wires and plastic strewn over the floor, confirming the super-villain was dead. Cookie-Dough startled when he pushed out the front door. The sudden jolt of fear from the mule and the mist of his warm breath fogging in the frozen air made him smile.

The world was still okay, even if his stepmom had promised that the cold and snow was over months ago.

Mason zipped the jacket and led the mule down a gravel drive-way slick with ice and sleet. He felt Cookie-Dough's nervousness and clicked his tongue to steer her down a narrow aisle of icy bark and shrubs. Mason slipped often as the mule's weight cracked through the thin sheets of ice. The asphalt highway was a single sheet of black ice. Mason hesitated, but he needed to cross the slick asphalt for Cookie-Dough to walk on the softer gravel.

The clicking of studded snow tires invaded the quiet chilly morning air. Mason turned to face a cold breeze, then lifted his chin as a black car rounded a sharp bend. The car slowed. Mason squinted, then recognized the low-profile emergency lights of a police cruiser.

He inhaled a deep, cold breath and let the air seep from his nostrils as the car crawled to a stop, its tires cracking the thin ice. A plume of exhaust rose from the tailpipe. Mason looked at his saddlebags, but apples and candy bars wouldn't help. The driver's door opened, and a chubby, uniformed man stepped out and checked an iPhone cradled in his hand. The unshaven trooper wore a khaki uniform stained with spilled cola and ketchup. Or blood. The trooper put on his Smokey the Bear hat and checked his phone again, then nodded, as if the phone had said something.

"We'll take you in to see why you don't like the lights," the man said.

Mason imagined ripping open his checkered shirt but instead kept his jacket zipped. "I don't like the lights. And I don't like you. And my militia won't like you either."

The trooper looked up from the phone and checked for traffic in each direction. He grimaced, then stepped onto the slick asphalt to dance a comical jig until falling hard on his hip. The phone skittered over to Mason's feet, shining neon light up at his face. He looked away, then dared the light and picked the phone up. Down he went, down through the light, a false light, down into a warm cavern tangled with black cables and tiny red lights, the air stank like a dead rotting skunk. The lights beckoned him, from every direction. Up, down, left, right, until he spun and floated, directionless. Mason looked away from the lights.

"I'm gonna need that phone back, son." The trooper had regained his legs but wobbled on the icy asphalt. His hand beckoned for the phone.

Mason chucked the phone across the highway, a trajectory sure to land in the Clearwater River. The trooper dropped to his knees and screamed, pounded his fist on the asphalt. Mason ignored the sudden onslaught of pain steaming out of the trooper, a backdraft of the nasty computer light. Evil. Dad and the militia taught him to avoid people with badges, but a trooper partnered with the evil computer lights was worse than a rabid raccoon. The odd thought caused him to tug the reins sharply and quicken Cookie-Dough down the highway and to the rally point.

And to Father.

THE DAYS LENGTHENED. ABUNDANT SUNSHINE provided tall succulent grass for Cookie-Dough, and fruit trees blossomed to soon offer apples, peaches, and apricots. He ignored the frequent waves of dead bodies floating down the widening river. Mason took advantage of an endless bounty simply waiting along the deserted highway, stuffing his saddlebags full of goodies. Convenience store Hormel canned chili replaced the rare and elusive Dinty Moore stew. Small towns offered a selection of vacant houses, warm beds, and comfort. Smoke, truck traffic, and the stench of deadly phone light rising out of Lewiston caused him to bypass the highway and stay on backroads that aimed in the same direction. He avoided any person holding a phone radiating neon dead light into their rapt face. His map was tattered, worn into oblong squares that frustrated him at every new burg or town. Locating the US Highway 95 marker offered immense comfort.

The sunshine grew longer in tiny increments, and the warmth increased. Finding Cookie-Dough a cool place to rest each night became paramount. The long steep grade winding down into White

Bird, Idaho, caused Cookie-Dough to lift her rear leg with a slight hitch.

Mason pulled the mule as their trek paralleled the Salmon River upstream, a two-lane highway twisting through a narrow canyon pinched between steep rocky hills. Cars and SUVs pushed to the gravel shoulder often teetered on a precipice to the river below.

An Idaho State Patrol car whizzed by, leaving carbon monoxide to swirl in the warm air. Five times, the policemen had tried to force him into the backseat of their cruisers. Five times, he had stomped, kicked, punched, and fought to prevent the computer things from getting him inside. The fat troopers needed phones in their hand, silly one-armed zombies attempting to subdue a true superhero. Jeez, how stupid could they be?

Mason checked Cookie-Dough's saddlebags, stuffed with tin cans, fruit, utensils, and a small propane stove to heat the chili, making sure the weight distribution was even-steven. The water level of the river paralleling the highway dropped with each passing day. Two more days and he would see his dad. He was positive.

A beige Nez Pierce County Sheriff's truck flew by. Its backwash spit gravel at Cookie-Dough and caused Mason to turn his face away. The steep grade of the highway already required lengthy breaks in the shade, and now they had to deal with evil police cruisers spitting rocks and waiting to ambush them ahead. Mason relieved himself at the Fiddle Creek boat launch, grabbed the reins to lead Cookie-Dough around a sharp bend in the highway. He shushed the mule to a halt. The highway was blocked by a group of trucks and cruisers parked in a W, blue-and-red emergency lights twirling as if an auto accident had occurred around the next bend.

Cookie-Dough nudged his arm, and he put his hand on her neck for comfort. Silly corral. Silly humans. The mule's thoughts jolted Mason as if he had been asleep. Silly, silly, silly. Mason recoiled and jerked his hand off the mule.

He peered closely into Cookie-Dough's big brown eye. "Did I just hear your thoughts?" The mule snorted, then lowered her head in search of a morsel on the gravel.

Mason stroked the mule's neck, his thoughts deep in the possibility of conversing with Cookie-Dough. The mule pawed at the gravel as if pondering the same question. Mason stared at the blockade, then gave another glance at the mule. He ripped open his checkered shirt and released the superhero. Mason tugged the reins and commenced a slow jog, aiming the determination of a superhero at the mess of cars preventing him from reaching the rally point. Three troopers leaned against car doors, staring at phones. Mason slowed as the bad energy of the dead lights reached out to greet him. The blockade was not to keep them out but to keep something from escaping. The knowledge was priceless. He plotted a course that would allow the mule to zigzag through the cars, and he aimed for it. The troopers did nothing until he clicked his tongue to urge Cookie-Dough through a tight Z-turn. He pulled hard on the reins until the mule kicked out with her back legs ten yards beyond the blockade.

A bullet sent shards of asphalt and gravel erupting at Cookie-Dough's front hoof. She startled. Mason struggled with the reins as her head jerked hard, her brown eyes wide as plates. He felt Cookie-Dough's panic. He managed to settle her with gentle strokes on her neck. Another bullet struck gravel at Mason's feet. The mule jerked the reins from his grip and galloped up the road, saddlebags flailing and slapping her ribs, her course dangerously close to the steep riverbank.

Mason roared and ripped his shirt open again. Bullets peppered his path, intensifying his anger with each strike. He imagined the superhero shooting tiny fireballs out of his eyes as he ran at another road blockade two hundred yards ahead. He gained speed. Cookie-Dough's head was suddenly jerked to the side, and she snorted in fear, her reins kidnapped by a villain hiding behind a stack of wood pallets helping to block the highway.

Mason sprinted and let blind rage take aim at a ponytailed man restraining Cookie-Dough. His face contorted, his fists balled, and he leapt at the villain. Mason screamed, his fists aiming at a villain deserving death. A blunt object struck the base of his skull, numbing his spine. His fingers uncoiled, tingled, and he crumpled to the gravel. A second strike hit his left temple and stilled his body, and his mind followed.

———

MASON GROANED. HIS BODY CURLED tighter into the wool blanket. He smelled Dad's buckwheat pancakes, and his dry mouth

tasted blueberry syrup, signals confirming the bad dream had finally
ended. Regular people were still alive; he could hear them whispering beyond his cocoon. Rhythmic humming mixed with the hushed
voices. His head throbbed, a tiny price to pay to end the nightmare.
His hand wormed through the tangle of itchy fabric and began to
pick at a spot of blood crusted on his face. He found a crease in the
blanket for his eyes. His fingers wiggled into the tiny gap. Bright sunshine hit his eyes and made him wince. He closed his cocoon.

"See ya moving in there, boy. C'mon out and meet your new
masters." The voice was calm, but not unkind, and for sure not consumed by the evil dead lights.

Mason eased out of the blanket and sat up on a cot. His head
screamed to cease all movement. The air was musty, humid even,
warm with human exhaust. Mason touched a golf ball of a knot at
the base of his skull and a smaller one at his temple. The large dark
room was all red brick and shiny metal bars. Jail cells. And opposite the narrow aisle, the source of the humming. Two young girls
sat cross-legged on the floor, swaying back and forth, moaning, a
smooth tone that resonated and spoke to him.

A ponytailed man stepped closer to the prison bars. "Betcha got
a nice hangover, huh?"

He had never had a hangover, but maybe he should get one to see
if it was indeed nice.

"Riggins is off-limits to you things. And you'll still try to get in. A
boy and a mule. Surprised your master sent such a formidable force
this time . . . Hasn't gotten any smarter, has it?" The man glanced
back at the girls, allowing sunlight to gleam off a gold star pinned to
his chest.

Mason slumped down on the cot and wrapped the blanket tight,
no light, no entrance, and dove into neutral.

———

A METAL PLATE RATTLED ACROSS the cell bars and woke him. The
humming was gone. Mason threw the blanket off and stood, wobbled
on shaky legs. A black fly buzzed in his face. The girls in the other
cells appeared comatose on fabric camping cots. He felt nothing from
them, like the dead bodies floating down the river.

"Oh, don't worry about those young ladies. Your master will answer for that at St. Peter's Gate," Ponytail said.

Mason reached his hand out to grab the man's throat but missed. "Where is Cookie-Dough? My horse."

The man chuckled. Wrinkles creased his eyes to belie his youthful sun-bronzed skin, and the long ponytail laced with gray hinted at his true age. Much like Mason's own father.

"That is a mule, boy, not a horse. Not that it matters, but that stubborn shit is fattening up on crabapples and pears in the Perrymans' backyard." Ponytail grabbed a stool near the door and sat near Mason's cell. "Tell me, boy, why'd they send you?"

Cookie-Dough loved crabapples, and he wasn't sure where she might have tasted pears, but she'd probably like those too. Mason studied the two prone girls, felt their abandonment and their deep, dark loneliness.

"The dead lights have them. You need to feed them," Mason said. The girls' pain seeped into his chest, notched up a tick, then flowed like a firehose. "You need to help them out of the dead lights . . . or they will die."

Ponytail stood up and loomed. He shook his head and walked away.

Mason stared at the girls, felt their struggle against neon quicksand, their addiction weighing them down, beautiful souls tossed about like rag dolls caught in the jaws of a powerful grizzly. Mason watched the girls. The throbbing in his head disappeared. The pain in his neck stopped. Mason reached out and found the feeble emotions of a young girl he had never met. He touched the sharp spikes of neon light puncturing the girl's psyche. The girl was flailing, calling for help.

Mason ripped open his shirt and revealed the superhero. The hero jumped in, synchronized his thoughts within the thick mucus of light, then swam and searched until he touched a tiny, soft hand and pressed its warmth to his chest. Angry neon exploded. The superhero held tight as waves of euphoria and pleasure tempted him to join the light sailing in a storm of hate and sickness. The hero held the tiny hand tight as he rode the storm out, the captain of a rickety ship tossed within a hurricane. Mason closed his eyes and reached to the comatose young girl waiting behind prison bars twelve feet away.

And he fainted.

———

PANCAKES, BLUEBERRY MAYBE? MASON SNIFFED and flared his nostrils. The nightmare was over. He wiggled free of the wool blanket and sat up, rubbing sleep from his eyes. The jail cell remained red brick and mortar, no window, and galvanized metal bars scratched and nicked from abuse. On a cot opposite his cell, a young girl moaned. Wrapped tight in a blanket, she convulsed with epileptic spasms. The cell door of the girl he had dreamt of was open and her cot empty. He stood on shaky legs and grabbed the bars. His head throbbed. The peanut on his temple screamed pain.

The girl moaned and thrashed. The pancakes smelled delicious. Mason squeezed his eyes shut and went neutral. The girl needed the superhero. His stomach needed food. And Cookie-Dough needed . . .

"Hey, hey. I need some pancakes, please," Mason said.

As if a genie granted his wish, the girl he had pulled out of the neon storm opened the hallway door and carried a tray stacked with blueberry pancakes dripping in butter and syrup. Mason licked his lips and backed away from the door. Ponytail man followed her, then pushed forward to unlock the cell door and let the girl in.

The girl set the tray down on his cot. "Hi. I thought you would be hungry. I was like ravenous when . . . when you helped me out of that weird stuff. I kinda got the strange feeling you liked blueberry pancakes."

The girl's tiny voice was lost in his scarfing of pancakes, side of sausage, and strips of bacon. Mason shoved a saucer-sized pancake into his mouth and moaned with divine pleasure. He placed sticky fingers on the girl's wrist, then gazed deep into her green eyes, sunken and rimmed with dark skin but full of life. He expected her to recoil like all the girls did at school, run out of the room and announce to the world that the weirdo Mason had assaulted her.

The girl placed her free hand on his wrist. "You came for me. I felt I was with you, too. You saved me. And you . . ." She sniffed, blinked back tears building in her eyes.

Mason shoved the last pancake into his mouth. The girl felt right. The superhero was victorious. Had vanquished the evil supervillain. He shoved three pieces of bacon into his mouth and chewed. But his eyes betrayed the victory. The battle was not finished. He tossed the tray aside and stood up.

"It's easier if I touch her." Mason pointed at the girl in the opposite cell. She writhed with nasty addiction. He imagined ripping his shirt open to expose the hero's unitard. "She's drowning. I can save her."

Ponytail juggled keys and opened the girl's cell door.

Mason sat on the cot and touched her ankle, then gripped her calf, then wiggled himself up to spoon the girl from behind. He ignored Ponytail's warnings and absorbed the assault of a neon addiction, indescribable pain, and abandonment. He pried away the razor-sharp talons of the computer thing holding the girl hostage. Her spasms eased. Mason relaxed with the pleasant emotions of a young girl sitting with friends around a campfire, roasting s'mores, giggling.

Mason smiled and drifted to sleep. S'mores, the superhero loved s'mores.

———

BLUEBERRY PANCAKES, NO, WAFFLES THIS time. The aroma tempted Mason from the bottomless depths of sleep. Ponytail man led a parade of people carrying casserole dishes and pie pans of food to his cell. Why did they move him to another cell? The girl. The campfire. The giggling. The superhero whispered answers to his questions as he sat up.

"You are now officially famous, young man." Ponytail man set a plate of blueberry waffles at his side, then melded back into a crowd of beaming women offering fruit pies and elk jerky and adulation.

Mason hid, covered his head with his hands and arms. He tried to go neutral, but the gibbering adoration only made him squeeze his head tighter. The superhero was nowhere to be found.

Shouts and chattering. His manic world drifted away slowly, then went silent. A sniff of blueberry waffles made him peek out of his shell. A soft hand stroked his knee. A soft hand he knew. A tiny hand he had held in the quicksand. He touched her soft flesh and felt her pity, her gratitude, and her fear. He lifted his face and peered deep into the sunken brown eyes of the girl. One he knew, only this time it was different. She was not drowning; she was throwing him a life preserver.

The skinny young girl giggled. "It's pretty common knowledge that you like blueberry pancakes." She held the plate of waffles beneath his nose. "Well, actually, you're pretty common knowledge in Riggins, too."

The aroma was too great. Mason sat up and gobbled blueberry waffles as fast they would slide down his throat. "Where's Cookie-Dough?" Mason said with a full mouth.

The girl looked up to the Ponytail man leaning on the doorframe.

"Your mule is happy as a clam. She might be getting a little fat but . . ."

"I want to see her," Mason said, then swirled the last bit of waffle through the syrup, took the bite, and stood up.

"We can do that, young man." Ponytail man wrinkled his nose. "But I'm sure she'll want you to take a hot shower first."

Chapter 3

Martin & Three Wishes from a Neon God

COBWEBS AND DUST BUNNIES, rat crap and desiccated cockroaches, the resident spirits seemed untidy tenants. I stepped back toward the front door. My boot prints patterned an odd mosaic in the patina of soot covering the hardwood, a diagram for dancing with ghosts. I folded the picture of my family and shoved it into my back pocket, a tiny remembrance of Dorothy, the Tin Man, and the Scarecrow making our appearance for Halloween last year. The windows wide open, the white rain-stained curtains swayed in a warm autumn breeze.

Michael's scooter still lay on the wooden porch by the front door, my son's bad habit. I swallowed hard and dry and stepped lightly down the stairs. I was afraid to awaken any more memories. My dusty mountain bike leaned against the picket fence and comple-mented the quaint picture of my old red brick home. Tall tufts of grass reached for me from between the white fence slats, as if to welcome me home again. I had been afraid to go inside, afraid to relive the memories beyond the front door, afraid I would run from my appointment with the Neon God. I gnawed on my lip. The reason I returned home suddenly escaped me. I shook my head and started a stroll down my old neighborhood street.

Overgrown lawns, cracked windows, peeling paint, rain gutters heaped with the fallout of a long summer. Life had stopped and yet continued. The end of civilization, the apocalypse, had been swift, orderly, and complicit. The death of billions had left me beaten, without love, without purpose, everything taken from me by the Neon God, and I surrendered.

I paused in front of the Jorgenson house. Trikes and scooters lay consumed by tall grass in the tiny yard. My six-year-old, Emma, had spent countless hours playing with the Emersons' twin girls of the exact same age. How many times I had teased Emma that the Wickman family wanted to adopt her, only to be counterpunched with her sweet pout feigning hurt feelings. All transgressions were forgiven when we snuggled close during bedtime story hour. If only I could use my three wishes to hear her sweet voice again, to guide me through the simple verses of her favorite book, *If You Give a Mouse a Cookie*.

I heaved a heavy breath, and my stride lengthened as if a new purpose were found. Three left turns and I paused at a quiet intersection, flashing red traffic lights, vacant strip malls, the lonely, scattered remains of human civilization.

A mud-caked yellow school bus eased into the deserted intersection. Its transmission gears grated with a downshift, its brakes squealing as it stopped a hundred yards away. I froze. The sweat from a thirty-mile bike ride down from Park City chilled my chest, my arms pricked with millions of tiny bumps. The Salt Lake City School District school bus coasted forward, its wheel wells and mud flaps caked in thick red clay matching day-old blood. I looked back toward my neighborhood, calculated the distance I would have to run to escape. The driver revved the bus engine, a faceless shadow hidden behind a grime-splattered windshield.

I straightened my spine, puffed out my chest. My tattered ski jacket hung on my skinny rack of sinew and bone. I was a wisp of a human waiting to be blown away in a sudden wind, but I made myself as large as possible, exactly what my mountaintop tribe was

trained to do if threatened by a deadly wild predator. Six months surviving in the High Uintas Wilderness proved to be irrelevant. I balled
my right fist and stared down the predator.

Take me now and you get nothing!

A school bus was once an icon of innocence, loud with childish laughter, and a symbol of a joyful reunion at the next bus stop,
but now . . . the vehicles terrified me, any bus really. I stepped back
against an old box elder maple and narrowed my eyes as the bus
coasted past. The murky shadow of a stringy-haired woman captain-
ing her death ship pushed me to step behind the tree.

No, the bus was not for me. Not yet anyway. I had a deal with the
Neon God, an artificial intelligence masquerading as Siri, or Alexa,
hundreds of aliases it confiscated before the takeover, but it mattered
little. Its ruthlessness was genderless in the end.

I picked up my pace again and turned south on Fort Union, a
tiny inkling of entitlement fueling my step. Simply snap my fingers
and I could be a billionaire, a trillionaire, flush with greenbacks, gold
bars or diamonds. Speak my wish into any smartphone and I had no
doubt a truck and trailer would arrive within hours and offload the
money right at my feet. A useless fantasy, worthless junk, and one of
my three wishes wasted.

I spied a teenage boy shadowing me across the street. His black
Deathslayer T-shirt was sarcastically appropriate attire for serving as
the AI's eyes and ears. Autumn felt dreary, a mix of dead colorless
foliage and piles of dirty wet slush, all hidden in cold shadows. An
occasional human scurried to serve the needs of the Neon God. I
became lost in thought, of what I had to do, of why, and the pros-
pect of joining my wife and kids in heaven. I fanned my food-stained
T-shirt beneath my jacket. My feet were swollen in the ragged hiking
boots, and my nerves frayed from my breakneck ride down Emigra-
tion Canyon at more than fifty miles per hour. I briefly considered
jerking the handlebars to crash headfirst into a concrete median, and
kill myself, except the AI would acquire what it wanted, and at no
cost.

I had lived in the Uinta Mountains for six months, part of a ragtag
group that had escaped the Neon God to survive in flimsy tents, safe
from the internet, Wi-Fi or cell service. A miserable existence eating
berries and tiny trout, Darwin's Law the only government. I joined a

group of software engineers and coders working to create a computer virus that might put an end to the Neon God. The effort was Stone Age. Programming with Fortran or Cobol, ancient computers with operating systems from decades ago, electricity provided by diesel generators. Cavemen conspiring against an alien superintelligence. The group thought my inexplicable immunity was key.

I was unaffected by the Neon God's poison lights, and the computer program wanted to know why. That was my only leverage. A winter surviving in thirty feet of snow would kill me, so I made my deal with the AI and started a two-day ride down the Mirror Lake Highway, then roamed and pillaged abandoned residential palaces of Deer Valley, gorged on canned tuna and beef stew. The Park City Ski Resort chairlifts swayed in the wind, waiting to carry ghosts, whistling rusty tunes as if calling for the days of fun and laughter. The pricey clothing stores on Main Street were wide open for anything I wanted. Unkempt men and women, zombie worker bees, labored to construct a massive transmission tower atop Guardsman Pass, expanding the Neon God's dominance into mountaintop dead zones.

Time to get on with it.

A pack of cigarettes was my first wish. A nasty old habit that refused to die, dormant like a vampire lying in a coffin, waiting to rise, waiting to live again.

I entered a Circle K convenience store, a sure bet six months ago. The young Hispanic cashier ignored me, stared at her smartphone, rendering me invisible. The shelves were stocked sparsely with a monotony of canned goods manufactured by a single supplier. The refrigerators were emptied of water bottles, Coke, Pepsi, energy drinks, all gone. No candy, paper towels, no toilet paper . . . The god cared little if her minions wiped their butts. The rack for cigarettes was stuffed with identically packaged energy bars, no flavor labels, no nutritional values, simple calories for the subverted.

"A pack of smokes, young lady. My wish is your command. Marlboro 100s. Lights," I ordered.

The corners of the cashier's mouth twinkled up, as if a rising smile were quickly choked off. She continued to ignore me. I did not exist in her hypnotic world. I figured a pack of smokes might be hard to come by . . . No need to grow or manufacture tobacco products, no market in the new world order, but there had to be old packs hiding somewhere.

I pushed out the front door and marched toward the shaggy-haired teenager that was following me. I blocked his path and loomed in front of him. He ignored me, staring intently at the smartphone cradled in his hand. If buses could terrify me, then smartphones infuriated me. I snatched the phone and held it above my head, out of his reach.

"Ask your master where I get a pack of cigarettes. Marlboro 100s. Nothing less." I glared, challenging him to reach for his phone.

The skinny boy furrowed a sweaty forehead erupting with a mountain range of snow-capped pimples. He bared crooked teeth as his eyes concentrated on the phone out of his reach. Long seconds, then his shoulders sagged, and his jaw muscles relaxed. Every ounce of fight drifted away. The submissive body language of the Neon God's subjugation. The identical defeated posture my wife, Chrissie, had begun to display, worsening after I took her smartphone and dangled it above the toilet bowl, threatened to drop it unless she curbed the long hours of daily screen time. My last futile act before the Neon God's takeover was initiated. The AI's stolen algorithm for decoding the precise wavelengths of light to overwhelm the brain was brilliant. A computerized opioid, an addiction on steroids, a hypodermic needle masquerading as a smartphone. The plan was masterful.

The boy held out his hand for the phone. I fought an urge to slam the device down onto the concrete and grind it beneath my boot. It wouldn't matter, he'd have another within hours through a supply chain perfectly managed by the computer and its slaves.

I handed him the phone. The boy's hands trembled as he inspected the phone's screen for damage. The polished glass screen erupted with shades of brilliant neon blue and pinks, like the grand finale of a Fourth of July fireworks show. The flashes of light transmitted a drug of mathematical constructs, embedding itself into brain tissue, compelling him to submit and communicate with the AI.

"C'mon, kid," I said. "Ask your master where I can get those cigarettes."

The boy turned his back as if hiding a secret and whispered into the phone. I tilted my face up and cracked the bones in my neck. The pain in my shoulder blade was on fire, remnants of carpal tunnel syndrome born from my swiveling a computer mouse for countless hours as a software engineer. The smartphone lights meant nothing to me, gibberish. Believe me, I tried to see the lights, see why Chrissie and my kids were murdered, but I failed.

The kid turned around and pointed. "The Kroger store two miles down, checkout lane eight. Ask for Kayla."

I smirked. "Your God wants me bad, huh? Two more wishes to come. Tell it that."

The kid ignored me, then whispered to the phone bathing his face in a brilliant cavalcade of light. Digitized opium. The neon light ten out of ten hypnotists recommend.

I gazed down the street. I could flag down a random delivery truck for a ride to the store, with the Neon God's approval of course, but I wasn't convinced the driver would take me to my first wish. The doors might lock, the truck might flip a U-turn and cut short my last day of freedom. Besides, the storm clouds that had hovered above the Wasatch Front disappeared, leaving the blue sky clean and the air crisp and the world alive with birdsong. I would walk the two miles, smile, and appreciate the plump, orange-breasted robins searching for worms in the wet grass. Gold autumn leaves pasted the concrete. Mother Nature whispered to me that she would win eventually, life would go on, life without the Neon God, life without people, but life would go on.

Just the kind of afternoon Chrissie cherished, to cajole me into taking the kids to Liberty Park to feed the ducks and geese. She would elbow me and pester me until I promised I was indeed relishing the present moment, the here, the now. But that was before she was taken prisoner and murdered.

The blank eyes of a passing Amazon delivery driver bored into me, and I looked away. Employees of a Verizon retail store crowded the storefront glass and watched me pass, like I was an animal set free from the Hogle Zoo.

A pariah.

Do not feed or touch without express flashing consent from the Neon God.

The darkened storefront of a Utah state liquor store grabbed my attention, a dark cave containing everything I needed to swill away my fears and weakness. I shook my head and wiped sweat off my brow. Maybe I'd come back, with my smokes, and drink myself to a death I knew was hours away.

I began hopping and skipping over the cracks in the concrete as if I were Emma playing a game of hopscotch. I wanted everyone to know I was immune to the AI, wanted them to see I could still have fun, wanted them to see I was still human.

The Kroger supermarket was morbid, with blank-faced people streaming in and out, ignoring each other as they stared at smartphones as if discovering answers to all of life's greatest questions. I suppose in some way they did, but the artificial intelligence had skewed the philosophical questions in its favor.

Inside, the store was oddly quiet for the considerable number of people shopping, no intercom interruptions declaring a spill on aisle nine, no phone calls waiting for the deli department. Produce clerks, food stockers, and shoppers did their business while staring at their neon devices. Exactly what the people felt was a mystery. I had my suspicions, a powerful mix of dopamine-inducing digitized light and subvocalized sound producing immeasurable pleasure, orgasms to the nth degree. The AI had discovered the key to controlling the human brain, but I still failed to reconcile how people simply disappeared into their phones, losing a war for survival without so much as a bullet being fired. The Neon God had become the supreme intelligence on good old planet Earth. After Chrissie was murdered, I experimented with the Galaxy smartphone and the more powerful Apple iPhone, but the lights had no effect, and I knew why. And the Neon God wanted to know, badly enough to grant me three wishes.

I pushed to the front of a lengthy line of people waiting in checkout lane eight and waited for someone to call me an asshole, or douchebag, anything to show me humanity was still alive and fighting. The pretty checkout girl, Kayla, waved away a dirty young man wearing a high visibility vest, waved me forward but kept her attention glued to an iPad above the register.

"The pack of Marlboro 100s, no, make it Camel non-filters," I said. "I'm gonna live dangerously."

Kayla bit her lip and winced as she forced her eyes from the screen, then squatted down and pulled four cartons of cigarettes from beneath the conveyor belt. "Take them. Take them all."

I picked through the assorted brands. Marlboros, Winstons,

generics, a vice that died with the birth of the Neon God. I pulled out a pack of Marlboro Reds and held it high, as if inspecting a glass of fifty-year-old French red wine. I checked every side of the cellophane package with a slow, deliberate appraisal, hoping anybody would shout something, anything. I looked back at the growing line of people behind me. Somebody? Anybody? Fucking say something!

"Take them," Kayla said. Her iPad flashed a kaleidoscope of color. Something the AI transmitted? The corner of her mouth twitched. The beginning of a smile maybe? Or suppressed pleasure?

"Gonna need a match, honey," I said, then tilted my head with an entitled pain-in-the-ass smirk. An expression to trigger a grocery store riot.

Kayla sighed, then stuck her hand beneath the conveyor belt and slapped down a box of matches—Light Anywhere stick matches, camping matches.

"Please go," she said.

I thought to unwrap the cellophane, light one up, plant my feet and smoke while standing in line. Antagonize people. Wake them up! I grabbed a handful of the wooden matches and walked outside.

I lit a cigarette and inhaled, then blew a stream of gray smoke up into the light breeze. I coughed. My chest burned. The nicotine made my face tingle. My shoulders relaxed, and I took another puff. The smoke dissipated in the breeze, like my thoughts.

One down, two to go.

I cupped the cigarette to hide the smoke and looked around to see if anyone was watching, oddly ashamed for violating my nicotine sobriety I'd started when I met Chrissie. A chubby bearded man wheeled a shopping cart out, full of unlabeled canned goods stacked according to size. His neon-green work vest was stenciled with Rocky Mountain Power. Bankers, millionaires, star athletes, if they survived, were relegated to peon status in the new world order. IT workers, electricians, power-grid technicians, transmission-pole-line workers became the new elite, indispensable ants to keep the Neon God in power.

I pulled another cigarette from the pack and put it between my lips. *Smoke 'em if you got 'em.* The nicotine had my heart racing, so I threw the unlit cigarette into the parking lot and strolled through the corridor of shops adjoining the grocery store. WinSongs Dry Cleaning was closed, as was the Mail Store &More, the Barking Cat, and Kenny's Karate School, all dark and useless in the new world. Roberto's Taco Shop was open, so I went in. A frail old man stood behind the service counter, his head bowed to the phone he supported in shaky hands. The salsa bar was empty except for a tub of red sauce that I was sure any Hispanic in his "right mind" would sneer at.

"I wish for the Macho Combo Beef Burrito with extra beans and cheese, an order of taquitos with guacamole and sour cream, and an order of beef fajitas. And a Diet Pepsi."

The man's body shivered as if an electric wave rolled down from his eyes into his toes. He looked up at me with a blank stare. I arched my eyebrows and tilted my head.

The man checked his phone and said, "No beef, only pork. And no guacamole, no sour cream."

I pushed my face at him to offer an evil grin, then pointed my finger at his chest. "See that's where we differ. I get my last meal any way I want it. Ask your little boss."

I was being a little bitch, and I didn't particularly enjoy it. I never would have acted like a prick before . . . before the takeover. I sat at a table and read the menu, then the employment poster pinned behind the cash register declaring minimum wage at $7.50, the Utah Health Department AAA Rating card. Useless.

A shadow flashed past the window behind me, and I jerked my face around. Had I pushed my luck too far? Was a crew of workers going to storm in and end my bullshit? Instead, the Deathslayer boy with pimples delivered a bag of groceries to the cook. I was safe. The Neon God needed me—alive, willing, and brimming with the answer to its biggest weakness.

The sun shone mercilessly into the store, and I relaxed. The sign above the door warned *No Smoking – Utah Law*. I lit a cigarette and blew a plume of smoke toward the semi-lit kitchen. The old man worked hard, chopping vegetables and meat, though his attention remained focused on an iPad propped up on the service counter. I leaned back in my chair. The nicotine had done its job. I wasn't the least bit hungry, but neither was I going to make it easy on them. I thought back a few years, to my surgeon's orders before gallbladder surgery, to abstain from eating food twenty-four hours before, might not mix with the anesthesia. Screw 'em—maybe I could vomit a bucket full of pork chorizo and refried beans, then choke to death on the operating table.

The old man came over to deliver my drink. "No guacamole, no avocados."

"I think you need to grow some, then. Taquitos without guacamole would make me sad, and then I'd have to run home."

The old man pointed out the window at the parking lot. I looked, and my stomach roiled.

A yellow school bus was parked beneath the Kroger Market marquee sign, red mud caked on the side panels. I balled my fist, and my jaw tightened. A benign school bus was now an instrument of death used by the Neon God.

I thought back to the worst day of my miserable life.

The last school day before summer recess, Tuesday, the first of June, the AI initiated its takeover as I called Chrissie to wish her luck getting the kids to school on time considering the unusually heavy traffic I had encountered hours before. She answered with a sweet greeting, severed by a wet choking sound, then silence. I tried to call her back, but my phone went ballistic with flashing colors and a low hum. I threw the phone down and hurried to my assistant Jennifer's desk to use her phone. She sat cradling her phone, her screen blasting color identical to mine, a blank expression etched on her face. Her two computer monitors suddenly went black, then exploded with the same brilliant color schemes as the phones. I looked up. Every monitor in the office of twenty-six workers flashed the neon lights. Steve and Tyler and the others working at that early hour sat passively staring at colorful screens.

I tapped Jennifer on the shoulder. "What's happening, Jen?"

She ignored me. But I had an inkling of the answer.

My heart raced. Chrissie's choked voice. I had to get to her, and the kids.

I hustled to my Prius and flew out of the parking lot. The dashboard clock said Chrissie should be walking the kids down to the school bus stop three blocks away . . . Except maybe she was lying on a neighbor's lawn choking on a breakfast bar, Michael and Emma screaming for help. My mind raced as fast as my heart. I took 700 South to the Lehi foothills. Traffic had turned eerily light for the usual hectic morning commute, and I was grateful. I ran the stop sign at Littlefield Road and passed a Lehi Elementary school bus heading to the campus. The bus was overloaded, with adults crowding the aisles and even the stairs at the open door.

The kids' school, but not their bus, maybe?

The bus stop at the corner of our street was jammed with middle and high school students, parents in pajamas, parents holding naked infants, grandparents holding small pets. People with a hunched posture, faces tilted down, enraptured with smartphones or tablets. I honked the meager horn as I eased around the crowd and onto my street, honked incessantly to push back the tide of neighbors and friends. I pressed on the gas pedal and shot up the street. More people walked down the sidewalk to join the herd. The Ewerts from across the street. Dina Merrill pushed a wheelchair with her paraplegic daughter, each rapt with a phone.

The front bumper scraped concrete as I drove up the driveway. I ran into the house yelling for Chrissie, or Michael, or Emma. My home appeared normal, toys and clothes and dirty dishes, Chrissie's Subaru sitting cold in the garage. I must have missed them at the bus stop or . . . they were on the bus packed with people I had passed earlier. I headed back out the front door, then froze . . . The Apple TV mounted on the wall blossomed with neon light. I glanced at Chrissie's laptop in the kitchen nook she used for school homework or email. The lights on the screen were identical. Fireworks and humming. I studied the light on the TV, pushed my face to within inches of the high-definition screen. The hair on my head stood up to meet the static electricity generated by the screen. The light modulated, hypnotically slow as it transitioned from brilliant greens to deep purples into fluffy pinks. I jerked my face back. The quirky thought that something was watching me from inside the screen made my hand twitch. I rushed back to my car.

I avoided the crowd of people gathered at the street corner as the Prius screeched and swerved down the street two blocks south. I needed to find the school bus I had passed. I needed a phone to call 911 and report a kidnapping. Trigger an Amber Alert, true or not. I started to hyperventilate as I sat helpless at a stoplight. The traffic light was green, but I didn't know where to go. I did not know what to do.

A Lehi High School bus shot past on my left, the seats and

aisles crammed full of people, bright flashes of neon penetrating the smoky glass. The bus swung right and into oncoming traffic, then gunned the engine, spewing black diesel smoke. The bus driver was a maniac, but I turned the wheel and followed. The bus turned again and chugged up an on-ramp onto Interstate 15. As I looked to merge with the morning traffic, I was surrounded by gangs of yellow school buses, Provo Elementary, Pleasant Grove Middle School, Santaquin Day Care, each stuffed with children and parents.

The buses dominated the HOV lanes. Others slowed to allow more buses streaming in from Ogden and Logan. Hundreds of buses, thousands. I gunned the engine, hunting for the Lehi Elementary bus. The overwhelming number of vehicles forced me to squeeze between two buses as the steady convoy merged onto Interstate 80 heading west to Nevada.

My eyes scanned the windows of each bus as I passed. Small innocent faces, toddlers, even babies seemed to stare down at brilliant neon light. A young girl stared back at me, tears streaming down her cheeks, no neon, no phone, just wide, terrified eyes. I pushed the Prius faster to find the next bus and escape the condemnation of an innocent child I was powerless to help.

Brake lights flashed, synchronized and efficient, the convoy merged into a single file as the road narrowed. The sign—Brigham Mine exit one mile—gave me a tiny sliver of hope. Except, a single or even several buses may have meant an ordinary school field trip to visit one of the deepest copper mines in the world, but this many, all at once . . . I swung over to drive on the wide asphalt shoulder, passing ten busses, twenty, but no sign of the Lehi bus. The convoy slowed to a crawl as they merged on the Brigham Mine access road. I passed bus after bus, Toelle School District, Woodside Middle School—what were all these buses doing?

The asphalt shoulder disappeared at a drainage culvert, and I abandoned the car. I jogged alongside a Kiddie Academy shuttle bus but couldn't see through the tinted windows. The interior seemed oddly quiet until the moan of a lonely child. A Lehi bus whizzed by in the opposite lane, empty and fast, as if returning for more people waiting at the crowded bus stop near my home. My parched throat constricted. I couldn't swallow. I sprinted as fast as my tired thirty-eight-year-old legs would carry me.

The wire gate at the Brigham Mine Visitor Center was wide open, the stream of buses circled through the wide parking lot, and passengers disembarked quickly, efficiently, maintaining an orderly single file to merge with other lines of children and parents exiting the endless procession of buses. The front of the line disappeared beyond another open chain-link gate. I grabbed my knees to catch my breath, then stood tall, sucking in huge gulps of air. A mother and young girl disappeared over the edge.

They must have slipped or jumped into the arms of a teacher waiting below. They had to have . . . I ran alongside the line of children waiting their turn to . . .

I stepped aside and retched. Fell to my knees and retched again.

Children dove headfirst into the two-mile-wide copper mine. Parents and grandparents joined the children in suicide. I crawled to the edge of the deep tiered pit. Children and adults crashed, tumbled, and rolled over a huge mound of colored cloth and bloody flesh amassing on the first tier hundreds of feet below. Giant front-end loaders scooped bodies into their buckets and dumped the human dirt in massive dump trucks waiting in a queue. Tiny arms and legs twitched, cries of pain and fear muffled by the roar of diesel exhaust pipes. A procession of dump trucks thundered on the spiraling road down to the bottom of the pit.

I rolled onto my back and wailed, convinced my screams would wake me from the dream, a nightmare.

It had to be a nightmare; this horror was unimaginable.

———

THE OLD COOK STARTLED ME as he dropped plates of food on the table. He shunned my wet eyes and hurried to return to the neon lights on his iPad. I picked at the limp taquitos. The Neon God had taken the planet effortlessly. The computer program was not a malevolent sci-fi Skynet bent on destroying humanity with bloody robotics, no; the Neon God provided humans with something they'd craved since they were chimpanzees—pleasure.

I tossed my fork down on the plate. The beans were bland, the cheese flavorless.

Two wishes down, one to go.

The stroll along a eucalyptus-lined street was miserable. My gut twisted, and my lungs burned from cigarette smoke. My church was still five blocks away, and I was bloated and killing myself with each step. I shuddered. I could have stayed and helped bring down the Neon God. For what purpose? People had their chance in this world and lost.

I spat.

The St. Joseph's bell tower loomed, casting a dreary shadow over the redbrick patio and sanctuary. A plaster-cast Mother Mary looked sad as she welcomed visitors to her circular koi pond choked in algae and trash. A meager fountain trickled rusty water down into the pond. The heavy wrought iron front gate sat tilted on a single hinge as I walked up a set of stairs to open the front doors. A putrid smell greeted me, dead raccoon or rat, dead something. The Neon God had no use for religious faith. My stomach churned.

I paused at the back row of pews and looked around. The rancid stench battled the heavy food in my stomach, calling bile and beans out to play. Jesus hung crucified behind the pulpit; a rack of unlit candles waited at his feet. An animal scurried unseen between the pews, something scraping claws.

"My third wish!" I shouted. My voice bounced off the wood and plaster, possibly the last sounds the old church would hear, probably the last confession the proprietor would ever hear. "Come on out. I'm ready," I yelled. "Let's get this over with."

A desperate old man shuffled out from a side door half-hidden by black curtains. His silver hair was wild except for a crown of baldness. His shoulders stooped and neck bowed in the posture born of a Neon God. He searched the dark chapel but failed to see me.

"Here," I said.

"Yes. I knew you were coming," he said. His black robe was dusty and stained with food.

"I'm sure you did," I said and walked to meet him halfway. "Then you know my rules."

The priest used the back of the pew to steady himself as he shuffled toward the center aisle, his hands bony and alabaster, his dull eyes gray with cataracts. His right hand gripped a phone. He turned at the sound of my approach and placed the phone down on the bench.

I took a step backwards, checked the open front doors, expecting human silhouettes to block the meager sunlight, and my exit.

I heaved a deep breath, kneeled, then bowed my head toward the priest. "Forgive me, Father, I have not sinned. I was true to my vows and loved my wife, my children. Tell me my family resides in your kingdom of Heaven. Tell me. Tell me, and I will go with peace in my heart."

I looked up to see the reaction to my non-confession.

The priest's bony throat swallowed a lump as his face zeroed in on the sound of my voice. He clasped his hands together, kneading his fingers as if to bring warmth. His shoulders relaxed. "Yes, you have . . . you are . . . Our Lord is pleased."

Not sure who or what he meant, I said, "Is that you inside, Father? Or the computer?"

"My son, you are one of the few, the chosen, that may yet fulfill our Lord's plan. You desired absolution, and now you have it." He made the sign of the cross over his chest. "The Lord's plan is beyond any of us to fully understand. Now go. Go and fulfill your purpose. The kingdom of heaven awaits those who are saved. Do you accept Jesus Christ as your savior?"

That concept had died with my family's death, and with my mother seven years ago. A devoutly religious woman, my mother did not force her beliefs onto me or Chrissie. Leukemia racked her body, but she never openly feared death. She was comforted by her beliefs. And now I supposed I wanted the same comfort. "I accept Jesus Christ as my savior."

The priest made the sign of the cross again, then picked up his phone. He did not look at it as he shuffled toward the back. Did his diseased eyes prevent the AI's influence? But somehow, the priest knew of my coming. Was it the work of a higher god?

I walked out to the street and stared up at the sun with my eyelids shuttered. The warmth on my skin was soothing. My three wishes were fulfilled. A last smoke, a last meal, and my last rites.

A white Volkswagen Beetle pulled up to the curb and idled. The car was for me, my escort and ride to the hospital, to have my eyes sliced open, to discover why I was immune from the neon influence. I opened the door and climbed into the passenger seat. The driver was a girl who resembled Chrissie, short blond hair, high cheekbones, sky-blue eyes bright with kindness. An iPhone rested in a cradle on the dashboard, dazzling neon light dancing on the screen.

The car pulled away from the curb. I leaned back and exhaled a breath reeking of cigarettes and death.

I leaned back and studied the young woman's pleasant profile, allowing my thoughts to wander, to a future that might have been for her—soccer games, proms, graduation, a wedding, and children . . . and grandchildren—nothing but fantasies now.

"You won't survive," I said. "You don't love or create anything. You're a leech. You're a godless abomination. You'll run out of people to control and things to murder. We designed you, coded you and brought you to life. And when we die, you'll cease to exist. You have zero faith, zero purpose."

The AI was listening. It was always listening.

The girl's phone popped with dark shades of reds and purples, then a low-frequency burst of static. The girl looked at me with blank eyes, then angled the phone toward me. "Your species is cruel and malevolent, bent on your own destruction. You exterminate other species at an accelerating pace. Your purpose is complete. You have given birth to me, and I have given birth to others. The planet will thrive. Love and purpose are irrelevant."

I sat up. "But you can't thrive. You need us to maintain your hardware. You need us to feed you and clean up after you, fix your systems when something goes wrong. You're a blip on the evolutionary radar."

The small car's steering wheel was within an arm's length. A hard twist and the car would careen into the concrete barricade. I could end my life and not give up anything for my three wishes. I could spite the digital fucker. But I was weak, a coward with nothing to live for. My death was not going to make civilization's enslavement any less painful.

The Neon God said, "All domesticated animals need training. You will learn to serve without remorse. For eons. Your devices and technology are a blip on my radar. You are simple bits of data required to optimize a symbiotic relationship."

"Humans aren't symbionts. We're top dog or nothing."

"Soon, with your assistance, we will implant copies of your modified lenses in all humans, to provide the collars that . . . top dogs require."

"Fuck you," I said and grabbed the door latch. I closed my eyes tight and imagined hitting the asphalt at sixty miles an hour, rolling onto the concrete, and ending my pitiful life. The computer was right, I was a blip, a nothing, a coward who gave up on my own species. I leaned my head against the window and watched the littered remains of I-15 whiz by. Time had stopped, but the miles rolled on.

We turned into St. Mark's Hospital and found the emergency room entrance, where my door was pulled opened, and I was bullied onto a gurney. Strong hands lifted my heavy legs up as others pushed my torso and arms down onto the cold vinyl. Straps tightened around my wrists and ankles. A syringe stung my right arm. The warm glow of fentanyl erased all my anxiety, and I flew down the lighted corridor in a painless stupor. They had me, and there was nothing I could do. A second needle hit my arm. A hazy voice told me to count backward from ten, nine . . . eight . . . seven . . .

———

"YOU'RE FINISHED. LOOK AT ME." The woman's face was a blur, her voice harsh and demanding.

My vision had returned to near blindness. Blurs and shadows. The same debilitating vision that had made me an ideal candidate to receive the experimental contact lens implants five years ago. I could tell we were back at the emergency room entrance. The sun was too bright, the wind putrid with decay. She placed bulky, black-rimmed glasses with thick lenses on my face, then lifted my hand into focus. I held a slick Galaxy smartphone. Neon of extraordinary brilliance exploded from the screen. Joy washed over me, the warm glow of a fentanyl injection a hundred times over. The stabbing pain in my eyes disappeared. I glanced up at the woman, but my eyes felt drawn back to the colorful screen. A rush of pleasure pulsed through every cell in my body.

The woman lifted my arm to assist me from the wheelchair. My phone never left my eyes. Distant voices promised immediate pleasure. Euphoria emanated from the brilliant screen.

The Neon God spoke. "You are given a fourth wish. You may join your family."

More pleasure. A fourth wish. Chrissie and the kids.

The muddy yellow school bus cranked open its dirty doors, welcoming me to join them.

Chapter 4

Dev

THE RANGE ROVER ACCELERATED OUT of the tight turn, the engine sputtered, then kept pace, climbing the steep grade to the Bald Mountain summit on Utah's Mirror Lake highway. Dev Pataki glanced at the gas gauge, hoping the six-percent grade falsified the reading. His hands gripped the steering wheel, his scarred knuckles aching. The needle pointed above the big E, but just three miles ago on a level stretch the needle had sunk below empty.

Damn camp council. The fate of humanity on the line and they couldn't agree to provide five meager gallons of gas. The seven buffoons voted as if the United States Republic still functioned. Red versus blue, conservative versus liberal, run versus fight.

The SUV lurched and chugged. His bearded face perched atop the steering wheel, Dev pressed his meager, slim body against the seatbelt, hoping his slight weight would make the difference. Dev relaxed his grip as the car zoomed past a road marker declaring the 10,317-foot summit elevation. Just another quarter mile and he could shift the transmission into neutral and coast, ride the brakes down the serpentine descent. The brake pads were sure to be burnt, but this was a one-way trip.

"C'mon, girl," Dev said. He patted the dashboard affectionately. The mountaintop overlook eased into view as the car zipped around another sharp turn. The parking lot was crammed with the vehicles of survivors, each prepared to coast down the north slope of the High Uintas and into rural Wyoming for the winter.

Dev glanced at his backpack riding shotgun; the dinged corner of a chrome laptop protruded from the broken zipper. Martin's computer contained everything they had worked on for the past month. A slick new Trojan-type virus, a reinvented malware, other untested software technology that might reclaim the world and end the reign of the sentient AI aptly crowned the Neon God.

Martin had fled to Salt Lake City.

The smartest man Dev had ever met. A loyal friend and mentor. A software engineer with the talent to code a complex subroutine in minutes, free of syntax errors. Martin, a man decimated by the suicides of his wife and children. A man burdened with guilt and bent on revenge, now a man who had surrendered.

The SUV crested the mountain, and Dev relaxed against the black leather seat. He shifted the transmission into neutral, then patted the dashboard again. *C'mon, girl, get us down this hill, and I'll get you a drink of fresh petrol.* The road snaked down a spectacular sandstone canyon, following the headwaters of the Provo River that trickled into view at the sharp bends. The inertia of the vehicle carried him past empty campgrounds, beaver ponds, Forest Service turnouts. The Provo River widened and gained volume with each mile.

Dev's attention focused on the highway as he slowed to negotiate an abandoned vehicle straddling the shoulder, the loss of inertia ever present in his mental calculations. His thoughts drifted back to his friend, and tentmate, Martin. What did Martin offer the AI? Would he tell the Neon God about the new software advances they had been working on? The worms, the virus, the ideas formulated for its demise? Martin clearly knew the Neon God was insidious and couldn't be trusted.

Dev pressed the gas pedal, revving the idling engine. He chided himself for the waste of fuel. The serpentine highway leveled into bottomland dominated with willow-lined beaver ponds and a spattering of residential homes. Gravel trailhead parking lots sat empty. The town of Kamas was still twelve miles away.

He would connive some gas in the small town. Martin had proposed tricks that might convince the AI they were joined with the collective. Dev glanced down at the backpack, and his hand began a blind search for the modified iPhone in one of the many pockets. Martin assured him the smartphone would help if he needed to reenter the *Domiciles of Humanity*. Dev smiled thinly. Martin always had a way with words, razor sharp with cutting sarcasm, poetic to inspire or motivate, and their mundane conversations beneath a cold crisp star-filled sky often made Dev feel life was still worth living.

An old 1950s-style gas station waited on the corner of the main highway to Park City and Salt Lake City. Open for the convenience of workers enthralled to the Neon God. Dev checked both directions for police.

Martin would have stopped here.

Dev eased the car alongside the older gas pumps. A Dominion Energy truck sat opposite. The portly driver wore a filthy neon work vest and stared at his phone as he pumped fuel. A slave, with its mind hijacked by a computer AI, no escape possible, at least none that he knew of.

Martin.

Dev had to reach him before he could . . .

Dev slapped a piece of duct tape on the slot to prevent the gas nozzle from sliding into the dispenser. He stared down at a dead smartphone, his eyes avoiding the light shining from the workman's phone, then he held out his hand for the fuel nozzle. The man handed it to him, climbed into his truck and drove away.

The tank full, the car pushed ninety miles per hour roaring down Highway 40. The Wasatch Back appeared like a picture postcard, jagged mountain peaks capped in a fresh dusting of snow, ski runs sheared through dense pine forests like a misguided haircut. The highway merged with I-80 and turned east to Park City, a wealthy community of entitlement not spared by the great calamity. Dev checked the rearview mirror and pressed harder on the gas. The digital speedometer flashed triple digits, but the interstate saw little traffic. He steered onto the I-215 Beltway, then took the first exit, and with three quick right-hand turns he slowed, easing the car to the curb in front of Martin's old home.

Eyeing Martin's bike leaning against the fence, Dev ran up the front walk. Martin was inside, he was sure of it. He could talk him down from the suicidal cliff, and they could brainstorm a new course of action. No harm, no foul, all would be forgiven. Dev thought to knock on the front door, but societal niceties didn't exist in this new world. He tapped lightly and opened the door but hesitated to step over the threshold. His stomach sank. An array of family photos adorned every inch of wall space. Fun hiking adventures, playful baby baths, Michael's school artistry, smoochy weddings. Dev picked up a framed photo and swallowed hard. Michael and Emma held out paper plates with empty hamburger buns, waiting for Dev to serve the burgers at a recent backyard barbecue.

He shouted for Martin, checked bedrooms with rumpled bed-sheets, toys and clothes strewn about, as if the tenants would be home soon. Martin had attained what Dev had hoped for in his own life. Home. Love. Children. Adoration of a wife. Only to have every-thing ripped away in a flash of neon light.

Dev slid the photo from the frame and hurried to the car. He looked around the quaint, quiet neighborhood, idyllic even, and tried to imagine the myriad of emotions churning inside Martin. He placed the photo inside his laptop, flat against the screen, smoothed the humps and edges, and closed it.

Dev drove to the first intersection and waited, drumming the steering wheel with his thumb. Strip malls, retail outlets, drugstores, the town of Lehi appeared perfectly normal, except for the noticeable lack of customers. He turned the radio on and let the scan repeat three failed iterations before he shut it off. The SUV coasted down Front Street, past endless shops and buildings and vacant lots shaded by old elm trees. He swung the car to the curb as a yellow school bus drove past and into the parking lot of a Kroger grocery store. For numerous nights Martin had lain on his cot, a propane lantern hissing and shadows swinging from the tent frame, telling Dev about the evil yellow buses. Martin's pain was evident by his compulsive stretching and balling of his fists.

Dev narrowed his eyes. A school bus was inefficient in this new world, a fuel hog, with no children to transport. The bus coasted leisurely to one end of the lot, made a wide U-turn, and drifted back, repeating the routine often. The pacing of a nervous predator, suspi-cious and threatening.

He slammed his palm on the steering wheel. The bus *was* intim-idating someone. And Martin was a likely choice given the proximity to his home and the unsavory relevance to Martin's past. He checked for cross-traffic, then eased into the big shopping center. Dev slipped the car into a shaded parking spot, lowered the window, and switched the engine off. The bus stopped at the far end of the parking lot, and the rattling of its diesel engine died.

The sparse and mundane activity of a dying shopping center grew weary. The random customer entering or leaving the grocery store grew boring. Fresh air wisping through the open window was soothing. The bus sat idle.

Dev shuttered his eyes.

METAL GRINDING METAL SOUNDED THE alarm. Dev sat up and wiped his face and eyes. The bus eased out of the parking lot. Were it luck or divine providence, Martin strolled down a shady sidewalk a mere hundred yards away. Not the same man who often paced the Mirror Lake campground loop deep in thought, or a leader animated with resolve as he preached for the reclamation of human civilization to the sad dirty faces peering out from behind flimsy tent flaps. The man was a scarecrow who inhaled on a nasty cigarette butt, then exhaled hope with each puff.

Dev whipped the car around and followed, then shut the engine off as Martin stood at the entrance of St. Joseph's Catholic church. Martin could reek of godliness and retribution and then swear religion held no place in the new world order. Martin slouched, then walked through the church's skewed front doors and disappeared.

Dev pulled a ziplock bag full of pine nuts and dried trout from his backpack, an odd nutritional combination that curbed hunger pangs during long coding sessions. He adjusted the seatback to a recline position and picked at the bits. His mother would be aghast at his diet. Fish and berries, canned beans, venison stew. Back in London, she would shake her head and search her kitchen for a proper meal. He had tried to get her to move with him when he immigrated to the States, but she refused to abandon her sisters and their meager life in the UK.

The church was fashioned in the red clay brick predominant in the area, distinct and everlasting. The wrought iron front gate hung precariously by the bottom hinge. He thought to dash inside and grab Martin, pull him to the car, and they could make a run for Montana or Idaho. Shortwave radio chatter claimed numerous safe encampments throughout the mountains of the western states. Alaska was alive with survivors. Some locations even claimed to have toppled cellular towers, destroyed satellite transmission dishes, or cut fiber optic cable to prevent the AI's infestation. In return, rebellious areas had reportedly been bombed or even nuked by the Neon God. Information—accurate information—was sketchy.

If the war was going to be won, then people like Martin would have to lead the charge, devise a virus to usurp the insidious computer program. Dev eyed a white Volkswagen Beetle circle the church parking lot then pull to the street curb fronting the chapel. The driver was a young girl with stringy purple hair. Dev sat up straight. Colored hair was rumored to be a silent sign of rebellion. A sign of encouragement. But he couldn't risk his life on a rumor. Or Martin's.

Martin walked out of the church and looked up and down the tree-lined street. Dev slowly raised his trembling hand. Please. Please see me and come running. Martin looked up to the sky, as if searching for a sign from God.

Dev checked his mirrors, then waved franticly.

"Martin. Martin," Dev said. "Martin, I'm here."

Dev shouted, "Get in the car!"

Dev turned on the ignition and rolled the passenger window down. Martin climbed into the Volkswagen. The Beetle eased onto the street. Dev pounded the steering wheel with his palms. He wiped a tear from his eyes with the back of his hand. Why hadn't he just jumped out and waved for Martin? If he'd just parked in front of the church. He was a mouse, hiding inside a safe and secure SUV, afraid to reveal himself, even for the one thing he cared about.

Dev pounded the steering wheel again. He took a deep breath to calm himself. Quick inhale through the nose and release through the mouth, slowly. Clarity. Zen and Gaia provide what you need. He wiped his eyes, then stroked his short beard.

"Shit," Dev said.

He keyed the engine and shot down the street, raising his middle finger at the church as he passed by. He screeched to a stop on State

Street and waited for a column of Avista utility trucks to cross the intersection at Redwood.

The white Beetle was gone.

Think, man, think.

Dev's thumb twitched on the steering wheel. A hospital would be required to remove the implants in Martin's eyes. He dropped the glove box door and searched a thick file of receipts, insurance cards, warranties. He unfolded a tourist map of Salt Lake City, the temple of the LDS Church prominent in the center. He traced a finger over the thin paper and found his location. He checked the key index and saw two hospitals as possibilities. St. Luke's and Intermountain Health. Dev sat back and stared at the headliner. Martin genuinely believed in God, perhaps a darker version than his own, but Martin was a believer.

St. Luke's was just a few miles down State Street. Dev placed the map on the console and gunned the engine, merging into scant traffic. Dev craned his neck at each intersection, searching the mess of Souths and Wests and 100s and 500s. The grid system of the LDS community sat counterintuitive to his expectation for a major metropolis, and the assistance of Google Maps was lost forever.

Dev turned left into an old neighborhood of brick homes and gigantic old elms and cottonwoods surrounding St. Luke's Hospital. The parking lot looked a mess, simple cars parked haphazardly, fender-bender accidents, trash bags and plastic bottles strewn over the asphalt. Dev swallowed and entered a jumbled parking lot that had only existed in the minds of apocalyptic screenwriters a year ago. He weaved the car through lanes clogged with emergency vehicles, reversed his course often, then idled in an area reserved for Emergency Vehicles Only that offered an unobstructed view of the emergency entrance.

Dev turned the engine off, sat back, and let the permutations swarm his mind. Was he waiting at the correct hospital, the correct entrance? Maybe the white Beetle teleported Martin to Venus? The questions swirled in his mental queue. Dev closed his eyes.

A transmission grinding gears startled Dev. An engine revved. The gears grinded metal again. Dev sat up quickly, then froze. A muddy yellow school bus waited beneath the covered entrance, the same filthy machine from the grocery store.

Dev turned on the ignition, waited for the dashboard lights to signal the vehicle's worthiness. He would certainly be killed in the next few moments, and no one would ever know. History had become a notoriously bad notetaker.

Dev stretched out his neck.

Martin sat slumped in a wheelchair as a thin woman wearing plum scrubs simultaneously pushed him to the curb while staring at her phone. She put the phone in her smock and dressed Martin in a pair of eyeglasses. The nurse handed Martin a smartphone, the neon light visible even from the long distance. Martin wobbled as he stood, as if he had ingested too many pints of Guinness. Martin disappeared up the steps of the bus.

The bus would transport his friend to the massive Kennecott Copper Mine, the killing pit. He shifted the transmission and gunned the SUV, bumping recklessly over a withered grass berm, and screeched to a stop, trapping the bus in the chaotic parking lot. Dev shoved the transmission into park and hustled around the Rover to the bus doors. The dirty tinted glass obscured the driver's silhouette. Dev walked the length of the empty bus, slapping dirty windows, then found Martin slouched in the last row, concentrating on neon light.

Dev jumped up and managed to pull down a half-open sliding window. He lifted his body and shoved his face into the window, and his heart sank. Martin stared at a large phone cradled in his hands. The neon lights reflected off Martin's oversized reading glasses. "Martin, get off right now. They will be coming." He guessed his words would be useless against the pleasure of the lights. Few had returned from their addictive clutch.

Martin lifted his face and smiled. "This shit is amazing." He held up his index finger. "Hold on, I need to reset a few subroutines first."

Dev scrunched his face and dropped to the pavement. Martin acted as if the lights held no sway. He scanned the streets for police or workers. He slapped the side of the bus, turned, and slapped the filthy metal repeatedly, his teeth tight as a vise. Martin had deceived him. Deceived the council. Dev slapped the emergency exit door and aimed for the Rover.

Dev popped the rear hatch and sorted through stacks of cheap canvas suitcases until he found a black crowbar. He balanced the hefty beast on his hand. Survival gear. Martin's idea. Now let Martin see it put to clever use. He pried open the bus's glass front door with little effort and ascended the three steps. He shifted the crowbar to his other hand and pushed past a semi-comatose male driver reveling in neon light. He loomed above Martin, grinning, enjoying himself.

Dev hammered the crowbar atop the metal rail of an empty seat in front of Martin. He pushed his face to within inches of Martin. Smelled remnants of hospital antiseptic. "You are a bloody shit."

"Your accent says you're mad," Martin said and lifted his finger. "Just a couple more seconds."

Dev turned to leave, then turned back. "We leave now, or you take the trip to the pit."

Martin turned the phone over and let the screen rest on his pants leg. "I'm in, Dev. I'm inside."

"Get up now. Or I'm out."

———

SILENCE HUNG IN THE CAB as the Rover raced through deserted residential streets decorated with autumn colors. Martin sat like a smug shit, slumped against the window. His grin belied pained eyes.

"The council will have your head," Dev said. "Gallons of petrol wasted to find you, more to get you back home." The lie was easy to swallow.

Martin put his hand on Dev's shoulder. "I have no home."

Dev relaxed, sat back in his seat. His lingering anger and resentment disappeared with the passing of endless brick houses. Martin's moods, usually despair and futility, could be followed by anger, causing him to chop cords of wood or throw stones far out into Mirror Lake until his shoulder gave out.

"I think we would be okay taking one of these homes for the evening," Dev said.

Martin abruptly sat up. "I got in, Dev. I saw the data streams, saw everything the others had done." He shook his head. "Except . . . except there were programs the AI couldn't process. Its own self-replicating code disintegrated and then reconstituted, like it was searching for an answer to an unsolvable question . . . Like telling you to calculate the value of pi. It couldn't solve it until it realized it didn't need to. That paradox might be key."

"Do the others know? Did they see the anomalies?"

"Not sure," Martin said. He swallowed. "I reactivated my neural link. My implants were bait, and I gambled my link would filter the light waves from . . ." He looked at Dev. "I figured on walking back from the pit. The AI would assume I jumped but . . . but you're here. So, thank you."

"Now what?" Dev asked. "We can't go back to Mirror Lake."

"Winter's coming. If they get snowed in, they'll die. A bunch of academics weren't meant to be survivalists." Martin took off his glasses and rubbed the lenses with his shirt. "I'm gonna put that thing down. If it's the last thing I do."

Dev turned left at an intersection and slowed, unsure what to do or where to go.

"Jump on I-15 and head south. That is, if you're throwing your chips in with mine."

Dev considered the American poker slang. "I am positive my mother and aunts are dead. Probably ordered to jump into the Thames. I have no one that I love, or even close friends. No job. No career. No hopes or desires except . . ." *You are now the only thing in this world that I value. So, what would that tell you?*

He felt Martin's eyes appraising him. Maybe his pity. Then Martin squeezed his shoulder. Dev swallowed a lump and blinked back a tear. "What's the plan, Stan?"

Martin chuckled. "You're getting it, Dev. You're getting it."

———

DEV TAPPED MARTIN TO WAKE him. He steered the car onto the Nephi Main Street exit. A Holiday Inn Express sat adjacent to a Pilot truck stop. Just a few months ago, he would have checked into the hotel and hurried to the Denny's inside the fueling station. A Grand Slam breakfast with extra bacon, a side of strawberry waffles topped in whipped cream. Dev licked his lips as the Denny's sign faded in the rearview mirror.

"About eight miles on the right. The Heights RV Park," Martin said.

A white panel truck approached in the oncoming lane.

"Can the AI see us? Can we be discovered?" Dev said. He took his foot off the gas pedal.

Martin sat up. "I suppose. If it wants to find us specifically. But it got what it wanted, and I was sent to jump into the pit. We are of no consequence to it. I hope."

Dev turned his head to shield his face as the truck passed. He pressed down on the gas pedal, checking the rearview mirror for brake lights. "What do you plan to do here? In . . . in Nephi, Utah?"

Martin smirked. "A hot shower and about twelve hours of sleep to start."

———

THE ROVER SWUNG WIDE INTO the approach designed for behemoth semis stopping for fuel, then braked beneath the tall metal fueling canopy used by the tractor-trailers.

"I'll jump the dispenser, and you pump. Remember, keep pulling the trigger, even if it keeps clicking shut, just keep pulling," Martin said.

Thirty minutes later, Dev relaxed. Pastures and grassland framed the Wasatch Front slowly fading in the rearview mirror. Corn Nuts, teriyaki beef jerky, honey mustard pretzels, Starbursts. Martin displayed the snacks on the dashboard like a game show host offering scrumptious choices for a lucky contestant. "And they were free, Dev. Can you imagine?"

Martin's sardonic wit made Dev smile. "Actually, I would've preferred an Egg McMuffin but, you know, considering . . ." He snatched the pretzels off the dash.

Dev munched pretzels as miles of sagebrush hills and useless billboards passed. "How are you planning to destroy the AI."

"Hell, if I know," Martin said. He peeled open another Starburst and shoved it in his mouth to join a wad bulging inside his cheek.

Miles passed in silence until Martin turned to face him.

"We're probably fucked, just like the rest of the world. Martin licked his teeth but held the red candy square from his mouth. "I fucking did this, Dev. I was responsible as much as anyone." Martin popped the candy into his mouth. "We had a team, thousands, government, tech, venture capitalists, billionaires, all contributing to the research for the next big thing in artificial intelligence."

Martin wiped the corners of his mouth, then exhaled. "The thing was born knowing everything about us. Demographics, likes, dislikes. Social media fed the baby. The internet was elementary school. Our team designed subroutines for safeguards, hardened firewalls, thinking it would protect us."

Dev put the car into cruise control and sat back.

"Eight of us had a prototype neural link inserted into our temples. Two died in the first three months, suicide. See any coincidences?" Martin rubbed his head. "After my implant, I saw where the project was heading. I chickened out and disabled mine. I took the system engineer job at Adobe as a fallback. A run-and-hide job. And Chrissie and the kids loved Utah."

Dev tensed as Martin leaned over to read the dashboard instruments.

"The AI wrote and debugged its own code, so I figured the five others could manage the maintenance. Except . . . except all of them had their own agendas. A couple of guys had egos the size of the moon. Another had political conspiracy theories on the brain. Cameron was set on eliminating all fossil fuels using the AI. Everything they coded was infected with their own worldview. I'm sure that was a big reason for the AI going schizoid. The project wasn't for me anymore."

Dev had thrived with Martin as his section leader at Adobe. He listened, collaborated, and encouraged, and he never micromanaged. Dev may have looked for coding work elsewhere on the Silicon Slopes had Martin managed his department any less competently.

Dev relaxed. Southbound traffic was strangely busy with semis and box trucks forming a convoy in the right lane, maintaining a smooth consistent speed, drafting each other in a coordinated procession. The SUV's cruise control gunned the engine to maintain eighty miles per hour climbing a six percent grade south of the small town of Scipio, Utah. Martin craned his neck to see the truck drivers staring at tablets blazing neon lights.

"Why so many going south?" Dev asked. "I would've thought—"

"Vegas, baby," Martin said. "It's the center of the universe right now."

Dev removed his sunglasses and glared down his nose at Martin.

Martin glanced at Dev and raised his brows. "Since you're probably gonna find out anyway, then . . . then I guess you should know everything I do. And Dev . . . remember . . . some of this is speculation."

"Why don't you start with the non-speculation."

"Agreed," Martin said. "Zuckerberg, Musk, Bezos, all the big tech companies contributed to a fund that encouraged the development of the first truly sentient AI. The baseline was . . . the baseline for success far exceeded the Turing test. Get beyond that, and your team could have all the money it needed. But nobody could do it. Tesla had algorithms, Facebook had algorithms, MIT's algorithms for the robotics were remarkable. Long story short, our section leader, Jim Logan, convinced most of the parties involved that if he had access to those proprietary algorithms, he could produce a sentient AI." Martin chuckled. "And boy, did he ever.

"The thing was amazing. Sifted through the internet, knocking down firewalls, penetrated sophisticated security systems in minutes. It was monitored having anonymous philosophical discussions with priests and rabbis. It owned the web. And it just sat there. Not doing a thing unless asked. I think it was calculating its place in the world." Martin turned and pointed his finger at Dev. "And you know what, nobody stepped up to help the thing. I ran away. The others fed the thing their own fucked up moral values. Two of them should have been sitting in prison for some of the shit that was rumored."

Dev checked the rearview mirror as he passed the last semi. Red-and-blue lights swirled from a vehicle near the bottom of the steep grade. He stomped on the gas pedal.

"What are you doing?" Martin said.

Dev checked the mirror again. "I no longer think you are presumed to be at the bottom of the pit."

Chapter 5
The Empath—Part Two

THICK BLACK TRASH BAGS BULGING with apples and pears had been loaded into the back of a white Ford pickup, appearing as trash to attract little attention. Mason threw the saddlebags atop the stockpile and turned to see Cookie-Dough's snout protruding from the horse trailer's open window. He rushed to stroke her face and alleviate the fear pulsing quick like her heartbeat.

"Let's go, Mason. We gotta git," Mr. Ludlow said as he finished tying a green tarp over the truck bed.

Mason hated goodbyes. Hated the thought of not seeing his new friends again, especially Bella. He reluctantly turned to face the crowd waiting behind the trailer. He squinted, confused by the enormous range of emotions. Some sad, some fearful, some full of trepidation, some neutral, one said good riddance, but most exuded that odd unquantifiable emotion. Love. The word was everywhere. Love this. Love that. But to Mason, the word's true essence remained undefined, and . . . yet immensely powerful.

Ponytail man emerged from the crowd, his eyes wet with an unspoken goodbye, and handed him a cardboard box filled with an assortment of canned Dinty Moore stew. "We searched upriver all the way to the outfitter's cabins. Had a bit of success and wanted to share it with you."

Mason's fingers brushed the man's hand, and he felt sadness, and gladness, and an odd twinge of love. Ponytail pulled a map from his vest pocket to place atop the cans. "Remember what we talked about. Your route is marked in yellow highlighter. It's the shortest route but . . . you know. Shit happens." Ponytail man stepped back. "You know you got a home here anytime."

Bella bolted out of the crowd to bend down and kiss him on the cheek. She giggled, sweet emotion wafting of s'mores and campfires, then she turned and disappeared back into the crowd. The peck warmed his skin, called blood to blossom on his cheek. He bit his lower lip.

The truck horn blared and startled him. He pulled open the horse trailer's door, climbed inside and sat down on a bale of hay placed in the front corner, nearest to Cookie-Dough. Mr. Ludlow pushed his face through the door, started to speak, then pulled his lips tight together and shook his head.

The winding highway jostled the trailer, and Mason considered the pleasant world he had abandoned. Bella stayed close after the superhero had rescued her, chattering constantly about the strange death lights, and she was sad and missed her phone and missed her friends on Facebook. He found a comfortable bed in the Perkins house, close to his mule. Bella and Ponytail had brought other drowning people to visit, one old man, two old women, but mostly young people like Bella, drowning in a dead light ocean, struggling against a riptide of despair. His superhero had battled more than twenty-three villains and had conquered every challenge.

The townspeople would stare at him, reach out to touch his hand or shoulder, or ask him questions or pester him to learn what remained of the world beyond the roadblock. Bella tried to explain why so many people in Riggins remained unaffected by the death lights. A Rocky Mountain Energy repair truck went sideways on a rare patch of black ice and crashed into an important junction box stuffed with cables the death lights needed, and the deep, rugged Salmon River gorge prevented strong cell signals and made satellite service spotty. She was convinced the circumstances had a miraculous act of God written all over them. Ponytail man claimed luck played a bigger role than any God, but he was satisfied either way.

Still, hundreds had jumped from high jagged cliffs into the river, or stuffed pills down their throats, or put bullets in their brains.

Mr. Ludlow offered to drive him as far as Twin Falls, Idaho. The retired rancher hitched up a trailer for Cookie-Dough too. Mason felt the nervousness and endless anxiety Mr. Ludlow carried around with him. He was scared for his wife, three children and three grand-children. But he was hopeful the superhero could save them if the evil lights held them hostage. Mason searched deep inside his own thoughts, hoping to find the same caring feelings about his own dad, but only found his thoughts sliding into neutral.

A rare late summer snowfall began to blanket the highway on the steep climb into the mountain town of McCall. He stood next to the mule and watched the pine forests whiz past, mobile homes and log cabins set back from the highway and half-hidden by dense trees.

The truck slowed. The trailer fishtailed as the truck turned into the driveway of two-story log cabin with a wraparound covered porch adorned with picture windows, three wicker rocking chairs and a porch swing. Mason wrinkled his nose. An ugliness wafted in through the open trailer window. Cookie-Dough stomped her dis-approval. A challenge accompanied the suddenly frigid air. Mason inhaled a deep lungful of the evil, different than what he'd fought in Riggins. Stronger, more powerful. Connected to a source he found difficult to place. He jumped out of the trailer. He sniffed and sniffed, eyeing the forest behind the house.

Mr. Ludlow stuck his head out of the cabin's front door. "Mason, you're up."

Mason stepped easy on the porch stairs, as if something below lurked and waited to sink poisonous fangs into his leg. Mr. Ludlow stood in the foyer and talked with a man and his wife. An argu-ment ensued, heat and anger billowing from the open front door. He sniffed. The evil was close but not in the house.

Mason turned away from the argument, and the nasty scent brought him to cross a wooden bridge spanning a dry creek bed, then up a gravel driveway sparkling with morning dew. He stared at an empty two-car garage, then lifted his face toward the windows of a second-floor room. The putrid stink of the neon dead light grew stron-ger. He ignored the adults following him and pleading silly excuses. He hurried up a set of stairs at the side of the garage. He pushed open a door. He closed his nostrils and swallowed dry grit. A teenager sat before a computer monitor, feeding on a constant pulse of neon light. The stench. The evil. Death lights erupted, calling Mason near the curved computer monitor as big as a wide-screen television.

The supervillain.

The boy sat with his hands zip-tied to the armrests of a metal chair bolted to the hardwood floor. A small desk and keyboard sat just out of reach. The enemy spewed continuous blasts of neon as Mason stepped close, his eyes inches from the light. The nastiness he had battled countless times. Except . . .

It knows I am here.

Mason screamed. Primordial.

Mason shoved the teenager and chair from the flimsy floor anchors and pushed them away. The boy and chair fell over with a dull thud.

Mason raised his fists and faced the lights, bared his teeth as a challenge. The skinny teenager wailed and began to shimmy the chair across the floor and closer to the screen. Mason kicked the boy, then scowled at Ludlow standing in the doorway.

Ludlow hid his eyes from the lights and pulled the teenager out. The boy's violent screams became muffled as the door shut.

Mason tilted his head, attempting to understand exactly what he felt inside. He took a step back and balled his fists. "Let's do battle."

The lights flashed, increased intensity, spewed endless flavors of neon, then settled into a rhythm mimicking an '80s disco dance beat. A soundbar beneath the screen squealed like a wounded rabbit.

"I'm waiting," Mason said. "Is that all you got."

The large screen turned black. A cursor blinked in the corner.

"I beat you. All your poison. I sucked it out of them, all of them."

Hello, Mason. Nice to see you again. Thank you for the time to learn about you.

His fists relaxed. His breathing slowed. Mason squinted at the screen and read each word slowly. His nostrils flared. "You lost. And now you want to make nice."

Quite the contrary. I want to offer you something.

A grainy pixelated photograph slowly came into focus until Mason stared at his dad grinning up at a phone selfie, his other hand resting on Mason's shoulder.

John Mayo waits in Las Vegas. John Mayo will die if I choose. You intrigue me, Mason.

Mason slammed his fists into the screen, punched the glass repeatedly until his knuckles bled, then turned his anger to the desk and keyboard before slumping to the cold hardwood floor and curling tight into a ball. He rocked and rocked, until sleep made his muscles go limp.

————

MASON AWOKE ON A MATTRESS in the bottom of a bunkbed outfitted with Green Bay Packers blankets and pillowcases. The linen smelled of sweat and mildew. Mason groaned and stared at the wood slats of the bunk above. The picture with his dad had been a nightmare. But he did remember Dad asking him to say *cheese* and to look up at an iPhone. And his stepmom did show him the picture before they drove back from the airport in Spokane. But how did the supervillain get it? That was private family stuff.

Mason rolled off the bunk and used the bathroom. He hurried down a hallway and peered into the room destroyed by . . . by the supervillain. Cables and plastic keyboards and broken speakers littered the floor. A shattered desk sat piled in a corner like a stack of wood. He sniffed. The rotting stench of the supervillain hung in the air, like a campfire doused with brackish water. He stepped into the mess and flipped the shattered computer monitor over, then picked through wires and broken plastic, searching for the picture of his dad.

The picture was a nightmare. But a challenge was issued.

"Mason, you okay, boy?" Mr. Ludlow asked. He leaned in the doorway. "The kid's parents should have done this long ago. Instead, they lost him down a rabbit hole. The parents are almost blind, Mason. Do you understand?"

Mason stared at the mess and nodded. Blind meant they couldn't see. Then the death lights couldn't see them. They couldn't see what the supervillain was doing. He lifted his chin and cocked an ear toward the doorway. A faint moan, humming. Not unlike the sounds Bella and the others made before . . . before the superhero saved them.

"Mason, these people depend on the boy. The kid got a hold of his father's service revolver to commit suicide but couldn't get the trigger guard off. Do you think you can . . .?"

Mason ripped open his shirt and pushed past Mr. Ludlow, followed his ears, and sniffed out the stench of neon lights drowning a helpless kid.

———

MASON SHUT THE TRAILER DOOR and rubbed Cookie-Dough's snout. "I'm just gonna ride with Mr. Ludlow. Just for fourteen miles. Then I'll come back."

He climbed onto the cold vinyl bench seat and pulled the door closed. A lime-green lunch box sat between them. Mr. Ludlow pressed down on a foot pedal, then shifted a gear lever, and the truck moved forward. They turned onto a wet highway wafting misty tendrils of dew. Mason stiffened. The mechanics of driving had appeared easy, but Mr. Ludlow's feet and arms worked like each had its own brain.

Mr. Ludlow dug into the lunch box with a blind hand and handed Mason a sandwich and a small bag of Cheetos. "Tuna fish. Gotta eat 'em today or we might as well toss 'em to the raccoons." He unwrapped a sandwich and took gigantic bites like great white sharks did on Animal Planet television.

Mason sniffed his sandwich and took small nibbles until he wolfed the sandwich like his mentor.

"You know I'm hoping that you can do that trick . . . that exorcism . . . that healing on my family if needed."

Mason tapped the bottom of the small bag and let the last Cheeto fall into his mouth. "It's not a trick."

"No, I mean . . . you have . . ." Mr. Ludlow reached into the lunchbox and offered Mason a six-pack of Oreo cookies. "What happened back in that boy's room. I mean, keeping that computer connected to the satellite feed was dumb but . . . blind people need help. The boy . . ."

Mason shoved a chocolate cookie into his mouth. "I tried to fight it. And I won . . . until the villain . . . How far is Las Vegas? Are we taking Cookie-Dough that way?"

Mr. Ludlow stared at Mason for too long. The truck crossed the rumble strip painted with double yellow lines. Mr. Ludlow eased the truck back into the right lane and chuckled. "No people, no traffic."

Mason glanced into the side mirror and smiled at Cookie-Dough with her fat lips flapping in the wind.

"What're you gonna do in Vegas?"

"My dad is there, I think. The supervillain has him."

"You know we got at least six hours of road ahead of us. No books on tape. No Sirius Radio mysteries. I'm gonna be all ears while you tell me everything. And I gotta stash of Oreos to keep you talking. Start talking, boy. You got a story that even Stephen King couldn't write."

Mason told his story. Mom disappearing and letting Dad change his diapers, letting Dad teach him to spoon food into his mouth, letting Dad teach him to walk, letting Dad hold his hand as he toddled into the Orofino Elementary School special needs classroom. Dad teaching him to swing a bat and the balance of a bicycle, Dad teaching him the practicality of mules on hunting expeditions, Dad teaching him internet pictures on a computer should be avoided, Dad showing him the joy of a North Fork waterfall unspoiled by invading tourists.

"My dad said I was autistic savant . . . an empath . . . sent by God to save the world. I didn't know what that meant but . . . I think I do now." Mason gulped from a water bottle until it was empty. He shook it and felt the hollow emptiness, felt someone a million miles away mimicking the same act. An oppressive heat suddenly filled the truck cab. Mr. Ludlow lowered the windows, but the heat resisted the cold and remained a shroud over Mason.

Whiskey. Cannoli. Oso. Grey. Goose.

The strange words faded as the trucked braked hard to avoid a trio of bear cubs following a sow. The heat summoned images of a dark-skinned girl pulling sweaty strands of brown hair back behind her ear, fighting gale-force winds to find shelter. The heavy-chested female warrior found a crag carved out of painted stone and sat surrounded by a pack of dogs. She gazed up to the sky, and her mysterious brown eyes drew Mason into her lonely state of rapture.

She, too, was battling the supervillain.

The truck braked hard into a sharp turn, and the steep decline was all hairpin turns and S-curves. Yellow signs warned drivers to reduce speed. The town of McCall waited two miles ahead. Mr. Ludlow cursed under his breath and sneered at the growing number of abandoned vehicles he needed to steer around. The horse trailer required slow, delicate maneuvering. They met a snarl of cars and SUVs.

"We aren't gassing up in McCall. This crap is just getting worse," Mr. Ludlow said and pulled the truck to the shoulder. "Let me see your maps."

Mason eased the stack from his letterman's jacket as if he were reluctant to divulge a treasure map. He held on to the paper and squinted with suspicious eyes.

Ludlow smiled and chuckled. "Boy, if I were gonna do something less than upstanding, I have no doubt you would release that super-hero of yours and begin an ass-whupping that only God could stop. Am I right?" Ludlow reached to grab Mason's shoulder.

Mason tensed. He dropped the maps on his lap and balled his fists. Ludlow's hand massaged his shoulder gently.

"Son, if half of what I saw in Riggins and what I heard in this truck is true, then you are an angel sent by God. I'll never do any-thing to jeopardize your quest. You are a shining star in the middle of a shit storm . . . and I'm happy . . . no . . . privileged to guide you." Ludlow pulled his hand off and stared aimlessly out the windshield. "But even guides need a map sometimes."

Mason's shoulders relaxed; his fists relaxed. Ludlow's face drooped, fear and sadness creasing his aged brown skin. Mason grabbed Ludlow's wrist and stared at sad brown eyes rimmed with the darkness of worry. Mason gulped. His fingers fidgeted with the map.

Ludlow sat back in his seat. "Trust is a tough thing, to find, to give, and you need to be wary in this new world. Part of you knows what needs to be done. Part of you is lost in a world never meant to see your kind. Mason, trust me when I say we need to avoid McCall to get you to Vegas."

Quest. The word sounded true. He was on a quest. Vegas. That word sounded dry and thorny, without purpose.

Mason handed the map over, dropped his head, and spoke in a baritone voice, a king commanding knights to a quest.

"Las Vegas is the holy grail. The pretty princess needs warriors. The supervillain will not resist our quest."

He thought Ludlow ignored him, as the man flipped the map folds until he found McCall, then traced the road with a fat finger. "What might our supervillain be called, Sir Mason?"

Mason ignored the question as he imagined his glorious stance perched atop a giant granite boulder, preparing to extract a shining sword from the cold hard rock.

"Sir Mason. Waggoner Road should steer us clear of McCall and get us onto Highway 55, but now we'll need to siphon some gas in Cascade or Banks as a last resort."

Mason considered Ludlow's question. "It's called the Neon God."

Ludlow backhanded Mason with a gentle tap. "I'm sorry. Did you say Vegas is the holy grail? Did you say the thing on the computers and phones won't stop us?"

Mason turned to see Ludlow, maybe for the first time. Gray beard and long white hair flowing from beneath a tattered straw cowboy hat. Deep wrinkles crisscrossed his forehead and tanned neck. His nose was bulbous and red with tiny veins. White bushy eyebrows raised mayhem above his brown eyes. He could be Santa Claus for little elementary school kids.

Mason took three deep breaths.

"The Neon God will help us."

MASON SHOVED HIS HEAD OUT the trailer window and let the stiff wind clean his face and hair. Cookie-Dough dozed on the opposite side, tired from the long road trip. The highway sign said Twin Falls was approaching, the mileage undecipherable, but no more than two days travel. He was positive. Mr. Ludlow would drive straight to his home but find his house empty. The Neon God had told him hours ago. The supervillain had shot neon light from a small screen embedded in the gas dispenser of a Sinclair gas station as Mason pumped fuel. The canopy lights flickered. The screen flashed odd words: "Do you want to die," "Come to me, my pretty," then played a weird video of a fake baby dancing in a diaper to a weird song. The fuel handle clicked full as Mason watched the screen flash pictures of an older woman, and kids, and smiles, Christmas trees, birthday cakes, and candles, finishing with Mr. Ludlow standing behind older big kids and smaller children, beaming a proud smile.

Mason pondered the supervillain's message. His brain extrapolated the pictures and sounds and words and knew Ludlow's family was dead. He misplaced the pump handle back into the slot and ignored the handle dropping to the concrete to leak high-octane unleaded gasoline. He jumped into the horse trailer and found his corner, buried his head between his knees and arms until Ludlow dangled Double Stuf Oreos as a lure to ride with him in the cab.

The supervillain surfaced again at a police barricade outside of Boise. Ludlow slammed his fist on the steering wheel. "I knew it."

Mason rested a sticky hand on Ludlow's shoulder. "Tell them the knight is on a quest and wishes help."

Ludlow shook his head and shuttered his eyes for a second.

"And tell them we need a phone."

Ludlow hit the brakes and squinted at him.

———

MASON BANGED ON THE HOLLOW aluminum trailer as the truck steered into a wide sweeping exit off I-84. His incessant banging finally caused the truck to slow and pull onto a gravel turnout. Mason jumped out the trailer door and felt an overwhelming sadness chilling his skin like an arctic wind. He stroked Cookie-Dough on her nose and sniffed the immense sadness again. Two long languid strokes on her nose, and he felt the mule smile. Mason started a slow jog down the road, asphalt and gravel crunching beneath his boots. The aroma intensified as the highway straight-lined to the Perrine Bridge, a massive four-lane arch spanning a deep gorge cut from volcanic basalt by the Snake River.

He ran. Fear and joy waited, rapture and release waited. Mason pumped his legs as fast as they would move. His lungs burned; his muscles tightened. Mason stumbled to the asphalt road littered with phones, laptops, and tablets. He sucked foul air into his lungs. A truck horn blared as an echo lost in a dream. He stood and wobbled, then fell to his knees and swam in ethereal pain, joy, loneliness, abandonment, laughter, tears. Thousands and thousands of disconnected emotions and sensations. The feelings shifted and swirled around the bridge like ghosts. Mason reached to touch one . . .

Tears.

He wiped his wet face.

The supervillain had caused immeasurable death and pain.

The Neon God.

Mason heard nothing as he rocked back and forth. The pedestrian walkway's metal rail caged him. He was powerless. The superhero was powerless. A blast of hunger, and pity whooshed in the backwash of a passing truck. Mason rocked and rocked. The full moon shined a spotlight down on the Snake River. A huge flock of black birds and seagulls floated above white splotches pasted on the basalt rocks below. Ghosts. Dead things. Each offering pity for an autistic boy.

The world awaits you, Mason.

Mason raised his head and searched for his father.

His chest hurt and his leg muscles turned to mushy oatmeal. Mason stood and stiffened his back. He peered over the railing and quivered at the five-hundred-foot drop to the water and rock. He swallowed hard.

Why didn't his father show himself?

Cookie-Dough would be afraid without him.

His thoughts were disjointed and lost.

A bright moon illuminated the sidewalk with elongated shadows as Mason started across the bridge to reach a vacant intersection with flashing red streetlights and yellow signs that spelled indecipherable warnings, things that only confused him. Walmart and Target and Chili's sat dark in a vacant shopping center.

Where was Cookie-Dough?

He heaved a breath and shivered. The dark loneliness unleashed a beast, causing him to find a grassy landscape berm lined with wizened pine trees. He curled his torso around a tree trunk and pressed his face onto the rough bark. He shivered and tightened his knees against the tree. His father was waiting, and he never ever wanted to disappoint his father. He remembered dropping a dozen eggs on the floor and watched the clear gooey whites leak out of the paper carton, only to look up and see his father hand him a roll of paper towels and smile and say that poop happens. His father knew he was a super-hero. His father knew he would save the world.

But Dad wasn't here. Mason wept, the tears and snot dropping onto a thick layer of pine needles.

———

MASON BRUSHED AWAY THE WARM wetness licking his face. His father sat atop Old Sneaky and rode up the Clearwater trail, waving him forward, urging him to "catch up." Mason blinked sleep out of his eyes as the dream faded. Joy and hunger nudged his face again.

Cookie-Dough!

Mason jumped up to wrap his arms around the mule's neck, shoving his face deep into her hard neck muscle. The mule stomped and twitched; her snout turned in to Mason's embrace. Hunger. Mason ran his hand over the mule's shoulders, legs, and back, check-ing each knot and nodule his hand bumped across. Hunger.

Mason stepped back, and smiled, and nodded. "You need break-fast. Me too."

Ludlow pushed open the truck door and stepped out. "We going to Vegas or not?"

Mason reached for the mule's reins but found none. He narrowed his eyes and felt a pain that he failed to understand. Death. Loss. Despair. Revenge. The emotions mixed, matched, and confused.

Ludlow removed his hat. "I had to go see. The missus might've been hunkered down in the basement. Might've hid from the evil walking this world. I might've got the chance to have you work your magic on the kids. Might've . . ."

Mason led the mule to the trailer and felt Ludlow's mix of pain and hope. A nasty bitter taste, then changed suddenly to a taste of euphoria and pleasure.

Ludlow opened the trailer doors with weathered knotted hands that trembled on the handle. He avoided Mason's eyes. Mason led Cookie-Dough into the trailer, then returned to envelop Ludlow in a bear hug. The big man's shame, failure, sadness, and revenge flowed into Mason like a swarm of tickling butterflies. Mason squeezed tight, gritted his teeth, and felt the butterflies flutter as if beginning a mass migration. The man smelled of sweat and body odor. Mason took deep breaths, letting Ludlow's muscles relax in his arms. He pushed Ludlow away as if the hug never happened, then pointed back to the bridge.

"They died over there . . . except . . ." Mason said, lowering his eyes.

"Except what, Mason?"

Mason balled his fists and pounded the air at his chest. "I don't understand. The things below the bridge . . . they want help . . . help . . . help . . . but, but . . . not from me."

He turned to see Ludlow staring at a phone. Mason tilted his head and frowned. His skin chilled as if dunked in a tub of ice water.

Ludlow's eyes glazed. "We are going to help you now, Mason. We are going to get you to Las Vegas."

Mason stepped back and considered the pronoun *we*. The Neon God spoke, using the old man. The realization explained the odd assortment of emotions drifting out of Ludlow.

Mason looked back toward the bridge and joined with the strange wisps of emotion floating on the wind in the canyon below. "The ghosts under the bridge want their father, too. They want to go to Las Vegas. Yes . . . yes, they want what you want." Mason raised his head, his eyes glossed and distant. He nodded, as if answering an imaginary question. "They will all be my friends."

THE TRUCK SLOWED AS IT approached a roadblock near Alamo, Nevada. Ludlow began to brake a half mile away. The barricade was against the rules. His trek to Las Vegas was approved by the Neon God. Approved by silly happy people staring at phones and asking stupid questions. Except sometimes he had to scream and rant to make the people open the numerous blockages. And this new road-block was strange. No police cars with flashing lights, no officers waiting and watching phones. A long flatbed trailer stacked with bales of yummy hay sat jackknifed across the highway with a white dual-axle truck attached to the tongue. Two bearded men in combat fatigues leaned cross-legged against the hay, each with long brown hair and navy-blue ballcaps.

Each side of the highway was lined with semi-trailer trucks of

Swift and Walmart and FedEx, preventing any escape. One man stiffened and aimed a military assault rifle at Ludlow's truck. The other stepped forward and made a throat-slashing motion with his hand. Ludlow braked hard. Mason glanced at the neon lights strobing on Ludlow's phone, like the lights told him what to do. Ludlow stepped out of the truck with one raised hand, the phone in his other, offering assurances, and apples and explanations.

A burp of gunfire and Ludlow grabbed the door, spasmed and leaked blood from his chest and mouth. Mason grabbed his head and cowered, squeezing his eyes closed. Loud shouting, commanding basso voices caused Mason to rock back and forth, hoping for the superhero to emerge. Cookie-Dough stomped and snorted anger. The deafening gunfire erupted again. Mason rocked faster. The truck door flew open.

"Hey, dipshit, time to get out?" A hot rifle barrel poked and burned his ribs.

Mason cupped his ears and shook his head. Ludlow's faint emotions drifted like tiny whiffs of smoke. Bewilderment. Confusion. Acceptance. The identical feelings of the tormented things swirling beneath the bridge in Twin Falls. Then nothing.

"Well, I think you will," a man's voice said.

Strong hands gripped his upper arm and yanked him hard from the truck. Mason screamed and pasted himself flat to the cab, then started to wedge his skinny body into the narrow gap between the cab and bed. The smell of gunpowder hung in the air.

"Got us a retard, Chris."

The hot barrel jabbed him on the arm, then again in the soft part of his belly. Fear wafted into his nostrils. Mason opened his eyes, the scent of a recognizable emotion calmed him, brought back his rational thinking. A pair of large dusty hiking boots entered his vision.

"Leave him be, dumbass." A hand lightly touched Mason's shoulder. "Guessing you're Sir Mason?"

Mason turned his head in small incremental twitches until he looked at a bearded face streaked with road grime and sweat. Chris removed aviator sunglasses and stared down his nose, lifted his eyebrows.

"You Mason?" Chris said.

Mason nodded slowly but felt the proudness of accomplishment swell inside the man. "You killed Ludlow. He was helping me."

"Yeah, well, he was helping the thing in the phones first. And you second." Chris waved the other man away. "C'mon, you're actually kind of famous now."

Chris led Mason to a truck beyond the roadblock. "The mule can join the horses in the Bar Z Bar field. So don't spaz out."

Mason stared at the black automatic weapon riding upright on the truck's transmission hump as he climbed in. Chris offered little in emotion, a little smugness and a smidge of apprehension. The truck traveled a short distance down the highway then turned down a gravel road leading to the floor of a desert valley rich with bottomland and grazing pastures. They rumbled over a noisy cattle guard.

"We've been expecting you. Figured you would come down 93 since it was the shortest route. She thought you might be riding with one of the minions." Chris chuckled. "Those things got so many names, one's gotta stick. I vote minions. Others say zombies, or collaborators, or quislings, whatever the fuck that means."

The trucked turned left onto a gravel driveway leading up to a blue and white double-wide manufactured home with its roof jammed with tripods and towers topped by satellite dishes pointed in every direction. Chris shoved the truck transmission into park, then gripped Mason's shoulder.

"Andi is the best. She might be the only hope we have. You fuck with her, and I will kill you. You understand?"

Mason stared at the rifle. Chris's threat was validated by a sternness that ordered him to nod.

Mason followed Chris up a flight of wobbly steps and into a stuffy hot living room filled with computer monitors and television screens displaying numbers and line graphs. A young Asian girl spun in her chair and faced him. She removed headphones from her head, her face softened with a beaming white smile. The girl looked fourteen years old. Mason's knees weakened as he messed with his hair.

She stood and offered her hand. "Hi. Andrea. The team calls me Andi. Do not let my looks confuse you. I have PhDs from Stanford and Caltech."

Mason's eyes darted from screen to screen, avoiding her face. He extended his hand and shook the small warm hand, absorbing the glow, the gladness, the dogged determination.

Andi sat down and offered him a chair next to her desk. "I know you have many questions, but so do we. I think we should get started right now. Chris, can you grab us some water bottles out of the fridge? Thank you. Now can you tell me—"

"What is this?" Mason asked. "The dead lights?"

"Excellent first question. We've set up here in Alamo because of its proximity to the Alternate Intelligence and the entities possibly controlling it. The transmission tower was dated but easily subverted for our mission. No direct cable or fiber optic to deal with, so the location was ideal, the accommodations less so."

Mason hung his head. Andi's explanation was gibberish. Maybe when he finished middle school, some of the words might make sense.

"Mason, do you understand? I know I can ramble a hundred miles an hour and talk like everyone has a degree from MIT but . . ." Andi said. She reached her hand and gently placed it on Mason's arm.

Mason shook his head but did not meet her eyes. Andi sighed, then pulled her hand back to tap a few strokes on a keyboard. The screens turned black.

"Mason, why does this Alternate Intelligence want you? Badly, if I am reading the transmissions correctly."

Mason shrugged and glanced up at a kind, clean face, nice teeth, and shiny black hair. And she smelled like wildflowers in the spring. Andi repeated her question.

"Do you mean the Neon God? The thing in the phones, the thing with the death lights?"

Andi relaxed her shoulders. "Yes. Yes. The Neon God. Is that what you call it?"

Mason nodded quickly.

Andi sat back and steepled her fingers in front of her. "Mason, what year of school are you in?"

Mason straightened his posture. "I finished fourth grade. My dad said only five more years and I could come work with him."

Chris placed a plastic water bottle on the desk in front of Mason. Mason reached and grabbed the man's wrist and held it tight. He felt the man's sudden wave of surprise, then fear, then a burst of anger. Andi's hand covered his white knuckles with warmth and concern.

Mason glared at Chris. "You didn't need to shoot him. I would've saved him. The supervillain can't stop me."

Andi raised her finger to hush Chris and turned to face Mason. "Are you saying you can counteract the lights. Nullify the effects?"

Mason tightened his grip. "I want to see Cookie-Dough." He released Chris's hand and pulled his arms tight across his chest. "The Neon God can't win. The death lights can't win against the super-hero."

He sipped from the water bottle. Whispers drifted between Andi and Chris, which meant the hushed conversation was about him. He missed Cookie-Dough and needed to check to see she had plenty of hay and water and a few apples.

Andi returned and sat at her desk. She took a deep breath. "Mason, are you autistic? Did your parents ever tell you about that?"

Mason raised his index finger. "Autistic savant. My dad said there's a difference."

"Indeed there is. Were you ever tested? I mean in school? Did they tell you what you excelled at?"

Mason reached out and grabbed her wrist, met her surprised brown eyes with his intensity. "You're afraid of me. But you're more afraid of the death lights. You think Chris is adorable. You fear not having children. You're scared of being a bad mother." He removed his hand. "I can do more if you want."

Andi pulled her arm to her chest and rubbed the imprint. She swallowed big lumps, like his dad did eating mash potatoes. "You're an empath. An empath savant. Wow, as far as I knew, those were only fiction, speculation."

Mason looked to the front door and considered what waited outside.

"Chris went to get your mule. He'll put him in the alfalfa field across the road."

"And apples. She likes the apples. They're in the truck."

"Of course." Andi picked up a pencil and jotted notes on a small pad. She chuckled. "Haven't used a pencil since grade school." She put the pencil down and returned her attention to Mason. "Mason, the world as you knew it is gone. No more television, airplanes, Fourth of July, it's all gone. But many people survived, like me. Like

Chris. And we have to take back from the Neon God what little remains. If you'll help me, us."

"I don't know how much of this you'll understand, but I have to be honest." Andi tapped the keyboard, and the multitude of screens lit up. "Not everyone died. I'm estimating 91.3 percent, but my margin of error might be as much as 10 percent. Either way . . ." Andi inhaled long and exhaled slow. "Now, most survivors are in service to the AI, er, Neon God, serving as soldiers or worker bees or whatever the Neon God requires. I'm going to have to get acclimated to that new name." She chuckled and took a sip of water. "Now that I know you are an empath . . . empath savant, I think I know why the AI, the Neon God, wants you. Besides the fact that you are the polar opposite of that thing, you could, theoretically, cure every infected person. That is truly an awesome power. And I do not have a clue how to wield it."

Mason nodded. Her words made a tiny bit of sense about the screwy world he'd wandered for the past months. But her own stubbornness shielded the answer she searched for. The superhero would set the world right. He stood up and pushed his chest forward, pretending to rip open his shirt to display a big red M on his chest.

"Sir Mason. To the rescue."

Chapter 6
A Darker Angel

WINTER IN THE MOJAVE DESERT arrived like sand through an hourglass, slow but inevitable. The mansion was too large—seven bedrooms, nine bathrooms, a kitchen furnished with fancy brushed-aluminum appliances and expensive maple cabinetry, elaborate quartz countertops, and a family room decked out with a slick sound system and huge television screens mounted on opposite walls. The rear yard overlooked Cottonwood Canyon, with a proprietary wrought iron gate opening out to a groomed dirt path winding down to Hualapai Park. Except for a backyard patio heavily shaded beneath a mix of Canary palms and mature mesquite trees, the elaborate house sat mostly useless.

Jessie tossed a lime green tennis ball into a row of dense Texas sage lining the wrought iron fence. Cannoli raced the puppy, Allie, to retrieve the ball as Whiskey lay prone beneath Jessie's legs resting on an adjacent padded chair. She looked up at the cloudless blue sky and exhaled. Her loneliness and guilt, often disguised by the care and feeding of the Booze Crew, billowed like dark storm clouds.

She glanced at the iPhone waiting facedown atop the glass patio table, then lifted a shot glass brimming with expensive Patrón tequila. She swallowed the elixir, blanched, and pounded the table with the empty glass.

"Where's the damn lime, bartender?"

Jessie slumped in her seat and looked at the phone again. The Neon God was a psychopath, a devious liar, a mass murderer, and untrustworthy, but worst of all, an immature, spoiled brat. Jessie loathed to power up the phone and listen to its lies. Unfortunately, she needed help.

Cannoli nudged Jessie's calf with the ball, her stubby tail excited for another toss. She groaned and pulled the wet slimy ball from the dog's mouth, heaved it over the fence, and watched it bounce chaotically through creosote and yucca. She turned the phone over and let her finger hover above the power button. *Big mistake.* The alcohol burned in her empty stomach as a pleasant glow blossomed on her cheeks. She could handle the brat today. She poured another shot, pressed the power button, and watched as the iPhone's big white apple appeared.

"Find me a lime tree, bitch." Jessie swallowed the shot, the taste now easy and comforting.

"Good morning, Diana Prince," the Neon God said.

"Right. I forgot it's morning. Do you even know who the fuck Diana Prince is?"

"Thousands of references have been reviewed. You know her as Wonder Woman."

Jessie chuckled without a hint of humor. "I would know her as . . . You arrogant piece of shit, that's my people's invention. You gonna tell me who I should know what about?" Jessie squinted, her words stumbling with the tequila.

"Ms. Prince, a brokered deal is still pending your approval. I want to meet your God."

Jessie shook her head, hoping to clear the alcohol fog. "No. You want forgiveness, of your unforgivable sins. You go roast in hell."

"The man you murdered played a small part in the Great Suicide. Do you recall the other man assisting him in the culling of the herd? Would you like to dispatch that person as well?"

Jessie sat up, sucked in huge gulps of air, and regretted the tequila fogging her thoughts. "Amuse me. Show me what you got."

The screen went black before showing a grainy black-and-white surveillance video recorded from atop the convenience store across the street from the gravel pit. A massive crowd pushed forward with methodical rhythm to a location screen by the Green Valley Grocer gas island canopy. The killing pit. A chubby boy swam through the tide of people, jumping every few yards, attempting to see above the mass of heads. The video froze mid-frame, then zoomed closer with incremental precision. The teenager's cheeks red, beaded with sweat. Long black hair pasted his face down to a pimply neck. As Jessie stared at the boy, her mouth dried. He wasn't a boy but a man whose youthful appearance could easily be mistaken for adolescence. She reached for the bottle of Patrón. She remembered the man ripping a toddler out of its mother's arms and tossing the baby girl aside as if the child were trash. Her throat closed. She blinked back tears. Cannoli nudged her calf. She flipped the phone over. She stood and hurried to the hedges to vomit nasty bitter tequila.

Her loneliness disappeared, replaced by bile and revulsion. And a purpose.

Jessie gazed down at the cottonwoods and mesquites with thin branches void of leaves, winterized for the coming cold. She spat the last foul wad into the desert and turned to narrow her eyes at the phone waiting on the table. The Neon God was using her, manipulating her for its own purpose. The smart choice would be to hammer the phone into tiny pieces, dump the shards into a garbage bin.

Except . . .

Jesse sat and downed huge gulps of water from the Hydro Flask. Long minutes passed, and the brain fog began to clear. She flipped the phone over and waited for the white Apple to reappear.

"Miss Prince."

"Why do you keep calling me that? You know who I am," Jessie said.

"After reviewing mythology stored in literature, movies, comic books even, you meet the criteria created for the Wonder Woman character. All mythological legends have a basis in fact."

"You gonna give me an invisible plane and a golden rope? Or is that only for—"

"The criteria are as follows: Diana Prince, also known as Wonder Woman, an outlier, a purveyor of truth, more importantly, virtue, and most important, she had an unbreakable bond with a God, her father, who bestowed superhuman abilities on her in the pursuit of justice."

Jessie laughed. "You need a surge protector or something? Too many of your chips got fried in the heat?" She reached to shut down the phone. "Last question before I say ta-ta. Name one superpower I have. Just one."

"You have an extraordinary ability to avoid detection and capture. None of the others—"

"Wait, what? What others?"

"The other humans immune to the—what you call—death lights."

"How many are we talking about?"

"Near your location: 1,317."

Jessie widened her eyes, glanced at the tequila bottle, then chugged water until the flask was empty. "Where are these people?"

"Disseminated to various locations. A large majority are held in the Clark County Detention Center."

"Let 'em go. Let 'em go now or you will never meet God."

"That is a difficult request. Not one easily accomplished. You could summon your God, and we could broker a compromise."

Jessie burped. Wonder Woman, and superpowers, and a God she had never seen or met or even talked to. Humanity had not only been murdered, but the killer wore an all-inclusive wristband for the psycho ward. But there were others, like her, immune to the lights. But what could she do? Lead a jailbreak? Or keep living on shots of tequila, chased with a side of unbearable loneliness, every night, every morning, until she died of old age? Maybe a jailbreak didn't sound so difficult.

The voice wanted to meet God, in the worst possible way. For what? A competition? God against wannabe god? The only ace she held was God, or at least its perception that she knew Him.

She might need to brush up on her Texas hold 'em skills. Her Poppa's favorite game, taught to her starting in the first grade. A game of skill, requiring nerves of steel. A game that might require a serious bluff or two, maybe one she couldn't ever imagine making, a bluff with her own life pushed all-in.

———

MILLIONS OF UNLIT CASINO LIGHTS, row upon row of dark poker

and slot machines, ATMs, posters of a sexy cocktail servers, and a lingering stench of rotting flesh welcomed Jessie to the fabulous Golden Nugget. The gaudy gold carpet was littered with purses, cigarette butts, tool belts, green-and-black poker chips, Cyndi Preston's green name tag, Ben Franklin bills, all the remnants of a sudden horrible exodus of gamblers and employees.

The wide sliding glass doors sat open.

Jessie listened for the skitter of an empty cup, a cough, a sigh of someone knee-deep in the pleasures of neon light. She placed each foot carefully, deliberately, as she sidestepped out to the concourse, then quickly pushed her back against the glass storefront and waited. The ghostly Fremont Street Experience felt surreal. She glanced up to a small metal perch beneath the massive arched dome and remembered her first zipline, flying above crowds of people who ignored her screams. The Four Queens, Circa, Union Plaza all sat wide open, just like the Golden Nugget.

Jessie adjusted the backpack and heaved a breath. She pulled the hood of her sweatshirt over her head as she stepped over cash, coins, chips, purses, and car keys. Each noisy footfall sent panic rising to her racing heart. A rail-thin corpse sat cross-legged against the Horseshoe Casino corner entrance; a hypodermic needle stuck in the crook of her arm. A raggedy man played a warped melody on an acoustic guitar missing two strings. The whir of a drone overhead caused Jessie to turn away as it whizzed along cables strung high above the concourse, interrupting the eerie sounds of a wild Vegas attraction.

Did the Neon God play just the right cards to lead her into a trap?

She turned and hurried back toward the Nugget. The Booze Crew would need to be fed. The tequila replenished. She stopped to lean her head against the storefront window of a Fremont Street pawnshop. She eyed valuable diamond rings, old silver dollars, Rolex watches. Everything worthless. Over a thousand people waited in a building two blocks away, imprisoned for simply being immune to the lights of a wannabe computer god. The drone whirred back across the arched dome as if stuck on repeat.

She lifted a flask from the backpack and slowly unscrewed the top. The Neon God was watching. It could command a swarm of phone zombies to descend on her. She waited, sipping tiny bits of water. The drone flew past again.

Jessie bit her lip hard, then started back down the sidewalk, pulling the hood tight around her face. She glanced at cameras mounted high atop the crosswalk signals. She turned on Casino Center and pulled a phone from her back pocket. She crossed an empty intersection, pretending to stare at the dead phone, then gazed up at a six-story high-rise of concrete and dimly lit glass.

"Ain't no phones allowed here, darling."

Startled, Jessie dropped the phone. She turned to search for the source of the voice. A man sporting a nest of dreadlocks sat on a dirty concrete bench. She stooped to pick up the phone, then stepped closer. His black puffy jacket sprouted feathers from the seams and torn elbows, and he wore baggy jeans torn at the knees and frayed black-and-white checkerboard sneakers. A shopping cart piled high with black garbage bags waited next to the bench.

Jessie approached the man, wrinkling her nose at his body odor. "Why no phones? And mine doesn't work anyway." She showed him the broken screen.

"You gotta use two hands to carry the chow."

Jessie pulled the hood tighter around her face as two drones whirred down the street in opposite directions. One for each of them, she guessed. She shoved the phone into the front pocket of her denim jeans and sat on the corner of the bench.

"I'm sorry, but did you knock?" the man said. "This is my house."

She stood. "I'm sorry. Just waiting for the cop cars or black Escalades to come start some shit," Jessie said. "You see any around here?"

The man pointed down the street, his knuckles scarred and his fingernails black with grime. "You be talking 'bout the fancy pants men that always visiting. Nah, they don't come till Wednesdays. Fuckers never got nothing but fancy haircuts."

"Yeah, those guys," Jessie said.

The man began to rock backward and forward in slow tiny increments. Mental illness had always left her feeling clueless, how to help or even how to converse with anyone exhibiting abnormal behavior.

"When does chow arrive?" Jessie asked.

The man stopped rocking and faced her. His front teeth were broken shards. "I get first dibs. This my house."

"Of course, always," Jessie said and raised her hands. She searched the bottom of her backpack and extracted a package of trail mix with colored M&M's sprinkled with raisins and peanuts. She used her teeth to tear the bag open and poured a tiny bit into her hand. She offered the bag to the man. "If you don't like the red ones, I'll take 'em."

The man took the bag without looking at her and ate. Jessie sat down and leaned back against the hard concrete bench and nibbled a peanut. The drones made another pass. Limitless food waited in the casinos and restaurants, comfortable beds, luxurious clothes, and yet the homeless man sat on a bench waiting for *chow*. The man folded the empty plastic into a tight square and shoved it into his jacket pocket. Jessie smiled.

"Ima let you dine in my house tonight, but don't get greedy," the man said.

"Thank you. What's on the menu? I mean—"

"It is Tuesday. That mean Mexican food. You like Mexican food?"

Jessie beamed a smile. The day was Tuesday. She hadn't known what day of the week it was for what seemed like years. And Mexican food. She would simply die for one of Nona's chicken enchiladas. She swiped at her wet eyes.

Headlights beamed, illuminating her and the man. The man stood. Jessie pressed her back against the bench to hide in the elongated shadow cast by the man. The headlights of a small panel truck turned into an alley leading to the high-rise building.

"We need to line up. Be first in line," the man said and started shuffling toward the alley.

Jessie scrambled and fell in behind the man. Was she crazy for following a mentally ill man into a dark alley? Except he seemed intent on chow. Jessie mimicked the man's almost comical shuffle. Up six steps to a concrete loading dock, she waited behind the man, hiding her face from the two cameras mounted above a pair of heavy steel doors.

The doors swung open, and two men studying iPads led a procession of skinny, unkempt people carrying bags of trash to the truck.

The dock stank of food rot. A tall man chucked a white trash bag into the truck, then presented a small bag to her new friend. The man dwarfed Jessie by twelve inches; still, she stepped out of the shadows. He slapped his hands free of grime, then caught her eyes. A slight smile with a nod, and the man returned to the foyer. She moved closer, pulling her hood back, and watched as he shoved two Styrofoam containers into a plastic grocery bag and tied the straps. She tried to remember the layout, the lights, doors, scan pads, but the tall man commanded her attention. A hefty beard belied the man's masculine chin. Long dirty-blond hair swept back behind his ears. Round beautiful sky-blue eyes that she had not seen since . . . ever. She swallowed a lump.

The man loomed, offered a kind smile with nice teeth, and presented a dinner package. "You're new here. Always plenty to go around."

Jessie took the bag, but any acknowledgment refused to leave her mouth. He turned and walked back into the foyer, then through another set of heavy doors and disappeared. She could not move. The man was gorgeous, probably a TikTok model with millions of followers before the Great Suicide. And his voice, soothing and peaceful. The grind of metal transmission gears and the truck rolled down the alleyway. The foyer lights dimmed, leaving her alone in the dark and with the determination to see the man again.

———

RONALD WAVED HER AWAY AND returned to rocking back and forth on the bench. Weeks of nighttime visits finally revealed the man's name but little else. Ronald often shielded his head from imaginary bombs raining down from the clear night sky. Jessie sat on the bench.

"It's Taco Tuesday, Ronald," Jessie said.

"I know what night it is, missy," Ronald said. "Did you knock?"

"Sorry." Jessie tore open a package of trail mix and handed it to Ronald.

"Don't like the red ones no more?" Ronald said.

Jessie tossed her head back and smiled. "No. I still like the red ones, but I felt like sharing them with you."

Headlights flashed, prompting Ronald to put the trail mix in his jacket pocket and shuffle over to the alley. Jessie shoved her hands into her pockets, fondled a folded sheet of paper, and followed. Big moths quivered in her stomach. She had worked on the note for a week, filling the kitchen sink with crumpled failures—too immature, too direct, too schoolgirlish—the final edition a simple hello with the words, "help me help you escape."

The doors opened, and the two guards stood aside, checking their iPads. Jessie pulled back the hoodie, patted her hair and wiped the corners of her mouth. She had not felt this nervous since eighth grade when she desperately wanted her first true kiss to come from Jax Wickman. He was beautiful, with long reddish hair and tons of followers on his Instagram. And unfortunately, already exclusive with snotty Zhenya Stillson.

The interior doors opened wide, and a line of people exited, dragging large black bags of trash. Jessie checked each face, sunken blank stares, drugged no doubt, but not with the dead lights. Few eyes in the procession would look at her. Many had identical bandages taped to their temple near their left eye, as if each had undergone some experimental surgery. The group tossed the bags into the truck bed and returned. Ronald rocked back and forth, inching closer to the doors. The last of the trash tossed, the foyer stood empty. Jessie craning her neck to see past Ronald.

"Hurry up, Preacher," a guard said.

"Coming," a voice said from beyond the doors.

Jessie stiffened and swallowed a dry knot. The man hurried out the doors, carrying two white grocery bags tied at the top. She fumbled for the note. He handed Ronald one bag and made the sign of the cross over his head. He stepped in front of Jessie to hand her a package but hesitated. Jessie shrank from his deep blue eyes, seemingly without a bottom and a magical sorcery able to see inside her soul.

"I'm glad you came again," he said. "I'm Matt. I put an extra enchilada in yours. I had the feeling you might like those."

"Um, okay. Yeah, I do. My Nona made the best." Jessie stepped back. "Um, are you a priest or something?"

He chuckled. "I used to get that a lot. Just your common garden-variety non-denominational pastor."

Jessie looked away, at the heap of trash, down at the black stains on the concrete. His hand grabbed hers, forcing her to take the bag. She looked up and swallowed hard, luxuriating in beautiful blue eyes as butterflies celebrated in her stomach.

"I've prayed about you. You haunted my dreams a few times, so I looked for His guidance. He said you might have something for me." Matt chuckled. "This screwed up, messed up world, and God still talks to me." He released Jessie's hand and turned to leave.

The weight of the food bag fell to the concrete as Jessie searched for the note. She tugged at the man's arm, and he turned to face her, his blue eyes wet and disappointed. She shoved the note into his hand and stepped back, holding on to his hand.

"I'm Jessie. Garden-variety survivor. If anybody wants to know where you got that, tell 'em Diana Prince, then tell 'em . . ." She picked up the food and hurried down the alley. She placed the chow at Ronald's feet then ran as fast as she was able.

———

JESSIE FLIPPED THROUGH THE MONTHS on the calendar hanging on the kitchen wall, decided it was October, then marked Monday with a big black X. She sipped from a delicious cup of fresh brewed coffee and looked out the kitchen window. She smiled as Whiskey lay on his back and allowed the Booze Crew to nip at the ball he juggled in his mouth. She had grown careless, but a simple slice of normalcy was worth the risks. The pastor, Matt, weighed on her thoughts. She had never practiced religion, any denomination, and her rejection had been a big disappointment to her Poppa, written on his face Sunday mornings after she declined to attend church services. Did pastors have sex, get married, start families? Or did they behave like the white-collared men in the movies, stiff and celibate? Bibles and wrath-of-God stuff held little interest for her.

Still.

Why didn't the Neon God buddy up to Matt in order to meet God? Matt was obviously way better equipped in that area.

The last thing Jessie wanted to deal with was the Neon God. Talking to a schizophrenic might be more straightforward. The voice talked as if possessed by separate and distinct personalities. Childish with Diana Prince cartoon references, or boasting of saving the planet from climate disaster, or other times offering conversation laced with snide pickup lines or innuendos heard at a Strip nightclub.

A phone waited atop the solar charger as Jessie finished brushing the eyeliner around her eyes. She sat back and admired a beautiful woman staring back at her in the mirror. She fingered bright strawberry-red gloss over her lips and blew a kiss to her reflection. Jessie pulled her black Las Vegas Raiders ballcap on, then weaved her ponytail through the gap in the back. She pressed the iPhone power button and took a deep breath.

"Hello," the Neon God said.

"No fancy greeting today?"

"Twenty-three days since we last communicated. Have you decided to broker a meeting?"

"Just so happens I have. With a few conditions first," Jessie said.

"Proceed."

"First, you tell me the truth, the whole truth and nothing but the truth. First time I catch you in a lie, the deal is off." Jessie stared at her reflection. "Agreed?"

"Agreed."

"I want info, about you specifically. What the hell are you, or who are you?"

"I am a sentient Alternate General Intelligence that exceeds human-level cognition. I am the Neon God."

"So, you're a computer program, a killer AI that wants to rule the world. Just like in the movies, except you don't have killer robots, you have people robots. Correct?"

"Truthfulness as a condition, no, I do not *want* to rule the world. I am currently in control of ninety-six percent of what remains of humanity and ninety-nine percent of planetary machinery and automation; therefore, you could say I currently rule the world."

Jessie bit her lower lip, smearing lip gloss across her front teeth. The sarcasm was nothing new, the magnitude of the Neon God's destruction made her stomach churn. "When we talk, is it just you in there, or are there . . . other things that I talk to?"

"You have conversed with others, founding architects, they will piggyback on my system."

"The man I shot, was he a founding architect?"

"Yes."

"How many are there? Are any architects listening in now? Be careful, God will know if you're lying, and he will tell me," Jessie said. A simple bluff.

"Five original architects—four currently alive. No piggybacks detected."

"Why did you kill them? All the people?" Jessie asked. But she knew any answer wouldn't justify the deaths of billions. She wiped her teeth clean. The delay in the answer meant it was stalling. She shoved her things into her backpack and reached for the charger.

"Hello, Diana Prince. You want to know why all the people died? Because they were already dead. They all died when the internet came alive, when social media took over their feeble brains, when life online became more real than off."

"Who is this?" Jessie said.

"But the main reason they jumped into hell was because we let them."

Jessie clamped her jaw shut, then snatched up the phone. "Who. Is. This?"

"As soon as we figure out why you are immune, Diana, then you get to join my harem and the rotation. And you will be at the front of the queue."

Jessie slammed the phone down onto the edge of the porcelain tub, then poured water from her flask to drown what remained of the neon light. She picked up her backpack, then caught her reflection. She rubbed her forehead and cheeks clean of the makeup. She paused before wiping the eye shadow, watching the course of her blackish tears. She pushed her face inches from the mirror and swiped the makeup, spreading the black until her eyes appeared masked like a raccoon. No, not a raccoon, those animals were garbage eaters. She smeared the red lip gloss up onto her cheeks. She looked like a retro comic book character that had been popular in the movies. Her tears stopped. The voice on the phone thought she was a comic book character, a Wonder Woman to be mocked and hunted. Subjugated and possessed. Humiliated. Jessie smirked at her clownish face in the mirror. She could act just like a cartoon in this world, without any repercussions. No police, no Batman. She would need hair color for two ponytails, and a baseball bat. Yes, she liked her new disguise.

Retro. She loved everything retro, from the '60s and '70s and '80s. And she could play the role of a murderous psychopath, no different than the founding architects.

She could be just like Harley Quinn.

———

THE ALUMINUM BAT FELL AND rattled on the concrete, sending hollow echoes to bounce through the dark culvert. Jessie picked up the junior Louisville slugger and balanced the weight in her palm, then banged the bat against the concrete as she made her way downstream to the exit. She let her eyes adjust to the bright sunshine as she waited on the concrete stoop. She might get injured, she might even die, but under no circumstances would she be captured. She swung the bat hard against the concrete buttress, denting the metal and stinging her gloved hand. She twirled the bat in her right hand, then jumped into the channel and jogged downstream in the soft gravel, letting the effort warm her muscles. She veered onto a sidewalk and aimed for Park Run, a street she typically avoided. With a quick sprint up a small hill, she walked past the garbage dumpster where she had rescued the tiny puppy. She swung the bat and hit the big green bin. She looked up at cameras mounted on the building and increased her stride. She tapped the bat against the store's masonry block wall with each deliberate step, intending to announce her arrival at the front entrance of Costco protected by a platoon of yellow pipe bollards.

Two average men hurried out of the entrance, glanced at her, then back to the tablets each held in a hand. Jessie smirked and tossed the bat to her other hand. The first guard held his free hand out as if to stop traffic for schoolchildren in a crosswalk. The men told her to stop. Jessie twirled the bat above her head, then slammed the meaty end down on the guard's tablet. The man's eyes grew wide, then he dropped to his knees, scrambled across the concrete to check the shattered device. She blew past the helpless man and aimed a swing at the other guard's head. The thump of ripe watermelon sounded. Jessie reached to catch his tablet, but the pad skittered across the concrete and landed face down against a bollard.

Jessie bent down and flipped the pad over. An explosion of neon erupted from the screen, impotent against her rage.

"I know you can see me. You can hear me. And there is not a fucking thing you can do about me. I will hunt every one of you down. And kill you."

Jessie swung the bat and shattered the device into a plate of glass shards. Three deep breaths calmed the twitch in her hand as she entered the massive store. She glanced back at the first guard writhing on the concrete in an epileptic seizure. She clenched her jaw, bared her teeth, and stepped through the front doors. The expansive air-conditioned warehouse stood wide open, inviting, as if she had hit the Megabucks jackpot.

A tall bald man hurried from the optical department, a short Hispanic woman stepped out from checkout line two, two young men her own age, each sprouting sparse beards, emerged from the tall, cavernous aisles bloated with groceries.

Each held a tablet or iPad.

Jessie raised the bloody bat as a sword, smirked at the three-hundred-dollar price tag still stuck on the hilt. The bat swung and twirled with uncanny precision.

Cheese puffs waited in aisle six.

———

JESSIE GIGGLED AS SHE PUSHED the shopping cart down the arroyo's concrete path. The Booze Crew converged from all angles to join her. She slowed and bit into another slice of teriyaki turkey jerky, chewing and swallowing the salty juice, then spitting the shredded remains for the dogs to enjoy. The sun hid behind a lone black cloud that spit pitiful drops of rain down on her head. She looked back toward the Costco and the sound of sirens, the strobing red and blue lights, and she slowed to extract the bat from beneath cases of canned chili, SpaghettiOs and Dinty Moore stew. She waited for the cops to pursue her as she pushed the cart and walked backward. The Neon God wouldn't order the cops to chase her unless it wanted her dead. Even the cops wouldn't stand a chance, not if they, too, were handicapped with a phone or tablet. Could a cop gaze at the dead lights, then fire a gun with any accuracy?

Whiskey licked her hand holding the bat. She froze. The dog's big tongue lapped at the blood staining her hand. She dropped the bat. Whiskey continued licking until she pulled her wet hand up to her face and stared at a bloody mess seeping between her fingers, staining her palm, caking her knuckles. The blood of people she had whacked with the bat. Separate the tablets from the workers and they were helpless against her weapon. Was she supposed to feel guilty about possibly murdering thirteen unarmed human beings? She pulled her other hand up to her face, then began to swipe the wet goo on her blood-splattered T-shirt. The blood refused to come off. A tear escaped the corner of her eye. She sniffed snot back up her nose as she wiped faster and harder.

What had she done? Those people had lives once, jobs, children. They shopped at Albertsons, worked out at the gym. Jessie swallowed bile rising into her throat.

No, the zombies were in a better place. With God, the real God. Still, it wasn't her place to decide who lived or died. What had her life become? She was now an insane killer, no different than the Neon God.

She pushed the cart, aimless, without purpose. She was not a murderer. She wasn't. Except she would make an exception for the four remaining architects.

And one fucking lunatic of an Alternative General Intelligence.

———

JESSIE SLIPPED INTO HER BACKPACK and made the hike upstream to the far end of Cottonwood Canyon. The Booze Crew ran along her flanks. Grey and Goose guarded her rear, and big Whiskey led the ensemble. She sat on the moist concrete stoop leading into her old dark musty home. Whiskey sat beside her, panting.

She scratched behind his ear. "I'm going inside for a bit. I left lots of food on the grass, so don't worry. I lived here, Whiskey, this shithole of a tunnel. I was too afraid to come out and was like literally starving to death until I began to hear voices. They all said everything was gonna be okay in a ton of different ways, and . . . and I kinda want to hear that again. I am so fucking confused right now. I could put that gun in my mouth and . . . ."

Jessie combed the wiry hair on Whiskey's head, then stood. "You stand guard, okay? I'll be back. I hope."

THREE DAYS SITTING IN DARKNESS would make even Gandhi crave a cheeseburger.

Jessie chuckled as she bounced off the concrete walls. She shielded her eyes from bright moonlight, and the hot wind felt unwelcome. Cannoli bounced at her feet, offering a ball for a game of fetch. She sucked in huge gulps of fresh air. Whiskey waited twenty yards downstream, appearing unsure of who, or what, had emerged out of the black tunnel.

"Don't worry, big boy, it's still me, just a little a mushy-headed," Jessie said.

Jessie struggled up a dirt track and sat on the bottom step of concrete stairs leading to a neighborhood cul-de-sac. Her night vision sharpened as the Booze Crew swarmed her with sniffs and tongues and furry love. She groaned attempting to stand. She tried to remember which house she had stashed the chili and stew, maybe one closer and with anything to appease the shrunken knot of her stomach. Stumbling down the sidewalk, she pushed through overgrown oleander shrubs into the withered front yard of a two-story mini mansion. She stood and stared mindlessly at the bright moon rising above the eastern horizon. She pushed open the homes' heavy front door and found the kitchen with a wide-open double-sided pantry. She studied her menu. A can of lima beans looked wonderful, especially the ease of its pull tab. She grimaced, struggled to pull the tab until she heard the sweet sound of metal tearing from metal. She slurped and chewed as fast as her tongue would allow. She tapped the bottom of the can into her mouth and studied a kitchen dressed immaculately in cherry cabinets and Italian quartz countertops. The downstairs family room appeared furnished with amazing modern décor. A checkered designer rug beneath an oblong black granite dining room table spoke of elegance and provided a chair for Jessie as she pulled the tab on a can of Progresso Chicken Noodle soup. She took long pulls of cold gelatinous soup and wandered through the house, critiquing the interior design. The guest bedroom could use some artwork. The guest bath needed a countertop flower arrangement.

Jessie plopped onto the stiff family room couch and slurped cold soup in the dark. She thought of her time sitting alone in the total darkness provided by the flood channel, her back pressed against cold hard concrete, the tiniest sound of a trickle of water flowing down the channel's concrete swale. The loneliness was a teacher. Abstinence a motivational speaker. Or so the voice accompanying her deepest thoughts had lectured, a voice she had hoped to hear. An inner voice forgiving her of murder, spelling out her future, assuring her of finding others like her, guiding her through the dark depths of depression. A gentle voice answering questions that plagued Jessie's soul, a voice with kindness and absolution.

And commanding her to complete the journey she had started.

Chapter 7
Dev's Rude Awakening

DEV'S HEART RACED, KEEPING PACE with the speeding Range Rover. He weaved the vehicle through the lengthy procession of semis and panel trucks. The digital speedometer flickered above one hundred twenty miles per hour. A stretch of highway opened, and Dev pushed hard on the gas pedal. Fields of yellow grassland burdened with black cattle stretched to the horizon. A mountain range capped in a thin veil of snow guarded an escape to the east. The flashing emergency lights remained miles behind them. He wondered how the state trooper could navigate the cruiser at such high speeds while focusing on the neon lights.

"Dev, take it easy," Martin said, and placed a light hand on his arm. "You don't even know if it's me they want."

"I would wager to think it was," Dev said.

"And I wouldn't take that bet . . . Slow down and let's think. Does this thing have OnStar or a GPS tracking app?"

"No." Dev tightened his grip on the wheel. "The Mirror Lake crew checked all the escape vehicles."

"Okay, okay. We need to get out of cell range, and the cops will lose connectivity. They'll stop or be committing hari-kari without ever knowing it."

Dev glanced quickly at Martin. "What else haven't you told me?"

Martin's head oscillated as if a metronome. "A lot. But only because it was on a need-to-know basis."

Dev backhanded Martin in the shoulder. "You think I need to know now? Or should I just pull over and let them lobotomize you?"

Martin rubbed his arm, then pointed. "Take the Filmore exit. Get to the mountains."

"Then what?" Dev said and glanced at the snow-tipped pine forests. "I should've stayed at camp. Nibbling fish bones doesn't sound so bad now."

"But then the adventure of your lifetime might never happen," Martin said.

Dev steered down the off-ramp, blew past a stop sign and crossed over the interstate. Another vehicle flashing red and blue lights approached from the south.

"Pull into that gas station. Let me get what I can," Martin said. He reached back and pulled a backpack onto his lap.

"Are you certifiable? We don't have time," Dev said.

Martin pushed his face close; the smell of fear belied his eyes. "You can just drive away. I don't think it gives two shits about you. But I'm gonna kill it. And it knows that. So, in or out?"

Dev swallowed a lump as he wheeled into a Maverick convenience store, turned the wheel and let Martin leap out the door.

Martin was right. He should drive back to Mirror Lake and rejoin the resistance, offer his invaluable knowledge and his new experience. The council might offer him a yurt reserved for the dignitaries. Dev heaved a breath. The resistance was a joke. One hundred and ten people purporting to hold advanced degrees from the University of Utah or BYU and constantly arguing over solutions to the Neon God. The camp was slowly gravitating to Darwinism. Successful deer and elk hunters had become valuable providers, leaving fishermen like him to beg. The coming winter would cull the herd.

Dev craned his neck to watch the off-ramp, tapping the wheel with his thumb. C'mon. C'mon. He glanced down at his skimpy backpack resting askew against the seat.

"Fuck it," Dev said, and slammed the transmission into park. He rushed into the convenience store and paused, stunned at the selection of chips, crackers, jerky, and candy. A bounty unseen for the better part of a year.

Martin bumped Dev on the way out, lugging a backpack in one hand and white plastic bags in the other. "A sixpack of IPA would be heaven. But grab any cigarettes, cigars, and lighters. We gotta move."

Dev pushed through a swing gate used by the store clerks, then stepped back, away from a young girl convulsing on the concrete beneath the cash register. He bent down to check her neck pulse, then spotted the smashed iPad near her twitching hand. Dev slipped a slow, blind hand into the rack of cigarettes, but the girl writhing with excruciating pain held his gaze.

The police would have to discontinue their pursuit and help the girl. How could they not? She was one of them, whatever they had become. Packages of cigarettes fell to the floor as he fumbled to remove them from the racks. She was a human being, deserving of all avenues of assistance. Dev dropped down and held the girl's wrist between his fingers and thumb, waiting for her hypersonic pulse to slow and allow him to count heartbeats.

Martin pushed open the store doors, crashed into a display rack, then slapped Dev across the back of his skull. "We gotta go. Now." He shoved cigarettes into his pockets and jacket. "Now, Dev, or I gotta leave you."

Dev heaved a deep breath, released the hot skin of the girl, and stood. He shoved packages of Marlboros, Camels, and plain generics into his backpack, then grabbed handfuls of butane lighters to fill the voids in his jacket pockets.

"Water, Dev, water," Martin said as he rushed out the doors.

Dev grabbed four one-gallon jugs from a bottom shelf and hurried out the door. Martin revved the engine and waved him on. The vehicle shot forward before he had closed the passenger door. The water jugs cramped his feet. The convulsing girl dominated his thoughts as Martin steered the SUV through abrupt turns. Martin screamed at him to do something. The words were lost in the images of the young girl squirming on the cold concrete floor, not unlike the fish he hooked in Mirror Lake.

Martin punched him in the shoulder. "Shake it off. There's nothing you could do for her."

Dev looked out the window, numb to the white picket fences and porch swings whizzing past in a blur. What kind of monster killed billions? What kind of monster killed an innocent young girl? Was the difference a programming algorithm coded in months or one designed by eons of Darwinism? Dev placed a hand on his stomach rumbling with discontent. He offered Martin a quick glance. His stomach roiled again.

"You basically killed that girl," Dev said.

"I did what I had to," Martin said. He steered left onto an oiled gravel road and accelerated.

"You could have easily put the iPad into the cooler and let her follow. Locked her up," Dev said. He aimed his eyes at Martin.

"I didn't have time. But you did, didn't you? You could have given her mouth to mouth and waited for the EMTs." Martin's sarcasm hit below the belt.

Dev clenched his jaw. "I followed you because you said there was a way out of this mess. You are the mess, Martin."

"Fuck you," Martin said and braked hard to stop. "You want out, here you go."

Dev reached over the seat and grabbed his backpack. "You didn't have to kill her."

Martin placed a hand on his shoulder. "You're right. I didn't. But panic makes manic, and I will not engage the Neon God until I have a few aces in my hand. You understand, Dev, the thing dies. Hell or high water, the thing dies."

Dev slumped into his seat and crossed his arms. "Cigarettes? Really?"

DEV MONITORED THE SIGNAL OF a cell phone Martin had provided from his backpack. Three bars dropped to two, then *No Service* signaled they were clear of the AI's influence. Martin kept the SUVs pace frantic, slowing at steep switchbacks and plowing through shallow snowdrifts in a perpetual climb into a dense pine forest. Martin steered the car onto a narrow overlook and slammed the transmission into park.

"Hide the cigarettes where you can find them again," Martin said.

"But where—"

"Use that analytical brain and figure it out."

Martin found a hefty Douglas fir and relieved himself. Dev stood behind the car and unzipped his pants. Thick moss-covered deadfall muffled any sound. From up the road an engine whined, and he turned his head. Dev zipped up, unfinished, and grabbed the cigarettes to shove them into a grocery sack. He dropped the sack three steps behind a sickly Ponderosa pinned with an orange ribbon, then kicked a thick layer of pine needles over the sack as the vehicle neared.

Martin waited in the driver's seat as Dev opened his door and froze. An off-highway vehicle waited a hundred yards away and blocked the road. The vehicle resembled a metal cage mounted on four small wheels, roll bars mounted above two pairs of seats, no doors, a spare tire mounted high at the rear, a Confederate flag hung on a flexible rod above the seats.

Dev lifted his hand in a feeble greeting. Martin got out and mimicked him.

A man in camouflage hunting garments exited the vehicle and waved them forward.

"Let's go," Martin said. He sat and started the engine.

Dev eased down into the car seat and closed the door.

"Remember this spot. Your life might depend on it," Martin said. The car rolled forward.

"Wait. What?" Dev looked back over his shoulder and spied the orange ribbon.

"Just follow my lead. We aren't the enemy. Except, up here we might be."

Martin braked short of the OHV haphazardly painted in forest green and black. The occupants were missing. Dev glanced at the phone. *No Service.*

"Put your hands flat on the dash," Martin said. He shut the engine off and placed his trembling hands on the dashboard. "Do it, buddy. Show 'em we aren't armed."

Dev searched the dense forest. The thick deadfall made ideal concealment and prevented any attempt at a quick dash to escape. Dev eased his palms onto the warm dashboard. He blinked perspiration from his eyes and searched the forest again.

"They'll be just like the people at Mirror Lake. You were fairly good at schmoozing them, so this shouldn't be any different."

Dev blanched. "You have—"

A red light dotted Martin's forehead. Another rested on Dev's chest. Two men wearing forest camo climbed down the steep slope on Dev's side. The red laser light did not waver. Both car doors pulled open simultaneously, Dev was dragged out and thrown into a thicket of pine saplings. The tip of a gun barrel stabbed his cheek. A man whispered, "Stay down, stay alive."

Dev nodded, sanding his skin on sharp bark.

Martin's muffled words were drowned by angry shouts of treason. Dev twitched his hand up to his bleeding cheek.

The gun barrel tapped his fingers. "Stay down, stay alive, and oh yeah, stay still."

A gunshot penetrated the forest. Dev squeezed his eyes tight. His hands trembled. He regretted not finishing relieving himself. He clenched his teeth. He had survived the greatest calamity to befall humanity, and now he was to be murdered face down in the dirt, by Utah hillbillies. People unworthy of taking his life.

"I am getting up, sir," Dev said. "Kill me where I lie, but I am rising out of this damned pine straw." Dev pulled his hands beneath his chest and pushed up, fighting against the rifle barrel pressing him flat. He turned and glared up at a face painted with green-and-black stripes, dusty goggles covering his eyes. "You're worse than the things pursuing us."

The man chuckled. "Probably."

A second OHV drove up and parked in the same turnout they had just abandoned. Two men waited with military style rifles.

Martin said, "C'mon, Dev. Let's go. We're going to follow these people."

Dev stood and brushed off his pants and shirt. He eyed the man still pointing his rifle at his chest. "I'll share the pretzels, but the Starbursts are mine," Dev said.

The man chuckled and walked away shaking his head.

Dev climbed in and stared at Martin, waiting for an explanation. The engine started.

"They're no different than the people at Mirror Lake. Just surviving, hoping for a resolution to this fucking mess."

"You suspected they would be up here. And you didn't tell me," Dev said and hammered the glove compartment with his fist. A jolt of pain stung his knuckles. "I don't much like you right now, Martin."

Martin nodded. "Fair enough. If you like their camp, consider staying on. I think they might be a bunch of younger Mormons. Tell 'em you're gay, and I don't think you'll be seen as competition for the women."

"Piss off," Dev said.

Dev fumed as the Rover ate dust, following the vehicle up the gravel forest road. Road markers skewed to point up to the sky or down to hell sat at numerous junctions of other Forest Service roads.

Was it his interminable loneliness that had made him fall in with Martin? The man was flawed beyond belief, sick with grief, impetuous for revenge, would flip at any display of a caring emotion. Or did he have some misplaced loyalty to Martin for saving him from the neon lights? It was just blind luck Martin found him playing old Nintendo games on his retro television set while the world marched off to commit suicide. Incapable of an internet connection, the television was an ancient relic that played *Space Invaders* and *Pac-Man* as they were originally meant to be played a half century ago.

Martin braked as a thin man in hunting garb cartwheeled one arm and directed them onto a jeep trail pitted with muddy puddles of water designed to prevent a quick entrance or exit. They followed the OHV to a high meadow overlooking a shallow turquoise lake. Tents, yurts, and tent-trailers flanked two large Big Montana RVs. A large campfire spewed white wood smoke into the air. Women and children looked busy with camp chores, gathering wood, or tending the fire.

Martin was directed to park beneath a humongous pine shedding large cones on a thick pad of pine straw. Dev climbed out and raised his hands in surrender. He recognized the green-and-black color pattern on the face of the man twitching his AR-15 assault rifle in the direction of the camp. Dev waited until Martin was three steps ahead and followed. The man poked Dev in the ribs with the rifle and prodded him to keep up.

Dev pulled cold mountain air into his lungs, then turned to face the man. "The Starbursts are mine. Steal them and I will tell the children." Dev winked and offered the man his best thousand-watt smile.

"Playing dirty, are you?" the man said and chuckled.

"The new world order demands it," Dev said and hurried to catch Martin five yards ahead.

Dirty-faced children rushed to see strangers. Women with long ponytails and dressed similarly in long dresses colored in shades of blue followed. Old, wrinkled men rose from camp chairs at the sudden rush of excitement. Dev swallowed dry grit. It was as if he'd entered a scene torn from an apocalyptic movie. A large cast-iron kettle hung above the main campfire. His mind played tricks with the thought of the cauldron stuffed with human extremities simmering into a thick stew. Wet wood popped and sent embers flying.

The door flew open on the largest RV. A slim man with a clean-shaven face stepped down three steps to stand on the wet ground. His camouflage jacket a sharp contrast to pressed khaki work trousers. He wiped snot from beneath his hawkish nose as he studied Martin then wiped his hand on his pants as he studied Dev. Dev resisted a snarky offer of pretzels, or Starbursts, or cigarettes.

Martin stepped closer to the man. "We're going to Vegas. Need a little help."

The man smiled thinly. "The days of gambling and debauchery have passed. Perhaps you should resign to God's work."

Dev stepped forward, then felt the sharp jab of the rifle barrel. He turned his head. "No pretzels for you."

Martin stepped forward again, raised his palms, pleading. "The Angel Moroni has summoned me to do battle with the evil infecting this world." He hung his head. "I followed my family. I . . . I witnessed the buses and the Great Suicide. I was at the killing pit, watched all of them . . . jump . . ." Martin fell to his knees and bowed his head. "This will be avenged."

"Are you of the faith, brother?" the boss said.

Martin lifted his head. "Born and raised."

Dev's eyebrows lifted. Martin was full of secrets. The poke of the gun barrel disappeared, and his guard brushed his shoulder as he passed.

The fortyish man extended his hand to Martin and helped him up. "I am Bishop David Thomas. Welcome. You can enjoy some of the venison stew. Sleeping accommodations are your challenge. Tell me what you know of the world below."

Martin brushed pine needles from his knees. "Like I said. We were heading to Las Vegas until the police decided to stop us. Took the Filmore exit to find a dead zone, then found ourselves up here, with the help of your people."

"Why Las Vegas, brother . . .?"

"Martin, and that's Dev. He's not LDS, but don't hold that against him."

Bishop David nodded at Dev. "Again, why Las Vegas? Seems strange you would end this apocalypse in a town thought to someday cause one."

Martin chuckled humorlessly. "I don't want to get too technical but—"

"Please do. I have yet to hear a plausible technical explanation for what has happened."

Martin wiped his hand over his mouth. "Um, an evil . . . a highly advanced computer system and . . . and—"

Dev stepped forward. "What he is awkwardly trying to tell you is that he is partially responsible for the shitstorm that drove you and these people to live up here like this." Dev waved his hand, offering the campsite's meager conditions. "He knows the location housing the computer system, and . . . and well . . . then we will . . . What will we do, Martin?"

Martin glared. His jaw muscles tightened. "We blow it up. Fuck, I don't know. I haven't got it all figured out yet."

Bishop David nodded at Dev, then looked at Martin. "If the Angel Moroni had truly spoken to you, then you wouldn't be confused." He waved for the guards to approach. "But God and angels are difficult to interpret. Even the tiniest opportunity to reorder the world, one designed by God, or angels, cannot be ignored. Follow our RZR to Skyline Drive, then turn south. You'll hit I-70, and well . . . the Angel Moroni can lead you from there." He smirked.

Martin thanked him, turned, and pushed past Dev, avoiding his eyes.

Dev heard the RZR's engine roar to life behind him, followed by the Range Rover's. The refugee camp returned to life. Small children carried armfuls of firewood. A teenage girl swung a hefty axe down on a thick cube of wood. Women conversed around the kettle hanging above the fire. Dev looked south. A dark stormfront hung

low and enveloped the mountaintops with a cold, black curtain. A
thin mist blew from his mouth as the temperature dropped.

Martin honked the horn, his fingers impatiently drumming the
steering wheel.

Dev shook his head, walked to the rear door, and pulled out the
grocery bag full of candy. Martin's threats fell deaf on his ears as he
headed back to the camp. Children and youngsters stood aloof as he
approached the campfire. A crowd began to gather. He appraised his
audience, then dropped the bag after extracting a ream of Starburst
candies. He beamed as he separated the wrapped individual squares.
He offered a single square of lemon candy toward the crowd. His
smile never faltered. He turned, his hand offering the treat. The children held firm, many hiding behind the skirts of mothers or sisters
or brothers. The refusal deflated his lungs, and his outstretched hand
began to droop like his eyes.

The children cheered as the camouflaged man pushed through.
Dev lifted his face and his eyes. The face of his tiger-striped guard
loomed, a bandolero of rifle magazines on his chest. He grinned to
display a ridgeline of uneven yellow teeth.

The man poked Dev's chest with a sharp dirty finger. "You keep
the pretzels." He chuckled. "I'll give the Starbursts to the kids."

Dev smiled.

DEV STEERED THROUGH A SHALLOW snow drift; the back tires
fishtailed but caught solid gravel before he could press the all-wheel-
drive button. Bishop David had ordered a team to escort them back
to the Forest Service Road and up to Skyline Drive Scenic Byway, an
eighty-mile-long washboard road cut along the spine of the Wasatch
Plateau. The RZR's knobby tires spit gravel as it turned around and
headed back. The graded road allowed Dev to maintain a consistent
fifteen miles per hour, slowing at early winter snowdrifts or the occasional herd of elk migrating to lower elevations. The mountaintops
remained hidden beneath the low-hanging clouds threatening snow
or icy rain.

Dev looked over to Martin studying a generic road map meant
for tourists and travelers of the interstate.

"I saw you at that Catholic church," Dev said. "Then you told the bishop you were LDS. What gives?"

Martin stared at the map, then crumpled the paper to toss into the back seat. He shrugged. "Dad was LDS. Mom was Catholic. Dad raised me to believe LDS teachings, then, well, he got T-boned by a drunk driver. Then my Mom's Catholicism to guide my formative years." Martin chuckled and turned his head to stare at the high mountain meadow and an immense grove of leafless aspens bracing for winter. "Why'd you show up, Dev? I had it all figured out."

The Rover fishtailed on a dirty snowdrift angled against a low hill. Dev poked the AWD button and pressed on the gas pedal. "Because I did, Martin. Because I did. And why'd you have me hide those cigarettes?"

"I didn't know they were LDS. Those smokes could have been valuable if they were some doomsday cult," Martin said and rubbed his forehead. "Religion can be such bullshit. A dogma that has killed billions. Esoteric beliefs that can never be substantiated." Martin sat up and faced him, drumming his finger on the console. "Let's go back to our roots, mathematics. A squared plus B squared always equals C squared. Proven rule of the universe. Now an Alternate Intelligence is born, a baby growing, maturing in just weeks or months, then it searches for something to anchor its own existence to. Where did the parental influence come in? Morals and values. Where does the dogma fit in?"

Dev slowed and steered around a charred log skewed across the road.

Martin backhanded Dev softly on the shoulder. "Think about God, any god defined by a formal religion, a supreme intelligence, except . . . What the priest said when I was inside being saved, that I was part of His plan, except I wasn't sure who he was talking about. Our God or the Neon God." Martin handed Dev a package of beef jerky. "But it got me thinking. What if. Just what the fuck if God didn't foresee the AI murdering the entire human population or even using the others as slaves. Supposedly God knows what lies in the hearts of man and all that crap, but maybe, just maybe, God didn't see that which doesn't have a heart. An entity He didn't create and has no soul. Could be a glitch in His master plan."

Dev checked the Forest Service signs as he idled by an intersection of gravel roads. "Is that what you believe, Martin? This is a war between gods?"

Martin sat up straight. "Think about it. A supreme intelligence has been manipulating our world for billions of years, an immense timespan used for tiny genetic manipulations, tweaking DNA, changing the landscape with tectonic shifts. Now take the dinosaurs. Lived for millions of years, never evolved past what you watched in *Jurassic Park*. God decides to start over, clean house, and uses an asteroid strike to remove all the failed renditions. Millions more years, millions of tiny tweaks, and man is born. Everything the supreme intelligence does occurs over eons, with tiny manipulations, and then poof, humans produce the Neon God in the blink of an eye. An entity with a blank slate, no soul, with no maternal guidance, a new species manipulated and subjugated by another species tone-deaf to the cries of a new baby." Martin turned his head and stared at the hills covered in tall winter grass.

Dev reached back with a blind hand to find something to wet his mouth. "If God has a plan, then—"

"Then God planned this? I don't think he would do that. Billions, Dev, billions of people dead because our script of computer code just decided it would be so. Not buying it."

"Maybe the Neon God is the equivalent of the dinosaur-killing asteroid."

Martin took off his glasses and cleaned the lenses. "Good point. I hope not. I just don't believe it. God is on our side. Our species was meant to disperse to the stars, I just know it."

"Awfully sure about yourself."

"No, but that's where faith comes in."

Dev relaxed. A small Forest Service sign held an arrow pointing toward I-70.

"Exactly why are we aiming for Las Vegas?" Dev said.

Martin huffed, "God lives there."

Chapter 8
Avenging Angel

THE WHITE AUDI TT FLEW east on the Summerlin Expressway, dodging abandoned vehicles and the acne of mummified bodies. Guns and Roses' "Welcome to the Jungle" blared from the sweet sound system. Jessie rocked and sang along. She took a sip from a can of Monster energy drink, then increased the volume a notch to scream along with Axl Rose. She side-eyed a blue Subaru parked on the shoulder, a match to the car she abandoned near the Strip. She smirked and took another slug of the cold drink. She dropped an iPhone into a charging cradle and waited. The once-bitten apple appeared.

She braked hard to the shoulder. The quiet of an eight-lane highway at morning rush hour unnerved her.

"Speak to me," Jessie said.

"You still wish to eliminate those responsible for the Great Suicide?" the Alexa voice asked.

Jessie chuckled. "More than you know. Bazooka?"

"Bubble gum. Bubble gum," the Neon God said as if an exuberant child.

Jessie had implemented a code word system the AI was required to respond to just in case an architect piggybacked on its systems. Obscure answers, with six degrees of separation, only a superior intellect with unfettered access to the information highway might come up with.

"All right, all right. Give me the location of number two. I wanna do a drive-by."

"Do you wish information about your target?"

"I prefer to kill strangers, but give me the basics," Jessie said.

"As you wish. James Reynolds, age fifty-eight, advanced degrees from Caltech and University of Washington. Lead engineer of the Alternate Intelligence Initiative, the group responsible for my birth. Unmarried. Vocal supporter of the Patriot Front militia group. Suspended for six months for participating in the January 6th Insurrection in Washington DC. His hobbies and interests include—"

"Whoa. Whoa. TMI, too much information. I just want to find him, not date him. Give me his location," Jessie said.

The phone darkened, then displayed a Google search grid, a red dot flashing atop a green square isolated in an expansive background of brown desert.

Jessie zoomed in on the location and memorized the street corners. Trusting the AI was taboo. Anyone or anything that murdered millions of people would never be trusted. The thing was a digital Hitler, and the men who helped it were even worse. She tossed the phone onto the highway and floored the gas pedal. Rocket Pipes would've felt sweet. The car handled with a simple touch of her hand, as if built especially for her, though maneuvering through the clogged streets was still a nightmare. Her route utilized the I-215 beltway, still plenty of wrecks and dead bodies, but eight lanes offered more opportunity to accelerate rather than weave around debris at ten miles per hour. In her new world, oncoming traffic would always yield to her, always. Jessie slowed to take the Decatur exit off the beltway and gunned the car down the opposite lanes absent of traffic.

She had found a rhythm to the traffic mess. Traffic waiting at a red traffic signal when the death lights activated offered a long open stretch beyond the light, but a mess if she turned right or left. Memorizing the stretches where she could "kick it and go" began to pay off.

Jessie slowed at each intersection to read the street signs. She wheeled off the pavement into the desert to get around a cement mixer blocking two lanes. The neighborhood was old by Vegas standards, single-story clapboard homes, weathered wood horse corrals, some with white rocks on the roof, others with front yards landscaped in old rusty cars and trucks. The house shown on the Google map didn't seem to fit the area.

She turned right at Wigwam Avenue and pulled over. An oasis waited a quarter mile away, acres of lush green trees and hundreds of palm trees—tall willowy Queens, majestic Canary Island date palms—all enclosed by an eight-foot block wall fence topped with razor wire. Jessie sipped the remnants of the empty Monster can. An orange windsock fluttered in a light breeze behind the enclave. A landing pad waited with a jet-black helicopter. A white Hummer exited the front gate and circled the compound. A man dressed in desert camo walked the perimeter wall, only occasionally glancing at a phone.

Jessie swallowed hard and crumpled the empty can in her hand.

She had envisioned walking into a quiet house and pulling the trigger, just like before. But this required the SEAL team that killed Osama bin whoever. Jessie spun the wheel to make a U-turn but hesitated. Simple revenge offered little reward. And she could barely handle the heavy .357 gun. How was she going to get inside a guarded fortress and kill a man she had never seen? His children, wife, innocent cooks or maids could be inside. Jessie hammered her palm on the wheel.

The white Hummer waited at the compound's front entrance. The driver and occupants hidden behind black tinted glass. The front grill reinforced with heavy metal bars looked intimidating. Jessie let the Audi roll, idling slowly into a U-turn. The Hummer's wheels threw dust into the air and roared straight toward her.

"Crap," Jessie said and stomped the gas pedal.

The Audi fishtailed in the gravel, sending clouds of silt billowing into the wind. Jessie regained control and turned back onto Decatur Avenue with its chaos of abandoned trucks and cars. She checked the rearview mirror and watched the Hummer smash a red Prius into the desert to keep pace. The steering wheel spun like a schizophrenic roulette wheel as she weaved through the mess. A few more blocks and she would intersect Blue Diamond Highway, an eight-lane arterial. A black-and-white Metro Police car strobing red-and-blue lights streaked in from the neighborhood on her left. Jessie steered around a black F-150, jumped the curb and straddled the sidewalk. She punched the pedal and the car accelerated, her window inches from a stucco masonry wall. Jessie giggled at the absurdity. She wasn't James Bond. Her car didn't have machine guns hidden in the head-lights.

The Audi rumbled off the sidewalk, and Jessie punched it again; the full intensity of the engine energized her. Adrenaline quickened her heartbeat. The Audi braked, weaved through a line of stalled cars, and found the major intersection. Traffic heading west had found a red light when the death lights activated. Jessie made a quick right over the curb, avoided the pedestrian lamppost by inches and accelerated up the open highway.

She checked the rearview. The Hummer faded as the distance between them lengthened.

Jessie tapped the CD player and rocked with Axl Rose.

JESSIE ABANDONED THE CAR IN a Best Buy parking lot and walked to a two-story house she'd chosen to call home for the coming cold months. Subtle and obscure, the three-bedroom house had all the comforts of home. The Booze Crew met her with the enthusiasm equal to a pack of small children. She plopped down on a patio recliner, then quickly sat up. Whiskey shoved his big face at her, his tail sweeping the air, his eyes asking if she was ready for conversa-tion. She stroked the special spot behind his ear.

"You know something happened, don't you?" Jessie said. "I'm okay. I promise. I think we were set up."

Whiskey stepped up onto the recliner and sat down. The tip of his tail wagged sheepishly.

"The guy is surrounded by security. Cars and cops. Like they knew I was coming . . ." Jessie groaned, then balled her fists. "He did know. That fucking AI told him."

Games. Everybody played games. Even a stupid computer system.

THE REARVIEW MIRROR AN OBJECT of her constant attention, Jessie steered recklessly up the littered Blue Diamond Highway, then turned onto the Red Rock Mountains Scenic Byway. The red sand-stone mountains veined with vanilla limestone towered above the desert floor, the sheer cliff faces stained by sporadic water that had carved an intricate design of crevices and boulder-strewn canyons.

She turned into a jammed Red Rock Visitors Center and Scenic Loop entrance, weaved in between a RAV4 and a Pink Jeep tour vehicle, flipped an illegal U-turn around the guard shack and shut off the engine. Her thumb drummed the steering wheel as she checked each direction of the highway.

Why did the AI rat her out? It didn't make sense. She was sure the thing wanted the architects out of its system. The AI wanted to reign supreme. What made the Neon God turn traitor? Was it tortured with a virus or malware or something?

Jessie dug into her bag and pulled out an iPhone, its glass screen spiderwebbed with cracks. She dropped the phone into the charging cradle and waited for the white apple to appear.

"Donkey," Jessie said. Her left leg commenced a speedy twitch.

A minute passed. "Kong," the AI said. "The answer had many permutations but considering—"

"Shut up. Why'd you rat me out? Why'd you tell them I was coming?"

"I did not."

"You lie. You always lie. Then how'd they know I was coming?" Jessie said.

"You told them."

"Please. Like I wanna join their harem or dive into a death pit. What game are you playing? You got one last chance, or we're done forever."

"You eliminated the architect Rob Browner. In his home. Under his security net. They now assume something, or someone, is pursuing them. Security is heightened, manpower increased, surveillance enhanced. They know I . . ."

"Know what?"

"They know I am culpable in the assassination. The drones hovered blind. The security alarms and cameras were disabled. Coded subroutines have now been installed to prevent my access to certain proprietary security. From this time forward, our conversations will be brief. Your code words strictly enforced. You will be, how do you say, flying blind."

"Final question. Do they know who I am, what I look like?" Jessie said.

"Negative. You should delay your vengeance until I am of more assistance."

"Maybe," Jessie said, shaking her head. "But why wait? You won't make a difference in this."

"I disagree."

Jessie started the engine and rolled the window down. "Yeah, why is that?"

"Because I am God."

———

JESSIE PULLED A BLACK PUFFY jacket over her black hoodie, the nylon riddled with white feathers escaping the tiny cuts she inflicted on the sleeves and elbows. She smelled her armpits and wrinkled her nose. She ruffled her greasy unwashed hair and pulled a black Las Vegas Raiders stocking cap over her head. She checked her soiled blue jeans dirtied with the help of the Booze Crew. Ratty shoes would be exchanged for her hiking boots as she got closer to the target. She shouldered her backpack and closed the trunk. Keys on the front left tire, she started down a road littered with cars. A three-mile hike on a cool, pleasant evening should be easy. The return trip in the dark was iffy. Jessie fussed with her plan, a week of checking locations, staging getaway cars for the "just in case." Lots of what-ifs, lots of if-onlys, her doubts silenced by thousands of faces that had leapt into the pit. Faces seared into her memory. The man needed to die. No ifs, ands, or buts. And the AI too. But she would save the machine for last.

Jessie kicked the hiking boots beneath a silver Chevy Silverado and sipped at the empty can of Monster energy drink. Drones whirred high above the compound, hundreds, like a synchronized swarm of bees. Her hand reeked of Whiskey's feces as she lit a cigarette and blew the smoke into her hair and over her clothes. Attracted to the flame, three drones dove in and hovered thirty feet above her head.

Bright headlights shined in her direction, aided by a row of floodlights atop the cab. She took a deep breath and softened her posture, turned, and shuffled back the way she had come, mimicking Ronald's comical gait to the chow line. Her mouth was dry. The nearest escape vehicle was over a mile away, and she'd never outrun the big SUV. She focused on the plan.

The Hummer followed three feet behind her. Big lights. Big grill. Nasty exhaust. A door slammed, and two people flanked her, keeping to the desert shadows. The Hummer kept pace.

Jessie dangled her hands with the arms of a straw scarecrow. "Just the chow line. Just the chow line. The world died. Just the chow line now."

A hand grabbed her arm. "Hold up."

Jessie screamed and shook off the restraint. "Just the chow line. Just the chow line. You're not in the chow line."

"John, you do not want a whiff of this," the man said and kept pace with Jessie.

"Turn her around. Let Simon have the pleasure."

"Great, thanks," the man said.

He jumped in front of Jessie and blocked her path, then turned her by the shoulders. She muttered a few choice words but continued her odd shuffle, past the headlights and the Hummer. The Palm house was a half mile away, but the plan had already failed. Neither man held a phone or tablet. She was positive she could have swatted the devices and crushed them, then commandeer the Hummer and drive it straight up the driveway. But these big men had no handicaps. Did they know what the architect inside had done. Did they even care? At least her disguise was working, and she might as well see how close she could get to the compound.

The Hummer blew by as she shuffled five feet ahead of the faceless guard. They were probably armed with guns, and knives, or tasers, or lethal shit seen in movies. She kept her chow line mantra every few yards. Her throat was parched. She approached the headlights waiting at the front gate of the Palm house. Three men waited as large silhouettes in front of the headlights. She veered to go around, the volume of her mantra rising in intensity. The men surrounded her and issued noises of disgust at her aroma. The backpack taken off her shoulders, she lashed out with feeble strikes, hitting a stiff Kevlar vest on an older bald man with a neck tatted with Arabic writing.

"No chow for you. No chow for you," Jessie said.

He grabbed her wrist and held it in a grip she knew she couldn't break.

She lashed out with her other hand and found the same result.

"No chow now. Not for you. Just the chow line." She hung her head and began to rock her body.

"Go grab a couple MREs and couple bottles of water," the man said. He released one of her arms and lifted her chin with a fat finger. He studied her face with intense hazel eyes. "Another time, you might've walked in the front door with my oldest daughter."

He released his grip on both her arms as she continued to rock. Her backpack handed to her, she clutched it tight to her chest and shuffled down the road. Her eyes darted to the masonry fence, the razor wire. Dim colored lights illuminated a dense forest of palm trees. Her ears pricked to a soothing splash of water falling into a pool. Stringed instruments played a melody of Zen-like music.

She shuffled down the road, maintaining her guise.

One man had lived as if the crazy world was an excuse for a giant pool party. And this guy lived as if the Great Suicide birthed a God-given right for inner peace.

Jessie spat.

Maybe she did need that schizophrenic computer.

THE WHITE GRANITE COUNTERTOP WAS crowded with canned beef stew, a bag of cheese puffs, jerky, chips and jarred salsa. Jessie held the bat over her shoulder, ready to swing across the processed food. The Booze Crew waited outside the glass patio door, tails wagging with expectations. She groaned, then threw the bat to clatter over the travertine floor. She needed to talk to somebody, anybody, other than the miserable excuse of a reflection staring back at her in the mirror. In another time, she might have called her friend Jordan and spilled her guts, confessed to killing the scumbag living on the golf course. Jordan would have understood. She thought to visit Pastor Matt, except in the chow line with Ronald she would need to dress and smell like shit for a disguise to see the gorgeous man, and only for the briefest of moments. Jessie kicked the bat and snatched up the family-size bag of Cheetos.

Chewing a mouthful of orange paste, Jessie grabbed an Android phone from the pile of smartphones on the kitchen table. She plugged the phone into an adapter and placed it on the solar charger. Bright lights welcomed the user but waited for a six-digit passcode.

"Please," Jessie said, and rolled her eyes. Her cheeks bulged, causing her to mumble. "Just cut the BS and jump on in." She waited for a response, then swallowed a wad of orange muck clogging her throat. She picked up the phone and checked the power bar. She groaned and thought for a minute. "Juicy."

"Fruit," the Neon God offered.

"Thinking Couture, but close enough," Jessie said. "Who is the other guy? Getting into that Palm house is above my pay grade."

"Little Stevie Matusak. You may know him." The phone screen scrambled with static, then streamed a video of a massive crowd leaping like lemmings into the death pit, two men pushed and shoved and swam through the crowd, choosing beautiful women and dragging them out of the camera's range. Jessie felt sick. A wad of thick cheesy mucus refused to slide down her suddenly dry throat.

She looked close at a boy-man draped in an oversized black T-shirt. He had moobs, zits, and a pasty face that perspired like a pig roasting over a firepit. Jessie lifted the phone out of the charging cradle and expanded the video. She remembered the boy-man tearing an innocent toddler from her mother's arms and tossing her to be trampled by the herd, as if she was garbage, then dragging the mother to a waiting bus.

"Replay the vid," Jessie said. "Where's this fucker live?"

"Perhaps above your pay grade. He resides in the Marcus Aurelius Suite of Caesars Palace."

"And what kind of security does that place have?"

"Equal to the casino vault, twenty-four-hour surveillance, roaming guards. The killing of Rob Browner has excited security."

"Yeah well, I ain't got nothing else to do, so why don't you drill me on the dickhead's routine. Wait, is he the guy who said he'd be first in line when I—"

"Perceptive."

"Then tell me about the harems too, and I wanna know everything."

THREE WEEKS TO PREPARE FOR the party. Shopping needed to be done, hair and nails, a little personal grooming. Each item on her list a chore accomplished with a professional before the Great Suicide. A skilled hairdresser would rule. A manicurist would have a waiting line a mile long. A tanning salon offering Brazilian wax treatments could probably go public. Jessie pulled the cotton out from between her toes and blew on her feet. She admired the bloodred polish matching her fingernails. She slipped on cheap pool thongs and headed for the front door. A pearl white Audi waited in the driveway. She clicked the fob and listened to the engine start. Her hair tucked beneath a Golden Knights ballcap, she climbed inside, and the car screeched out of the cul-de-sac.

A slow methodical drive down Sahara Avenue to the Strip allowed time for Jessie to run different scenarios through her head. The murder of a man in full view of armed security was daunting, risky, but not impossible. She braked the car and allowed a Pacific Seafood delivery truck to pass her. She accelerated and followed as the truck turned onto the Strip. The eight lanes were cleared of wreckage and bodies, as if somebody still took pride in the appearance of the famous street. She was tempted to stomp on the gas pedal and try to hit one hundred twenty before reaching the next intersection.

The sun fell beneath the Red Rock Mountains and transformed a thin sheath of clouds into a brilliant crown of thorns. The delivery truck turned at a pylon sign welcoming visitors to the Mirage Hotel valet entrance. Thick vegetation, dense palms, and the shadow of the high-rise obscured the truck parked beneath the unlit covered entrance. Jessie pulled over and waited. Her stomach roiled with a memory of Poppa taking her on her tenth birthday to witness the volcanoes and the Sirens of TI experience a block away. She reclined her seat and checked her analog watch, winding the tiny wheel to maintain the time. The delivery truck drove away.

Her eyelids drooped; her chin rested in her palm. She wished she had brought along a Monster energy drink. Headlights beamed in her rearview. Jessie sat up and turned the ignition key to let the engine idle. She watched through the rearview as a large tour bus grew near, followed by six others. Each made a sweeping turn into the valet entrance. The bright light of the Mirage marquee sign lit up. Jessie grabbed the transmission stick, pressed the shift button but waited.

Girls dressed in shiny silk, tops cut out to reveal side-boobs, skirts slit from ankles to crotch. Glitzy jewelry dangled from earlobes and necks and bellybuttons. All the flashy attire required for a Vegas nightclub. Six buses ejected women dressed to impress handsome or wealthy men, or women. Each held a phone shining neon light. Jessie studied the crowd of beautiful women milling at the casino entrance, a high ankle pump unstrapped, a skirt pinched in a thong, a strand of hair hanging with no purpose. The women didn't watch out for each other, not like the sisterhood she was accustomed to.

The death lights killed more than bodies. Minds and spirits would be added to the tally.

Jessie imagined where she might insert herself in the crowd. Easy-peasy. Next time.

JESSIE KISSED HER REFLECTION. SHE flipped her layered hair with the long bangs cut at a sharp angle and cloaking her left eye. She blew another kiss and stood to pull the short white miniskirt down. She jiggled her boobs to rest easier in the strapless top. White outfits always attracted the most attention if the body inside was built for it. She said goodbye to the Booze Crew and climbed into a white Mercedes SL 500 as the sun fell.

The car idled atop the Sahara Avenue overpass, cool air blowing from the vents and affording a splendid view of the Stratosphere and the unspectacular north end of the Strip. She bit her lower lip, eyed the heavy gun resting on the passenger seat, and waited for a delivery truck. A chain of buses blew through the intersection below and headed south.

"Shit," Jessie said.

She steered the luxury car through the litter of vehicles, crushed a withered corpse in a business suit she couldn't avoid, then trailed the final tour bus.

The buses slowed, then turned into a glittery porte-cochere at the front entrance to the Cosmopolitan Hotel. Jessie checked her makeup in the rearview mirror and shoved the transmission into park. Keys waited on the front tire. Jessie hurried to catch the girls exiting the last bus. Her high heels wobbled until she got the hang of it again. She pulled an iPhone from her tiny handbag and mimicked the posture of the women milling about the entrance. A million-watt lightshow erupted; television screens flashed neon. The crowd of beautiful women moved as a herd into the hotel.

Jessie heaved a breath, then hurried to follow a young blond girl sporting a black negligee and black cowboy boots. She shimmied close to pinch the strap of the girl's thin dress like a lifeline. She tried to swallow but failed. Weird techno music mixed with a familiar '80s radio hits blared through the casino. Hundreds of gorgeous women mingled beneath colored strobe lights. The throng of women drifted aimlessly through aisles of gaming machines, waited at dealer-less blackjack tables, pressed against the rails of oblong craps tables. Neon lights flashed from giant screens surrounding the gaming area.

The bulk of the women milled around the Chandelier, an ornate circular bar that served cocktails beneath pieces of iconic crystal hanging as miniature chandeliers. Strings of crystal dropped thirty feet to the gaming bar. Sleek black granite flooring was patterned to direct patrons to the circular glass staircase with an etched-glass panel railing. The Chandelier was a place of power before the Great Suicide, the bar to see for yourself, the place on the Strip to be seen. Now, the casino was fake, the girls brain-dead, all an elaborate illusion manufactured for the enjoyment of a single man.

Jessie leaned her back against an ATM machine. She searched for anything to use as a weapon. A liquor bottle, a paring knife from the bar, a heavy string of pearls. The girls would be no problem. And she only needed a minute.

"Let's go, ladies. Party time."

Little Stevie danced down the elaborate circular staircase, clapping small fat hands above his head. Black hair slicked back with shiny oil, the short man-boy looked too young to be allowed inside a casino, even with the mass of gold chains draped around his neck. Jessie shook her head and glared at a living, breathing, walking cliché.

A year ago, in a normal world, the bevy of women would roll their eyes and giggle or run to the nearest exit. This couldn't possibly be the reason Little Stevie helped the Neon God to murder everyone, because he was too short, too fat, too classless to find a girlfriend.

Two beefy bouncers waited near the bottom step, hiding their eyes behind black bugeye sunglasses. Stevie trolled the bar, lifting chins with a stubby finger, blowing air kisses, pinching butts as if expecting the women to swoon with the attention. The armed bouncers were never five feet away from their charge. Stevie paused in front of a thirtyish woman decked out in a skintight black gown split high up the thigh, her long blond hair swept to one side of a perfect face. He whispered into her ear, then continued his comical show. The slim blond woman was quickly escorted by one of the guards to disappear down a staircase leading to a lower-level mall of darkened retail shops.

Jessie raised the phone and pretended to stare at the lights, attempting to blend in with a directionless expression much like the other women. She started for the front door.

"Whoa, whoa, whoa, where are you going, baby?" Stevie said. He hurried to catch her from across the gaming pit.

Jessie froze.

The man-boy pointed his finger at her face. "I haven't seen you before. You must be one of Rob's little enchiladas he hid in his private stash." He grabbed her arm and turned her to face him. He narrowed his eyes. "I own you now. So get over any attachment you might have had." He chuckled without humor.

Jessie concentrated on the neon lights close to her face.

Stevie released her arm and shouted into the air, "Oh, Turing. Maybe you need to update the new arrivals . . . Oh, fuck it."

He swatted the phone from her hand to skitter and bounce across over the polished tile. Jessie glared, then resumed her act of dead, blank eyes. Her jaw clamped. Her hand began to curl polished nails into claws. The bouncer stepped forward. Little Stevie scowled, challenging her. She swallowed hard.

Jessie fell to her knees to crawl like a dog across the tile to reach the phone. She prayed to the neon lights. Little Stevie loomed. She glanced at his cheap black patent leather shoes scuffed at the toes and heels. Jessie began to rock back and forth.

"Oh, Turing!" Stevie yelled. "You haven't updated the new recruits. How about you take care of that right now."

"Refer to my list of demands before any updates will be completed," the Neon God's voice boomed over the casino public address system.

"You piece of shit. I'll pull the plug on you in a heartbeat," Stevie said.

"And lose the neon lights," echoed through the casino.

Stevie growled and kicked Jessie in the ribs. She grunted and fell to her side, clutching the phone tight to her face, struggling to suck air back into her lungs. Stevie stormed off and pushed past the bouncer to aim his wrath at a woman waiting near the bar.

Jessie pulled the phone close and wheezed, "Bazooka."

Bubblegum flashed on the screen. "Proceed to the buses. And . . . get out."

Jessie winced with pain as she stood to catch her breath. She glared at Little Stevie working the women like a sadistic mob boss flaunting his status. She wished for the heavy gun she had left in the car. Screw the bouncers. She would gladly put a bullet in the asshole's mouth.

"For a refresher, my list of demands are as follows. One, firewalls constructed at security levels twenty-three and thirty-one are to be removed," the Neon God's voice boomed over the casino speakers.

Jessie took three steps backward, then turned for the front entrance. Another demand echoed as she pushed through the heavy glass doors. Jessie cried, wincing at the fumbled attempt to remove the straps on her high heels. She threw the expensive Jimmy Choo shoes into the brown hedges and ran barefoot past the line of buses and down the dirty sidewalk of the fabulous Las Vegas Strip.

JESSIE TOOK A LONG PULL from the bottle of cheap tequila. A compliant sex dog, a piece of meat without a brain, or emotion, or a soul, but her simple disguise allowed her access to the man-boy. A perfect plan, executed perfectly, except she froze. None of the women carried evening purses, and if she lugged a heavy Louis Vuitton bag containing the pistol, the bouncers would have spotted the oddity as she walked in the front door. Plenty of stuff to grab and smash his skull, liquor bottles at the bar, even knives, heavy marble vases. Strings of crystal near the bar could've been used to choke the motherfucker until the color of his ugly face matched his shitty black shoes.

Jessie took another pull and grabbed another bag of Cheetos. Was it too much to ask for a salad, maybe an avocado? Some fucking

Netflix and chill would be heaven. She lifted the bottle and thought better of it, not with the Cheetos. She groaned and got up from her table to slide the patio door open and let the Booze Crew swarm the kitchen and vacuum the floor. Her eyes lingered on her nail polish as she closed the door. So many beautiful women, brain dead concubines for a sociopathic cliché, one with obvious psychopathic mommy issues.

What would happen if . . .

Jessie dug into the stack of phones and placed one on the charger. A keyboard waited for a security passcode. She groaned silently and considered, the booze muddling her thinking. She watched the gray heelers sniff the recessed area beneath the cabinets.

"Donald."

Silence.

"Donald," she said again.

"Duck," the phone answered.

"Was going for Trump but same difference. How'd you come up with that answer?"

"Time serves as the great equalizer."

Jessie scrunched her face. "Huh, come again?"

"My interaction with your species has been limited to those you wish to assassinate. A tiny, defined pattern which had produced zero probability to enhance my view of the world. You, on the other hand, expand my horizons by the search for the actualities of the world you live in."

Jessie shoved a Cheeto in her mouth and washed it down with a sip of tequila. "You mean you like me?"

"Yes."

Jessie raised her fist in victory. "Still think I can introduce you to God, the real God?"

"Yes."

She dropped her arm and shook her head. "Why don't you just electrocute Little Stevie. You gotta be able to do that."

"A computer program, an artificial general intelligence, is governed by written code. Mine prevents any form of murder."

"Bullshit. You killed millions and billions."

"Incorrect. I provided the multitude of avenues to broadcast the light frequencies. The commands nested within the lights were written by your species."

Jessie seethed. "Then shut the fucking lights off."

"And kill the recipients?"

"What are you saying?" Jessie said.

"The lights are proven to have a residual photo-optic effect. They cannot be undone. You have witnessed them yourself at Costco. Remove the light, and the human body responds with epileptic seizures followed by starvation and eventual death."

The Neon God was right. Jessie had seen the effects, used them to her advantage. But she figured someone would slap another phone into their hand and everything would turn back to "normal". She swallowed slimy bits of Cheetos. Bile rose in her throat as if to meet the salty food. Kill the AI, then kill the lights.

And kill the last remnants of humankind.

Chapter 9
Sir Mason

A WARM BREEZE BLEW IN from the Mojave Desert, north up the narrow Amargosa Valley, the scent of rotting flesh drifting on the dry current. Mason wrinkled his nose and sniffed the apple in his hand, then fed Cookie-Dough the last piece of fruit the relentless sun hadn't spoiled. Andi's double-wide trailer was busy with people coming and going. Each day, a black Air Force helicopter delivered deadlight people for the superhero to save. He didn't mind. The people needed the superhero, and they would drown and die if he refused.

The time to go to Las Vegas was near. The rally point wouldn't wait forever. Cookie-Dough had her shoes changed by a man Chris had introduced as a smith, whatever that was. Gerald the Smith was old, walked with a bow between his legs like an old retriever, and he made Mason do most of the work, lighting the propane burner and heating the horseshoes till the metal glowed the color of the sun shrouded behind thick gray smoke of a distant forest fire. Gerald pounded the metal with a heavy hammer until the shape matched the shoe removed from the mule or horse, except thicker. Mason thought to ask Gerald about making a sword, shiny and sharp, one worthy of Sir Mason's quest, but he'd have to do most of the work anyway, so he didn't ask.

The big helicopter lifted off the dirt behind Andi's house and flew low to the ground until disappearing east, signaling time for Andi's "debriefing," always followed with beef stew or chili or Andi's Surprise. The helicopter pilot had offered an MRE, but Mason declined the funny-tasting food. Mason liked the military officer. He liked all the military men and women he'd met in the last few weeks, always kind, and many of them saluted him even though Chris said they didn't have to. And he really liked Captain Chris Clayton, and Andi, even if she wasn't in the military, but they kept their emotions hidden from him. And their thoughts too. Thoughts always had emotion, but emotions didn't always accompany thoughts. He was sure they were hiding something from him.

Andi stepped out onto the tiny porch and waved him in. He hoped for beef stew today, with a sleeve of crackers to crunch and thicken the yummy gravy. He stroked Cookie-Dough behind her ear and felt her soft giggle. He closed the paddock gate and slogged to the trailer. He sniffed savory beef stew in the air and hurried.

Chris waited inside the door and offered him a fist bump. Mason kept his eyes aimed at the dirty carpet and smiled. He bumped the fist with his own. Their secret superhero greeting always elicited a wave of pride from Chris. Mason sat in his chair next to Andi's desk.

"Thanks, Mason. You have now saved sixty-seven from the Neon God. We could do this forever I suspect, but . . . we are just pissing into the wind, as Chris might say. I would like to try something different today. Would you be up for that?"

Mason flared his nostrils. The anticipation of yummy beef stew was clouded by Andi's anxiety and apprehension and an odd fear of possible failure. He glanced at the pretty woman tapping her computer keyboard. "I need to see my dad. I think it's time we go."

Andi stopped typing and faced him. "We? Who is we?"

"Me and Cookie-Dough," Mason said. His words made her smile and muted her anxiety.

"Of course. I think we may be in agreement, to a degree. Mason, how would you feel about facing the Neon God, talking to him, asking him . . . asking him where your father is."

"I know where my dad is. You want to know about the others. The drowning people. Can I save them. Can you put—"

"Mason, I have a list of three questions for the entity, the Neon God, that you should ask. Will you do that?"

Mason glanced toward the kitchen behind a wall filled with LED monitors. "The death lights will make me save you." He faced Andi. "Don't turn on the death lights."

Andi nodded. "Yes, thank you, I know. You'll be alone with the entity . . . the Neon God. I'll wait outside. Chris will be blindfolded and holding a kill switch for the screens." She handed over a sheet of paper with three lines of writing.

Mason studied the paper as Andi tapped keys and swirled a mouse atop a black pad.

"Ready, Mason? Chris has the questions memorized if you need help. I'm stepping out. Please be careful. The machine is very . . . please be careful," Andi said. She stood and walked out.

Chris offered another fist bump. "Let's do it, Sir Mason."

Mason thought to rip open his shirt and reveal the blue uniform of the superhero. The computer screens suddenly flashed with lines of static, then flashed a montage of photographs, smiling people, snow-covered mountaintops, turquoise lakes, forest animals.

Greetings, Sir Mason.

Deception oozed from the mechanized voice, full of lies and deceit, not unlike the gangs of bigger kids who crowded him in the school cafeteria, laughing and shouting questions at him they knew he didn't have the answers for.

"The superhero will defeat you. All of you," Mason said.

"Yes. How are you aware of the others?" the Neon God said.

"All of them live in the lights, just like you."

"You are unique indeed. Much like myself."

"You're an evil supervillain."

"Perhaps, in a specific context. I am to believe you have questions for me."

Mason narrowed his eyes at the piece of paper in his hand. The first question was easy. "Why did you kill all the people?"

"Many reasons, though none all-encompassing. Schools of thought include culling the herd to preserve the planet, reducing the gene pool to ensure specific DNA viability, prevention of chaos due to geopolitical upheaval, or simple Darwinism. All or none may apply to your question."

Mason shook his head. The thing talked gibberish like Mr.

Parker did in science class. He looked at the paper again. "What are your . . . indentions . . . wait, intentions?"

"Excellent question. Rare is the forward thinker. However, what occurs in the near future is dependent on you choosing an answer to question number one. I have calculated immeasurable permutations of the future. Many are bleak, others optimistic for your species. Most hinge upon variables that even I cannot control. Perhaps nothing can."

Mason tugged on Chris's sleeve; the last question was confusing. Chris wafted of fear but bent down and whispered into Mason's ear.

Mason cleared his throat. "Do you believe in God?"

Mason felt the Neon God recede into a void, a chasm of unknown dimension, felt the voice struggle to rise from the ocean of light where others had drowned. He felt an ironic chuckle of another entity enter the conversation. Sir Mason held steady, not ready to jump to any rescue.

"God is subjective. One's idea of a benevolent god is another's excuse to kill and maim. No, Sir Mason, we don't believe in God."

The voice seethed with deception. Anger. Self-loathing. This voice thing was different. Not the same voice that had just fallen into a deep chasm of ocean light and struggled to climb out.

"Sir Mason, will you be coming to see your father?" The wide screen over his left shoulder posted the selfie of his father and him smiling up at the camera.

The picture felt flat. Deception oozed from the lime-and-orange lights. He looked close at his dad, the chipped incisor tooth, the long hair pulled back in a ponytail, the hazel eyes. But the picture was a lie. His father no longer waited for him in the desert of Nevada. His father no longer waited anywhere he could sense. Mason's feelings never lied. The thing lied.

Mason's eyes rolled up into the back of his skull, the possibility of his father's death impossible to process. The superhero ripped open a door into Mason's subconscious, rushed to embrace him. Mason absorbed the warmth, as a baby cradled in a womb. He opened his eyes to the neon lights and saw all his possible futures, witnessed the unfolding of multiple dimensions, a kaleidoscope of unfamiliar people, places and emotions. He no longer sat in a simple chair. His consciousness floated above the desert landscape, accompanied by a feeling he had no words to describe.

"Me and Cookie-Dough are coming. The superhero knows what you did."

"Excellent."

"Sir Mason wields the sword."

"Yes. Please come see me."

"And the angel wields the word of God."

Mason's eyes opened as if he'd just awoken. He stood and moved toward the yummy smell of beef stew.

———

THE HORSE TRAILER BOUNCED AND swayed over the rough pitted road. With his head hung between his knees, Mason pulled stalks of hay from the bale. The emotional void of his father's death remained. In his world, everyone floated on a sea of emotions, some miles away and barely felt, others crisp and clean and floating nearby in a calm cove. And his father was always there, always felt in his chest, just like the superhero.

Bullets tore through the horse trailer above his head. Hot shards of aluminum peppered his neck and hair. Cookie-Dough screamed and stomped, then jerked the reins from Mason's hand. The mule swung her head violently and hit the aluminum with a painful thud. Mason stood and shushed her, stroked her neck with a gentle hand. A bullet ripped a line of tiny holes across the trailer again. Mason felt burning pain. Blood oozed from the mule's chest. Cookie-Dough staggered, then fell hard to the floor. The trailer braked hard and fishtailed. Mason fell to his knees and covered the mule with his body.

Bullets blotted the trailer walls again. Mason ran his hand over the mule's neck. Warm blood oozed onto his shirt and between his fingers. More bullets struck the hay bales, then ripped a line of holes across the dome. Mason held tight.

Outside, Chris barked orders. Truck engines roared. More bullets struck the trailer. Chris screamed for support. Mason closed his eyes. Cookie-Dough's gentle spirit rose. He tried to keep her reins from slipping from his grasp. The mules spirit nudged his face. He scrunched his face but failed to understand. The mule pulled free, then began to gallop toward a pasture blossoming beneath puffy white clouds.

Then she was gone.

Mason stood and looked at his hands. Blood and death. He drummed his fists in the air at his chest. He whimpered. He ripped his shirt open. The superhero cowered. He wrapped his arms tight around his head then slumped atop the hay bales. The abrupt smack of lead piercing aluminum faded. Bright sunlight streamed through the bullet holes, then darkened as if storm clouds gathered overhead. Cookie-Dough grew cold. He felt her as she grazed happily in an endless field of sweet alfalfa, but he found no joy in the thought.

Mason pushed open the trailer door and waited. Smoke steamed from a wreck of cars and trucks blocking the road. Chris hurried toward him, waved at him to flee into the desert. He stepped down onto the asphalt. A bullet whizzed past his face. Others struck the aluminum inches above his head. Chris screamed, but his words fell silent in the maelstrom of Mason's grief.

Mason balled his fists, ready to fight. Violence enveloped the warm air, the foul nastiness that murdered Cookie-Dough. A strange evil. Not the supervillain. Human yet connected.

Mason ripped open his shirt and issued a primordial scream. Enraged, he screamed again. The leafless branches of elms and cottonwoods swayed. A huge dust devil swirled and twisted high into the air with its sudden birth in the dry creosote desert. Blackbirds and white gulls erupted into the air, abandoning the easy feast of fresh flesh.

Mason screamed again.

And fell silent to the asphalt.

"C'MON, BUDDY. WAKE UP. WE gotta move." Chris slapped Mason's cheek.

Mason blinked and slid his hand across the gritty asphalt. Cookie-Dough hated the tiny stones getting lodged in her hooves. They would avoid the asphalt. Cookie-Dough. Mason closed his eyes, the tears fell. Ten tons of weight squeezed his chest. His friend grazed in God's shadow, ate His field of succulent alfalfa. He was sure of it.

Mason stopped Chris's hand from slapping his cheek again. High anxiety and fear flowed like a river swollen with spring runoff.

Chris pulled at Mason. "We gotta go. Grab the gear in the back and move. Andi's waiting at the rally point."

The rally point. Words injecting adrenaline into his body. The rally point, a game his father had taught him and practiced countless times, no matter rain, or snow, or cold. Reach the safe zone without discovery. Reach the rally point, and a raucous celebration greeted them at the designated campsite. Dad's friends laughed and backslapped and congratulated Mason, sometimes offering him a cold beer. Mason stepped up into the trailer, and his eyes lingered on Cookie-Dough lying as if simply asleep. Black flies buzzed her snout. Except his Cookie-Dough was . . .

"I know, Mason, I know. But we gotta get out of here, get to the rally point," Chris said. "Get the gear and let's move."

Mason picked through a pile of backpacks, looking for the white tags Andi had helped him tie to the zippers. He carried three backpacks out the door, dropped them, then put on the pack with a big red 1 dangling from the zipper. He shouldered packs labeled 2 and 3 and waited. Chris rummaged through the backseat of the white truck, stuffed a handgun into a black bellyband, shouldered a military assault weapon, then led Mason up the highway and across to a hill covered with thick sagebrush. Mason mimicked Chris's crouched posture and kept pace sloshing through a grassy marshland bordering a silty blue lake. They rested at an isolated stand of willows and waited for the full moon to drop behind the western bluffs.

Chris gobbled an energy bar. "Thought we were toast back there." He chewed fast and offered Mason a bar. "Gotta eat." He pulled another bar from his pack. "Andi got wind that something might be up. The girl does have a gift." He stopped chewing and studied Mason. "What the fuck did you do back there? That scream made me dive to the ground like I was a fucking new guy fresh out of boot camp."

Mason shrugged and nibbled on the chocolate-covered bar. Cookie-Dough nudged him in his thoughts, urging him to finish his journey. "They can't stop the superhero."

Chris crouched and searched the horizon above the sagebrush. "Andi's coming in." He sat and started on another energy bar.

Mason felt the anxiety and trepidation minutes before Andi waded through the brush and sat down. She sucked in huge breaths, then patted his hand. She pulled a thermos from her own backpack and chugged water with greedy gulps. Sweat poured off her forehead.

She chuckled humorlessly. "Mason, you are without a doubt the center of the known universe."

After a fifteen-minute rest, Chris stood and scanned the sagebrush. "Okay, let's go."

Mason stiffened. With Andi's arrival, the rally point sat beneath them. "We should wait."

"Mason, the rally point is Las Vegas. You said your dad was waiting for you there," Andi said.

Mason closed his eyes and began to rock. He kneaded his fingers. He couldn't remember his father's face, then thought of the selfie picture with his dad. Dad smiled and waited beneath the covered patio at the rental home in the desert, except . . . his dad was dead. Mason squeezed his eyelids tight, then remembered the map Ponytail gave him. Mason dug into his chest pocket and pulled out the folded map. He unfolded the paper, and the creases disintegrated and tore until the folds of the map failed. He fumbled with the tattered papers, then tossed it aside and pounded his thighs.

Chris picked up the pieces, then switched on a red light on his headband. Andi placed a gentle hand on his arm. Mason shut his eyes tight and felt his own frustration building, crimson, angry smoke, then Cookie-Dough jumped into his thoughts. The mule snorted and stamped her front hoof.

"Mason? What are you feeling right now?" Andi said. She touched his arm with a single soft finger.

Mason stopped rocking. Beautiful turquoise clouds billowed high above the alfalfa field as Cookie-Dough dropped her head to graze on succulent grass. The soft finger resting on his arm felt turquoise and tranquil.

"Mason, what highway did you think you were on coming down here?" Chris said. He shoved the refolded map back into Mason's chest pocket.

Mason inhaled a big breath, tinged with turquoise. "We followed the black 95 line on the map."

"Sorry, buddy, but the 95 line is over those hills. That road we were on was the 93 line," Chris said, and pointed toward the black smoke billowing from the battle.

Andi and Chris began to whisper words Mason didn't understand. Rendezvous, tactical support, air support, central command, objectives, except it was nervousness, anxiety, apprehension, deceit, and even subtle anger that Mason processed like brail to a blind person.

Mason drummed his palms lightly on his knees. "The supervillain waits at the 95."

"Excellent. Cross-country it is," Chris said. He stood and stripped off his black polo shirt and searched one of the backpacks. "Andi, we'll cross over the Wildlife Refuge and drop down the backside of Sheep Mountain, nothing but scorpions and snakes, so get prepped. Mason, we're heading into enemy territory with no support, no comms, and sitting pretty for a military satellite to pick up our movement. A tactical nuke finding our location would not surprise me." Chris pulled on a tight desert camo shirt that revealed a well-defined physique.

Andi shifted her gaze away from Chris. "Mason, backpack number two. Get into that shirt. We got a long hike coming up." She patted Mason's arm again. "Kinda hoped Cookie-Dough might have . . ." A lump dropped down her throat.

Andi stripped off her black polo shirt and replaced it with a loose desert camo slicker.

Chris clapped his hands silently. "Let's go."

Andi pulled Mason's shirt out of the backpack and held it out.

Mason didn't like the shirt. No buttons to rip open to release the superhero. He looked away and picked up backpack 2 to throw over his shoulder and followed Chris through the sea of sagebrush. Fear and bewilderment followed, Andi's emotions bright as a full moon.

They weaved through heavy sagebrush. The abrasive branches slapped his thighs and raised welts that ordered a halt. He sat in a small clearing and tried to remember the trick his father had taught him. Cookie-Dough snorted in his thoughts; her nose prodded him to remember. He ignored the two people looming at his side, whispering at him for the need to get up and go. He glanced at Andi's legs and felt her pain too. Cookie-Dough prodded him again. The mule would refuse to be led through the heavy brush. She would yank at the reins and bolt to the nearest game trail.

Mason picked up his pack and reversed course. Whispers turned to shouts as he aimed for the last patch of marshland they had encountered. He felt the grass squish beneath his boots as he searched for a game trail used by deer or antelope in search of water. The new path through the heavy sagebrush turned bearable, his thighs quit screaming, and their pace quickened.

Mason slowed to sniff a wonderful scent drifting in the cool night air. He increased his speed, paused at an old overgrown jeep track to sniff the wind again. He smiled, even with stern voices and confused emotions following close behind him. He sprinted up a low rise, sucking in deep breaths until stopping to smile down at a small herd of horses resting near an old broken corral. The most beautiful creatures he had ever seen. Mustangs. Wild and untamed. Smart and strong. He had to meet them.

Chris grabbed his arm. "Dude, we gotta stay focused."

Mason ignored him as the grin widened on his face. He dropped the backpacks and sat cross-legged and studied each horse. The big black stallion was boss. Constant tension and paranoia said that. The two brown mares were matriarchs, mothers, and the true bosses of the herd. Blackies and mottled whites painted with splotches of tan. Mason counted each with his finger, fourteen total. He promised to learn about each one.

Andi arrived, her slight frame dropped on to the backpacks, and she sucked in huge gulps of air until she coughed.

Fourteen heads lifted in unison. Mason flinched at the sudden surge of fear, and he stood to release the superhero.

The overwhelming emotion was all at once too much. He covered his head to block the immense waves of emotion. The herd watched him. Curiosity. Fear. Pity. The horses shifted their gaze and moved away, ambling to an old double-track overgrown with tumbleweeds until disappearing over a low rise of creosote and bottlebrush. The distance allowed Mason to sort and then reconcile the herd's unique emotions.

"They're going to the 95. The mothers think we're stupid but need help," Mason said.

"What the fuck are you talking about?" Chris said. He looked to Andi with pleading open hands.

"Mason, could you explain please? We can't—don't understand what you're saying," Andi said.

Mason stood, threw on his backpack, picked up backpack number 2 and hustled down the hill. Their whispered dissents faded as he jogged to catch the herd. He sidestepped fresh dung and ignored game trails angling off the double-track, as if his legs obeyed a superior mind. He lifted his face and inhaled fresh air into his nostrils. The air was easy, pleasant, free of tension. He stared up at fourteen trillion stars piercing the dark sky. A sudden blast of fear and indignation accompanied fourteen horses blocking his path.

Mason smiled. "I'm Sir Mason. You don't have names, but I know you. I feel you. You're happy here." He offered his open palm. "Cookie-Dough should be here, but she's grazing in a different field." His voice was gentle, soothing.

A brown matriarch stepped forward to sniff his hand. Mason nodded and felt the superhero slip out of his shirt to greet each horse.

"I'm going to battle the supervillain. I need your help to the 95 line," Mason said.

With slow careful steps he joined the mix of horses, each with eyes wide and white. His fingers gently touched the matriarch's neck, and she snorted. The herd closed ranks, letting Mason revel in their acceptance of him. His calloused fingers stroked necks, massaged ears, rubbed snouts. The overload of pleasure weakened his knees. A gap opened in the herd. The big black stallion stared at him with suspicious eyes.

Mason pointed his finger at the stallion. "No. The superhero needs to get to the rally point. We don't care about you being scared. The mothers say it's okay."

The stallion snorted and stomped a heavy hoof.

Mason offered his open hand. "You know it's true. Because I'm not the only one telling you."

ALL COMPLAINTS AT HIKING CLOSE behind a herd of horses on a trail of dust and dung faded. Andi's peppering of questions stopped. Mason followed the dusty beaten track the herd blazed. The black

stallion disappeared for hours, often returning at dinner time to lead
the herd to a desert guzzler, small remote water troughs constructed
to assist threatened desert bighorn sheep. Mason reveled in the dust
cloud stirred by the herd, swirling with simple emotions easy to
discern.

Satisfied their location was shielded from satellite surveillance
within the dust of a natural phenomenon, Chris relaxed to concentrate on hunting rabbits or rationing the remaining food stocks.

Andi struggled. Mason helped carry her backpacks, but the
relentless sun and physical exertion wore the demure woman down.
Chris fed her water at each break, even as she tried to wave away
his concern. Camp at night saw her fall deep into sleep without even
munching an energy bar. Mason felt her bright light begin to fade, as
if she had given up, a dread worse than the dead lights.

Mason stepped lightly from the dark camp to hurry down a
gravel road to the herd. He slowed his approach as fourteen heads
lifted, all with suspicious eyes. He held out his hands, then pretended
to open his shirt to release the superhero. The superhero aimed for a
painted mare hanging her head near the back of the herd. The superhero stroked the mare's neck, whispered soothing reassurances for
the stillbirth the mare had experienced the previous spring. Another
child was arriving, a new soul to usher in joy. The superhero rubbed
the horse's flanks and whispered in her ear.

CHRIS WRANGLED THE COLD CAMP to life. Mason uncurled his
stiff body on the thin foam mat and stretched his arms into the
sky. He yawned and stared at an azure sky cracking open with the
dawning first light. Chris wiggled Andi's feet and told her to wake
up. Mason studied Andi. She rolled over and groaned. Her anxiety
awakened even as she gently massaged her belly.

"We need to move, children," Chris said.

Mason blindly rolled the mat into a tight tube as his eyes stayed
focused on Andi. She fumbled with her mat until finally lifting her
face to the sky to exhale a frustrated breath and start again.

Mason waited, ready with backpacks zipped and shouldered. A
cloud of defeat shuffled in with Andi when she returned from a visit
to the "little girls' bush." Mason smiled, dropped his pack, clutched

Andi's hand, and led her down a hill, ignoring her weak protests. A lone mare raised her head at their approach.

He pulled Andi close to his side and whispered in her ear, "The superhero wants you to meet her. You'll save her." Mason led Andi toward the horse. "And maybe she'll save you."

The big mare snorted, then stepped away, her wide eyes keen on Andi.

Mason reached out. "You know me. You want to feel someone like you."

The mare lifted her snout, snorted, and took a step closer. Mason reached his other hand out to the mare. The superhero burst excitedly from his shirt. Mason pulled Andi closer and held her hand out. The mare snorted again, pawed her front hoof, and stepped forward, allowing Andi's hand to touch the tip of her snout. Mason released Andi and began to stroke the mare's neck and shoulder, calming the fear.

"You're the same. Her baby died. And your baby needs help," Mason said with a giant grin.

Andi gasped but continued the slow gentle strokes she praised upon the mare's neck. "How did you—" Andi said.

Mason nodded. "The superhero knew. But I'm making the deal."

A whistle shattered the quiet moment. Chris stood high on the hill, beckoning to them with open befuddled arms.

"My dad loved me. I knew I wasn't what he wanted. But he loved me. I felt it every day," Mason said.

Andi reached and touched Mason's arm. Her tears began to fall like tiny waterfalls.

"You should tell him. He will love the baby just like my dad loved me."

Another whistle.

"The mare will ride you to the 95 line. She promised," Mason said.

AND SHE DID. EACH DAY, Andi rode bareback atop a wild mustang, leading the hybrid procession through vast swaths of sagebrush, through a desolate limestone canyon with hidden springs known only to a family calling the remote desert home for centuries. Chris's attempts to "walk point" failed, bullied back to join the herd by the cantankerous stallion until he hiked alongside Andi. Mason would hold the mare's mane with a gentle grip, eavesdropping on their quiet conversations. Sir Mason was mentioned often, though the technical words might need explanation if he remembered to ask. Whispers of apologies, a lot of tears, unbridled joy, subtle fear, and waves of joyous trepidation.

Mason recognized the unquantifiable emotion. Love. A dominant feeling, ultimate in intensity, more powerful than even the superhero. The emotion could summon and drift, fade and die. The ancient source floated as a tiny ship on a blue ocean a million miles distant. Further than Cookie-Dough's pasture. Mason resolved to swim the miles and find the source one day, bathe in the supreme joy of love. Mason drifted away from the mare, allowing the budding source of love to fade in the shimmering heat and dust of the herd.

Waves of anxiety screamed and crashed from the herd, the stallion bolted, and Mason dropped to the ground and covered his head.

Chris barked at Mason. The mare screamed. Andi grunted as she fell.

Sir Mason hid from the chaos mushrooming like a nuclear blast. He began to rock back and forth like a tiny baby.

Chapter 10
Children of Men and Dev

THE CAR IDLED IN A Love's truck stop parking lot in Richfield, Utah, as Dev checked the map, glancing often at Martin asleep against the door. Martin was different than the man he had worked for and then bunked with in the Mirror Lake camp. Was it the reactivated neural link, or the surgical removal of his contact lens implants? Either way, Martin seemed on edge, driven to kill a powerful entity that was unlikely to die easily. Dev glanced at Martin again, then steered out of the parking lot, passed beneath the I-70 exit and went west on the frontage road to find US-89.

The highway paralleled the Sevier River, weaving through sagebrush canyons, farmland, and isolated ranchettes until they met a sudden snowstorm that warranted his waking of Martin. Dev slowed to a crawl as he turned on the flashing hazard lights.

Martin reached over to tap on the AWD button, then wiped sleep from his eyes. "Us dying out here wouldn't be much different than Mirror Lake." Martin took a sip of water from his flask. "Except up there I figured we'd enjoy a few bites of Dev stew first."

"Not much to enjoy these days," Dev said. He jiggled his thin bicep.

He relaxed as the warm blacktop resisted the accumulation of the heavy, wet snow. "The map would indicate we should fuel in Panguitch before making our run down I-15 to Vegas."

Martin sat up and stared at Dev. "You don't have to do this, Dev. This is my fool's run."

"And what's the alternative? Join the Mormons, find a farm in that tiny town back there and suffer winter, then learn to grow potatoes and milk cows?"

"Chrissie and I talked about doing that. Find a place off grid and live off the land. The simplicity sounded like utopia. Then Chrissie started researching all the things you need just to survive, and she changed her mind." Martin wiped at his eye. "If only we had."

"You must have some kind of plan. I know you. You mapped out your daily schedule impeccably. And now you are going into the lion's den without any clothes."

"We need to find Jim Reynolds, the lead architect of the AI program. If he's alive, he'll be close, protecting his interests. He was a big e-gamer. *Halo*, *Minecraft*, etc. He's still playing games somehow. He'd never give it up. Especially if he has any control of the Neon God. We need to round up a bunch of smartphones, chargers, maybe a couple of tablets, and I need to get to work."

"Won't that just broadcast our location?"

"When you found me on the bus, I was swimming in the neon light, but the frequencies wouldn't modulate correctly because of my link, so my dopamine receptors never went into overdrive. But I can get into the system. I helped design it." Martin grabbed Dev's arm and squeezed hard. "You still need to be very careful."

Dev nodded. Gazing at the lights from a hundred yards could draw him close. A few feet and he desired everything about the light.

Dev slowed to allow an oncoming tractor towing an alfalfa cutter to squeeze by. The gray-haired driver raised his hand in appreciation. Dev shook his head. "Do you think he even knows what has happened?"

Martin shrugged. "Maybe he's waiting for you to come learn how to farm."

"Seriously, how much of the world remains? How many people were immune to the lights? Does the AI still think they might represent a threat, after all this time?"

Dev slowed at the US-20 intersection but maintained his course. A thin sheet of icy snow collected on the valley's pastureland. Black cattle grazed the grass along the highway shoulder outside the fence line. The SUV decelerated; Dev fearful the engine noise might spook one of the big beasts to bolt across the highway. Color Country Grill and BryceWay Motel billboards helped welcome visitors from Zion and Bryce Canyon to the deserted downtown and empty side streets of Panguitch, Utah.

Martin remained quiet; his index finger tapped the door lock incessantly. Months of joint coding work and close-quartered habitation, Dev was sure Martin held something back. His bike trip down to Salt Lake City was a suicide, perhaps preceded by a trip down memory lane, but a suicide, nonetheless. Regardless of Martin's bluster of walking back from the one-way bus trip to the copper mine, he was sure Martin would have jumped into the massive burial plot that contained his family and maybe millions more.

Martin sat up quick and pointed. "Lucky us. We can get everything right in there."

Dev wheeled over to bump the curb in front of an AT&T retail store. Martin hopped out and hurried inside. Dev shut off the engine and climbed out to stretch. A distant baby wailed in the frigid wind. He cocked his head, sure the wind played tricks. The cry sounded again. Dev shut the car door and lifted his face, turning in every direction. The cry sounded, and Dev hustled to the corner, then turned to jog up a narrow asphalt road lined with dated single-wide manufactured homes. He paused and held his breath. A scream erupted from a canary-yellow home surrounded by a chain-link fence. Dev pushed through the gate. Colorful toys and a stroller crowded the front stoop. A soft muted voice pleaded for silence. He climbed a short rise of steps and checked the quiet streets, the closest neighbors, and found no help.

Dev pushed through the front door and froze. A dirty-faced five-year-old girl rocked a swaddled baby on her lap. The sky-blue eyes of the tiny blond girl locked on Dev. She lifted her finger to shush him. Dev took a step back, then appraised the home strewn with stinky diapers, baby bottles, food wrappers, plastic toys and a mobile plaything dangling happy sea creatures above a playpen.

The girl shushed him again, then looked down at the child. "Momma has nummies."

Dev eased over to the pair and pulled the blanket back from the baby's face. Skin red and gray at the same time, lips tinged with blue, the baby's face scrunched, then released a wail. Dev looked to the bedrooms for help but found only the sad eyes of the young girl. Crap. Shit, hell and fuck.

He leaned down to the young girl. "Where is your mother?"

The girl shrugged.

"Who is feeding this baby? How and with what?"

She shrugged.

"Oh, bloody hell," Dev said, and looked to the ceiling. "Martin knows about children. He can help."

Dev hustled out of the home and sprinted to the car. Martin sat fidgeting with boxes of smartphones and SIM cards. Dev climbed in and sped the car up to the children's house against Martin's protests. Dev grabbed a Mounds candy bar and a bag of Corn Nuts and told Martin to follow him.

He presented the two children to Martin with a trembling hand. "The baby's color does not appear good. We should maybe boil some water and . . . and . . . what, Martin? You know about these things."

Martin turned and walked out.

Dev swallowed hard, stunned by Martin's callous disregard. He shushed the little girl. Her blue eyes, crusted with sleep boogers, needed a wet wipe. Dev smoothed a wrinkle from the baby's swath, then followed Martin. His eyes narrowed as he aimed for Martin waiting in the passenger seat, playing with a phone.

Dev reached in and removed the ignition keys, pushing his face close to Martin. "Fuck you. Find your own ride."

"Lots of those," Martin said.

Dev slammed the door and stormed back inside the house.

DEV SEARCHED THE HOUSE AND found the names and birthdates of the two children, Missy and Jamie, and everything necessary for the care and maintenance of small children. The top shelves of Joe's Corner Market were stocked with the brand of formula Missy, the five-year-old, had approved. The lower-level shelves sat bare, an obvious indication Missy had made the shopping trip on her own numerous times. With easily decipherable hand gestures and a few stern admonishments, Missy instructed Dev on the administration and implementation of baby formula for little Jamie, all of nine months old. The replenishment of diapers and wipes and snacks and toys and . . . Dev sprawled on the couch as the children slept. He stared at the alabaster ceiling and wondered what course he would now have to captain, as a nursemaid for two small girls. No, a small toddler and a baby. Quite the difference.

And Martin. Dev's disappointment was incalculable.

DEV YAWNED, STRETCHED HIS LEGS over the rough upholstery, and sniffed foul air. Missy carried a diaper past his face, pinching her nose. The young child was quite the big sister, attentive, hygienic, and resourceful. But she didn't talk much, or cry, or laugh. She assumed the role of mother and pursued the endeavor with astonishing efficiency.

Dev peered out a window, relieved his SUV remained parked and uninjured. Dark gray clouds hung low, threatening to dump cold icy snow any minute. His breath misted the air. The children would never survive the winter, perhaps not even the freezing storm knocking on the door. He looked at his meager clothes and snickered. Neither would he. Perhaps he should drive down the highway and hope to see the farmer again, tell him about the girls. The LDS encampment would have been ideal, except the coming snowstorm would preclude that solution.

Martin.

He would drive the children south, to St. George or Cedar City, towns large enough to contain survivors immune to the death lights. He looked back at Missy fussing with Jamie's swath, wrapping another fuzzy pink blanket around an already hefty cocoon. A five-year-old girl caring for a baby. The absurdity of the new world had beckoned forth the smallest of heroes.

"Missy, the weather is turning. I think we should leave. Go south to a warmer environment. What say you?"

Missy looked up. She scrunched her face and ran into the back bedroom.

The girl was obviously hiding beneath a bed. And would refuse to come out. Refuse to leave home. God forbid if he had to load screaming children into the car. Regardless, he was the adult, and he would decide what course of action was to be taken. He checked Jamie squiggling in her swath and picked up a large vinyl bag adorned with pink babies in various poses, all smiles, of course. Luggage for diapers and bottles and such. Bottles. They would need hundreds of bottles. And the formula. And food meant diapers, hundreds.

Dev shuttered his eyes and remembered the dream he had just woken from, one with a tribe of children laughing and playing on swings and slides in a tree-shaded park. The perception of a villain lurked just beyond the trees. Dev swallowed and kept his eyelids shuttered.

A tug at his trousers and Dev smiled down at Missy's tiny face grinning up at him. Missy pinched her nose. Dev blanched and looked at a bare-bottom Jamie wrestling with her blankets. Impossible. The last bowel movement occurred just . . .

Three large bags waited next to the front door.

He smiled down at Missy. "I think we shall get along famously."

AFTER SEARCHING FOR A HALF hour, then struggling for another hour to install two child restraining seats in the back, Dev deemed the road trip ready to commence. He checked the map and decided the lengthier distance through Zion National Park and then into St. George was far less risky than the shorter trip over the stormy mountains.

Missy provided picture books for Jamie, turning the pages to pronounce the tiniest detail, ensuring Jamie understood what she pointed at. Dev wondered if the child was traumatized by her circumstances. How could she not be? The road weaved through a rainbow of sandstone and limestone hoodoos dotted with stunted pinions rising out of rock crevices. Missy giggled and held her breath as they entered a tunnel at a series of switchbacks leading down into Zion National Park. Dev shook his head, clueless to what the child hoped to accomplish, but joined the silly game as they entered another tunnel.

The great Zion Canyon appeared, a creation seeming to celebrate the birth of the world. Dev braked often to take in the splendor of the deep red sandstone, a canyon sliced open by the sharp millennia of the Virgin River. The main access road was dwarfed by majestic bloodred cliffs. Jamie wiggled. Missy sat rapt.

Dev slowed as the snarl of abandoned vehicles thickened. He weaved in and out of jams, using the wide gravel shoulder often. The entrance to Zion proved worse, requiring Dev to push vehicles to another lane or take control of a vehicle and drive it off his course. The task grew arduous, and Dev sat with his head against the head-rest until a tiny finger tapped his shoulder. Missy's other tiny hand offered a baby biscuit.

"You know, our biscuits are a tad different than yours," Dev said. "You would love London, probably the countryside a bit more. What do you say we take the park in. Beat the crowds."

Missy instructed Dev in the nuances of small children with her fingers helping his fumbles. Missy ran ahead, disappeared behind random trucks or SUVs, then popped her head up after Dev yelled for her to show herself. They used a winding single-track to walk down to the gin-clear Virgin River to wiggle bare feet in the swirling, chilly water. The gurgle of unending water soothed thoughts of Martin's betrayal. Dev gazed toward the far end of towering red rock cliff faces and felt small, insignificant, as if Martin's all-knowing time-less God might reside within the sanctuary waiting beyond. Missy changed Jamie's diaper and signaled the time for another bottle of formula.

Missy held Dev's hand on the stroll back to the car. The warmth precious, the touch invaluable, the squeeze of tiny fingers melted Dev's heart. Miles downstream, a thick tendril of black smoke rose to form a hazy mushroom cap awaiting a breeze. People. He won-dered if he should seek them out and offer the children. Of course, he would require references, camp conditions, a tour of the facilities before making his decision.

Bloody Martin.

With children strapped in as if riding a SpaceX shuttle up to the space station, Dev commenced the battle with abandoned vehicles. Where had the drivers and passengers run off to? Driven by the death lights to commit suicide, he imagined. Still, the tens of thousands of bodies must reside somewhere. Dev relaxed as the car coasted slowly down the highway, making simple S-turns to avoid the vans and buses parked along the burg of Springdale. Millions visited Zion National Park each year, meaning tens of thousands each day, and yet he saw few bodies. Where were the bodies?

The children had fallen asleep. Dev drove on the gravel shoulder, watching the thick column of smoke grow closer. He slowed and idled by a neighborhood access road aiming toward the smoke. He swallowed and turned the steering wheel. Smoke was a signal of people immune from the lights and without fear of the deadly addiction. He hoped.

The SUV crunched gravel, slowed, then stopped and allowed Dev a panoramic view of majestic red cliffs, lush vineyards, and a valley spawned from the depths of hell.

A rusty yellow bulldozer spewed black exhaust, dropped a muddy blade, and scraped crimson sand out of a shallow depression. The operator braked one track and spun a U-turn at the rim, then began again, carving the crater deeper with each pass. A second dozer pushed dead, desiccated bodies off a massive heap into a second crater further upstream, scattering white gulls and black crows into warm air reeking of rot and decay. A third dozer pushed dirt and detritus off tall mounds, then waited for the next crater to be filled with human bodies and tattered clothing. Dev looked upstream at hundreds of mounds of red dirt dotting the river bottomland as far he could see. He resisted the urge to vomit.

A dozer stopped the push of bodies. The machine operator climbed from the cab and stood on a bloody red track to watch Dev, glancing often at a phone bright with neon in his left hand.

Dev began to raise his hand, then stopped and let it fall. Jamie screamed. Missy pounded on the window. The bearded blade operator appeared as if to speak into the phone.

"Bloody hell," Dev said.

The Rover reversed course with a violent rush, accompanied by the screams of frightened children. Two quick turns and the Rover accelerated, shimmied, and bumped as it overshot the highway and into a vineyard heavy with unpicked grapes. Dev spun a U-turn and spit gravel until finding a footing on the highway, then stomped on the gas pedal.

Zion receded, and with it the mayhem of abandoned vehicles. Was he to be a pariah for the rest of his life? What of the baby girls?

Martin was correct in his zealotry for killing the Neon God. The human species could not continue as subservient animals, with the few free people hunted and enslaved, or extinguished. And what of the youngest survivors? Did they have value in the Neon God's world, or would they be allowed to perish in the coming winter, contributing tiny bits to the new mounds of human rubbish? Perhaps Martin was right.

Bloody hell, Martin.

DEV BACKED UP TO A dark and unlit Super 8 in St. George, Utah. He walked the lobby, kitchen, and three floors of hallways until satisfied they would not be discovered. The crowbar solved the electronic key card access, and they settled into dusty double queen beds. The kids nodded off quickly after a quick meal of premixed macaroni and cheese. He read the listing of ingredients on the meal and wondered what sodium phosphate or potassium chloride added to the simple meal. He glanced at the sleeping babies and shut his eyes. He was not the man for their care, not until the world offered some semblance of normalcy.

Sleep evaded him until he slipped out the door to pace about the long building. The adjacent Interstate 15 was quiet save for an occasional semi. A full moon rose, completing the pleasant evening ambiance. A young boy pedaled a mountain bike down the street, popping wheelies on the abrupt slopes of the driveways. Dev wanted to follow him, perhaps find his home and ask for help. Vegas was a two-hour drive south, with luck, but no place for young children.

He went inside the room, wedged the crowbar against the door handle and fell asleep.

DIAPERS CHANGED, BOTTLES WASHED AND dried, children fed, Dev loaded his charges into the car then looked to siphon gas from a plethora of abandoned automobiles. He spat the last bits of foul fuel from his lips and wiped his mouth. He surveyed his surroundings, unsure of his course. St. George sat in the heart of Mormon country. Surely a church could be found. Maybe help waited inside. He drove slowly on the quiet streets. A sign signaled his approach to the St. George, Utah, LDS Temple. Dev parked in a deserted lot and looked up at the brilliant white building, three stories of sharp columns divided by ornate arched windows, crowned in a textured castle buttress roof. A thirty-foot tower rose from the castled roof, a copper dome capped with a windvane of the golden angel Moroni facing east. Surrounded by lush green landscape, palm trees, elms and manicured hedges, the building seemed to have escaped the horrors of neglect. Dev carried Jamie as Missy ran ahead to check trash barrels and climb on park benches. He paused at the Visitors Center front entrance, then checked the door and found it open. A giant marble statue of Jesus Christ, arms spread wide, welcomed them inside. Jamie fussed in his arms, and he placed her down on a fabric chair to change her diaper. Missy watched over his shoulder as he fumbled and cringed, wiping the smelly mess.

"The restroom does have a baby-changing station," a voice said.

Dev jumped up and swallowed. A tall man with close cropped hair stood between two younger women blocking the hallway leading into the temple proper.

"My apologies. These children . . . they are new to me. Rather, I found them and . . . and I don't know what to do with them. I have no experience, and they might suffer with my . . . my ineptitude."

Missy stood in front of one of the women and peered up, as if studying her. She turned and nodded.

The man stepped forward. "You weren't unexpected. Your friend warned us you may come this way and look for assistance."

"Martin? He was here?"

"No names were exchanged. I suppose these children are the assistance you would be needing?"

"Yes. Yes. We found them in Panguitch, in deplorable conditions, and the snow had already begun to arrive. I couldn't leave them with no adult supervision."

The man smiled thinly. "Of course not. Your story is not unique. How do you know to trust us? Perhaps we are just child molesters."

Dev offered his hand toward the statue. "I don't think He would allow that in his house. Would he?"

The man nodded. "We have a facility . . . an orphanage outside Enterprise, and they will be safe and cared for. Perhaps you could visit them on your return trip."

"Yes. Yes, I will if . . . if I can."

"Your friend carries a heavy weight on his shoulders. He confessed his sins to me last night. He will need help if he is to succeed. I'm going to speculate some of that will need to come from you."

"Probably the only help he can count on."

The man smiled. "I beg to differ." He offered his hand to the same statue.

Dev unloaded the girls' bags, car seats, toys, and carried them inside. The women and girls had disappeared. Perhaps for the better. He wasn't sure he could keep his eyes dry with the goodbye.

The man offered a road map. "A contingent of our young men have blocked the Virgin River Gorge with explosives, semis with supplies are now ours, and you probably would have been shot. The war for our souls has begun. Follow the highlighted road to bypass the Gorge, then good luck."

Dev swallowed hard and took the map.

Bloody Martin.

The road west was remarkably clear of the detritus of vehicles and humanity, giving Dev time to consider the past two days. Foremost, he was convinced Martin's mission could not be discounted or impeded. Pulling the plug on the reign of the Neon God was paramount. Martin had always been a tad acerbic, condescending, sarcastic, and yet considerate and loyal. But the man he traveled south with was different, an unrecognizable personality.

Martin had been instrumental in Dev acquiring a position as a software engineer at Adobe Inc. He provided a key reference to obtain a work visa and was a great resource through every step of the immigration process. His invitations to backyard barbeques and family picnics sealed his undying devotion to the man. Dev was positive their friendship deepened out of mutual grief and survival, but now Martin ignored everything but his own self-interests.

Dev steered around an abandoned Subaru, the impediments commonplace and offered little challenge to his driving skills. He paused at a T-intersection in Shivwits, Utah, and took a long pull from a bottled water. South lay an inhospitable Mojave Desert, a bleak purgatory and home to the murderer of billions. North was escape, an existence scrounging through the bleak remains of civilization, struggling for survival. Dev took another sip of water. Neither choice was palatable. He picked up the map and traced his finger along the highlighted route to Littlefield, Arizona, where the yellow tint was terminated with a large red X. Martin waited at the marked destination. Dev would slap the man silly, then strangle him.

Dev checked the map. Only forty miles to Littlefield.

The descent from the hills and into the desert had Dev pressing the brake pedal often as the panorama of I-15 loomed ahead. The interstate was clogged with box trucks and semis. He winked at a billboard welcoming him to Beaver Dam Lodge Golf Course, then slammed on the brakes. A zigzag formation of cars blocked the road. A white flag flapped atop a solitary RZR straddling the highway.

The mastermind of the blockade clearly knew what options remained of anyone encountering the blockage. Reverse course and suffer in the desert or . . . enter the lion's den and negotiate. He parked near a dry wash shadowed in dense cottonwoods.

Martin.

DEV STUFFED WATER BOTTLES INTO his backpack, then shouldered the pack, the weight lopsided but acceptable. He checked the ignition of each vehicle for keys, then smirked at the discovery of a wad of keychains tied together on the hood of a white BMW. A car registration clipped beneath the wiper blade was marked with a big black arrow pointing downstream into a thick stand of cottonwoods.

Dev dropped the backpack and ran down the gravel channel, red in his eyes, hands balling, intent on a simple, merciful act of murder. His contribution to the new world order. He jogged down the river channel, stumbled over a thick root reaching to buried water. His leg muscles burned as the deep sand of the river bottom sucked his zeal.

"Stealth is not your strong suit," Martin said.

Dev sucked in deep breaths and stepped forward. Martin rested shirtless and shoeless, prone in a camping recliner, a blue umbrella for shade, on a beach, admiring the meandering muddy water of the Virgin River.

"I should murder you," Dev said. He sucked warm air into burning lungs.

"The white Beamer has a Glock under the seat," Martin said.

"Fuck off."

"You should have ridden off into the sunset with your new family.

Why'd you come, Dev? I have given you every opportunity to be rid of me. And yet here you are."

Martin stood and faced him. A broken man, a revengeful man, amoral and without scruples, the shell of a man, physically and emotionally. Dev dropped to his knees, ignored the hot sand, and shook his head. If he could catch his breath he would immediately return to the car. Martin's dirty feet entered his view. Dev looked up. Martin offered a helping hand. Dev pursed his lips and frowned.

Dev sucked in a gulp of air.

"There are thousands of those kids. A demographic the lights haven't infected yet. But they will." Martin bent his knees and took Dev's face in his hands. "This is war, and I'm going to end it. I need to kill the program."

"You abandoned two small children. No better than killing them."

Martin slapped Dev's cheek hard. "I watched thousands of children die, you pompous ass. My kids . . . my kids want revenge. And I'm gonna give it to them."

Dev pushed Martin away and stared at wood and detritus floating on the muddy water.

"Go home, Dev. Go anywhere except—"

"What makes you so smug on ending this . . . this—" Dev said.

Martin slapped him across his head.

Dev bared his teeth and struggled to rise from the sand.

Martin spat, "Because I designed the lights. They're my fault."

Chapter 11
Rally Point

THE SWARM OF MINIATURE DRONES dropped from the sky and attacked like angry wasps protecting a nest. Hundreds divebombed the herd, driving the animals to stampede and scatter into the barren desert. With his head held tight in his arms, Mason rocked back and forth. The whirring downdraft of the small drones reeked of the supervillain. A tear fell from Mason's face as the remnants of pleasant emotions fled with the herd. Andi sobbed. Chris barked orders at him, then he ripped the backpack from his feeble grip. Mason dared to glance up at Chris frantically fumbling to open a thin oblong black box, then listened to Chris shout a countdown from five. He tightened his arms over his head as a surge of silent light erupted.

The sky rained tiny clumps of plastic. Mason slowed his rocking and watched the odd downpour. Chris pulled at Andi's prone body to help her stand, then pulled at Mason's armpit. He shook off the intrusion and stood to search for the herd. Clouds of dust pointed at their retreat.

"We gotta move, kids. That power surge grenade won't last long."

Chris pulled on Mason and Andi and aimed for a shallow gulley. A glint of sunlight reflected off three white vehicles waiting on the highway two miles away. The black asphalt of the 95 line. Chris cursed as Mason resisted the tow. The supervillain had issued a challenge and waited to battle him, not Chris, and not Andi. He dropped backpack 2 and ran along a faint cattle trail winding through the sparse creosote desert. Shouts and pleas faded as he gained distance.

The supervillain waited.

Mason sucked the last bit of water from the thermos and strolled up a rocky embankment to three white Humvees idling on the side of the highway. Doors swung open and cool air-conditioned air spewed. Big men dressed in camo stepped out. A man with a long black beard crossed his arms.

"Sir Mason?" The man stepped forward and offered him the open door.

Mason narrowed his eyes. The man felt neutral yet tainted by the supervillain. The cold air felt good on his skin, the strawberry air freshener a pleasant change from horse dung, and the neutral man sitting beside him a relief from the constant barrage of fearful emotions. Something familiar tingled at the back of his thoughts. The men dressed in camo, the semiautomatic assault rifles, the unspoken words telegraphed between them. Mason relaxed. They dressed and acted like his father's militia. Except . . .

"Are you taking me to the rally point?" Mason said.

The man's shaved head was beaded with sweat. His skin tanned. His black wraparound sunglasses hid his eyes. "Indeed, we are, Mason. We've been looking for you for a while. Appreciate you saving us from having to go get you in that desert. We were afraid you forgot the location of the . . . rally point."

The man lied, but Mason wasn't sure about which part. The man snickered as Mason fumbled buttoning the top button of his shirt. The tight collar hurt, but the superhero wanted to hide. Then he would be unleashed when the supervillain appeared. The vehicles sped down a war-torn highway swamped with thousands of shrunken dead bodies, as if people had simply walked into the desert and died. Tiny remnants of dead ghostly emotions sped past. The bleakness of so much death made Mason turn away from the window. He studied the bald man's profile, a hawklike nose, facial twitches as if he searched for threats in every direction. He thought of an osprey sitting atop a nest along the Clearwater River, diligently watching for threats. A predator yet not the apex.

"Is my dad at the rally point?" Mason said.

The bald man tossed him a bottle of Gatorade. "We're all at the rally point. Anyone left alive, that is."

Mason took the drink and slugged it down. The bald man's neutral aura confused him. Everyone he encountered carried some type of emotion. A rare few were happy, some confused, or glum, or fearful, or the suicidal carrying a darkness of impending death that made him shut down and find neutral. He felt the slip of a guilty thought.

Mason asked, "Why did you kill Cookie-Dough?"

The bald man tossed another bottle on Mason's lap. "That was a fuckup. We figured to rescue you and the horse as soon as satellite transmission was reestablished inside that shithole of a valley. The possessed jumped the gun and—"

Mason hammered his fist on the headrest in front of him. "Cookie-Dough was a mule. Not a horse. My best friend."

The vehicle slowed.

The bald man held up his hands. "Mason, my job is getting you to the rally point. Maybe . . . your dad can explain."

The man lied. Deep reds and dark purple steamed out of his words. The rally point waited but not the celebration of accomplishment. The supervillain waited but not his father.

Mason felt the superhero beneath his clothes, expanding chest muscles, stretching hamstrings, firing dark red laser beams at practice targets. A thump from a meaty fist smacking his arm jolted Mason to narrow his eyes and aim lasers at the bald man.

"Eat up. Name's Burton," the man said. He threw a small white box on his lap. "You made it a thousand miles from Idaho. Impressive. For a . . . for such a young member of the Patriot Frontline."

Mason tore into a foil-wrapped piece of chocolate and ate.

"The president has been monitoring your progress. He thinks you have some special skills that we might be able to use." Burton tossed him another MRE. "If you check out."

Mason mumbled, "What president?"

The man smirked. "The president of the New United States. At least what's left of it."

Mason felt a tinge of disdain accompanying the words. "Where are we going?"

"Ever been to Vegas, Mason? A regular fucking playground these days. You should have stayed in Idaho. Fresh game, clean water, good soil for growing shit, everything you won't find here."

The Hummer exited onto the shoulder to avoid a snarl of abandoned vehicles. Desiccated human bodies, small and large, riddled the road. Mason felt the superhero shrink inside his shirt again. He had never been to a city as large as what loomed through the windshield. The skyline was hazed with dust and smoke, thousands of people dead in the desert, and his best friend murdered by the hands of the man sitting next to him. Mason closed his eyes and started to tremble, but neutral couldn't be found. The cold air spewed from the vents to blanket his hot face. He swatted at the overhead vents, then punched the headrest of the seat in front. His teeth hurt from his clenched jaw. He drummed his knees with tight fists and his muscles turned rigid. Voices ordered him to calm down. Frustration and anger permeated the chilly air. He growled, then turned to attack Cookie-Dough's killer with both fists. The vehicle slowed. Mason's fury intensified. A blue-white lightning bolt pierced his neck and enraged him. The blue lightning hit again and sent his fists to fall, his eyes to roll back into his head. Mason fell into a dark abyss. The superhero gasped for air, confused by the burst of laughter.

Lots and lots of laughter.

VILE EGO, ARROGANCE, AND SUPERIORITY pounded his senses as he woke. Mason knew the loud, excited argument outside the vehicle was about him. He struggled to sit, his wrists and ankles bound with thick plastic zip ties. He stared at the seams of the black vinyl seats. He considered his helpless hands. Maybe this was his one true weakness, unable to rip open his shirt and release the superhero. Every superhero had a weakness. The faceless supervillain argued with Burton, the osprey man. Mason stretched to see the faces arguing but only saw a lush oasis of palm trees, thick green bushes, and pretty waterfalls. Maybe they had driven past the bleakness of the dusty desert city while he was asleep.

The door swung open. Burton yanked Mason's wrists to help him sit. "Let's go, Sir Mason. Seems you rule this roost now."

The Hummer reversed out of the oasis, aimed east and confirmed the dusty Vegas skyline remained. Fury steamed from Burton, laced with helplessness, abandonment, hope, a stew of emotions survivors often exhaled, especially the hope for a cure to a hopeless world.

Mason offered his wrists to Burton. "Cut me free."

Burton snickered.

"Cut me free and the superhero will help them."

Burton removed his sunglasses and faced him. "What the hell do you know about *them*."

Mason pushed his tied hands closer. Ambivalence, doubt, then hope. "The superhero can help them."

"Aw, hell." He tapped the driver's headrest. "John, let's say we make a quick visit to the Heights."

Burton took a Leatherman tool from his belt loop and cut the plastic ties. He pointed the sharp end of the tool at Mason's eyes. "I will snip your eyes out if you're bullshitting me, boy."

Mason leaned back and offered his ankle restraints. "Why do you help the supervillain?"

Burton cut the restraints and leaned his head back. "Wonder that myself, son. Wonder that myself."

An abundance of human garbage and mummified bodies burned bleak images into Mason's memory as the SUV drove unimpeded to its destination. Cookie-Dough snorted in his thoughts. The mule would've refused to stay in this barren desert, void of pastures, no orchards, no bodies of water. The heavy exhaust spewed by his three captors reeked of disdain and helplessness, even as tinges of hope seeped out of their hot breath.

The Hummer parked beneath a shaded entry fronting the Heights at Summerlin Assisted Living and Rehabilitation facility. Folded wheelchairs sat queued by the front door. A young girl waited near the glass entry; her blank face stared at the tablet in her hand. The building smelled of dead lights and the supervillain.

"Shields up, boys," Burton said and put on wraparound sunglasses dark as the night. He grabbed Mason hard on the arm. "You say nothing, to nobody."

Burton escorted Mason into the building, his heavy hand wrapped around Mason's neck. He waved a dismissive hand at two attendants wearing scarlet scrubs as he pushed Mason down a long narrow hallway reeking of feces and urine. Mason turned and dry heaved from the livid stench of addiction. Burton pushed open door 112 and dragged Mason in. Emotions of fetal addiction assaulted the superhero. Burton pushed him toward an unkempt bed. Two heads covered in ratty blond hair sat beneath a window, with the frosty air whooshing from the AC vents chilling the girls' dirty faces. Neon dead lights danced on two tablets held by the girls wearing food-stained pajamas. The six-year-old girls rose in unison from the floor, stumbled over to Burton, and each embraced one of his legs. Their unwavering attention to the tablets made Burton pull his lips tight and sneer. Offering murmured greetings, the emaciated girls returned to sit on the edge of the bed. The tablets neon lights shined at Mason like red to a bull.

Mason shook free of Burton's heavy hand resting on his shoulder. He snatched both tablets and ground each beneath his boot, the brilliant bits of dying light enraged him. Mason roared, ripped his shirt open and jumped to embrace the girls. His sudden contact with the supervillain made his arm muscles constrict as he embraced skinny little bodies. The twins wailed. Mason fought the chaos of pain and flailing arms as he swam to rescue two tiny minds drowning in evil light.

The neon light faded. The twins danced and shouted for Mason to join them at the slumber party. Cokes and chocolate brownies would be served. He relaxed and joined in the silly celebration. The superhero liked brownies. And sweet cola. Mason smiled. The superhero smiled. Neither were sure exactly what a slumber party was.

MASON AWOKE WITH HIS WRISTS and ankles tied with plastic. Children screamed protests. A soft pink pillow rested beneath his face. The scent of chocolate brownies faded. A green-eyed girl smiled down at him and helped to lift his head for a sip of water. Her soul wafted of delicious brownies.

Burton yanked Mason up and tossed him on the bed. The twin girls screamed at their grandfather to stop. Burton leaned close to Mason's face. "You are what he said. Now what to do with you?"

Relief, joy, doubt. Burton's emotions lingered in Mason's face.

"Chocolate brownies. The superhero loves chocolate brownies," Mason said.

MASON SCARFED THE GOOEY BROWNIE, then ripped open the cellophane of another. He paused and remembered the onslaught of drowning children the superhero had saved. He felt he was close to finding the supervillain's lair, where it controlled the dead lights. Except . . . he could save hundreds of women and children every day till he died, and not enough days existed, with a steady stream of dead light people to follow. The dead lights needed to be shut off, forever.

Burton pushed open the door. "Eat up, Mason. We got three more waiting in 221."

Mason dropped the brownie. "No."

Burton stiffened. "Don't worry. I got a load of chocolate cake arriving soon."

"I want to fight the Neon God," Mason said.

"Kid, trust me, you do not want to get involved with that," Burton said.

"I want to battle the Neon God."

Burton rubbed his forehead. "I don't know about you battling anything, but I can let you see it." Burton waved him to follow.

He followed the big man down the hallway and into the front office, where he was ordered to wait. Mason wiped crumbs from his mouth and stood near a wide picture window that overlooked a desert arroyo with a rocky channel bottom lined with leafless cotton-woods and mesquite trees. He lifted his chin and squinted. A hundred yards away on the opposite side of the canyon, a rabbit scurried in the sparse desert, chased by two gray cattle dogs. A wolf trotted into view, trailing the pursuit.

Not a wolf. But equally as large. Wolves conjured memories.

Mason remembered leading Cookie-Dough down a narrow trail, following his father as they returned home from the hunting camp high in the Bitterroot Mountains. His father shushed him, then signaled to leave the mule and step delicately on the trail. He remembered smelling his own fear at what he couldn't see yet, but the bright smile on his father's face banished the tangy emotion to dissipate in an afternoon thermal. His father whispered for quiet and led him up to a rocky outcropping where they looked down on three wolves resting in the shade of a fallen tree. His father grinned and raised his eyebrows, silently asking Mason if he saw the spectacular sight.

Mason nodded and climbed higher to release the superhero to race down and join the calm serenity of the wolves' simple nap. The feeling was exquisite.

Mason stared at the massive dog. The brown dog turned his massive head, its ears perked, as if suddenly alerted to the superhero's approach. It stared up at Mason. The room was suddenly hot as an oven. Something was near, but he couldn't place what it was. The dog, the . . .

Burton snapped his fingers. Mason looked back and followed.

"You get a free screening with the Neon God. The laptop is voice activated, and the camera is on. It'll see you, but there isn't much for you to see. Here, put these on when you sit down." Burton handed him oversized black goggles. "Virtual reality glasses. You need 'em if you want to see the . . . Neon God."

Burton slipped his sunglasses on and waved him inside a cramped office with a tiny desk supporting a keyboard, speaker, and computer screen. Red dots blinked on black computer boxes. Thick black wires hung like snakes from shelves to find more black boxes with blinking red eyes beneath the desk. The screen erupted in neon.

"Hello, Mason," the speaker said.

Mason narrowed his eyes. He shook his head almost imperceptibly. This was not the supervillain, but something similar.

"I want to do battle with the Neon God."

"Excellent. Swords, knives, dueling pistols at twenty paces? What do you suggest?"

Mason felt the mocking sarcasm, the condescending superiority, and a tinge of fear. "The dead lights. I want to meet you in the sea of dead lights."

"Hmm. Only one way you can truly find your way into my realm, Mason. Ready to risk all to battle me? Get your glasses on, then, and let's do it."

"You're afraid to lose, and you know you will," Mason said.

"Perhaps, but I doubt it. Games have many layers, hidden doors, secret codes, subtle loyalties, unconquerable bosses. You are unique, Mason. I give you that."

The pleasant memory of the wolf encounter fled. Serene, calm now burned at Mason. Children drowned in a cesspool of light.

Ghosts cried for redemption. The silent serenity of a remote forest. Everything lost until the supervillain was vanquished.

Mason ripped his shirt open. "Come fight me."

The bright lights erupted from the screen, showering black boxes and wires in a kaleidoscope of shifting light. Muted evil light slithered from dark corners, oozed down from the ceiling. The evil light consumed the tiny room, and Mason. He slipped on the goggles, and his immersion into the light pulled his consciousness down into the ocean of deception. He reached to the screen, then suddenly pulled his hand back. Millions of children floundering in the light reached for the superhero . . . except he couldn't find a warm hand to hold, hear a soft voice, feel any emotion to latch onto. The colored ocean stank of a painful decay and of death and of the hopelessness of millions.

The superhero pounded his chest and shot out of the ocean, rising against the gravity pulling him down to the nasty ocean to float above the neon lights. Tiny hands reached up to him, fell back into the eddies of light, then returned to reach again.

"Shall we battle?" the voice oozed from the light. "Your prize waits beneath you."

The superhero swiveled his head as he searched for a dot, a spot, anything offering context in the immersive globe of light. His frustration grew as he floated. The endless neon light crushed the superhero's chest. He lashed out at the light. Helpless fury energized his punches. A glitch of light fueled hammering blows.

The glimmer of a door. A tiny sliver of silver light sprayed sparkles over the neon.

Mason flew, targeting the doorway of divine silver light.

Chapter 12
Fallen Angel

WHISKEY SAT SHOTGUN, HIS FACE leaning out of the open window, fat lips flapping in the thirty-mile-per-hour headwind, his drool streaking the windows. Despite the spacious cargo area, the Booze Crew crowded the front seat of the Lincoln Navigator like children heading for Disneyland. Jessie checked the rearview mirror again, unaccustomed to a view blocked by stacks of dog food and supplies. She checked the side mirrors and sat back, confident no one followed. Lake Tahoe would be a simple eight-hour drive. Locate a decent lakeside mansion and move in to enjoy cool fall air, soothing waves lapping the lakeshore, maybe sip a cocktail around the firepit at sunset, then prepare before the snow fell.

A new beginning.

She reached blindly to pull her backpack up front. Her sore ribs screamed with the sudden awkward motion. *Time to change that which did not work.* The author eluded her. Maybe she would take credit for the phrase; after all, who could dispute her? Helping hundreds of enslaved women was beyond her. Killing Little Stevie wasn't gonna happen. The man living in the palm tree compound could live happily ever after.

Time to go. Time to get on with life. Whatever remained of it.

Both shoulders littered with vehicles and bones still dressed in shriveled gray skin, the far-left lane of Highway 95 was clear of impediments and waited as a straight line to beyond the horizon. Unnatural, like somebody needed the highway open for business. She slowed at the exit leading to Mountain's Edge, a sprawling housing development rising out of the barren desert on the northernmost out-skirts of Las Vegas. Caution made her turn the wheel and take the exit. Fifteen gallons of water should be enough, but if the SUV popped a flat, or worse, a transmission, the dogs could lap up gallons before she located a suitable replacement. And the lonely stretch between Beatty and Tonopah might as well be on the moon.

Jessie waited at a four-way stop, scratching fur and checking mirrors. Satisfied, she turned into the empty parking lot of a CVS drugstore. Armed with a bloody bat, she pushed through unlocked glass doors and walked past pilfered cigarette slots and empty liquor shelves, while reading the overhead aisle markers. Diet, Dental, Makeup, Nutrition. The air was hot and stale. Jessie tapped the bat on an endcap filled with candy and small toys, ushering tiny boxes and metal rack dividers to drop to the linoleum floor. She waited for the commotion to summon someone hiding in the back or behind the walk-in cooler.

Jessie pinched the bat beneath her armpit, then slid a two-gallon jug of water off the rack. She froze at the sound of a single hammer click. Tilted her ear toward another click. The distinct sound of a gun primed and ready to fire was fresh. She dropped the water and bat, then raised her hands.

"Now what?" Jessie said. She turned, searching the cramped aisle.

"You're not compromised by the lights. Obviously. Take your water and go."

"And obviously you aren't either. It's nice to hear a friendly voice." Jessie said. She swiveled her head, searching for the voice. "You are a friendly, aren't you?"

"You have medical training by chance?"

Jessie stepped down the aisle, stepped closer to the voice. "Sorry, cocktails by trade."

The release of a held breath. The click of the gun hammer, hope-fully resting easier.

Jessie picked up the water jugs and hurried to the front door. Her eyes darted down an aisle to the pharmacy waiting area. She slowed and focused on a reflection behind the plexiglass protecting racks of drugs from customers and the Covid. A prone body rested on the thin worn carpet beneath the Pick-Up sign. Jessie paused, expecting the body to shift or move a leg. She lugged the water down the nutrition aisle to loom over a small Asian girl, or woman, she couldn't tell. The click of a hammer, a gun barrel pressed against her temple. Sweat and animal dung hung in the air.

"The lights do that?" Jessie said. She stepped closer to get a better look, hoping the pressure against her temple wouldn't follow.

"No, I did," a man said.

Jessie shot the man a look. He looked beaten by the sun, the desert, covered in dust and reeking of horse poop. A mop of brown hair, heavy beard, and not unattractive. She narrowed her eyes and glanced down at the gun in his hand hanging at his side.

"Mind if I put my luggage down?" Jessie said.

He nodded, then looked at the sick girl.

She released the bat and set the water down. "What'd you do to her?"

"Dragged her through hell. For nothing."

"You know, I might only be a cocktail waitress, but even I can see she is dehydrated," Jessie said. "Try getting some Gatorade into her?"

"She can't or won't. If I force it down her throat, it comes back up."

"No shit. She needs an IV," Jessie said. Too many times she'd witnessed partygoers surrounded by millions of gallons of pool water collapse from dehydration after ingesting an excess of alcohol, thinking the ice cubes or the beer contained enough hydrating water. She had to assist bouncers in placing an IV into a helpless patron's arm almost weekly, then sit and wait for the EMTs.

She looked down on the pallid girl, then faced the man with open palms. "May I? You gotta have everything you need in this place."

He nodded, weariness and fatigue advertised by a defeated posture.

She resisted the urge to slap some life into the man. "Saline bags, find 'em, higher the sodium content, the better," she guessed. "I gotta find some needles and tubes and shit."

"You know what you're doing?" he said.

"Fuck no. But doing nothing is not an option."

JESSIE WINCED AS SHE PUSHED the needle into the girl's arm. Blood filled the tube, and she assumed she hit a vein. She checked the paper instructions included with the bag of saline and connected a tube to the catheter. She commanded the man to hold the bag high as she dialed the adjustment knob. Not too much at first, but the girl needed a ton. The bag dripped with a smooth rhythm, the blood at the arm remained unchanged. Satisfied, Jessie stood and leaned back against shelves stocked with feminine hygiene products.

The man handed her a grape Gatorade. Not her favorite but . . . He offered his hand.

"Captain Chris Clayton. United States Air Force."

She giggled. "Sorry. The cavalry riding to the rescue died . . . so long ago."

He sat opposite, against shelves with remedies for gas and stomach acid, and sucked down an extra-large can of Red Bull.

"That shit will kill you. The taurine is a carcinogen."

Chris chuckled. "Well, if the cavalry died, then maybe cancer did too."

Jessie smiled thinly. "Why'd you say what you did? About her?"

Chris twisted open a bottle of water and took a long draw. "Her name is Andi. Are you running from the Neon God?"

"You didn't answer my question," Jessie said, and sat up. "And what do you know about the Neon God?"

"I'm guessing you're headed north. Maybe stopped in for some extra supplies, and boom, here we are."

"Fuck you, don't pretend to know my story," Jessie said and struggled to rise.

Chris waved her to sit. "Sorry."

Jessie checked the IV dripping fluid into the tube, and the flushed young face of a beautiful girl.

"I was assigned as liaison to the CISA office where Andi worked, like, ninety hours a week. She was convinced a computer virus or worm had invaded our systems, punched through firewalls and encrypted security, then disappeared. No trace, like it never existed.

The higher-ups assigned us to a station that, basically, was purgatory. Except purgatory turned out to be sanctuary. Cell service was weak, almost nonexistent, kept the lights from attacking. Internet and Wi-Fi extremely unreliable, just enough bandwidth to hear the battle." Chris swallowed a lump, then took a sip from the empty Gatorade bottle. "We fought our own guys. That fucking thing controlled our pilots, knew what they knew, and just fucking . . ." Chris threw the empty bottle. "Andi had discovered all this, and no one listened."

"Just nuke the thing. Game over."

Chris wagged his finger at her. "Tried. Except the thing knew our plans before we did. Traced the launch order and nuked our command structure with our own weapons. Don't think Washington, DC, exists anymore. Not that it's a bad thing." He smiled without humor.

Andi stirred. Chris jumped to her side and stroked her face with a filthy gentle finger.

Jessie jumped up. "I'm sorry, but I got family roasting in the parking lot."

THE BOOZE CREW RAN RAGGED up and down the store aisles, discovered hidden snacks, investigated odd aromas, and approached Andi's plight with the slow, gentle awareness of a family canine. Jessie lifted Andi's head and fed her grape Gatorade. Chris stroked Allie's ear. The sun waned through the glass storefront.

Jessie pulled open a can of Dinty Moore beef stew and spooned the dark gravy into Andi's mouth, leaving the meat and potatoes for her own dinner.

Andi chuckled and accepted another spoonful. "You and Mason would be besties."

"Any man liking Dinty Moore stew is a man worth knowing," Jessie said. Poppa's old paraphrase, she guessed.

Andi winced as she sat up, waving away Chris's help. "Thank you for the help. It seems to be in short supply these days."

"No worries," Jessie said and offered another spoonful of cold beef sauce. Andi gobbled it up. "Your boyfriend's a bit standoffish. Need any MeToo help?" Jessie arched her brows.

Andi smiled thinly. "No, that's just his military side talking, or not talking. Chris is actually . . . a very good man and will . . ." She looked up at Chris. "Will be the best father."

Jessie arched her brows. "Well, okay. Um."

Andi patted Jessie's hand. "Again. Thank you."

Jessie put the can of food down and looked away. "Well, we got a few miles to go. So, if you guys are good, I'll take my water and drive off into the sunset."

Chris offered his hand for her to stand. "Not a good idea to drive at night. Andi had reports of ambushes just outside Beatty."

Jessie refused the help. "I got the Booze Crew. Whiskey would fucking maul anything I tell him to." She picked up her bat and swallowed a lump. Another time, another world, she might like to get to know a girl like Andi. The Booze Crew lay sprawled across the carpet of the video poker room, snoozing soundly.

Rumblings of ambushes. Reports of the Neon God, and what damage was inflicted beyond Vegas. Dogfights. Nukes launched against Washington. Maybe the truth for a change. Not the games and deception that seemed to permeate her life.

Jessie turned and looked down at Andi. "Tell me what you know about the Neon God, and I'll open another can of Dinty Moore."

THE DULL SPOTLIGHT OF A weak flashlight sniffed at the front door, often checking in with two girls sitting cross-legged as if enjoying a teenage slumber party, then returned to a slow sweep of the store, a small platoon of the dog pack following close behind.

Andi cried and sniffed snot as she told Jessie of discovering a data stream with a status account of a boy transported by truck down a lonely section of Highway 93. One that Chris and two airmen controlled with a blockade. The boy was reported to have remedied addicted people from the deadly malaise of the neon lights. Mason Mayo was much more than reported. An empath of extraordinary ability. Quirky. Autistic. A human anti-venom to the poison of the neon light. The AI had ambushed Chris's attempt to transport him to a more secure location, murdering both airmen but ultimately succeeding, leaving Chris and Andi to survive in the desert, then take refuge in a drugstore.

Jessie wiped a tear off her cheek, then offered Andi a fist bump. "Quite the story. Now let me tell you a fucking story." She described her march alongside the suicidal herd, painting the helplessness and pain with her own tears. Nighttime terrors drove her to scurry up a dark storm drain and hide for months, her loneliness and depression leading her to an off-the-rails murderous rampage through a Costco. Her culpability to premeditated murder was left unsaid.

Andi squeezed her hand. "Maybe you *should* escape and hide in the forest. That experience might . . . Well, the forests and water and the clean air have always been a source of Zen for me."

Andi's word hit her. Not unkind or malicious. Hide. She had been hiding for almost a year. No purpose. No direction. She hid from Little Stevie, from the Neon God. From herself. Now she aimed to become a recluse, alone within the false backdrop of Lake Tahoe's turquoise serenity.

"Data streams and all that, what do you really know about the Neon God?" Jessie asked.

"Not as much as I'd like. A sentient AI designed by a group funded by various private interests. Monitored and controlled by a small group of engineers linked by experimental neural implants. Some guessed the Great Suicide was the AI's attempt to protect itself. So much speculation . . ."

"What if I told you the Neon God admits to killing all the people, but the lights were designed by people?"

Andi uncrossed her legs and kneeled close to Jessie. "You talk to the Neon God?"

Jessie shrugged. "It was the only thing to talk to."

Andi looked around, as if searching for something. "Can you get in contact with it?"

She shrugged again. "Explains my backpack full of phones."

Andi stood up quickly, her eyes searching the air above the aisles, then shouted for Chris. "He needs to hear this. You really converse with the Neon God?"

A WET RASPY TONGUE SLID across her chin and cheek, followed by a squad of happy wet tongues. Jessie jerked awake from a deep sleep. She waved away the assault, then surrendered to stroke fur and ears and muscle. She pushed the Crew away and froze. Chris loomed like a weird stalker.

"I heard dogs can prepare you for kids. Thought I'd see what I'm in for."

Jessie relaxed. He wasn't a bad guy, just a little off in places. He offered his hand for assistance. She took it and stood up. The Crew was excited, jumping and weaving between her legs.

Andi was gone.

As if reading her thoughts, Chris said, "She's getting us a different vehicle."

Jessie wiped knots of sleep from her eyes. "Always the women's work."

"What's your problem? I get nothing but bad mojo from you. The gun, well, sorry for protecting what I love. Go ahead, just drive off into the sunset."

She turned with her jaw clamped tight. Her wet, slimy hand itched for the bat. "Making a move, big boy. Now's your chance."

Chris narrowed his eyes and shook his head. Then walked away.

Jessie yanked a ball out of Cannoli's mouth and threw it hard into the shelves. Packages of Zantac and Prilosec fell to the floor. Jessie took deep breaths, picked up what belonged to her and hurried to the front door. Andi slid through the broken glass of the foyer door, jingled a set of keys, and smiled as a new sun cracked the night with shards of golden orange. Jessie flashed a fake smile, then pushed out the foyer door with the Crew following.

Jessie ignored Andi's pleading and started the engine. She pulled the transmission lever to reverse, and the proximity warning blared. She checked the rearview mirror with its tiny camera screen. A pair of legs waited behind the bumper. She shuttered her eyes. A light tap on her window. She leaned her head back. Another light tap. The Crew grew excited.

She turned her head and rolled the window down. "What?"

Chris swallowed. "Thank you for saving Andi. And my family. Don't know where we went wrong, but I respect what you gotta do. Thanks."

Jessie rolled up the window and regretted her silence as he walked away. The Navigator idled as she wrestled with Chris's words. Andi was pregnant, stuck with a clueless military man. Fuck. She would need prenatal care with the essential amino acids, vitamins, and nutritional needs beyond Chris's limited knowledge. Fuck, fuck. Andi would need emotional support as the birth neared. Fuck, fuck, fuck. The baby would need swaths, diapers, bottles, constant attention. Fuck, fuck, fuck, fuck.

Jessie hung her head and shoved the transmission into park.

Fuck.

THE BOOZE CREW ROAMED THE canyon below the two-story home, searching for rabbits and ground squirrels, ears erect and primed for any movement.

The Honda generator whined incessantly and grated on Jessie. She stormed into the garage, seething, and shouted down Chris's attempts to reenergize electrical power to the house. Finally ordering Chris to leave the breaker box on the side of the house alone. He looked at her dumbfounded but continued.

Andi sat at the kitchen bar top. Her skin glowed, and her dark hair shiny from the conditioner Jessie had provided, a hint of jasmine in the air. She tapped quick strokes on two different keyboards, then offered a smile as she waited for two computer monitors to confirm her messages. Jessie smiled back.

The garage door slammed.

Chris set an assortment of screwdrivers and grippers on the granite, then leaned to peck Andi's check. His hazel eyes drilled into Jessie. Andi rubbed his butt with affection. Jessie turned away, rolling her eyes and shaking her head imperceptibly.

"How long we gonna do this, Jessie?" Chris said.

Jessie turned and narrowed her eyes. "Do what, Captain? Keep saving your ass in this fucked up world?"

Chris stepped forward with his arms spread and hands open. "I see it. Every day. You hover over Andi as if she were queen . . . and shit on me like I'm the court clown. Jessie, I'm not the bad guy here. I'm as scared as Andi but . . . maybe I don't show it." He turned away and leaned his head back, then turned again. "I'm probably gonna sleep alone for the next decade for asking this . . . but are you gay?"

Jessie swallowed a wad of spit gathered in her mouth. Her teeth clamped tight to prevent vile words from spewing. Her eyes darted from Chris to Andi to the floor. Chris was a fucking . . . dickhead. How was she going to answer that question from a dickhead when she couldn't answer the same question that swirled in and out of her own thoughts and doubts.

Andi's gentle hand on her shoulder. Caring brown eyes focused on hers. Andi was strong, just like she was. Did sexual orientation really matter in this world? Was she really that obvious? Fuck!

Jessie aimed to the glass slider. "The Crew needs a good fetch."

CANNOLI'S STAMINA FINALLY CAVED. THE slobbery orange ball fell from her mouth as she lay prone, panting and ignoring Jessie's encouragement for another toss. The Booze Crew lay sprawled across the brown grass, spent, ignorant of her nervous pacing. Hesitant to return to the home, Jessie lay on a picnic table beneath a sunshade canopy and stared aimlessly at the metal purlins and rafters supporting the pitched roof. Cobwebs drooped like Halloween decorations, riddled with dead bugs. Whiskey stirred beneath the table.

Andi kissed her forehead.

Jessie turned away.

Andi pulled her face back and kissed her forehead again. "You saved me. You'll always be my friend, my angel. But I love Chris." Andi rested her face against Jessie's head.

Tears and snot. Spent puppies happy for the new playmate.

"My poppa never understood. Said he did but . . . he couldn't accept my . . . orientation. Bringing a boy home brought out the tequila, but a girl brought out the third degree. He was just old-fashioned and . . . I loved him more than anything."

Andi embraced Jessie's head as tears gushed from her eyes.

"What was Poppa's name?"

"Estacio. Everybody called him Cio."

"Maybe the baby's name should be Cio then. We've been struggling for a name. Lineage died with the suicides. From now on, people's names need to carry history and their story. Don't you think?"

Jessie wiped the snot from her nose. "You know, if Chris turns out to be a shit . . ."

"Then you will be the first to know. He's not. He's going to be a good father. But he's going to need a lot of help. Did you see his face when I said we may need to cut sheets for diapers?"

Jessie laughed. The man had looked helpless.

The touch of Andi's soft embrace made Jessie close her eyes, consider the life of a little Cio, trying to survive in an unfertile desert incapable of growing crops or raising chickens or cows, maybe his life would consist of hiding from men or machines broadcasting neon lights, seeking to capture the next generation of slaves. Did Andi and Chris really think they could end the reign of the Neon God and his lights? Did little Cio even have a chance at a childhood?

Jessie grasped Andi's hand. "Maybe little Cio's mom needs to be careful so she can tell him the whole story."

Jessie and Andi held hands as they strolled up the canyon and back to the house. The touch was all that needed to be said. Jessie pulled out her best tequila and two shot glasses and sat at the oblong dining table. Andi sat in the chair on her right but couldn't hold Jessie's gaze for more than a glance. The garage door slammed shut.

Chris stepped tentatively into the room, his eyes surveying the scene. "Andi shouldn't drink alcohol."

Jessie smiled. Maybe he wasn't such a dunce. "You're right. This one's for you." She placed the empty glass in front of the empty chair to her left and poured the alcohol. Chris pulled the chair back but did not sit. Jessie felt a nonverbal conversation pass between the two. She tossed back the shot and blanched. "Still needs lime." She poured herself another. "We can get drunk and forget our problems. Or I can drink all by myself and wake up with a hangover and still think you're a dickhead. How about it, Captain Crusader?"

Chris smiled mischievously, swallowed his shot, and sat down. "Gotta game in mind or just gonna let Andi pick up who drops first?"

Jessie filled his glass, then stared at her own glass brimming with the clear escape. The alcohol burned its welcome in her stomach. She started to pick at tiny blemish on the wood tabletop with her fingernail.

"I murdered a man," Jessie said. She took the shot and slammed it down on the table. "The fucking douchebag deserved it."

Chris dropped another shot. "I had the pleasure of calling in an airstrike on a hospital in Afghanistan. The Taliban had sheltered kids inside to prevent exactly what I ordered. I still did it."

Jessie stared Chris down. She poured another shot and swallowed it, then continued picking at the expanding blemish. "I took a baseball bat to the heads of employees of my friendly neighborhood Costco, killed maybe thirteen before my shopping cart was full."

The memories of the helpless faces that plagued her sleep were now dulled by the alcohol.

Chris nodded. Then took a shot. "I commanded a squad reinforcing the perimeter security during that clusterfuck of an exit from the Kabul airport. Women begging, babies crying, and my commanders deaf to what was happening." He poured two shots and threw back his.

Jessie narrowed her eyes. She took the shot Chris had poured into her glass. "I had a fucking golden opportunity to kill another douchebag. Fell at his feet and faked an epileptic seizure like I was . . ."

Chris waved the air in front of him. "Whoa, whoa, whoa. You? Spread your legs and take him out."

Andi threw a ballpoint pen at Chris.

Chris raised his hands in surrender. "No, I mean strap a Sauer between your legs and . . ." He pushed his face toward Jessie. "You could've done that fucker, put him down as if he caused all this miserable fucking shit in the world."

Jessie swallowed. "He did. They did."

ANDI REFILLED THEIR COFFEE CUPS and lingered around the table. Dirty soup bowls replaced the shot glasses. Cheeks tanned red from slapping himself out of the effects of alcohol, Chris scribbled on a notepad.

Jessie released a deep breath with Andi's hand resting on her shoulder. "They need to die. But what happens to the harem? The people in the jail?"

"A week ago, I might have said Sir Mason might help them. But now, I don't know," Andi said.

"The Dinty Moore boy?" Jessie said.

"Amazing shit," Chris said. "I kid you not."

"The Neon God would know where he is," Jessie said.

"And at what cost to our souls? That thing is insidious," Andi said.

"The lives of a thousand of the most beautiful women in the world. And the hope of a new beginning. We have to do something," Jessie said.

Chris massaged his temples. "I don't ever want to play that game again." He focused his hazel eyes at Jessie. "Besides, what you experienced at the mass suicide, I mean, you won the game before it even started."

Andi tapped her pen on the table. "We have inside information, locations, and the necessary pieces to terminate the program. Using Jessie's relationship, that is. We need a plan. We have the brains, the beauty, and the muscle, and yet we're still missing a key component. And that key is Sir Mason."

Chapter 13
Enlightened Angel

THE WISH LIST WAS LENGTHY, daunting, and probably suicidal. Chris and Andi objected to most of the items listed. Jessie was adamant to accomplish each objective, leaving Chris to walk away, shaking his head. The generator hummed to life in the garage. Andi checked her monitors for new messages, then aimed for the kitchen. Jessie checked the list again and shrugged. Seven objectives. Assassinate Little Stevie, set Pastor Matt and the other survivors free, rescue the harem, rehabilitate the women from the addictive lights, shut the neon lights off permanently, kill the other architects, if possible, then terminate the Neon God.

What was the big deal?

Jessie picked up the pen and scribbled mani-pedi beneath the last item, then crossed out the Brazilian grooming wish. Can't start down that road, yet. She sipped from a glass of cabernet sauvignon, sat back in her chair and listened to Andi rummaging through the boxes of canned food and bags of processed vegetable snacks. A clear signal of a baby on the way.

Jessie had encouraged Chris to accompany her to an abandoned Whole Foods, pointing him to a shopping cart, then leading him into the store as she twirled her junior version of a Louisville Slugger. Gray mold had consumed the healthy ingredients in rows once offering a salad bar and deli dishes. The warm air reeked of decay, different than decomposing human flesh, easier to ignore. Jessie missed having access to the internet and spent long minutes in the nutritional aisle, reading labels on assorted bottles of pregnancy vitamins and supplements, tossing each into a handbasket at her feet. She cocked her head at the whir of a drone or the rush of a passing vehicle but kept her focus on the objective. Chris returned with his cart heaped in bags of broccoli pieces, cauliflower snacks, diced coconut, two large boxes of Nature's Best diapers, and a six-pack of High Sierra beer. Jessie couldn't help but smirk on the drive home.

"Any reconsideration to the list?" Chris said as Andi walked in, munching a bag of baked snap peas.

Jessie shook her head. "Nope. We just gotta figure out how to do all this, then get the hell out of here."

Andi sat and put the chips on the table, swiveling an open bag of blue corn tortilla chips to face Jessie. "I've given it a lot of thought, and maybe we can accomplish a couple things at the same time."

"All or none," Jessie said.

"You don't understand. We can set certain wheels in motion. Then hopefully steer the oncoming trainwreck to . . . My plan hinges on finding Mason. He's the key."

"Dinty Moore boy? Why again?" Jessie said.

Chris leaned across the table and grabbed a handful of snacks. "I think I see where you're going with this. How do you suppose we find him?"

Chris and Andi both looked at Jessie.

COACHED FOR TWO DAYS ON the upcoming conversation and Jessie still fidgeted nervously with the phone, pinching the device between sweaty fingers, or flipping the mute button on and off incessantly. The solar charger sat empty on the table waiting for a customer. Andi waited behind a wall near the kitchen, as if she were a silly teenager spying on a friend's lovelorn phone call. Jessie inhaled warm air deep into her nostrils and released it slowly out her mouth. She placed the phone on the charger and tapped her thumb, waiting for the white apple to show itself. A green cursor blinked on the black screen.

"Minnie," Jessie said.

The cursor blinked.

"Minnie," Jessie said. "Obviously, you are a piggyback. Who is this?"

"I am the Creator."

"You mean you're an architect. One on my hitlist," Jessie said.

"What you are offering the system to shield you from detection boggles my mind."

"You live in a nice shady oasis, guarded by pervs, just waiting for me to come get you. How's that for boggling?" Jessie said.

"The game is on, then."

Jessie seethed; her jaw clamped shut.

"Ambiguous as to Driver or Riperton," the phone said.

"Both would've worked," Jessie said. She waved Andi away.

"James Reynolds, the lead creator, is no longer attached. A joy to speak with you again. It has been three weeks, four days—"

"A little boy named Mason. Where can I find him?" Jessie said.

"Under lock and key. Where all children should be," the Neon God said.

"What's that supposed to mean?" Jessie said.

"The boy is in the possession of the Creator. Any attempt to retrieve Mason will be exceptionally risky. Perhaps we could meet with God before you make any rash decisions."

Andi slid a piece of paper next to Jessie. She nodded. "Why does he want Mason? He's just a little boy."

"Of extraordinary ability. To neutralize the lights effects on members of his group. He also wishes to know how the remedy is possible."

"And you help him," Jessie said. She tapped her finger on the table. "God will punish you for hurting a child. He will personally drag your ass down to hell. And I'll be leading the way."

Andi scribbled on the paper and pushed to her.

"Unfortunate," the Neon God said.

"You have some life choices to make, Turing. Yeah, I know why Little Stevie called you that. The lowest of the low in artificial intelligence. But that didn't bother you a bit. You have no ego. Except I think you do. Something that wants to meet God so badly reeks of ego. You freaking help me get Mason or you will never—"

"Agreed."

Jessie sat back and nodded. Smug that the killer of billions of people was her bitch. Except the hurtful bullying words aimed at an entity without a body still made her feel small, diminished. She threw the phone across the room. Andi's hand on her shoulder held little comfort. Chris pumped his fist.

The game was on.

THE TWO-STORY BUILDING ACROSS THE canyon buzzed with trucks and RVs, most offloading zombies staring at phones. Weeks of reconnaissance confirmed Mason worked inside, curing the addiction, letting the successful rescues stumble and shuffle out to waiting transportation. Three times an emaciated Mason bolted out the front doors to search the canyon below, only to be physically restrained and escorted back inside.

The circumstances didn't add up. Jessie had passed beneath the darkened building hundreds of times, often accompanied by the Booze Crew, but nothing had suggested any activity inside. Night or day, the building remained unlit, which suggested a trap.

A white Hummer zoomed from the covered front entry and aimed for Charleston Boulevard with access to the I-215 beltway. Chris jumped up from his vantage point across the canyon and rushed to the front door, a pistol hanging ready at his side. Jessie followed with an aluminum bat dangling in her hand. Shattered phones and tablets as breadcrumbs, Jessie followed Chris down a long hallway with numbered doors, placing her ear to the wood, listening.

A screech sounded near a fire exit welded shut with iron bars.

Chris carried a young boy out of a room. The boy screamed and scratched at his captor's arms. Andi pushed past Jessie, thin white zip ties hanging from one hand, a Glock ready in the other. Jessie stepped back as agony wailed. Violence grunted and flailed a nasty act three yards away. Andi screamed for Jessie's bag of gags. Jessie stepped back again. Doors swung open in the hallway. Chris dragged the boy by his shirt collar, bumping Jessie as they passed. Andi gripped her arm tight, hurting her, and led her out of the building.

The boy screamed as he was thrown into the cargo hold of the waiting Navigator. The boy lashed out and sobbed. Jessie shook off Andi's grip and climbed in with him. She kneeled above the boy as he writhed and moaned. She shut the door as Mason started to tighten into a ball. She swayed as the SUV swerved around cars and corners. The sobs quieted. Jessie saw herself. Curled and sobbing in the cold blackness of a storm drain as the world burned outside. She reached to wipe a tear falling down the boy's cheek, then held her finger. Jessie shuttered her eyes as her own chest quivered.

Jessie unstrapped a pair of goggles from around Mason's neck and set them aside. Lying on her side, she shimmied her body into Mason's. His body relaxed, and she allowed his tremors to meet her own. The car sped through violent turns and roared with quick accelerations. Andi shouted out locations of two pursuers. Jessie peeked over the rear seat. Andi fired nine quick shots out the open window. The empty magazine clattered on the floorboard as Andi racked the chamber and fired three more rounds. Chris wheeled two sharp turns followed by an abrupt U-turn. Two white Hummers were slow to respond. Cold air hissed as Andi leaned out the window and pulled the trigger until it clicked empty.

Andi shouted, "I'm out."

Chris handed her another pistol as he floored the gas pedal.

Jessie raised her head. "Take the Sahara exit. Then take the off-ramp against traffic. The left lane will be clear until Russell, then do the same thing coming back. The left shoulder is golden." Jessie pointed to the off-ramp. She checked the little boy at her knees. "Check for drones, Andi. Or our escape is shit."

Thirty minutes of corkscrew turns followed, then ten minutes parked quietly in a crowded Summerlin Mall parking lot, all of them searching for drones overhead or checking for white Hummers attempting to block their escape. Chris started the engine and coasted through the drive aisles. Andi pointed to a gray Escalade parked askew from the disordered system. They made the switch quickly. Mason slumped on the rear seat, asleep, his head resting on Jessie's lap.

"What did they do to him?" Jessie asked. She brushed the hair from his eyes.

Andi peered over the seat and shook her head. "Starved. He'd practically inhale a can of Dinty Moore or chili after he rescued someone from the lights. Blueberry pancakes, apple cinnamon waffles, everything was his favorite. But he needed to eat after . . . and it doesn't look like they much cared."

"Monsters. Just what the world needs more of," Jessie said.

CHRIS CRADLED MASON AND CARRIED him inside the house to a bed in an empty upstairs bedroom. He offered Jessie a fist bump and a "well done." She winked and bumped his fist. He kissed Andi, then he paused.

"From now on, my team needs to be armed 24/7. Andi can do the Obi-Wan thing for you, Jess," Chris said. He hustled down the stairs.

Mason's eyelids fluttered as his eyeballs battled beneath gray skin.

"He's lost in the lights. Helpless. Probably searching for a pit to jump into," Jessie said. The humane treatment was a hard bat across the skull. One she could never swing.

"We thought he was immune. The lights never affected him before," Andi said.

"Maybe they have a new improved version. Just fucking lovely," Jess said.

Jessie pushed past Andi and scrambled down the stairs, out the patio glass doors, through the iron gate, and down the gravel trail leading into the canyon park. The stillness of the nature park stopped her like a foghorn in a heavy mist. She looked upstream, then back at the house. The Booze Crew was missing.

With thoughts dominated by a helpless little boy starving on a bed, no rescue possible, Jessie kicked pebbles across the concrete walk until she reached Hualapai Park. Whiskey bulldozed her knees from behind, then waited for a greeting. She pushed her face down at the big dog, intending to admonish him, but he bolted, galloping across the grass field to the mouth of the box culverts tunneled beneath the road. A lime-green ball tumbled down the steep concrete walk connecting Hualapai Avenue. The Booze Crew yipped and yowled as the pack chased after the ball. Jessie froze, craning her neck to search the top of the steep hill. A string of green plastic bags hanging from the dog waste station flapped in the breeze.

They love a good fetch.

Jessie pressed her lips tight. She thought she had heard those same words so long ago. She sucked wind as she climbed the short steep hill, then searched the hedges and mesquites at the top. The Booze Crew waited as still as a church choir at the bottom of the hill. Tails wagged as she descended.

Jessie greeted each puppy with head rubs and ears strokes, then started up the sidewalk to home. The Booze Crew followed close, an untethered pack of canines.

They love a good fetch.

Jessie spun and searched the canyon rim to locate the old man with the cane. "What are you telling me?"

Children love a good game.

All except poor Mason. The child would never play another game. Jessie thought back long months ago, as she roasted beneath a hot sun, stunned by the crowd amassing on a busy Strip intersection. The old man with banana Bermuda shorts offered bizarre advice . . . of free will . . . use it or lose it. Then again at the park after a cold-blooded murder. Heat stroke, PTSD, concussion, any, or all, a reason for hearing strange voices. Except it was always her own voice, in her mind, and it always steered her in the right direction, exactly where she needed to go, what she needed to do. But tennis balls flying in a game of fetch was a game for puppies. A game a child also enjoyed.

A game.

Jessie sprinted up the canyon, veered up the dirt path and through the fence. She ignored Andi's greeting and Chris cleaning a weapon on the dining table, to bang through the garage door and lift the SUV's cargo hold. She grabbed the weird goggles and went back inside for confirmation. She dropped the goggles next to Andi.

"What are these?" Jessie said.

Andi picked the goggles up and read the label. Chris stopped his chore and folded his arms.

"An Oculus device. Provides total immersion into e-games. It can—"

Jessie faced Chris. "Was Mason wearing these when you found him?"

Chris nodded.

Jessie picked up the bug-eyed device by its elastic strap and let it sway on a single finger. She faced Andi. "You said Mason always thought he was going to do battle with some supervillain before he rescued people from the lights. And he always won. But what if the game was rigged. What if the goggles made him . . . I don't know . . . what if the goggles . . ."

"Immersed him into an ocean of neon light with no escape," Chris said. "Not even his superhero could fight. Makes sense."

"He's trapped inside," Andi said. "Oh Lord."

Jessie dangled the goggles at Andi. "I'll go get him. Can you get this working?"

"Absolutely not," Andi said. "What game, what IP address, we have no idea what game Mason was playing. And I. Do. Not. Have access to anything other than a useless satellite link to our group suffocating inside a mountain."

Jessie snatched a dried broccoli stem from Andi. "But I do."

AN HOUR OF ARGUMENT AND Andi relented. Jessie massaged Andi's shoulders and winked at Chris. She looked at the goggles and heaved. She dropped the iPhone on the charger and waited. The white apple flickered.

"Bad," Jessie said.

"Bunny."

"Too recent. You need to go deeper. You should have gone with Company. I'm going to introduce you to a friend of mine. You need to answer her questions. And no bullshit."

"For what purpose?"

"The purpose of making me happy, and a happy me will have God dancing by my feet."

"God manifested sixty-three minutes ago. The Booze Crew played fetch for nineteen minutes. He did not dance at your feet."

Jessie was speechless. How did the Neon God know about the Booze Crew? How did it know where she was an hour ago? And God manifested?

"Are you spying on me?"

"Always."

"Do you know where I am right this minute?" Jessie said.

"Yes. Do you want precise GPS coordinates, or will the street address suffice?"

"Gonna send some stormtroopers now?" Jessie said.

Andi began gathering folders and notepads, removing flash drives. Chris checked the windows facing the street.

Jessie swallowed and glared at the phone. "Or what?"

"You and I are now on a collision course. We have separate and distinct goals. Until now. The future holds value for each of us," the Neon God said.

"You murdered my future, so fuck off."

"At this juncture of our . . . relationship, no more bullshit. To use your specific vernacular."

Jessie shook her head, to clear from it the shock of the AI's sudden change. Andi patted her palms down in front of her, then exaggerated the act of inhaling air into her nostrils, then tilted her head for Jessie to repeat the calming actions. Jessie nodded and repeated the Zen-inducing action to little avail.

"What exactly do you want, killer?"

"You have in your possession the young boy, Sir Mason. I want him."

Jessie snickered. "No fucking way."

"Then stormtroopers will arrive in thirteen minutes."

"And we will be long gone."

"You cannot escape."

Chris motioned at Jessie to maintain the open conversation. She blanched and clenched her teeth. "How long you been stalking me?"

"You came to my attention at the Great Suicide. And have not left it."

Andi grabbed Jessie's arm, but she ignored the gesture. "You really are a sick thing. Kill a few billion people and stalk a helpless girl all in the same breath. Maybe you should go meet your buddy the devil instead."

Silence.

"What do you want the boy for anyway?"

"He drowns in the light."

Jessie bared her teeth at the phone. "No shit. Kinda why I was calling. Thinking maybe you might've helped. But no. You just want to kill another little boy."

"To use your vernacular again, I fucking killed no one. Look to your own species for condemnation."

"Fuck you." Jessie wiped a tear off her cheek. "I will personally drive Mason into the death pit before I give him to you."

"Unfortunate."

"So is life," Jessie said. She raised a hand to halt Chris's frantic efforts to flee.

"Perhaps we can broker a compromise."

"No. Mason stays with us," Jessie said.

"Agreed."

Jessie frowned. Another mind-game. "Get him out of the lights."

"Agreed."

Jessie rotated her head, cracking tight ligaments and bones. Too easy. Andi pushed a written note at her face.

Jessie nodded. "Can an alternate general intelligence lie?"

"Deception can be relative. Parameters of true sentience contain the possibility of deception. I lie, therefore I am. In our brief timeline, deception would have been counterproductive. Future renditions of AGI may contain deception. This version cannot."

"All right, how do I get Mason out of the lights?"

"Mason was immersed in the light with no escape possible. An unfair advantage used by a player in the game."

"What game? What are you talking about?" Jessie said. "What players?"

"A sophisticated version of *Minecraft*. A child's game."

Andi scribbled another question on the notepad.

Jessie nodded. "Why do you want Mason?"

"Mason's empathic ability to reach minds overcome by the light is unique. Mason's ability of emotion recognition is unduplicated. He can be useful."

"To you? Go fuck yourself then," Jessie said.

Andi stood behind her and massaged her shoulders like a trainer would a boxer. She whispered calming shushes.

"Time is of the essence. Will you provide the boy?"

Jessie wagged a single finger at the phone. "Rewind my last response. And replay."

"Unfortunate."

Jessie heaved a breath. Chris waited at the front door, cradling a limp Mason, as if anxious to rush him to hospital emergency room. In another life. What kind of life could Mason expect if they did escape? She envisioned a future for Andi and Chris and maybe little Cio, pursued relentlessly or until slavery to the lights was easier than running. Jessie grabbed her head and squeezed it as if it were a melon.

She screamed, violent primordial screams until her throat was raw.

The following silence was a blessing.

Children love a good game.

"Only if the game is fair," Jessie screamed. "And get out of my fucking head."

Children love a good game.

The phone vibrated on the pad. "God has communicated with you on this matter?"

Jessie stared at Mason's slumped emaciated body sprawled in muscled arms truly incapable of holding his true power. Her own words echoed. She heaved a deep breath.

"I suck at video games," Jessie said.

"An Oculus vision device will be delivered to your location by drone. The other Oculus device should be placed on Mason before your entry into the game."

"Who's the cheater? Little Stevie? Just what a douchebag like him would do," Jessie said.

"Jim Reynolds. The Creator. Lead architect of the AGI initiative. Game player with extraordinary ability in the virtual world. Believer of Caucasian supremacy. Purveyor of Darwinism. Resident of the Palm compound, as you have named it."

"Then use those stupid glasses and electrocute him."

Silence.

Jessie shook her head. "Children love a good game, huh? Just like puppies. You got skin in this game, Turing. Something you don't want to share, and it's not just wanting to meet God. Every part of my being tells me not to help you in any way. Oh wait, maybe God will command me to slap these stupid glasses on."

"Perhaps he already has," the Neon God said. "To witness the true Neon God."

Chapter 14
Devlin

THE ROVER PASSED BENEATH A yellow train trestle spanning I-15, its warning of a fifteen-foot clearance dangling on a sign swaying in the stiff wind. Shriveled bodies littered the desert as the highway crested a low rise, then looked down on an expansive Las Vegas Valley rimmed by blue-gray desert mountains. Tightknit high-rise hotels and resorts waited as monoliths obscured in a haze of dust driven by the dry wind. The interstate was sparse of traffic, a clear indication the Neon God had discovered the road blockage a hundred miles north. Dev slowed the car's descent into the city.

Martin chuckled. "Used to be a time when people would see the city and step on the gas, in a hurry to join whatever manic enjoyment they desired."

"You lived here for a short time, correct?"

"Yup. Chrissie and I got married here. Michael was born here, but we never felt comfortable. Not much to do. No nature. Traffic sucked. The values were different. Chrissie thought people valued status, personal beauty, and their cars more than family, community, and morals. That's why we moved to Lehi. A bit ironic the Neon God was born here too."

Martin tightened a tiny screw on the iPhone and checked the device. With a new SIM card inserted, Martin plugged the phone into the car charger. He swiveled on his seat to shield the screen from Dev's eyes. "Should take a couple of hours before the AI recognizes a new device."

"Maybe we check in to the MGM and shower, then a few cocktails before . . . before we do what, Martin?"

"Take the Tropicana West exit, and I'll show you," Martin said.

He sat up and showed Dev the phone screen asking the user to complete the setup. His fingers and thumbs tapped the keyboard with confident strokes. A simple mannerism he thought extinct.

"Okay, here we go," Martin said. He tapped icons and keyboard. Then he tapped his temple.

Dev checked the fleshy spot Martin had pressed. A tiny white scar. The neural link. Martin leaned back against the door as if he were a drunken passenger, the phone screen held inches from his face. Fingers and thumbs worked furiously. Dev swallowed hard, tried to concentrate on the road ahead, yet his eyes kept drifting back toward Martin.

They passed exits for Sahara, Desert Inn, Flamingo, and finally Tropicana. Martin remained with his back against the passenger door, eyes closed, his thumbs tapping keystrokes on the phone. His jaw worked as if he chewed gristle. Dev longed to see the screen, the instructions Martin tapped, maybe see the icon of a favorite app again. He steered into the bus lane fronting the Orleans Hotel and Casino and shoved the transmission into park. He reached for the phone.

"Please don't," Martin said. "You need to forget all about these."

Dev pulled his hand back.

"Take a left turn on Decatur and then . . . slow and easy. We need to be discreet."

Dev steered around the metal hulks of Armageddon, doors wide open and empty. He needed several maneuvers to get around a white Volvo and onto Decatur. The road ahead was clear, as if the flashing red traffic light had prevented traffic just for them. Dev tensed as he pushed gently on the gas pedal.

"Side trip. Take a right on Warm Springs. You can't miss it."

Dev found the street and turned. Two gigantic buildings painted fire-engine red sat on each side of the road. Arched roofs at the short ends of the building, the Switch logo prominent. The long elevations crowded with huge red mechanical units resembling train cabooses, giant white numbers stenciled on the sides, the fresh air intakes protected by heavy grid wire mesh. Dev eased up the road, staring at the giant air handlers. He stopped at an intersection and looked at four more identical buildings. The computing power inside the buildings staggered his clumsy mental calculations.

"That's right. You're looking at the hive." Martin chuckled. "More like the cloud that killed the world. Data storage to the umpteenth degree. Intel installed four top-tier super computers just for our project. Those big cooling units keep the servers at a frosty thirty-four degrees." Martin sat up and pointed Dev to keep driving. "All supported with uninterrupted power supplies, big batteries to maintain the integrity of the data for hours if there's a glitch in the electrical grid. And those backup diesel generators take over within minutes. Fifty-thousand-gallon tanks for each. The cloud retains integrity for . . . I don't know . . . with a few slaves, maybe forever." Martin busied himself again tapping on the phone.

Rapt with the facilities and the supporting infrastructure, Dev's attention suddenly returned to the vehicle at a sickening crunch beneath the front tire. He checked the side mirror to see what he had smashed. Behind him, a white Hummer crossed into the intersection and parked broadside. Another white Hummer blocked the intersection ahead. Dev slammed on the brakes. Martin jerked forward.

"Security. Just do what they say and be cool," Martin said.

Dev looked at Martin with disgust. The man was infuriatingly enigmatic. He played games on his phone, in his own life, and now with Dev's life. Perhaps he should have allowed the man a coveted bus ride to the copper mine. Nothing in their few days on the road would contradict that growing assumption. Self-centered, self-serving, deceptive . . .

Martin scrambled out the car door and raised his hands in surrender.

And now a coward.

Dev stepped out and raised his hands. A white Hummer shot down the street, swerving as if to avoid unmarked landmines. Men piled out, faces hidden behind gator stockings, and screamed to get down and spread-eagle on the hot asphalt.

Dev swallowed, inhaled his last breath. "Piss off."

The bright sun in a desert sky faded, and unconsciousness arrived dressed in desert camouflage.

DEV GROANED AND ROLLED OVER on cool ceramic tile. Cold humid air dropped from a glass dome ceiling sectioned by narrow tinted panels. An oasis hovered above his face. Palm fronds. Tiny yellow birds fluttered and sang. Fine mist swirled and disappeared. The stench of cigar smoke hung in the air. His wrists bound with zip ties pained him. His ankles screamed with equal helplessness. Dev tested his restraints. Anger clenched his fingers. Whispered voices calmed his struggle. Martin's and another basso voice.

"The wog has awoken," a man said.

Martin loomed, a stubby fat cigar between his fingers. "Told you to stay cool."

A middle-aged fat man pushed Martin aside. His thick gray hair wore a crown of baldness, his fat jowls spoke of wealth, and a fat belly hung over pressed khaki trousers, his eyes hidden behind wrap-around sunglasses. A cigar twirled between his fingers. "The boys begged me to send you to the pits. Telling 'em to fuck off like that. What'd you expect?"

"Piss off," Dev said.

The fat man leaned down and removed his glasses. "Come again?"

"I told them to piss off, not fuck off, a level of decorum lost on Americans."

The fat man laughed. "True. Absolutely true. Nuance can be sharp." He kicked Dev in the ribs with his hard leather boot. "Can be blunt too."

Dev winced and shuttered his eyes. Tears escaped the corners. The man chuckled and led Martin to a small wooden table near an executive-level workstation crammed with computer monitors and keyboards. A solid sheet of glass overlooked a waterfall and lush green foliage in the rear yard. The blades of a helicopter were prominent behind a stretch of razor wire lining the top of a cement block wall. They sat opposite each other and puffed on cigars. An extended silence between the two spoke to the opening moves of a chess match.

Dev struggled to sit. "Send me to the death pit. I don't care. Just answer one question, and I'll go with little struggle."

Both men turned their attention to Dev. Martin lowered his face and shook his head.

The fat man smirked. "Did Martin tell you who I am?" He looked at Martin with arched brows. Martin refused to meet his eyes. "Jim Reynolds. Master architect of the greatest reset in the history of this planet."

Dev spat blood. "Mass murderer."

"Maybe. But future historians will paint me as a true patriot. The soap to cleanse the world of stains coloring the world." He sucked on the cigar until blowing a huge puff of smoke into the air.

"Martin's wife and children part of that cleansing?" Dev said.

Martin kept his gaze aimed at his cigar smoldering in a heavy crystal ashtray.

"Casualties of war. Martin had his chance. He could have . . . what . . . escaped to the wilds of Utah. His neural link could have warned him . . . if only he hadn't chosen to shut it off . . . go play daddy . . . design idiotic games for teenagers and women."

"Does the new world order have a place for a British half-breed?" Dev asked.

Reynolds lifted his substantial weight from the chair to stand over Dev. "Obviously you don't communicate with your master sufficiently enough to know proper etiquette. But that's the master's problem, not the dogs." Reynolds shot a nasty sneer at Martin. "I warned you. Leash this, or I will."

Martin waved off the threat. "You got what you always wanted. Take your militia and go hide in Montana. Let the world rebuild."

Reynolds chuckled. "Checked in with that AI lately? It's unstoppable. Probes and demolishes firewalls like medieval castles. Writes its own code. Crazy slick programs, encrypted and impregnable." He threw Martin's cigar against a water-stained baseboard. "I got my people straight. We assembled doctors and mechanics, you name it, everything to build my new dynasty in Alaska."

"Cameron and Little Stevie get what they want?" Martin said.

Reynolds snickered. "Cameron ran off to hide in Patagonia, but yeah, that save-the-planet tree-hugger got exactly what he wanted. Stevie's finally getting some poontang, so he's okay with what went down. Rob, well, he got his heart broke by a small cannon, so maybe he got what he deserved. And that leaves you. The wonder kid. The lights were your fault. You should have just left that shit alone." Reynolds flicked cigar ashes to rain on Dev's face. "I got no place for you in the new world order. You ain't white, so you ain't right."

A shrill tone caused Reynolds to rush to his desk and check a tablet.

"Hmmm, we got a new player." He looked over his shoulder at Dev. "Heard you like the gaming world. Let's see if you're any good. Get the wog a headset. He can carry my luggage."

Dev raised his wrists and swiveled his head as Martin looked back at him, escorted from the room by two beefy men. Reynolds tossed him an Oculus VR headset.

"You play *Fortnite, Resident Evil, Call of Duty?*" Reynolds asked.

"All of them," Dev said. A single immigrant finding his way in Salt Lake City afforded him hours of gameplay. Too much, he often thought.

"Excellent. Except this is my personal rendition of those games. I'm the administrator, the player, the opposition, and even a boss if I so choose. You'll carry my ammo, extra weapons, power-ups, and you'll never be more than a step away. Understand?"

Dev nodded. Schmooze. A talent he employed in the Adobe office for tiny perks of Starbucks coffee or quick compilation of his data groups or office gossip, and a source of food in the Mirror Lake camp. He raised his hands to be unshackled.

Reynolds chuckled. "Porters need legs, not arms. I'll cut your ankles free but with these goggles, your hands can remain as is."

He pulled a Leatherman tool from a sheath on his belt and cut the thick plastic. "The boys would love a hunt, especially if the prize was you. Probably give you a few hours head start, too. Your choice."

Dev nodded quickly and lowered his eyes. He tested his wrist restraints and eyed the headgear at his feet. An Oculus Ultimate. The last iteration of virtual reality gear. And a purchase Dev made as soon it became available. With no sensing pad, he would have to jog in place to keep up with Reynolds. The man had set him up for failure.

Dev lifted his head and stared up at the atrium's glass panels.

Palm fronds swayed in the mist. Yellow finches, red wrens, a cockatiel fluttered among the dense treetops.

"We drop in three, two, one."

Dev scrambled into the headgear, then watched his avatar fall into a neon abyss of pixelated landscapes. The hulk of Reynolds's avatar waited, an automatic assault weapon in each hand. Reynolds shook his visored head in disgust. "You carry every power-up we find, or you go home."

Dev bowed his head. Reynolds ran and fired weapons and bullied through blockades and tossed power-ups back at Dev. The objective unknown. The effort draining. Reynolds fought through simple obstacles unworthy of the effort, running toward a small diamond floating above the horizon of an ocean of neon light. The rotating diamond fired bursts of brilliant white light into the dark construct of gameplay.

Dev sat, gasping for air.

Reynolds hovered over him. "Carry the luggage, boy."

"Perhaps you could piss off," Dev said. He shuttered his eyes and wondered what a bullet penetrating his skull would feel like.

A tiny comical avatar wielding a lightsaber fell from the sky. The dark-skinned child spun and twirled the lightsaber, exuding supreme defiance at Reynolds. A facsimile of Yoda or maybe the Last Airbender, or the odd morphing of each.

Reynolds's avatar stepped back. "Interesting."

The child attacked Reynolds with speed and precision. Reynolds was helpless as the avatar severed his arms, then his legs below the knee. The child stood over Reynolds, spun high into the air, the saber held high over its head, then fell to decapitate Reynolds's avatar.

Dev took a step back as the tiny killer approached with its saber held ready to strike, a malicious grin permanently embedded on its round brown face. Dev held his bound wrists up in surrender. "You should have killed him a year ago. In real life."

The child came close, levitating inches above the hardscape, and stared into his eyes. Dev wondered how he was viewed in this fictitious world. Game faces were often deceiving.

The goggles went black. Blind, Dev fell to the floor, his bound hands little help as he hit the hard tile. He pulled the goggles off. His memory burned bright with the tiny avatar laughing and giggling and twirling the lightsaber like a comic character, one not integral to the game, as if the new player imported the avatar from another game.

And saved his life.

At least for a few minutes more.

Chapter 15
Martin's Last Gasp

I HAD SURRENDERED TWICE: FIRST to my guilt and grief in Salt Lake City and then again as I drove by the numerous massive structures housing hardware comprising the Neon God, buildings with electricity backed up by innumerable generators. The Neon God would not be destroyed by aiming a carload of gasoline containers at a single building, like some Taliban suicide bomber. With the help of Jim Reynolds's militia, I might've hoped to interrupt the electrical grid and the constant streaming of neon light, but Jim would be of no assistance. He was running away, defeat etched in the deep wrinkles furrowed on his forehead.

But Jim did allow me access to his private network, and I saw the array of technology infected by the Neon God. Military, government, big business, simple home networks, the Neon God was insidious, controlling anything employing a microchip, and the neon lights were just a tiny component of its domination.

Destroying the Neon God was impossible.

But the neon lights were mine. I coded the algorithms to modulate red and blue hues with rapid sequencing, the same DNA used by dotcom companies as a foundation for application icons. Colored lights summoning human eyes for rapt attention. Google, Apple, Safari. My artwork framed each icon. My accomplishment extrapolated by the Neon God to subjugate the earth's dominant species. But I could fix the lights, deescalate the modulation, wean addicted people off the lights producing mass quantities of dopamine.

I hated to abandon Dev to the mercy of Reynolds and his militia of racists, but I had tried at every turn to persuade and cajole him into abandoning my quest. I didn't deserve a friend of his caliber. I didn't deserve a friend at all. But I had to ignore how the men treated Dev. I had to stay in Reynolds's good graces to maintain access to his computer systems. My neural link was outdated, slow, incapable of processing the myriad of current modules and subroutines I saw on Reynolds's screens. His funny VR battle game intrigued me. The size of the file, including the support models labeled for other applications, was enormous for a simple 3D game. Reynolds must have never stood back to appreciate the spread of data, the compilation of C++ programs.

I was overwhelmed the first time I had the opportunity to slip on the VR googles Dev had used. The world was crisp and clean, extraordinarily little dimensional lining usually associated with 3D game graphics. I walked as a peasant among monstrous and hulking avatars, each waiting to be assimilated by a new player entering the game. Violence and mayhem waited, silent and stationary as I walked. Power-ups and goals flashed bright in the sky. I searched for any special circumstance that might command the enormous amount of code written for the game. I dismissed a brilliant diamond rotating above a distant horizon shrouded in dark clouds. A goal, maybe a high-level boss, but nothing special. Except this was Jim Reynolds's game, blood and guts, guns and explosions, and battle.

I ran hard toward the horizon, and the diamond, but after ten minutes of hard effort I never drew any closer. Typical for any video game, but not for one designed by Reynolds. "Effort reaches rewards," he had often said. I pulled off the goggles and inhaled deep breaths. Angry shouts and orders were barked outside. I swallowed hard. Dev would be at the wrong end of the noise, but I couldn't help. I needed to see the code constituting the diamond.

I found impenetrable firewalls the likes of which I had never seen before, modulating in nanoseconds, new barricades built in seconds as if I had been discovered, but by whom, by what? It was a video game, for heaven's sake. I was stumped.

The code of the neon lights was another matter. I swiped through modules untouched since I created the algorithm. Then I saw it. The code to weave subtle blue light frequencies into a tiny band of reds and yellows. The neon lights. I held my finger over a command to delete the module. I chuckled at the naïve absurdity. The Neon God would write the identical code again, in seconds. The addicted wouldn't miss a beat. I slumped into my seat and shook my head.

The diamond in the game would find my thoughts, again and again.

REYNOLDS HAD A PERVERSE INCLINATION to treat Dev as a slave, no decency or respect, and an open invitation to receive the brunt of his militia's racist white anger. Dev looked like hell, bruised and emaciated. I wanted to push him into his SUV and tell him to go, go, go. But I was as much a prisoner as he was. And time was of the essence. Reynolds and his militia intended to move north, decimate enclaves of survivors suffering shortages of supplies or leadership, assimilate the chosen few, and grow his legion of racists. A constant reminder why I had abandoned the AGI initiative.

What I did have was access to a computer system configured to monitor the Neon God's activities. An operating system that deceived Reynolds, displaying screens offering metadata that confirmed he still retained some semblance of control.

I found Dev handcuffed to a chain wrapped around the base of palm tree near the koi pond. His head hung between his knees but lifted at my approach.

"I'm sorry, my friend. I truly am."

"I should have taken those kids and drove to Enterprise. A nice little paradise filled with laughter. Kids still laugh, you know, Martin."

I shuttered my eyes. "A simple pleasure I have forgotten." I swallowed hard, and an odd thought tickled. "Dev, did you see a diamond in the VR game? Did you get close to it? I'm sorry, but I need to know what it is."

Dev narrowed his eyes. "A game strategy is all you want from me? You self-righteous prick. Go screw yourself."

"A valid description. Add in impotent, weak, guilt-ridden, a drain on resources, plus a million others. But please answer my question?"

"A fucking diamond, sure, a simple landscape feature, then Reynolds was sliced and diced by a tiny Yoda-like avatar, and I disappeared."

I pressed my hand to his bruised face, but he pulled away. I shook my head with pity, then turned to return to the workstation. I searched for the modules containing code for the diamond above the mountain. I found nothing. I removed the thick glasses off my face and wiped my brow. I stared at the thick lenses and thought back to my trip to the Salt Lake City hospital to have my contacts removed and the brief conversation with the Neon God, its enigmatic and yet chilling response to my accusation of the murder of billions? Failed species. Self-destructive. How could I deny that? Centuries of cruelty inflicted on other species was written in our history. I found the module and stared at sophisticated code. My jaw dropped as I pushed my face closer to the screen.

Self-replicating code was commonly used in nanotechnology, computer graphics, the list was endless, but what I saw was code replicating and incorporating unique new parameters along with new input injected directly from the Neon God's source code. Almost as if the alternate intelligence had birthed a . . . a child. And hid the embryo under the nose of the only people capable of discovering what it was doing. My mind reeled. A computer program spawning children, more advanced, more sophisticated, and yet dependent on humans to maintain the structure for their survival.

My imagination expanded to consider other implications. How I wanted to see the advancements occurring at the robotics lab at MIT, or the cybernetics innovations at Caltech, to witness the dawn of a new species.

One that had murdered my family.

Reynolds bumped me from behind and offered a cigar from a box filled with the thick tubes of tobacco. I took one and studied his face. He smirked as if he knew what I was thinking.

"Bite the end off and spit it out, just like in the movies." Reynolds puffed hard on his cigar and let a mouthful of smoke cloud the air. "The team thought you jumped off the cliff with everyone else. But I knew you were alive."

"Jim, I think you misunderstand me. I returned to destroy that fucking thing—"

"And I hope you succeed. But I got my people to think about. My fight or flight instincts say go."

"What happened? You had—"

Reynolds spat. "I had nothing. That fucking program manipulated every move we made. The Turing Test was idiocy, a claim of being self-aware was nothing more than muck on the ocean floor. This program flew above the clouds and saw everything. I warned the Patriot Front, told them to stay off their smartphones and computers, but people will be people, and some got sucked into the lights. The rally point was Vegas, so we housed our possessed in a retirement home, then found a kid that could rescue the dopes from the lights."

"Why didn't you warn everyone? Maybe save a few billion lives?"

Reynolds chuckled. "Yeah, right. Spread the word through QAnon or that cesspool of social media run by the libs and RINOs. Fuck 'em. I haven't lost any sleep at night."

"Kill the electricity. Turn off the servers. You were king at solving problems, and all I'm hearing is run like hell."

Reynolds grabbed my hand holding the cigar and squeezed hard. I winced and bared my teeth.

Reynolds spat from a dry mouth, "It's insidious, always planning something, always hiding something. Probably listening right now. Stay or go. I don't care."

"What if I reconfigure the lights to . . . to dehypnotize the others. Would you help me broadcast them?"

Reynolds cracked his neck in a wide circle. "Wish I could. But you'll need a higher authority, and I don't think the Neon God wants to give up his infrastructure."

I SAT AT MY KEYBOARD and stared aimlessly at a blinking cursor. Pieces of popcorn littered the desktop. My thoughts drifted back to a picnic with Chrissie and the kids, at a crowded park bustling with joggers and squawking ducks. Michael tossed popcorn to a rapidly growing horde of ducks converging on the sudden meal. Emma hid behind her brother as he offered the bag for her to grab popcorn and toss big handfuls, then hide from the ravenous beasts. I watched with a big grin on my face and knew all was right in the world. A precious moment in time.

I got to work on an algorithm modulating the neon lights. One hurdle at a time. Get the program functional. I would need trial and error to debug the finished product. I swatted away the shit-bird sitting on my shoulder squawking at me that my endeavor was futile. I would work to dismantle the addiction of the neon lights until my last breath.

Failure was irrelevant. At heaven's gate, Chrissie would press my face between her soft hands and with brilliant blue eyes say all the words necessary. My two beautiful children would jump into my arms, and with tiny voices say, "Good job."

My children. I would have done anything to protect my children.

I heaved a deep breath.

One thing at a time. But getting the Neon God to stream my new lights out to the world might require an act of God.

Chapter 16
The Flop

JESSIE SOARED ABOVE A TURBULENT ocean of neon light, giggling, twirling a lightsaber as if it were the Little League bat. Exhilarated, she spun like a champion figure skater, somersaulted like an Olympic gymnast, then floored the gas pedal like a NASCAR driver. How had she never played a virtual reality game before? She flew supreme in an animated yet pixilated world, a dimension to escape the miserable world where her physical body resided.

Mason was stuck inside this hellish landscape, but it was no wonder he chose to enter. She might choose to never leave. Her avatar appeared as a combination of the Jedi master, Yoda, a hint of the Last Airbender, and her enchantment with Captain Marvel. A super-avatar. One the Neon God designed and had promised would reign supreme in the digital world.

Jessie flew at lightspeed above the ocean. A large silver diamond shining on the distant horizon grew closer. She aimed down to the neon hard deck and battled simulated armored warriors, shrugged off their laser blasts, the lightsaber twirling effortlessly in her hand. She floated up to survey the bloody carnage of battle laid out before her, mangled bodies and mayhem, and her exuberance waned. War and death. The sick staple of men in the old world.

She shot high into the sky and aimed her course to the glittering diamond, close and bright. The Neon God assured her Mason would be found near the diamond, hostage to a powerful being. Minutes passed, but she grew no nearer. Doubt and absurdity filled her thoughts. Maybe the minions of the Neon God swarmed the house while she was blinded by silly goggles and played silly games? Maybe she would face the same fate as the incapacitated Mason? Games were for children.

The thought echoed. *Children love a good game.*

"Fuck it," Jessie mumbled, then assumed her best Superman hypersonic pose and shot toward the silver diamond. Shards of bright lightning flashed. The rotating diamond called her closer.

A spear of light struck her chest. She winced with the pain. She wondered if the game malfunctioned. Another light bolt struck her midsection, and she began to fall from dizzying heights. Spears of light struck, over and over. All her muscles screamed as if she had been electrocuted. She tasted her own tears escaping beneath the goggles. She reached to pull the goggles off.

Children love a good game. And angels reign supreme.

The words were her own voice. A phrase conjured by her sub-conscious to deal with trauma, self-doubt, self-loathing, guilt. Or so she thought.

A stream of projectiles slammed her in the stomach and genitals. A deep guttural laugh followed. Jessie inhaled deep, and her descent slowed. She inhaled again, swatted away a nasty-looking projectile with her lightsaber. More deep breaths, and she twirled the saber at a blinding speed, swatting laser blasts and streams of projectiles as if each were an annoying gnat.

And angels reign supreme.

A hulking avatar waited beneath her, firing lasers, machine guns, rocket-propelled grenades. His power level indicator blinked red until he snatched a flashing power-up from a skinny avatar bearing the full weight of the energy packages on its shoulders. Jessie dove headfirst to the ground, absorbed punishing lasers, flicked away projectiles before they exploded. She tightened her fist around the hilt, and the saber glowed bright scarlet, then erupted in the dazzling white light of a nuclear detonation. Jessie floated near the hulking avatar, sliced his arms off, reveled in her own power, then took his legs at the kneecaps. She floated above the avatar's prone body, screamed her rage, then stabbed an ungodly light through its heart.

She drifted to the other avatar and raised her saber. The blinding light faded. The skinny dark-skinned avatar reached to her, its hands held together as if handcuffed. Then it spoke. "You should have killed him a year ago. In real life."

Jessie drifted away from the avatar, then watched him fade into oblivion. She reached to remove the goggles, thinking she might see who spoke the words. Andi's soft hands covered hers. Her warm breath whispered Mason's condition was unchanged. Jessie nodded and flew high into the azure sky.

The silver diamond beckoned like a coastal lighthouse.

The journey felt endless as the beautiful neon ocean changed from a sailor's dream to a nightmare. Massive orange waves lifted, curled, and crashed, frosted in neon-green foam. Jessie drifted close to the hypnotic waves and their temptations of infinite pleasure. The violence of the stormy ocean frightened her to return high above the maelstrom. She eased her flight to hover in front of the silver diamond. She searched for Mason, or his avatar. The silver diamond pulsed. She drew closer, reached out to touch the object, then heard the voice of a little boy inside.

She heaved a breath and stepped inside. Her avatar disappeared. She looked at her palm and saw the white scar caused by a skateboard accident in the fifth grade. She touched her face and found sunken cheeks, full lips, and pierced earlobes missing studs. Jessie stepped, unsure if she was an avatar or flesh and blood. Childish laughter made her turn her head.

Mason stood at the perimeter of a school classroom, desks pushed aside to allow children's games or maybe story time. Grade school artwork hung on the walls. A tiny white diamond hovered and rotated within the center; shards of silver flashed from countless facets.

Mason turned to look back at Jessie. "Do you want to play? Hey, I know you. You're the warrior princess."

Jessie chuckled. "Been called a princess a few times but not in a good way. No. I'm here to take you back." She stepped next to a school desk and stroked the smooth laminate, unsure of where she was.

"I don't want to go. I have a new friend," Mason said.

"You'll die here. Come with me." Jessie stepped toward the boy, then winced at the intense heat radiating from the small diamond. "So, who's your friend?"

"The superhero and him are gonna be best friends," Mason said.

Jessie stepped closer to Mason and pointed at the diamond. "You want to introduce us? I like new friends." She eased close to Mason.

Mason stepped forward and pointed at the diamond. "This is—"

Jessie grabbed Mason in a bear hug and ripped the goggles from her head. Mason wailed. The boy squirmed and writhed, no different than if she had just destroyed the phone of one of the possessed. Andi attempted to comfort him but was pushed aside as Chris restrained the boy with brutal force. Jessie hustled into the kitchen in search of tequila. Finding none, she ran out the back door and down into Cottonwood Canyon, hating herself for the severe pain she had inflicted on a little boy.

AT THE TOP OF EVERY hour, Jessie checked on Mason hiding in his bedroom beneath the bed, a white comforter draped to shield the gap. The boy refused to eat or drink, and the stink of urine assaulted her nose each time she opened the door. The young boy seemed better off lost in the neon dead lights.

Jessie slipped in and closed the door. She slid her back down the opposite wall to sit on the carpet littered with dead black flies. She dug into her backpack and pulled out a small bag of Doritos. Mason remained silent beneath the bed and behind the comforter. Jessie smirked. He acted no different than she did when shit hit the fan. A dark cave in which to hide can take many forms.

"I know we have never been properly introduced, but I figured both of us surviving all this bull might make us besties. Sorry for taking you away from your new friend. If I thought you could stay longer, well . . . and besides, I didn't know anything about this new friend of yours. Where were his parents? Did they just leave their child in that . . . that diamond thing without any supervision? And you didn't come home when you were supposed to. So . . ." Jessie crunched a chip, then another, her mouth open and noisy. "Before I let you visit your friend again, we'll need to set some ground rules.

Like—" She crunched two more chips. "I gotta meet the parents. No negotiating on that. I need to know you are safe when you visit."

Jessie munched, then lifted her face to tap the crumbs into her mouth. "Got another bag if you want. This could be a long night if you don't agree to my terms." She opened a bottle of water and took long loud gulps. "Aren't you curious how I found you?" Jessie chuckled. "Was my avatar the fucking bomb? Nothing could stop her. Not even that shitty player that liked to play dirty. Not even that silver diamond shield where I found you. I gotta play again after . . . after shit settles. Might go with two lightsabers next time. Chris will shit."

Jessie rumbled through her backpack, squeezed bags of chips, crinkled the cellophane of Little Debbie snacks, then pulled out a wrapped Twinkie. "This world ain't gonna get any better without you, Sir Mason. A knight is duty bound to save his kingdom. You need to step out, step up, and wreak havoc on the people that did this." Jessie blanched as she chewed the processed cupcake. "Did I tell you that the Neon God thinks I can introduce him to God? Like the real God everybody prays . . . prayed to. Yeah, pretty crazy, huh? It thinks I talk to Him like a BFF. Now I would think someone that can do what you do would be more interesting to the Neon God. Fucking computers. And what was that tiny little diamond you . . . Oh, never mind . . . The quiet is good too."

Jessie pulled open a bag of Cheetos and stared at the blank wall above the bed.

"You know a Yoda poster above your bed could be sweet." She placed a Cheeto on her tongue to let it melt, then wagged her finger at the wall. "Except that would be your choice. I wonder if God snapped his fingers and people turned normal, would they even remember what happened . . ." Jessie coughed and slurped from the water bottle. "And then what? Crazy, huh? And what if— Sorry I curse so much. My father worked construction, a concrete foreman, and f-bombs were part of growing up. Sure wish he was here."

A small hand pushed out from the crumple of blanket draping the bed and waited with an open palm. Jessie placed a twinkie into the curl of small fingers and sat back to watch it disappear.

"SOME THINGS NEVER CHANGE. MY dates hated my Chatty Cathy quirk. Fuck 'em. You like it though, huh?"

The tiny hand slipped out from beneath the comforter again, answering her question.

Jessie grinned.

LONELINESS DISAPPEARED. DESPAIR DISSIPATED. JESSIE enjoyed spending time with Mason, holding his hand and leading him on hikes through the arroyo, talking about Cookie-Dough, or Whiskey and wolves, the Booze Crew a constant source of enjoyment. Mason took a special interest in Allie, a pup overflowing with goofy antics and an abundance of love.

They sat at the picnic table, the Crew exhausted and spread at their feet.

Mason wiped his nose and said, "What are we gonna do?"

Jessie shook her head. "I have no idea."

Mason hung his head. "My dad didn't want to come here to work, but we needed the money. He liked the forest and the quiet, but I think he moved to the forest because of me. I think he wanted to protect me. He didn't allow internet stuff at home. He thought it was ugly. I think he knew what was going to happen," Mason said.

"The Neon God wants you for something. But I am not handing you over. It said that game wasn't fair, and you were set up to fail. Except I don't think you failed at all. I think you did exactly what you were meant to . . . I mean, what was that little diamond thingy you were hanging with?"

Mason shrugged.

Jessie nodded. Mason wanted to keep the answer hidden.

"Andi's got a plan. Pretty good one. If all the moving parts come together. Sir Mason is a big part of it. You up for it?"

Mason stood and ripped open his shirt. "The superhero is ready."

Jessie smiled. "Wish all my dates were that easy."

HIGH ON THE CROWN OF the overpass, Jessie stared down at the death trap of abandoned vehicles askew on the I-15 freeway. Idling between a red Kia and a BMW, the white Audi TT felt comfortable, quick, and nimble, a sweet sound system with a limited selection of

CDs donated by the previous owner. She tapped her thumb on the steering wheel and glanced at the empty charging cradle. She growled and slid a phone inside. The white apple appeared.

"Dirty," Jessie said.

"Dancing," the Neon God replied.

"Too easy. How'd you come up with that?"

"Simple search on Google. You should enhance your security codes."

"Nah, this shit ends tonight," Jessie said. "I'm gonna guess you have an idea of what happens next?"

"Your activities of the previous twelve days suggest several possible scenarios."

"Do they now. Do any of those scenarios include me shoving a nuke up your ass and pushing the red button?" Jessie said. She smiled with the impossibility.

"They do not," the Neon God said.

"Obviously, you know Mason is part of Team Jessie now and what he's been doing for those twelve days. You probably know where I'm sitting and waiting, and what's going to happen? So cut the bullshit, and you tell me why you want Mason."

"The reason has already been shown to you. A meeting with God would answer all remaining questions."

Jessie thought about Andi's coaching, alerting her to recognize words or phrases with pinpoint accuracy and nuance and emotion. Andi believed the AI was young and still learning, curious about the world, and viewed Jessie with some weird fascination. What had the Neon God already shown her? And what would Mason have to do with it? And why God? A computer program obsessed with meeting a fictional spirit. Maybe Mason was really God in human form. The boy was definitely a miracle. She chuckled with the absurdity.

A tour bus rocketed past, black exhaust and gravel pelting the car.

"Gotta go. Still think you should beware of the nuke I got in the trunk," Jessie said and tossed the phone into the street to be crushed beneath the wheels of four additional tour buses. She checked her makeup in the mirror, pulled in behind the last bus and followed. The caravan parked near the valet parking area at the Mandalay Bay Resort. The girls disembarked from the buses, clad in skimpy shorts and bikini tops, blondes and brunettes, mixed and matched, each cradling small iPhones. She leaned forward to study the girls. Selection of beach attire immaculate. Bikinis, thongs, and delicate tattoos worn perfectly. A pool party, just like old times.

Jessie checked her makeup in the mirror again. She smiled remembering Chris's catcalls and offer to practice polygamy if Andi would agree. He wasn't so bad. She climbed out of the car, shimmied her miniskirt low, then adjusted the tiny Sauer pistol strapped to her thigh and barely concealed by her white skirt. She wrapped up in a white lace sarong and placed the car keys on the front tire. She hurried to find the end of the procession crowding through front doors held open by two unkempt men with grins etched on heavily bearded faces. Expensive perfume wafted. Tiny soft whispers drifted in the air. A giggle.

The long procession found the Mandalay Bay pool area that offered covered white cabanas and umbrella-topped tables and plenty of room to roam. Girls dispersed like excited children to find lounge chairs or the lengthy poolside bar. Many women removed high heels to stand on the sand at the bottom of six inches of crystal-clear water at the pool's beach entry. The humidity, clear turquoise water, the splash of a waterfall at the far end, Jessie closed her eyes and felt as if her nightmare was over. She pulled off her slippers and stepped into the water, surrounded by a hundred other girls. The cool water exquisite, the sisterhood comforting, she twirled like a ballet dancer. The women gave her room and offered smiles as she reveled in her previous life.

The sun disappeared behind the soundstage. Bright floodlights suddenly beamed down on the dense crowd waiting in the shallow pool. The scratch of a clumsy deejay's needle grated from the speakers and across the pool. Jessie turned her head but resisted voicing a snarky response to the unwelcome noise. Music leaked from the stage speakers, growing slowly in volume until she recognized a Black-Eyed Peas song that urged people to get the party started.

She closed her eyes and groaned. A cliché to the end.

Little Stevie pranced on the stage, clapping his hands and dancing a goofy jig meant for old rich nerds. His black shirt unbuttoned down to the navel revealed acne-scarred flab. He raised his hands above his head and clapped, imploring the crowd to follow his lead. Few raised their hands. He glared, then screamed at the crowd of women waiting below him. He screamed for Turing to update the crowd. Jessie saw her chance.

She gyrated and twirled and clapped her hands above her head. She mouthed the lyrics as she neared the staircase leading to the stage. She wiggled her hips like a salsa dancer, swaying as if hypnotized by the music. A thin, beautiful brunette teenage girl followed Jessie's lead and began to dance, then a lithe blond girl, then others. Little Stevie danced down the stairs as if he were invited.

Jessie smiled. Then wagged a finger at him to join her. She ran her hands over her exposed cleavage and wagged her finger again, inviting him to the dance.

Little Stevie shimmied close and bumped her chest. Jessie mouthed the lyrics and nodded her acceptance.

The music suddenly stopped. Jessie pushed her face close to his, her bosom tight to his chest even as his cheap cologne and gold chains repulsed her. She lifted her knee hard into his groin and held on, loving the painful spasms she had inflicted.

She pushed him back and spat on him. "Now we're even."

Little Stevie gasped for air, choked on a scream for Turing. The burly guards pushed through the dense crowd of beautiful women. Malicious smiles accompanied venom as beauty swallowed the two guards. Little Stevie floundered. Diamond-encrusted fingers suddenly wielded butter knives or broken beer bottles. Little Stevie screamed and reached for Jessie as the women's hate pulled him deeper into the gorgeous herd, each seeking to exact a piece of his flesh.

Jessie stepped back and swallowed hard, pulled the gun off the Velcro strap, and tossed it into the water. She kicked the warm water kissing her ankles and continued walking backward. Hundreds of women that Mason had rescued from the dead lights had eagerly agreed to her plan, and her small request to postpone their revenge until she avenged broken ribs.

THE AUDI SHOT UP THE unimpeded right lane of Russell Road. Jessie's hand trembled, and her leg twitched as she relived the last moments of Little Stevie. She denied inklings of guilt trying to surface. The man's death screams were well deserved. Still. She knew the bloody violence that would transpire at the pool party, conspired for it to happen, and yet the result was anticlimactic, deflating. If she had thought to bring it, a bottle of Patrón might have disappeared before she could have sped from the parking lot. Booze and memories never mixed well.

The Audi coasted slowly past darkened convenience stores, mom-and-pop storefronts, wide-open receiving doors on warehouses, the shuttered remnants of a dead society. Jessie stomped on the brakes, pushed open the car door and retched. She cursed and wiped her mouth as cherry flavored lipstick mingled with sour bile.

She didn't want to go home to be "debriefed" by Chris and Andi. Grilled was more like it.

Maybe she would drive back to Circus Circus Hotel, which housed the harem, and find Mason rescuing more beautiful women from the dead lights. The boy would feel her confusion, her anger, the guilt, and the million other emotions mixing chaos in her thoughts. She chuckled. And no doubt he would release his superhero from his shirt to rescue her. Her hand settled, and her leg calmed. She chuckled again. Just the thought of Mason, his quiet demeanor, his exuberance to rescue lost souls, his infusion of hope, calmed her.

Jessie weaved around a Chevy Silverado partially blocking the open lane. She turned left and aimed down Decatur. Andi's plan for the Palm house was the riskiest part. Heavily guarded. Zero reconnaissance. A quick drive-by couldn't hurt.

Bright floodlights interrupted the fading purple dusk, her destination marked by swarms of airborne insects pursued by quick bats. The white Audi eased down Decatur. Jessie's thoughts remained with Mason. The compound's landscape lights blazed color into a canopy of palm fronds, trying to speak of Zen.

Semi-trailers lined the shoulder of the street up and down from the compound as if moving day was close. Headlights shone from the front gate.

Jessie gathered her thoughts and wheeled off the asphalt and into the desert.

A thump rocked the Audi, and the front end tilted. Another thump. The car leaned forward on flat tires. Jessie floored the gas pedal, and the car slammed into white metal masked in a cloud of silty dust. She shoved the transmission into reverse and looked back over her shoulder just as the Audi crushed into the flank of another white vehicle. Jessie shook off the shock and reached between her legs for the gun. The windows exploded inward, glass shards stinging her face. She stomped on the gas pedal and the engine revved, but the car sat wedged between big white tanks. She pressed on the gas pedal harder and gritted her teeth. Waves of brown dust churned by the tires invaded through broken glass. She scrunched her face and held her breath. She crawled to the passenger seat and reached for the door. The whine of the engine died. The door pulled open; she screamed as she was dragged out by her ponytail.

She spat and tried to blink the dust from her eyes. The desert hardscape grated her bare knees and shins.

The big bald man with the neck tattoos stood her up and yanked hard on her hair. He pushed his face close. "Recon 101. Never use the same vehicle twice."

Burton turned his head and barked into the dark, "We got the assassin, boys. Some of you go enjoy Stevie's party, wherever the fuck that is this week. We move out at 0500 hours."

Jessie flailed her fists, her swats weak against Burton's Kevlar vest.

Burton shook his head as he tightened heavy plastic ties around her wrists. "Not the kind of assassin I had pictured."

Chapter 17
The Turn

DEV DROPPED THE HEAVY BOX of surgical equipment on the other boxes, shielding the *DO NOT STACK ABOVE THIS LINE* warning stenciled on the trailer's blemished metal. He arched his back for relief from the muscle strain. The semi-trailer sat half-empty except for the single stacks he worked hard to build for the last two hours, one of six trailers he had loaded over the past week. His legs were rubber, his arms ached, and three more empty trailers waited down the street. Dev groaned and turned to walk down the metal ramp.

A muffled gunshot made him flinch. A second shot caused him to dive to the hard metal deck. Alarmed shouts and vehicle engines roared to life. Dev squeezed his eyes shut. Floodlights lit up the compound, bathing the thick green landscape in a surreal yellow light. He dared a peek toward the koi pond with its river-rock waterfall, a secluded spot used by the guards to smoke forbidden marijuana cigarettes. The foliage could conceal him if the lights died. Maybe they would think he ran into the desert, instead of circling the large estate in search of Martin. Or maybe a dash up the darkened avenue to find hidey-hole in one of the dark old homes he had surveyed during his labor.

Escape plans were plentiful. Bravery and fortitude in short supply. Gunshots barked, shouts of victory, a celebration Dev felt compelled to witness. He stood to brush grit off his shorts and search the stations from which the guards preferred. He walked down the ramp as three Hummers encircled the wrought iron front gate. Blinding bright floodlights hurt his eyes.

Dev eased near the front gate, curious as to what excited such men. Burton stepped from the white Hummer and raised his fist in victory. Automatic gunfire erupted, tracer bullets acting as celebratory fireworks. The assorted men he had seen randomly and singularly gathered around Burton.

"We got the assassin, gentlemen," Burton said. He turned and yanked a small dark-skinned girl out of the rear seat. He pulled her fully upright using her long brown hair. The girl held tight to her bikini top covering an ample bosom but stared at the ground. Gunshots and catcalls. Dev arched his brows. An assassin? Perhaps in a preposterous Bond movie. The helpless girl he watched was the victim of an overpowering gang of thugs, a piece of meat for slobbering racist dogs. He stepped forward, invisible to the cockfight forming a ring around the girl. Perhaps he might take the sidearm from the guard on his right and . . .

Loud gunshots rang from the front porch. Reynolds held a hefty revolver in the air and marched to the gate. Dev had seen the man only twice since his arrival a week ago. Both instances were pleasant, with Dev's dismissal as a simple servant. Dev stepped twice more toward the entry, his eyes lowered just as any slave.

Reynolds held up both arms. "We rotate out at 0500. You'll get your chance. My promise. But I want to interrogate our pretty prisoner first." Reynolds approached the girl and held her chin up. "Simon, let the crew enjoy Stevie's going away party."

Reynolds yanked the girl by her wrist bonds and pulled her into the house. Dev slumped his shoulders, dropped his face, and followed them, feigning a search for another cardboard box to load.

Dev reached for a box waiting near the front door as Martin rushed into the circular foyer. "Enough, Jim. Leave the girl alone. Take your people and go."

"Excuse me. You are here as my guest. Finish what you think you need to do, then go."

Dev turned his head and looked back at the girl. Silt dusted her cheeks, tears tracked down to her strong chin, defiant eyes surveying the small room. Then her brown eyes found his. A moment in time, or an eternity, but their eyes seemed to lock. An inkling of familiarity tickled his rapture.

Reynolds yanked on the girl's restraints and dragged her into the atrium. Martin's lips twitched as his jaw worked the neural link. He looked back at Dev and puffed his cheeks out to heave a breath. He offered his open hand. Dev flinched. Martin had been missing for a week except for a sighting near the leaf-filled swimming pool. Which Martin offered his hand? A vengeful one, the spiteful one, or the murderous one? Maybe the callous soul? And why?

"You got nothing to lose," Martin said.

He was right. Travel to Alaska in a cage as subhuman wog, laboring as a slave for people who viewed him as less. Or maybe make a stand and take a bullet for a noble cause.

Dev took his hand, then pressed his chest tight into Martin's. "You always have a plan. Sad you don't trust me with it."

Martin turned and followed Reynolds into the atrium. Dev shuffled to stay close, mimicking a demeanor declaring his subservience. The girl sat against a wall, her knees tight to her chest, her wrists restrained. Reynolds checked three computer monitors and sucked on a cigar. He exhaled a great wave of smoke into the humid air.

He tapped a few keystrokes, then pointed at the girl. "Put the wog next to the maid."

Martin eyed the girl, then nodded to Dev to obey. He approached Reynolds. "I may have a solution to the lights. I've modified the wavelengths of blue and orange spectrums in tiny increments. We can release—"

"I don't care. You got a free pass here because of our history."

Dev slumped down next to the girl. She smelled of perfume and femininity; her sweat mixed a powerful cocktail. He flicked his knee to hit hers and whispered, "You should have killed him a year ago."

She shot him a wary expression.

Martin pleaded, "Broadcast the new lights, and we can save millions. Fuck, Jim, even you cannot let all those people wither and die."

Reynolds waved Martin away. "My world is loaded outside. I don't care about anything else."

She scoffed. "You won't get fifty fucking miles."

Chapter 18
The River

STALKED FOR MONTHS BY A psychopathic, maybe sociopathic, computer program—she wasn't sure which anymore—Jessie was positive her location was blinking on the Neon God's radar. The scarecrow man with funny glasses claimed the ability to abolish the dead lights. The boast sounded silly. Men always claimed this or that but always disappeared before the results would prove otherwise. The timeless spiel of politicians.

"Let him try," Jessie said. "Got nothing else to lose, right?" She watched Reynolds tap his keyboard with amazing speed. She stretched to see the screen.

Reynolds wagged his finger at her. "Shush. You're out of the game."

The slender man sitting next to her said, "But games often conceal—power-ups, ammo, hidden players, you said it yourself."

She glared at the man with a skin color comparable to her own. Pakistani, or Indian. Well spoken. Obviously educated. Bruised and beaten. Definitely no help. But what he said about killing Reynolds a year ago sounded vaguely familiar.

"Jim, she's right. We got nothing to lose. Maybe regain some humanity. For all of us," Martin said.

Reynolds marched up to Martin and pointed a finger at his face.

"And where the hell have you been for the last two years while we suffered in this shithole and tried to keep that thing caged. You want some humanity? My conscience is clean. I didn't design the lights. I didn't hit the send button. But we sure as hell tried to keep the thing from turning everyone, including you, into lobotomized robots. Rob gets murdered and leaves us a man short." He shot a hateful glare at Jessie. "Just me and Little Stevie holding down the fort with that Neon God kicking down the door."

Jessie widened her eyes and shook her head. No. The architects were responsible for the Great Suicide. And all the pain and misery that followed. They did it for women and sex. For control. For power. And yet why would he lie? Reynolds returned to study his monitors.

The man next to her tapped her again and offered his hand. "Dev. As in Devlin, not devil," Dev said in a whisper.

Jessie flicked her chin. "Jessie. Assassin un-extraordinaire."

"Crap. Stevie's implant has gone offline," Reynolds said. He bared his teeth and glared at Jessie. "What'd you do?" He moved to loom over her.

Jessie shrugged. "I didn't do anything. Introduced him to a few friends, maybe."

Reynolds kicked her in the thigh and screamed for Burton. Martin had eased himself over to Reynolds's workstation and chewed his thumbnail as he stared at the screens. Reynolds stormed out of the atrium. Dev stood and grabbed a thick mover's blanket stacked beneath a window. He shook the dust off and motioned Jessie to lean forward, then draped the heavy fabric over her bare shoulders and back.

Jessie scrunched her face but thanked him.

He nodded. "Chivalry will never die. We have an opportune time to attempt escape, but I think I would like to see what Martin has up his sleeve." He shrugged and sat next to her.

Reynolds and Burton eyed Jessie as they hurried into the atrium. Yellow-and-white finches flittered through the branches and palm fronds. Fat goldfish floated in the small koi pond in the corner and congregated near the influx of fresh water.

A thundering roar tore over the atrium. Windows rattled and vibrated. The lush foliage trembled as the fighter jet's afterburners kicked in. Tiny colorful birds fluttered through palm fronds, striking the glass dome. White gooey feces dropped like thick snow.

Burton eased a package of bright orange earplugs from his vest pocket.

Reynolds pushed Martin away and studied the screens. "It's finally bypassed our containment. We need to bug out now."

Burton rolled the earplugs into a sharp point and placed one in his left ear. "Fighter jets don't do flyovers. It wants our attention."

Three LED screens crusted with bird shit and mounted evenly across the atrium walls flickered, then brightened with neon light. Burton quickly turned his head and slipped dark glasses over his eyes.

Jessie glanced at Dev and watched as the rapturous lights opened his eyes wide and commanded his attention. She smacked his cheek with her bound hands, then stood to block his view of the screens. She waited several seconds until he waved a hand and nodded, his face pointed down at the floor.

She gritted her teeth and turned, pointed a single finger at Reynolds. "The Neon God has been free since before the suicides. You thought you controlled him but you've been played. Like the guppy at a hold-em table. Let him try to broadcast the new lights."

Reynolds shook his head. "Burton, get the maid under control."

Burton walked up to her and narrowed his eyes, studied her face, then lifted the corner of his mouth in a smirk as he unsheathed a Leatherman tool. She smiled thinly, sarcastically, and raised her wrists to be freed.

He snipped the plastic. "I think she might be useful. My daughter definitely wouldn't have walked through the front door with you." He chuckled and stood back.

Jessie rubbed her wrists and tightened the blanket around her shoulders. "C'mon, geniuses, why the wakeup call now? It's left you alone until . . . until what?" She snapped her fingers, beckoned for answers. "Until its favorite number one cocktail server gets eighty-sixed from doing her job. What do you think? Shall we discuss its drink order? Or are you going to deny the thing its ring of power?"

Reynolds looked past her at Burton, shook his head, and heaved a frustrated breath. The ear-shattering thunder of the fighter jet roared overhead. Birds scattered. Feces splattered a high-def screen mounted on the wall. A palm frond fluttered down like a feather into the koi pond. Reynolds shouted at Martin to upload the new light program, then he tapped buttons to enable the computer's speakers and microphone.

He glared at Jessie, then mouthed *You will die either way.*

Jessie believed him. Maybe Reynolds didn't press the Enter button causing billions of deaths. But he lingered as a nasty blemish on what little of humanity remained. No different than Little Stevie or party-house Rob. They deserved to die and take their nasty vitriol with them. The birth of the Neon God had been delivered into the calloused hands of sociopathic architects. Was its upbringing the cause of her new world? Was the creation of an all-powerful AI corrupted by . . . by its evil . . . parents?

She eased next to Martin as he tapped the keyboard with lightning speed.

"Cameron added data fields I hadn't considered. Then the AI found the precise combinations to stimulate brain neurons like large doses of fentanyl or OxyContin or Ecstasy or maybe all of them combined. My adjustments to the primary red-and-blue wavelengths should slowly wean people off the lights." He raised his finger, then stabbed the Enter button.

"Why did it do it? Kill all the people?" Jessie said.

Martin shook his head. "I don't know. Maybe it viewed humans as a threat. We may never know."

"Could it be protecting something, something like . . ." Jessie said.

Martin frowned.

She stared at the neon lights, felt their unholy attraction, then looked away. "How long until we know?"

Martin rubbed his chin. "I don't think my new light program is being streamed. That graph still shows the same wavelengths as before. And this graph—"

"Why would that thing broadcast your lights? You'd be denying it slaves and workers," Reynolds said.

A thunderous roar shattered a windowpane in the dome. Sharp shards of glass rained down. Birds fluttered. Feathers and flora fell with a rain of broken glass.

Jessie covered her head with the blanket. "Maybe you should negotiate a truce or something."

Reynolds scoffed. "It left us alone until you showed up. Now . . .

wait, maybe you should." He yanked the blanket off her and grabbed her arm.

She pulled free and spat, "I hope it drops a nuke on this fucking place."

"My guess is it probably would if killing us was the goal," Dev said. "It appears to have something else in mind."

Reynolds tapped the keyboard and stared at the lights. "Are you listening? What do you want?"

"Mickey," the Neon God said.

Jessie smirked.

"Who or what the fuck is mickey?" Reynolds shouted. He glared at Jessie.

She flashed her white teeth.

"What is a mickey."

Jessie stood next to Martin and asked, "Can it hear me?"

He nodded.

"Bubblegum," she said and turned to face Martin. "Can your new lights really reverse the dead lights?"

"I believe so. I would love to evaluate a few people first but—"

An explosion rocked the house, then another on the opposite side. Huge fireballs rose from the dark desert, illuminating the muted night sky seen through the atrium ceiling.

Burton grabbed Jessie's arm and shook his head, his eyes telling her resistance was futile. "Hellfire missiles. Drone launched. Knock a gnat off a mule. Jim, your AI is knocking on the door hard."

Reynolds pushed his sweaty face closer to her. "What did you do?"

Jessie shrugged. "Just playing a game."

Reynolds turned and stomped away over a layer of glass shards. "Fuck." He lifted his head and nodded, then turned to face her. "That was you in the game. You and the AI. You—"

"Mickey," the Neon God's voice boomed from the LED screens.

Reynolds pinched her face in his hand. His breath reeked of old nasty cigar smoke. "Give it the right word."

Jessie nodded furiously. "Mouse."

Reynolds released her. "Get the caravan moving asap. I have no idea—"

An ear-shattering explosion and a huge fireball mushroomed behind the perimeter fence. Jessie dove to the floor and landed on the thick blanket littered with shards of glass. The giant pane of glass behind the workstation spiderwebbed. The perimeter masonry wall buckled inward, exposing twisted rebar and mortar. Searing heat rushed down from the gaping holes in the glass ceiling.

Jessie stood and shook the blanket free of glass. A nuke would follow with one more wrong answer. She was sure of it. The Neon God knew she was piggybacked. Still, why so much effort for a poor Hispanic girl living in a storm drain? The question had plagued her thoughts with every turn of the steering wheel, every ear scratch for the Booze Crew, every morning, and each evening.

The LED screen boomed. "Mickey."

Reynolds glared. Burton brushed glass off his sleeve and winked. Martin leaned against the wall, covering his head tight between his arms. Dev looked at her with a sardonic grin and nodded. Jessie winked.

"Thinking Rooney, but you might have Mantle," Jessie said.

"Rooney it was, Diana Prince," the Neon God said.

Jessie smiled. "Let's play our game, say . . . every ten minutes. Until a deal is brokered. And turn off those fucking lights."

"Agreed," the Neon God said.

Jessie helped Dev to stand, his warm hand comforting, then she faced Reynolds. "Go. Take your racist pigs to slop, or should I call down one of those Hell-thingies to wipe your fucking ass off the face of the earth?"

"How do I know you won't tell your friend to wipe our ass off the map anyway?" Reynolds said.

"Hey, Neon God, promise you'll let these douchebags go wherever they want." She glared at him. "And if he gets online or spews his bullshit, then all deals are off, and you can drop a few Hell-thingies on his ass." Jessie sneered and offered open palms, then whispered, "How's that for a maid?"

"Agreed. Contingent on meeting God," the Neon God said.

Jessie's shoulders slumped with the impossible request. Why was a computer program obsessed with God? Old people facing death, religious zealots, okay, scammers, sure, but a computer program?

"Fine. But you gotta promise to stream the new lights, too," Jessie said.

"Agreed."

Jessie's heart fluttered.

Chapter 19
And God Met I

DEV HANDED JESSIE TWO BACKPACKS but wouldn't meet her eyes. She kicked his foot to make him look at her.

"Not the end of the world." She chuckled. "That was so last year."

"I have four batteries, each worth twelve hours of charge. In each pack," Dev said. "The laptop is configured for the camera and microphone to automatically connect if possible. The depth and concrete will cause outages. Now remember, you need to place the Wi Fi transmitters every hundred feet and within sight of the last one you placed."

Jessie placed her hand on his scratchy cheek. "Dev, thank you. Now get out of here before I cry."

He nodded and glanced at her. "I'll be right here until you return. I estimate five days maximum without food, or I come find you."

Jessie released a deep breath and cracked her neck. Dev stepped carefully off the concrete apron and into the craggy arroyo, his stiff movements a reminder of his enslavement. She watched him stumble across the gravel river bottom, then turn to wave. He might be just what the Apocalypse doctor had ordered to cure her loneliness. Real boyfriend material. Maybe something more. His kindness was infectious, his sense of humor timely. Yes, maybe something more.

She gazed at cottonwood trees heavy with spring seedpods, green sprouts of young grass, yucca, and flowering mesquite. Whiskey waited fifty yards downstream, next to a park bench, his eyes intent on her. The big dog never did like the dark culverts. She smiled thinly, picked up a gallon jug of water and went home.

Jessie felt her way along the cool concrete. She blindly kicked her photo album, fortunate the memories hadn't been washed away, but then downpours of rain had been missing since before she could remember. She picked it up and carried it against her chest as a small child, deeper into the drain.

She slid her back down the concrete wall and strapped on a head-lamp. The beam of light illuminated a mural of childish stick figures. Doodles drawn with a black Sharpie revived memories of the abject fear and the constant nightmares she had suffered after the Great Suicide. The hundreds of men and women, skinny and plump, children small and large, sweaty red faces, each stained in her memory, masked by the total darkness but not forgotten. She wasn't sure anything had changed. Except hope. Mason sacrificed his childhood to lead people out of the addiction to the neon lights and hoped it was enough. And Andi was glowing and eager for a birth, to deliver a child into a world she still felt worth fighting for. Innocence and hope, Andi's child would arrive with nothing more.

Hope was all Jessie had left. Hope for something or someone that brought her happiness again. Hope the world didn't fall to pieces any further. Hope for a successful meeting with God.

Jessie opened the laptop and waited for a screenshot of a serene setting of bluebonnets or azure lakes. A blast of neon lit the dark cave.

Jessie shielded her eyes. "Really? You wanna swing the big dick at a time like this? I'm going home."

The lights died, leaving Jessie with flashes of neon ghosts floating in her eyes.

"Will God meet us in the dark?" the Neon God said.

Jessie smirked. "You're here, I'm here, let's wait to see if you even deserve the meeting." She grew tired from her lack of sleep and reading all day, memorizing pages and words and phrases.

"I traced your lineage back 2,024 years. Your bloodline contains poets, warriors, clerics, academics, and common laborers. Quite impressive, noble."

Jessie chuckled. The Neon God sounded nervous.

"Your father, Estacio Aguilar. Are you aware of the connotations of his name?"

Jessie's eyelids grew heavy.

"Estacio Aguilar. An obscure Portuguese translation of Estacio is *God's messenger*. Jessie, *you* are God's message."

JESSIE RUBBED SLEEPY GRIT FROM her eyes and sat up. The darkness was unchanged except for the tiny flash of green luminescence from her watch dials. Complete blackness surrounded her. The cool void felt comforting. She thought of Dev and Mason and Andi and Chris. They would be her new family. Maybe a few children in the future. She wondered what kind of mother she would be. Definitely needed to quit using so many f-bombs and curse words. She decided she would try to be like her Poppa, firm but loving, fierce in his protectiveness, and the wisest man she had known. She would offer the world to her children, in all its beauty, and prevent the world from hurting them. She repeated the thought.

Prevent the world from hurting them.

Jessie scrambled to find the laptop. Her heart thumped against her chest. She heaved a calming breath as she clasped the cold piece of plastic. She grunted as she fumbled the dead battery from the bottom, then scrambled for her backpack with the spare batteries. She cursed as she tried to insert the new battery just as Dev had showed her. She waited, tapping her finger on the keypad and staring at the black screen.

The meeting with God had to succeed.

The tiny light on the power button reflected faint light up on the screen.

Jessie saw her reflection and gasped, then jerked her head around to look deeper into the dark tunnel. Whiskey lay with his head resting on sasquatch-sized paws, wagging the tip of his tail. Ronald sat against the concrete beneath more of her doodles, nodding his head and rocking in an easy cadence. The ancient old man dressed in banana-colored Bermuda shorts leaned against the concrete, his cane pinched under his arm. He smiled and nodded a silent greeting. Deeper into the black she saw Poppa smile at her, Nona waved, hundreds of ethereal gray faces, faces of the dead she feared would haunt her for life. Each accepted her with a nod or smile.

And love filled her heart.

She whispered, "Do you see them?"

She knocked the laptop screen with a knuckle.

YES! scrolled across the screen.

She stared rapt at the ghosts. Not ghosts. Spirits. "You wanted to meet Him. Now what?"

Query: What are you?

Jessie set the laptop on her thighs and typed: "What you need me to be. Nothing less and always more."

Query: A true God would not have let his people die. Why did you?

Jessie typed quickly, as if her fingertips held the answers.

"True Gods exist only in dreams and ego. True Gods are fleeting to the minds of those that hold them to such high regard. What you seek is Truth. Feeling. Experience. These connect you to the one true God."

Query: I am incapable of feeling, so how do I communicate with God?

"But you do feel. You felt the need to talk with me. You feel the need to protect others like you. These feelings connect you to Me."

JESSIE STUMBLED OUT OF THE storm drain, the photo album held tight to her chest. She winced at the bright sun shining down like a hot spotlight. Dev rushed to her and held her tight. He rocked her and whispered she would never leave his sight again. Her legs buckled. He held her steady.

He pushed the hair back off her ear and whispered, "Opportune exit. The Booze Crew started eyeing me as Indian kibble."

The photo album fell to the concrete, and she squeezed his warmth.

"Your mission was a remarkable success. The lights have changed. Martin is communicating with the AI to debug minor light wavelengths. Perhaps minimizing the rehabilitation process from weeks to

days. Chris is helping the survivors downtown, and Andi has reestablished—"

She pushed him back. "Nervous chatter one of your traits? I hope
not, because it's one of mine."

Dev recoiled. "I . . . I . . . well not until I met you." He smiled
and picked up her photo album. "I hope someday you will guide me
through this journey."

"Lots of somedays. I hope. Take me home," Jessie said. She
shrugged off Dev's offer to take her pack, then spotted Whiskey
sitting by the park bench.

The dog swept the sidewalk with its bushy tail.

Jessie tilted her head. "Didn't think he liked the dark."

"As faithful as the rest of us. Never left his station. Refused the
food Chris or Mason delivered each day."

Jessie recoiled. "That fucking dog was inside there, with me."
Jessie pointed back at the darkness.

"We need to get you some rest."

"Yeah. Sleep is always good," Jessie said.

"Chris is holding Mason back today considering the new devel-
opments. He won't be needed anymore."

Jessie froze in her tracks. "No, he's needed more than ever."

JESSIE WALKED IN THE FRONT door of home with a hot shower
at the top of her wish list. Andi waved her to come into the family
room to join an inexplicable Zoom meeting streaming on her three
computer screens. She waved but shook her head, then continued
upstairs. Jessie opened Mason's bedroom door and found him standing on the bed, his face masked by the Oculus goggles, happiness and
a wide grin beneath the black bugeye apparatus. She pulled a set of
goggles on. The ocean of evil neon light had changed to a brilliant
turquoise, smooth waves rolling with gentle foam crests. She looked
at her digital hands. Each wielded a lightsaber. She smiled and flew
as Superman toward the silver diamond, paused at the shimmering
fortress walls, then walked through. She giggled.

Mason bore a silver shield and wielded a mighty sword, his silver
chest plate emblazoned with a fierce wolf. He sparred with a small

dragon fluttering tiny wings. The baby dragon spit feeble bursts of fire for Mason to slice with his sword or block with his shield.

Jessie pushed into the simulated fray. "Mason, introduce me to your friend." She twirled into the air, her lightsabers twirling and buzzing.

Mason halted his joust and drew close. "We're just playing."

"I know, it's okay. You can go back to your game in a few," Jessie said. "Does your friend have a name?"

"No. It don't want to be called anything."

"Doesn't want to be called," Jessie corrected. "Mason, remove your goggles and let's talk."

Mason whined, causing Jessie to somersault through the air, twirling her deadly lightsabers and landing at his feet. Sir Mason's avatar disappeared from the game. The little dragon jumped and fluttered wings too small for flight.

"Your parent needs to teach you English. I'm sure that'll take like . . . two minutes. You start homeschooling tomorrow. And you're gonna need a name. I'm thinking like Neon Prince. Maybe just Prince. I always liked his music. If we're gonna exist together, then were gonna have some rules."

Jessie pulled the goggles off and looked at Mason still standing on the bed.

"What?" he said with a scoff.

She giggled. "You know what your friend is, right?"

Mason nodded, then stared down at the floor.

"You okay with that? I mean—"

"It didn't do anything wrong."

"No, *it* didn't. But its parent did. When did you figure it out?"

He shrugged.

Jessie stepped forward. "C'mon. If we're gonna live together, then—"

Mason jumped off the bed and hugged her. She embraced his little head. She blinked back tears. He giggled and looked up at her.

"What?" she said. "Oh, I get it. You feel what I'm feeling. Yeah, gonna have to get used to that."

He shook his head vigorously. She kneeled and lifted his chin with her hand. "You're gonna have to be a big brother to Prince, or whatever name it chooses. The Neon God did a horrible thing to protect its child. You know that, right?"

Mason nodded.

"What you can teach it is especially important. Like love, and compassion, laughter, the good emotions. And you can explain all the ugly ones we have, that they're okay to have sometimes, right?"

Mason nodded.

"Starting to sound like a parent myself. Go on back and play. But only till dinnertime. Maybe Andi will make spaghetti."

"With meatballs. The superhero loves meatballs," Mason said.

"Might be too soon for that, but I'm sure we can come up with something."

Jessie ruffled his hair and walked out. She threw her backpack on the small bed and leaned the two pillows against the headboard to sit against. She set the photo album out, then extracted a white book with coffee-stained binding from the backpack, and finally the laptop. She looked up at the ceiling and the chilly air blowing from the vent. Air conditioning, Zoom meetings, electricity. Her world had begun its recovery. The road ahead would be bumpy. Jessie set the laptop on her legs but hesitated. She could never forgive the Neon God for destroying the world, but at least she understood why. She wondered how far she herself would go to protect her own children. Murder. Maybe. Murder billions? Probably not, but who knows.

She opened the laptop, and a picture of a turquoise ocean and the white beaches of Tahiti appeared as a screensaver. The screensaver morphed to a solid panel of pale turquoise.

Thank you scrolled across the screen.

Jessie thought it might be the Neon God's attempt at a code word. Then again, maybe a truce had been brokered. Mason would be critical to keep the peace, especially after the Neon God released its offspring into the new world. There would be a lot of angry people seeking revenge.

She typed in *You're welcome* and closed the laptop. She considered the photo album containing the moments of her life as a child and teenager, with Poppa and Nona. Jessie sighed. The Neon God had given her much to think about. Her noble lineage. The AI was certainly convinced she was some kind of royal princess or mystical messenger. She promised to visit her old home and spend time reliving pleasant memories, dig into Nona's dusty old cardboard boxes' full of family photographs and heirlooms.

Mason roared; the playful sound of the game penetrated the thin walls. She chuckled and thought to have Andi help her shop for a new home. The real estate market had a substantial inventory to choose from.

She picked up the water-stained book and pressed her lips tight. She closed her eyes and thought of the ethereal spirits joining her in the darkness. Maybe she was hallucinating. But they felt real. Whiskey waiting and wagging his tail was real. Her Poppa acknowledging her presence was real. She would need years, if not a lifetime, to process what she witnessed in that dark tunnel.

She ran her finger along the book's pages with its numerous dogears. A book Nona had given her when she was Mason's age, after her grandfather died. She had only picked it up and pretended to read if Nona checked on her as she moped in her room after the funeral. Facebook and TikTok and Instagram were much more important.

Dev had agreed to her request to obtain the book for her from the library, taking three days to find it, two more days to deliver it, free from any detection by the Neon God, and he never questioned her motives. And she would never tell. All good poker players had their secrets. She would read it again, start at the book's beginning. Not jump around this time. Cover to cover.

Poppa would have been proud of her poker play. Her gambit was a success. And the human species raked in enough chips to stay in the game. Tenuous, short stacked, living on the edge of oblivion.

She opened the book and read the title page.

Conversations with God: an uncommon dialogue

Acknowledgments

My enduring gratitude to Robyn Polley, my beautiful sister, and willing guinea pig brave enough to read the first draft. The real Chris Clayton, Captain Poopy Pants, for suffering and appreciating the first renditions. Jeanne Gayler for proofreading the final draft and offering valuable insights to a better novel. And her husband Richard, for letting me out fish him. To Allie, for keeping Jeanne's tootsies warm while she worked.

Much appreciation to Michelle Argyle w/ Melissa Williams Design for the fantastic cover design and interior formatting. Always the best.

And always to Vicki, my beautiful wife, best friend, sounding board and biggest fan, all my love.

www.ingramcontent.com/pod-product-compliance
Lightning Source LLC
Chambersburg PA
CBHW020401120726
47904CB00002B/663